DEAL WITH THE DEVIL

"Mainly, Jonathan," the Devil said bluntly, "I can give you a life. Bottom Line: you're a loser of a cop who'll never get his Dick Tracy badge and decoder ring. You're a loser of a husband whose wife went thataway with the family gene pool. And tonight, to nobody's surprise, especially your own, you're a loser of a son whose dad got stiffed before you could wave him bye-bye and whose mom plays mum for forty years cause she doesn't know better...or does she? Either way, you're on the outs in all departments, J.H. and I'm the only ride you got left outta here."

DEAL WITH THE DEVIL

Robert DiChiara

A TOM DOHERTY ASSOCIATES BOOK
NEW YORK

This is a work of fiction. All the characters and events portrayed in this book are fictitious, and any resemblance to real people or events is purely coincidental.

DEAL WITH THE DEVIL

Copyright © 1989 by Robert DiChiara

All rights reserved, including the right to reproduce this book, or portions thereof, in any form.

Cover art by Thomas Canty

A Forge Book
Published by Tom Doherty Associates, Inc.
175 Fifth Avenue
New York, NY 10010

Forge ® is a registered trademark of Tom Doherty Associates, Inc.

ISBN: 0-812-51692-8

First edition: July 1989
First mass market edition: December 1996

Printed in the United States of America

0 9 8 7 6 5 4 3 2 1

To my student and secret sweetheart, Elaine Nash
To Francesco and his bride, Frances Kathryn Czerwinska
To Hye Sook, flying across an ocean and into my heart
To Big Wal, El Wayne-o, Bob "Humble," and friends who would
call me Deech
To everyone with former identities and pasts to go with them

All events depicted in this book are fictional except for the case in Illinois involving the Holdberg Technicality; all characters are fictional as well, except for the Devil, of course.

When she had finished, he grimaced impatiently. "That's silly. Mamma's not really dangerous. She's just a case of arrested development. Most of us have outgrown ethics and morals and so on. Mamma's just not grown up to them yet." He frowned and corrected himself thoughtfully: "She might be dangerous, but it would be like a child playing with matches."

"And what do you think of your father?" I asked.

Gilbert shrugged. "I haven't seen him since I was a child. I've got a theory about him, but a lot of it's guess-work. I'd like—the chief thing I'd like to know is if he's impotent."

—Hammett
(The Thin Man)

Queen. Do not for ever with thy vailed lids
Seek for thy noble father in the dust.
Thou know'st 'tis common; all that lives must die,
Passing through nature to eternity.
Ham. Ay, madam, it is common.

—Hamlet
(I. ii. 70–74)

· one ·

The Devil, flanked by Officers Kramer and Fanelli, walked through the high-arched, wooden portal of the San Marco Police Department, and not surprisingly, nobody noticed.

Not that the Fifty-second Precinct was particularly busy midnights; in fact, it was dead. Desk Sergeant Walcott propped a weary head in his left palm while his right cradled *Popular Mechanics*. The long bench against the wall was occupied by two brawlers from the Crestview Bar on Ocean Street; earlier targets to each other's knees and knuckles, now both punchy and drunk, they unknowingly used each other as props, leaning shoulder to shoulder so as not to slide into each other's laps, two sides of beef in a symbiotic stupor. The two arresting officers, Hall and Van Dam, were questioning the alleged cause of the battle—a girl, tanned with bare feet and tight ragged-cut shorts and lots of leg in between—and they were enjoying their work.

But any life at all came from farther back among the tables where patrol cops were trying to complete their paperwork and go home, and the midnight-to-eight shift milled around, waiting for cars or partners or both. Between these two groups, Sergeant Howard "Beans" Fowler lumbered, gripping his clipboard and pencil, matching names and cars, always feeling this responsibility as he would an extra tug on his belt in order to achieve the next hole—it squeezed the sweat from his heavy torso onto his face and forehead. Every night he cursed the heat, the breakdown of cars, the absence of men, and the deep blue stain that soaked his shirt from neck to waist.

The Devil, meanwhile, stood quietly and, at a glance, absolutely motionless. He was arrested—that was true. His eyes slowly shifted, unseen behind the dense gray shield of his sunglasses, observing what little activity the station house offered at the moment, but mainly searching. His eyes were shifting and searching.

"Harding!"

Sergeant Fowler's fat finger had slid down the clipboard and found the name, but the face had not produced itself. A dozen faces looked up when the sergeant had suddenly shouted out, but none belonged to the man they all knew had Sgt. Fowler's guts knotted up and shaking. Fowler looked up and twisted his neck.

"Harding!" He spat the name out as he would a piece of gristled meat on a plate. The tables' activity gave way to a heavy silence. Even Officer Hall took his eyes off the tanned girl's breasts. The silence annoyed Fowler, and he spread his hands in a questioning gesture and cocked his head defiantly. The message was clear: Keep working.

Pencils returned to reports, cops to patrol cars, eyes to bosoms, and Fowler to his task.

Fowler swung into the locker room, the door banging against the broken stop. Officer Curry tried edging past the ranking bulk at the door, but a pincer grip caught him at the elbow.

"Curry, you seen Harding?"

Curry shook his head and slipped out the door. The sergeant pivoted, and his eyes lit up in the dimness between the tall metal lockers. There, adjusting his holster, stood Officer Dale Stone, lanky and becalmed, readied since the door slam.

"Stone!" Fowler bellowed, though now only a little more than a yard away. "Where's your burnout of a partner tonight, huh? You two got coast patrol, and I mean now."

Stone didn't look at Sgt. Fowler until he set his gun properly on his hip. It had to feel right. "Okay," Stone said even-voiced. "Ease up, Sarge. I'll get him."

Stone tried to move away, but Fowler planted his sweaty hand flat on Stone's chest. "Ho!" Fowler said; his brow unwrinkled, his grin grew wider, as though the physical contact blessed him with insight. "Sure . . . I know where he is."

Stone finally looked from Fowler's hand to his face, then at Fowler's drenched back, the sergeant having turned and barreled toward the door with a satisfied grunt. Officer Stone raced a few steps and snatched at Fowler's arm, only to have his fingers slide off.

"Hey, Sarge! I can—" Sgt. Fowler turned on his heels and stopped as Stone nearly collided into him. Fowler stuck his face in Stone's.

A quiet voice eased its way between clenched teeth. "Get to your car, Officer Stone."

Nose to nose, Stone held his ground as long as he could, his eyes locked on Fowler's. But the sergeant's stare was too crazed, his lips too puffed, his breath too strong—something about the mass of the man, the years on the force and on his face, the empty pit in Stone's stomach—Officer Stone backed down. Fowler licked the sweat from the corners of his mouth and nodded, then he flipped open the locker room door and left. Stone sat down on a bench, staring at the floor. His gun pulled at his right side, so he shifted the holster less than an inch to the left. No good. The balance was off. The gun hung off his hip like an extra appendage, heavy and useless.

His eyes kept searching.

The hot winds blew across midtown, baking buildings and leaving a cloudless nighttime sky. The heat surrounded the city and forced its surrender. Officer Jonathan Harding, in full dress blues except for his cap, which lay beside him like an openmouthed pet, sat above everything: the heat, the patrol that lay ahead, the incessant stir of people and traffic. Harding leaned against the short wall that circumscribed the roof of the police station, his body hidden from other rooftops, other eyes. The black tar-coated roof merged with the surrounding black walls; the walls merged with the dark horizon—only the sky itself was spoiled by stars. He felt tired. The night had become an inky blanket that covered a shiny sky with thousands of bright holes worn through.

Harding heard the roof door open. He barely glanced toward the noise. He could tell by the outline that it was Fowler, his shape unmistakably like an oversized inverted bulb. Harding pressed his head back up against the wall, wanting to feel the wall's pressure and the slight pulse that comes with it at the back of the skull.

The sergeant hesitated at the door for an instant. His

little confrontation with Officer Stone was nothing. Officer Stone was a boy in a uniform playing cop; he obeyed the game rules, understood the fist of authority. Officer Harding was another matter. Fowler was tired of complaining that Harding wouldn't even try the new "psycho service" the department offered. Fowler would alternate between being a buddy, his arm like a leg of lamb slung across Harding's shoulders, and being the man with the orders, "the bigger badge," as he put it. As self-designated morale officer, Fowler felt stuck in this one-two combination punch.

The wind continued to blow hot on Fowler's face as he stepped up slowly to the seated Harding. The sergeant's voice was even and low.

"Daydream's over, Holdberg. Patrol time."

Harding rose, almost levitated, to his feet, stiff, head down. He tugged on parts of himself and his uniform in rote motions of preparation.

"On my way, Sarge," Harding said.

He moved slowly across the rooftop toward the door, head still lowered, Sergeant Fowler watching Harding's broad shoulders recede from view. Fowler spoke to those shoulders.

"You know this—hiding-out business. This sulking crap. It's no damn good for the guys here."

Harding stopped and listened. He waited for Fowler to mention his wife next.

"And how about down there?" Fowler said, pointing his finger out past the low wall. "What kind of good you doin' out there, out in the street, with you all—all in that—that—" Fowler's voice rose. It wasn't what Fowler meant to say. "You're not doing—" Fowler stuttered and froze. He hated words and his lack of them. Harding stood there facing the door until Fowler finally shouted.

"Harding!"

Harding turned around and looked at Fowler, though his expression remained blank.

Fowler's low growl crawled across the tar pitch roof: "To hell with you, Harding."

Harding slipped the cap on his head. "Like I said, Sarge . . . *on my way.*"

Harding opened the rooftop door, and the red light from the EXIT sign above splashed down and filled his face with a crimson hue as he descended the stairs.

The Devil wasn't paying much attention to Officer Fanelli, who stood by the bench beside him. Instead he sat, arms folded, eyes moving from face to face: the barroom bruisers now wearing shamed looks; the girl, her brown bottom lip curled like a cinnamon stick, scolding; Officers Hall and Van Dam standing back and smiling at the scene. The Devil tried to peer behind them, almost through them, past milling cops to the corridor of cells and their occupants.

Officer Fanelli's face had offered only features best fitting a mule, a long protracted nose and spread eyes that blinked slowly, heavily. Swaying to no music whatsoever, Fanelli waited for Desk Sergeant Walcott to finish his magazine article, not out of politeness but because of an unspoken policy.

Officers, especially young ones, who interrupted Walcott's reading, his concentration, somehow felt the repercussions later through Fowler and the shift assignments he issued. Like getting cars with air conditioners that spit, or being handed lost paperwork recently found and needing immediate attention. Some officers thought the magnitude of the offense was determined by what reading matter Sergeant Walcott was unplugged from. Once a first-week patrol cop asked Walcott about the precinct's attendance procedure in the middle of a *Playboy* interview with Bo Derek. The patrol cop was transferred to the Forty-third—"another inner city winner," as its new precinct members are called—the very next week. Officer Kramer, Fanelli's partner in the current arrest, conveniently had to "hit the john," a bad bladder always the excuse for not attending to Sgt. Walcott's ritual.

"What's doin', Fanelli?" Walcott had suddenly looked up and caught Fanelli by surprise; midsway, the jolt nearly toppled him. Fanelli quickly made sure the Devil was still where he put him and walked to the desk, placing a short form in front of his superior.

"It's a six sixty-six, Sarge. Possession and sale of the hard stuff to some of the Cub Scouts we brought in earlier. Got some coke here, too."

Fanelli fingered a small bag of white powder from his breast pocket and placed it on top of the short form. Sgt. Walcott looked as though Fanelli had dumped a collection of roach droppings on his desk. "Nice," the sergeant mumbled.

He wrote an indecipherable notation on the form, then pointed his pencil at Fanelli's beak. "So bring your boy up here."

Fanelli jerked his arm for the Devil to stand and come to the desk.

Sgt. Walcott peeked up from his jottings to see what kind of street creature was approaching him. The Devil wore a brown shiny leather jacket that embraced his upper body like a thick coat of skin. His black cotton shirt fell open two buttons down to where a coffin-shaped charm sat just above the V plunge and was hooked to a thin gold necklace. Boots gave his already towering frame an even added measure of dominance. Not that Sgt. Walcott felt challenged by the oncoming figure. Just your standard Vegas drifter peddling dope for another gambling go-around, he figured. Still, two things bothered Walcott about this character. For one, the scarf, probably silk, that draped his shoulders was the fashion touch that labeled him artist or fag or a custom blend. Two, and more important, Sgt. Walcott couldn't get a lock on this guy's age. Sunglasses hiding his eyes was a factor, but his face at once looked like the cream of youth and then like something soured, something not old, but hard with age. No matter. This analysis was only a temporary mental structure Walcott quickly demolished and replaced with an edifice more traditional and more solidly built, one he always felt secure placing people in: the guy was a creep.

Walcott sighed and wrote the date, July 8, 1986, then poised his pencil above another line. "What's the name?"

The Devil's taut body transformed and melted into a humble posture. His tone was pure, his diction perfect; his voice was very sincere. Some would call it an FM voice. "Ah—well. It depends, you see, on which one you would like, Officer. I go by some biblical ones, some literary ones. There're a couple your average Joe calls me . . ." He paused in thought, then added, "Need something with a first *and* last name?"

The sergeant stared at the deadpanned face before him. He turned to Fanelli. "Where'd you get this guy? The fruitcake factory?"

Fanelli felt helpless and squirmed. "No ID on him, Sarge."

Walcott let out another breath and surrendered.

"All right," he said to the Devil, "just gimme one—your pick."

The Devil's face remained still; then his lips puckered. "The old ones are pretty strange. I'll just give you my latest. It's kind of good when you think about it."

Sgt. Walcott raised his left eyebrow. "Shoot," he said.

"Berner," the Devil replied. "With an 'e.' Sol Berner."

Walcott wrote quickly. "Sol . . . Berner. Okay." He stopped a moment, then glanced up at the Devil. "I don't get it."

The Devil did not reply. Instead his flat face cracked open like molten rock and out gushed a hot, Hollywood smile.

"I'm telling you, man. Forget making detective if Fowler parks on your ass." Stone had one foot up on a squad room table as he leaned in over his knee toward Harding, his hands out like a beggar.

Harding folded some papers and stuffed them in his shirt pocket; he put on a pair of dark sunglasses, which at least dimmed the bare bulb glare from the cheap metal table lamp aimed at him; swiveling in his seat, he looked up at Stone.

"Detective?" he said mockingly. "I blew that number long ago." Harding almost laughed. He pointed his thumb toward their waiting patrol car outside the metal-grated window and stood. "No, Stone, I'm afraid that down these mean streets a few big jerks must go." He tilted his head toward the back door, and Stone followed his lead.

"Whatever you say, Jonathan," Stone replied, shaking his head; then he laughed through his nose.

Suddenly shouts and scattered footfalls outside stopped the two patrolmen cold. The smoky glass panes of the precinct's front doors were being darkened by animated figures from a Punch and Judy shadow play. Harding, Stone, and a few fellow officers moved as one toward the noise, when first an intense beam of light struck the frosted glass and diffused on through; then the doors burst open with the urgency of an explosion: four patrolmen hustled in two teenaged boys with brown paper bags over their heads, their wrists cuffed, feet trying to keep pace;

followed by two television crews, each with a miked reporter and cameraman whose portable lights threw beams that turned white everything in their rambling pathway—suspects' backs, protective palms in front of eyes, the Devil's bright medallion; a local newspaper reporter tagged behind with archaic writing implements, shouting questions. Everyone was shouting except the bagged suspects. Sgt. Walcott stood, trying to pitch his voice above the din, telling Officer Fanelli with his eyes to move his suspect back. The Devil retreated one step voluntarily but looked intently at the new arrivals.

Word spread among the thicket of cops who watched from just beyond the front desk that one of the suspects was the son of the district's congresswoman. Kicked out of UCLA, he now was part of a protection racket that recently plagued the renovated specialty shops on Euclid Street near the boardwalk. Officer Van Dam had heard that the upstairs bulls with their wrinkled blue jackets, and ties as wide as bibs, planted a setup tonight. "And here's the payoff," Van Dam mumbled to Stone. "A celeb's kid, his pal, and media up the ass."

Sgt. Walcott got the arresting officers' attention while newsmen were being ushered back by Hall and Fanelli. When the jostled camera lights panned the onlooking clump of patrol cops, they quickly ducked their heads and scattered. Stone also dodged away, feeling guilty somehow. Harding, however, remained a witness. An anger inside him had ignited, and when the more snappily dressed of the two suspects bent down and elbowed the cop beside him, Harding jumped the boy like a hungry panther. He slammed the boy against the wall and yanked his hands together behind his back and would have made a knot if the boy's arms were long enough. The attending officer who had buckled over with the blow stood up straight and waved off any assistance. Immediately the paper bag jerked from side to side; the muffled words from inside the bag said it was an accident. Harding still gripped the boy's elbows tightly, not sure what to believe.

The Devil, meanwhile, having examined the boy's attire, focused in on the paper bag before him. His jaw imperceptibly tightened; his ears pulled back. In a fraction of a second, a tiny pearl of fire burst at the bottom of the bag, sped around its circumference to form a thin circle of flame, then, shooting upward, engulfed everything above the boy's shoulders, his head becoming a massive burning torch atop a contorted frame.

Harding fell back in shock as the boy let out a cry of horror; then the cry ceased with a jolting suddenness, like a needle quickly lifted off a record. The bag had evaporated as fast as it had ignited. The boy's face looked startled but wholly unscarred, not even singed. Undaunted, the television cameras focused in on their newly revealed subject, zoom lenses whirring. The Devil, disappointed with the face uncovered, pursed his lips. Harding, after hesitating, leaned into the boy's ear and said, "*Now* wave 'hi' to your mother." He had always wanted to do that—to somehow rip and tear or burn the bags right off these punks' heads every time he saw rapists and thugs on television with their K mart hoods protecting them, always imagining them laughing underneath like little pranksters: I-see-you-you-can't-see-me. Now, as if possessed by a demonic tickle, Harding laughed at what transpired, loudly, in a burst that hurt an unused muscle in his stomach. Stone, Fowler, Walcott, all were still frozen by the sudden fireball from nowhere, but Harding had enjoyed the moment too much to need to understand it. His laugh echoed in the front hall unshared; unshared except with the man who, unknown to Harding, was only a breath to his left. Then Harding turned his head, and finally he saw the smiling face, smiling like his, satisfied like his, with the camera's lights catching it all and glaring off two pairs of matching sunglasses, their reflections merging in the short space that separated Jonathan Harding and the Devil.

· two ·

S quad car 29 carrying Officers Harding and Stone
sped through downtown San Marco toward the
shoreline, leaving behind the buzz of wonderment
and speculation stirring up the precinct house over the
burning bag incident. Some fifteen-year-plus men barely
managed a shrug and said they'd seen a lot weirder and
went home to bed. Many others talked and joked about
it, feared it somewhere in the back of their throats,
and accepted Sgt. Walcott's explanation about "external
spontaneous combustion," probably because they all
wanted first crack at the new-model patrol cars due Sep-
tember or maybe because he *was*, after all, reading *Popular Mechanics*. In any case, the event itself, however scary and exciting, was becoming less so than the
anticipation of its telling—the Palm Tree Lounge would
be riddled with two A.M. off-duty anecdotes for nights on
end.

In sharp contrast, Stone and Harding said next to nothing for a good half hour into their route. Stone made sure he drove tonight. Even with the light traffic on the coast roads, Harding behind the wheel would have meant being chauffeured around the city by a cursing Jehovah who wanted to bust every slow turner, jaywalker, and stop-sign roller on the spot. "Diddlyshit," Stone would say to try and separate Harding from his intensity. But even though he would successfully deter Harding from making the collar and especially, thank God, from initiating the needless car chase, Stone would suffer the lectures, ones about the diddlyshit here and the diddlyshit there and the crap up to your nose. Somehow Stone would acknowledge that vision without a trace of condescension, and for the rest of the patrol, at least, Harding would feel appeased, his shoulders laid back a notch.

In the passenger seat, Harding gazed out the side window, his eyes unfocused behind the useless silver shades, watching things pass by in dark smears.

Stone bit his lip and circled the silence with his thoughts until he felt confident enough to grab hold and break it.

"Fowler mention June at all?" He looked to Harding as he would a locked closet door from the inside.

"Not this time," said Harding, still facing away. "Not directly, anyway."

"Happened to him, you know," Stone said. Harding's head flipped toward Stone. "I mean, his wife divorced him."

"I know," Harding said flatly, removing his sunglasses, an act Stone took as loosening the first brick from a wall.

"I heard from Van Dam and Hall that the sarge was pretty much of a wreck for a while." Stone looked for a response and got none. "So maybe he's trying to help," Stone explained. Harding's and Stone's eyes met and lingered for a moment.

Harding had to give his partner a quick smile. Stone always thought every open palm was a helping hand and never the first step to a slap in the face.

"Maybe," Harding said. "But if he wants to help so bad, maybe he could get June to move back downstate so I could see my kids more. So they're not some sort of ghosts from a past life."

"Still think he means well," Stone said.

They looked at each other more openly now, their bond reconnected, reinforcing the precinct's theory that Stone should have been a social worker, which could have been why four years ago they teamed him with Harding in the first place.

The patrol car cruised by the 7-Eleven store on Beecher Avenue where Chuck Sherry and his pals usually partied and piled the beer bottles up in the parking lot, some finding their way under customers' tires once in a while. But tonight there was no sign of the young toughs that had become a steady checkpoint on their post.

"Quiet, huh?" Stone said, pulling around the lot, catching a peek at Marty, the 7-Eleven owner who punched the register like a one-fingered piano player, then moving back onto Beecher.

"Mmmm," Harding said as he watched a bird's silhouette darken one of the low metal lamplights that lined the renovated block. The patrol car soon slipped into a residential area of San Marco known as the Tweenum section, a name recently popularized by the San Marco press. It was the area for people who could afford neither the rebuilt beachfront apartments and condos nor the older onlookers, the Victorian spreads that graced the hills along the ocean. It was the area "'tween 'em." It was where the blue-collar workers who drove to Kingsfield and its power plant lived. It was where all the civil servants who flew in and out of city hall and the county courthouse and clogged Seacliff Road at seven A.M. sharp lived. It was where Jonathan Harding had lived all his life.

"I'd still like to get my mitts on the deadbeat who told Sgt. Beans about my short stint in law school." Harding glared at Stone, but this time Stone remained silent. Stone never thought it was much of a mystery, not the way Harding spat out trial records and even occasionally threw in a Latin phrase that once made Van Dam roll his eyes so hard his contacts flew from his sockets and into a nearby mop bucket.

Stone looked concerned. "You mean he pulled the Holdberg bit again?"

Harding shook his head in disgust. "He loves that Holdberg routine because he knows it burns my butt."

Stone made a face. "So why do you let it?"

Harding couldn't answer him; he fingered his belt buckle and shrugged. The answer seemed locked up with an image of his mother and her stare, one of accusation mixed with sad disappointment at his becoming an officer in the first place. "People are going to call you 'copper,'" she said as the first words out of her worry-lined mouth when he had finally made up his mind to apply at the police academy. He would shake his head as if to shake loose the non sequitur from his ears. His mother had envisioned him as a lawyer, the trim-suited professional untouched by the gutter, which was why he attended law school for two years, a concession to her vision before he quit. Later, as a rookie cop he would try to explain to her the difference. Harding did not see law enforcement as sword-bearing heroes out to slay society's foes—he wasn't that naive. A cop was like a garbage picker, poking his pointed stick in all the dark city corners and dimmed alleyways, skewering any and all two-legged trash that skittered down sidewalks making life unsightly by their presence and dangerous by their penchant for gathering violence. Cops dutifully hauled this trash to prevent it, as an accumulating force, from smothering the city. "Lawyers," Harding told his mother, "all they do is dump the garbage back in the street." In response Mrs. Harding, untouched by metaphor, had simply performed her stare, the one perhaps Sgt. Fowler, too, had perfected with a scowl to underline his intent.

Harding thought he heard Stone say something about food or God; he couldn't tell. ". . . this late night," was the tail end of it. "What did you say?" he asked.

Stone dropped his mouth open a notch as he waited for a red light and turned to his puzzled partner. "You know, Jonathan—the big sarge has a point—you *do* kinda get yourself lost in there, man, in those thoughts."

Harding stared straight ahead at the crossing strings of streetlights that dotted the hills and veered off into all directions, twisting. He shook his head. "It's outside them where I get lost," he said.

Ralphie Moranis sneered at Sgt. Fowler, who passed his holding cell and looked at him, at least in Ralphie's mind, as if he were a lean and mean young animal captured from the wilds and hungry and the big-bellied sergeant, his keeper; as if the sergeant were fearful that the caged creature would be set free, knew that he would, or even better, that he would gnaw through iron bar and human bone and break loose and leap upon the city, claws out and ripping. In truth, Sgt. Fowler glanced at the glaring face with a professional blankness: another punk in the tank. Sgt. Fowler jangled his keys and left the jail area.

Ralphie pulled his fingers through his beard and laughed to himself, saw himself smile at himself, and strutted around the cell. More than once in the last several years, C. L. Poser, his lawyer, shook him loose before the night faded into day; he had no reason to think otherwise tonight. Looking at his two partners, Rick Hernandez and Tommy Longo, laid out on two parallel cots, sleeping off the vodka and pills, Ralphie started to giggle. It had been a good time these seven or so years together. The money could choke you, the women could wear you out, and the drugs, whether you were dealing or using, flowed easy as if passing through one communal bloodstream; the city and "the boys" were flying. Ralphie smoothed out his new seven-hundred-dollar suit, then, leaning back, closed his eyes to feel the bars cool his hot back.

Then he heard approaching footsteps, saw the neighboring cell door creak open, and watched Officer Fanelli deposit a man inside, a man whose eyes burned through his own sunglasses and into the eyes of Ralphie Moranis. The cell door slammed shut, and with it Ralphie felt his heart constrict and collapse upon itself. His veins and arteries shook, the drugs kicking in like a SWAT team, as he staggered back a step, then another. Slowly he drifted back, withering, stumbling backward to his cot, sitting, still facing the man in the next cell. Only Ralphie's eyes began to glaze, and every drop of his dreams drained from his soul. He sat there shriveled like a wild jungle flower exposed to a heat far too intense even for its exotic makeup. Ralphie didn't bother to wake his friends. They would know soon enough.

The Devil, still standing, still staring, eyes smoking in a victory pyre, felt relieved. His search had ended.

The fire surged and puffed up like a bright, red balloon, then another explosion spewed charcoal-gray clouds like a giant can of sooty shaving cream oozing and growing and swallowing the building that stood as its source and its victim. Harding spotted the fire a mile or two off up on the western hill, maybe halfway up. It dominated the hillside and the sky, as the sirens became just audible inside the patrol car. Stone watched his partner more than the nighttime show, watched Harding leaning over, his nose just above the glove compartment, gazing so intensely through the windshield.

"Looks like a four-alarmer," Harding said, not moving. A ladder truck turned a corner three blocks ahead and onto their street, speeding ahead even farther.

"Looks mean, man," Stone injected. No question he was now especially glad he took over the driving duties tonight. He knew Harding would have pumped his foot on the gas pedal and radioed in that they were going to the scene "as an assist." He knew Harding wanted him to do that right now, but the pact to which they had agreed since the beginning of their long partnership originated from their favorite game of poker: dealer's (read: driver's) choice. Stone had the wheel; Stone held the cards. Otherwise any excuse would have been good enough for Harding—traffic blockade, first aid, crowd control. Not that these weren't legitimate assignments for a fire, but they were to be just that—*assigned*. Otherwise, you were to keep to your post.

Many a Fowler tantrum erupted from a Harding sidetrip to a local blaze. Once a liquor store on their post was robbed of about fifty dollars while Harding was tailing Engine No. 16 to a burning warehouse. The store was only a block away from where at that hour they probably would have been scarfing down free Chinese food behind Wing Lo's. But by the time they swung back and reached the crime scene that night, the crook was gone. Out of guilt, Harding pulled fifty dollars from his next paycheck and sent it to the liquor store owner in a letter signed by a made-up neighborhood fund established for such catastrophies. "I fucked up," Harding said as the reason for the mailing, sort of an evening up, which left a clean slate for his next excursion because the fire chasing did not stop.

Stone remembered one time in particular when "Beans" Fowler actually appeared at the burning of the old Clothes Barn on Fairlawn. Fowler appeared only because he was off duty, and the heat and commotion were rumbling through his own neighborhood. Wearing street clothes as wrinkled as his uniform blues, he popped Stone on the shoulder, much to Stone's surprise. And then, even further to Stone's surprise, he said absolutely nothing. Off duty was off duty, so Fowler stood and observed his boys, including Stone, keep the surging people back and the "hosers" (Fowler's wit) aim their nozzles toward the smoky blaze. Then Fowler blinked, did a double take. There was Harding, twenty feet in front of him. Not controlling crowds (which Stone knew he never did), not redirecting traffic (again, never), but standing hypnotized by the fire. Not by the fire fighters in their struggle, but by the actual fire, as it licked its way up corners and burst its way through windows, commanding the scene and Harding's eyes like a war-whipped soldier shooting up a storm in a last blast of shot and shell.

But what dumbfounded Fowler was that there wasn't even a hint of excitement in Harding's gaze. His eyes were dead; his face granite. His body was bowed—he looked like a shadow with such a fiery backdrop. He looked lost.

Fowler turned to Stone, puzzled and even worried. "What's he looking at?"

Fowler wasn't the first person to ask Stone that question at such a time—he heard it from firemen, fellow cops— but to Stone it was never the right question. The right question was—"What's he looking *for?*"

Stone knew, and he pulled the car around Gaines Avenue. The view of the hillside conflagration was quickly eclipsed by a series of six-story, brick-front apartment buildings. Harding slid down in his seat, his head awk-wardly back on the squared vinyl top; his view the car roof. A long, shaky breath was released seemingly from his whole body as if it were full of leaks.

"What do you figure?" Stone said. "It had to be more than one of those Victorian places with that kind of smoke, huh? It's a shame."

Gaines Avenue curved westward, and the hillside was alight once again, now adding a pink glow to the trees that bent with the heat. With the renewed spectacle came the question Stone never asked, wanting to, turning to Harding even now, then letting the words float idly through his mind alone:

"Your father always come back to you when you see a fire?"

Just as well Stone didn't ask. Harding would not have heard him, as a fire truck, loud and clanging, flashed past the squad car and down the deserted street like a hysterical woman screeching, running from the sight of her murdered husband.

• three •

A quick peek down Holden Street off Gaines, and Stone's eyebrows lifted. "Hey, that was Gardenhire, I think."

Harding raised himself in his seat as Stone made a compact U-turn and fast right onto Holden, where squad car 33 was positioned in front of a battered green Buick half a block down.

"Yeah, that's him," Stone confirmed.

"Gardenhire, huh?" Harding said, trying to sound interested. "Knopfler with him?"

Stone saw Gardenhire clearly; he was leaning an arm on the Buick discussing something with the driver, then looking into the backseat where the silhouette of a head appeared.

"Maybe Knopfler's on the radio," Stone said, squinting, "'cause I don't see him."

Harding grimaced. "He's probably calling in for a

three-squad backup." Stone chuckled. Officer Knopfler, a known lagger, was always letting his partner approach vehicles first. He hated confrontations and had little fondness for talking overall. The dispatcher, Officer Mary Gates, whose radio voice was often likened to a factory whistle, would yell into the mike for Knopfler to stop chewing his socks when he talked and speak up. Knopfler said such exchanges reminded him of talking to his wife on the phone, a comparison he revealed, not to complain, but almost as if to explain the comfort he derived from being on the receiving end. Somehow there was security in the shrill tones from a known screamer not found in the grumble of an unknown motorist.

Gardenhire, on the other hand, was a perpetual mouth flapper. He would yack to a deaf-mute or a snarling dog without a blink or need for response. Something with ears was his only qualification, though the house plants that garnered his bachelor studio were surely susceptible.

Stone stopped the car across the narrow street from the Buick, which faced the other way, south back toward Gaines.

"Gardy! Say, fella!" Stone shouted.

The stocky officer glanced behind him and smiled a gap-toothed smile that made him look like a country boy when in fact he was born in the slum center of San Marco, the Bradley district.

"Stone . . . well." Gardenhire crouched to stare at Harding. Harding stared back. Gardenhire straightened and directed his punctuated speech toward Stone.

"You on your way up to or down from the big to-do on the hill?"

"Neither," Stone said.

"What? Passing this baby up?" Gardenhire turned and

stuck his flat hand straight across his brow like a statue of Hiawatha. "Yeah," he said, acknowledging the sight. "I thought anything greater than a Zippo gone haywire and your car was there." He snapped his fingers.

Stone felt Harding's presence grow behind his back like a threatening storm cloud.

"No, man, not tonight," Stone said, hoping to change the subject. "So what gives here? Any problems?"

Gardenhire flapped his hand as if it were cardboard. "Nah, couple of bad boys is all." He lowered his head back to the Buick's window. His voice went from mush to marble.

"I thought I said to step outside."

The young man forced air through his teeth, puffing his cheeks and closing his eyes, then slipped out of the car to his feet, flipping shoulder-length hair away from his stubbled chin. Harding peered over Stone's shoulder and out the window. It was Chuck Sherry. Harding wondered what Sherry was doing out of position, way over on the north side of town. He also wondered where his buddies were. Then he craned to see who the dark image was in the backseat.

"Glad you could make it," Gardenhire said to the leaner, taller boy before him.

"Big fuckin' hassle, man," Sherry said, flexing his tattoo and shifting his feet. His hair flopped from side to side in a split-second lag after his face moved. Stone laughed to himself how this sixties Neanderthal looked as ridiculous as an Eisenhower crewcut, though he knew how he sometimes, out of habit, touched two fingers to the back of his own ear and slid them through to the base of his neck, then up, moving the ghosts of a thick mop that had once cascaded to his shoulders like a brown waterfall.

"What's the charge, Gardy?" Stone asked.

"Yeah, what's the fuckin' charge?" Sherry parroted, his left hand pointing down and tapping an invisible table, a freaky lawyer making his case while lung-soaked with weed.

Gardenhire talked to Stone as one eye kept fixed on the wobbly suspect. "What's it look like? Flying without a license. Usin' this stuff as fuel." Gardenhire displayed three joints in his hand as though he had eight fingers. "Found these in his shirt pocket." He laughed. "You should get clips for them next time," he advised Sherry. "Clip them next to your pencils like me." Gardenhire stuck the left side of his chest out in front of Sherry's nose, showing off the three number-two pencils and one ball-point peeking over his pocket in a neat line.

Small dribblings of knowledge penetrated the dope and started seeping through to Sherry's brain. "Ya sayin' I was drivin', man? I was sittin' here. No way I was driving! I was fuckin' *sittin'* here!"

Harding looked at Gardenhire make a face and knew Sherry was telling the truth. There was a souped-up, eight-cylinder engine pulsing in that Buick that green-streaked up and down Gaines Avenue like a neon flash and never once gave in to a patrol car in pursuit. Gardenhire just liked to bust chops and long-hairs, and he got double his money with the loitering Sherry. Sherry would think twice about ever leaving Harding and Stone's post, where Stone, once having backed Harding off, would have chased Sherry home and pocketed the loose joints for a Monday Night Football game at Harding's apartment.

"You bustin' me 'cause I was *drivin'*, ya say?" Sherry was hopping around in a small circle, his sneakers together, his fists flailing. "Oh, man! Shit!"

"Probable cause for the search, babe." Gardenhire turned to Stone. "This guy's a scream," he said, then his face threw on a serious expression. "Hey, you in the back," Gardenhire yelled, "we have to go downtown. Come on!"

Harding saw the shadowed head move toward the rear side window as the streetlight cut down the side of his face, displaying only shard pieces—a flat nose, a shiny upper cheek, and then eyes, blurred and strange and stoned on something far more potent than marijuana. Those toys you hold one-handed and pump with your thumb and watch the wheel—all colors and sparks— spin; those wheels were his eyes.

Harding looked at Sherry, knowing the kid was now dangerously out of his depth, that that stupid leftover hippie was trying to move up in status and years, twenty years, past the homegrown highs and prescription poppers and up into the 1980s. That meant cocaine and maybe worse; not uncommon to San Marco, just not the stuff of 7-Eleven turf kings.

Harding shook his head and sensed he had better get out of the car. The shadow in the backseat was no gang member, was an outsider, was more than likely not to know the rules. Gardenhire had stumbled onto an exchange, and his chatter at once insulated him from his awareness of it and revealed how he, like Sherry, was dangerously out of his depth.

"How about my rights, pig?" Sherry was almost crying. "You didn't give me my rights!"

Gardenhire planted a puss on his face. "You want Miranda—shit." He exhaled, then grimaced. "You have the right—face the friggin' car," he said, pushing Sherry down for a frisk. "You have the right to remain silent. Everything you say—I mean, anything you say—" Gardenhire stopped, then shouted toward the front. "Knopfler!"

Then in a low voice back to Sherry: "I only got the tune, he knows the words." Knopfler stuck his head out the window, stunned, looking like a kid called home early from stickball.

"Mirandize this chump!" Gardenhire shoved Sherry toward his partner, then bent over toward the Buick's back window, toward the patchwork-lit head with eyes like a spiral staircase. "I want your friend," he growled to himself.

Harding jumped out of the car, startling Stone. Sherry jerked back toward Gardenhire, suddenly afraid, suddenly shouting, "No!" loud, almost loud enough to smother the sound of the shot.

The barrel of the gun approximated the size of the brass shirt button above Gardenhire's belt, and at that point, the bullet, having been fired point-blank, bored a bloody tunnel, drilling its way through his stomach, past his spine, and fleeing out his back cleanly, leaving behind a hole of equal size no button could plug. Gardenhire's eyes and mouth, however, grew far wider than that, and the killer's grin wider still.

Then the puzzle-face and the hot gun barrel quickly vanished as Gardenhire's body slapped against the Buick's open back window. Harding pulled his gun, diving back behind his rear fender. Stone screamed, "Gardy!" then flung himself back toward the passenger seat, his hand grabbing once, twice, for the radio, his eyes hurting.

All twisted up, Chuck Sherry almost flipped over his own wiry legs, but regaining balance, he ran madly past the front patrol car; his hair, a straight brown streak, shot from the back of his head, giving him the look of a speeding comic book character. Knopfler by reflex jerked the car in gear and swerved the hood toward the fleeing man. He clipped Sherry just below the left thigh, catching his heel in the right tire and cracking his leg as the bony gang leader then bounced against a stop sign and fell, screaming, his hands outstretched, wanting to touch the center of his pain, yet not being able to do so.

"Jerk," said Harding to himself. Not only did Knopfler slam into a nonentity in this shooting, but he unblocked the Buick's pathway. The killer, after firing another shot that assured all heads were down, dove over the front seat, started the car, and rammed the gas pedal to the floor. The Buick jerked, the front tires leaping up like attacking panthers, and swerved down the road in a roar of exhaust and speed that made Harding cringe.

He leaped in the middle of Gaines Avenue and, with his boots straddling the double yellow line, locked himself into firing position, both fists squeezing the butt of his .38. The Buick looked invisible now, the dark green body faded into nothing between the distant pools of street-lamp light; only its taillights shone, burned red and round and full, like eyes that never dared to blink but smoldered in the dark. Harding aimed between those eyes, and his gun kicked with both shots fired—one, two—into the night toward the retreating beast. But the beast only roared in disgust and let loose a plume of exhaust that blanketed the street, its distant eyes smaller and beadier still in the smoky shroud.

Harding clambered toward the squad car, stumbling. Chuck Sherry screamed at him just as he screamed at the world at large, screamed at his motherfucking leg, a leg he felt was no longer his, felt detached from, a thing disowned, bloody and misshapen.

Harding answered Sherry's screams with a yank at the squad car door and its following slam. He pushed Stone's hunched form onto the passenger seat. Stone fell onto his side and against the glove compartment as his hand still gripped the radio transmitter and his heart thumped in his ears. He wasn't sure he had radioed in. He wasn't sure he had a voice at all.

"Unit fifty-two! Code fifteen! Code fifteen! Bring the wagon to Holden off Gaines! Hurry!"

"Heard you the first time, fifty-two," Officer Gates said, her voice pitched and shrill through the radio's crackle.

Harding pushed his foot to the floor, and the jolt flipped Stone upright on the passenger seat like a kid's inflatable punching bag. Stone looked up, startled. He looked past Harding's stern profile toward the street and at a slumped Knopfler crouched over his inert partner and staring at the blood-soaked hole that spewed red throughout Gardenhire's sky-blue shirt. Knopfler ignored the siren's burst and the haunted screams of Chuck Sherry, ignored the squad car careening past, flinging loose stones off his cheek and arm. This was his place, the hole was his place; he crouched motionless and watched a piece of a man he could never fill.

Stone's image of Knopfler vanished with the car's jump start and was replaced by the pumped-up cop in the driver's seat next to him. Harding was at the wheel, and the fire he was chasing wasn't up the hill anymore or even blowing gas fumes down the street but somewhere buried in his heart. Stone clipped his seat belt: he knew he was in for a ride.

The Buick skidded into a right turn two short blocks up, its tail bobbing as it caught the corner curb, then scraped a few sparks loose when it landed. The patrol car followed, screaming its way down Holden in the Buick's smoky wake. Harding's foot was fixed flat to the floor; he jerked the wheel—the backside of the patrol car swerved out, then joined the front in its own sharp turn right.

Stone sat tense, his right hand holding the badge on his

chest as though his heart were suddenly exposed and tin an eighth of an inch thick.

Harding spotted the Buick up ahead, only a block away now. He straightened his lips in a suppressed smile: he'd get him on the turns; he was no match on the straight-aways, but he'd take large bites out of the street on the turns until he was close enough to swallow that Buick whole.

"Report your position, fifty-two. Report position, fifty-two," the radio intoned.

Stone, who still unknowingly had not released the microphone, shoved it toward his mouth. "We're on Bolton Avenue heading east past Carmine Road. We're approaching the city limits on the north side. Request assistance, fifty-two."

The radio buzzed, then cleared. "Assistance uncertain, fifty-two. Fire at East Hills grabbed a lot of units. We'll see who is northbound."

Stone grimaced. "Do that," he grumbled to himself.

"I intend to," Officer Gates replied.

"Always the last friggin' word," Stone said to no one in particular.

The radio responded, "Always."

Harding glanced toward Stone. "Maybe if you let go the button . . ."

Stone saw his thumb still pressing the red button on the microphone. He muttered, "Shit," and quickly flung the mike down. It struck the dashboard, then danced like a puppet on its coiled wire, banging in punishment against the floorboard with each high-speed bump, Officer Gates strung up by her flat heels and fat ankles.

The Buick pulled into a hard left and nearly struck a pair of winos, who clutched at their tattered sacks and fell to the street in fear; prone, they lay indistinguishable from the bags of clothing they clutched and cursed upon.

Harding barely missed one of the crumpled bum's boots as he streaked past in a siren whine, driven on by the satisfaction of knowing that another turn meant another stretch of pavement closer, closer to the red eyes and the puzzle-faced killer ahead.

He felt lucky, too. The streets at the north end were especially deserted past six P.M., let alone past midnight. Blocks of beat-up factories lay dormant, spooky by their bulk and silence; you felt like an echo driving between them—they were the twentieth-century equivalent of antediluvian caves. The few bedraggled dwellers were homeless, aged men who now watched the flash of two cars career past their quiet alleys and briefly shock them into their nightmare world from a dream state induced by cheap vino and a dulled mind.

The vacant streets and vacant minds meant a deserted world divorced from the rights of pedestrians and the clockwork beam of red lights, of demands from stop signs and school crossings. It meant speed and unbridled release, of gunning engines and skidding turns; it meant catching something outside oneself at full tilt like racing naked after a bear in a thicket. It meant being "outside" it all: the city, the people, the law; the deserted northside meant all that to Harding and was precisely why he felt lucky.

". . . the fuck this guy going?" Stone said.

"What's that?" Harding asked.

"I said, 'Where's he going?' You think he's going somewhere in particular? Some destination? Where in hell's he taking us? And where's the friggin' backup?"

"I don't know," Harding replied, eyes dead on the road.

Stone cocked his head. He thought he heard Harding add, "I don't care," and in truth he heard right.

Stone didn't like what he was feeling; he didn't like the

buildings whipping by or the fear swimming in his stomach. He wanted the chase to end, a patrol car to jut out a side street like a bolt in a lock and cut it all off . . . *now*.

It was precisely the click of the jail cell lock—not the shuddering groan from the next bunk or the flick of the match from the next cell, not even the clang of that cell's door shutting—which jarred Tommy Longo's heavy lids open.

Through a squint he saw Fowler's fat ass walking away from the jail area. He sat up on his elbows, bleary and dry-mouthed and more than a little scared. The click of the lock next door shook him up, closed him in, like something reached into his head and shut down the system. The drugs were playing on him bad, or maybe just easing off enough to let the world crash in too fast. He liked the control, the chemically induced power to push it all out, to allow just the sweet stuff in, liked being his own psychic doorman.

"The dream is done, T. L. It's wake-up time," Longo said aloud to himself. Or did he? He didn't feel his lips move. Longo ran his tan, tapered fingers along his mouth. He hadn't felt his lips for days, so maybe it *was* him. Only it didn't sound like . . . it sounded like . . .

Longo quickly pulled his body up and faced something beside him he thought was his main man, Ralphie, but, leaning in, started thinking otherwise. He could barely recognize him. Longo was looking at a slab of fear lying like cold butcher's meat next to him, some white-faced son of a bitch who got the blood sucked out of him, his brains mangled, *something*, 'cause Ralphie just lay there, more scared than alive and sweating like a goddamn steam valve.

Longo heard the voice again, not from his lips for sure, and certainly not from Ralphie's shivering, blank mask. It was from somewhere behind, far off in Longo's head, like an echo inviting him to look down a dark well: "Tommy."

Longo turned slowly, his heart rate tripled, his mouth numb and open. The Devil sat on a cot in the adjacent cell, one leg up, his hand dangling over his knee holding a lit cigarette. "How they hanging, Tommy? They still hanging? You got any left?" the Devil asked, not smiling, not condemning, just showing a curiosity for the facts.

"What's going on, man?" Longo said, his voice dry, his throat feeling all rotted out like an old lead pipe. He said it like he was passing time, being cool, but all that came out was a sudden spurt of water in his pants he didn't notice.

Longo noticed, however, the silence and the Devil's stare, and he moved about his cot uncomfortably, unable to stay still. "So what's going on?" A little more desperate this time. Longo tried to laugh. "You got arrested or something?"

The Devil shrugged. "I got myself arrested a few times tonight," he said casually. The Devil liked jails, liked going in the "normal" way, too. Getting arrested got you in closer to the other prisoners, got you to hear about their stories and, more important, their needs. Popping in and out like a spook only scared the crap out of them, which he liked to do, too, but he'd save the special effects only for certain times: to have a laugh, to make a point, to punch out an "arrangement."

Jails were good places to meet old clients with debts due and new clients with fatal dreams. Jails smelled of desperation, and that always meant an opening, like a vulnerable cut, a wound the Devil could walk through like a vaulting archway and, quite simply, make a deal. It was all about making deals.

"Hit a few jails," the Devil continued. "Figured I'd bump into you gents eventually. Slumming around. . . ."

Longo now squatted with both feet on his cot, his body pushing against the far wall, wishing the stone would move, would give him room. "The fuck you *want!?*" He knew the answer somewhere, but if the stone could move, could make a hole, a loophole—

The Devil snapped the thick, folded paper open with a sharp flick of his wrist, the noise making Longo flinch. He looked wide-eyed and innocent as he pointed. "The contract, Tommy. The contract."

The cars both veered east again, then back south, then east, then north; circular at times, dizzying, the patrol car gaining at each turn. Harding could almost see the green now. He shoved himself a few inches closer to the wheel. He could see the green paint shimmer between the crimson lights.

The cars were no more than three lengths apart, and they stayed that way for some time throughout the northside. It had become not so much a chase, but the head and tail of the same animal, winding and twisting its body through alleys and up curbs, whipping from side to side, skittering along, testing itself, enduring.

One last left and the patrol car found itself nearly up against the green trunk, the Buick almost veering into a newspaper stand and beyond on the turn; Harding broke just enough to whip the front tires into position and cut clean the corner.

"Yes!" Harding said as though slam-dunking the word down his pursuant's throat. Then the Buick suddenly swerved onto a ramp that became Primrose Road, a coastal two-laner that snaked up the ocean bluffs on the outskirts of San Marco. Harding struck the steering wheel with the flat of his palm. "Damn it!"

Stone fished for the weaving radio mike. He snatched it

and called in. "Fifty-two. Fifty-two. Suspect out of north-side moving up shoreline on Primrose. You got backup in the district or what?"

Harding already knew the answer. Primrose sat up above the water, overgrown and underpopulated and too close to the city limits for San Marco to care. The Winston Beach force might care if they stationed some sleepy-eyed motorcycle jockey on the borderline, a practice more than one tourist filed complaints to the state board about. But not at this hour, not on this night. No—he and Stone were flying solo, and somehow Harding felt that was the point.

"Units eighty-three and seventy-two in northside," squawked Gates. "On their way, fifty-two."

"We're not *in* northside," Stone snapped.

"Heard you the first time, fifty-two. They're right behind."

Stone felt helpless. "What about Winston Beach? Suspect ready to cross the line."

"We'll try contact, fifty-two." Gates's voice sounded anything but soothing.

Stone threw the mike back at the floor and shook his head. ". . . believe this, man."

Harding hadn't paid any attention to the radio or to Stone. He felt his guts were slowly pulling away from him, as was the green Buick, six feet, ten feet . . . The upward slope and Chuck Sherry's overdriven engine worked to allow the killer's car to drift ahead gradually, as though in 75 MPH slow motion. Only the lack of straight road, the constant coastal curves, kept the patrol car from watching its prey immediately jerk away in a great streak of speed and disappear into a far bend of foliage.

Harding began to sweat; the red lights were accusing again, becoming eyes again, the green fading, the night closing in the widening gap.

Harding twisted his head toward Stone. "You ready?" he said.

Stone's eyes shifted toward the hunched driver. He knew what Harding meant. "Hey, man—"

"No 'Hey, man,' man," Harding cut in. "We're losing the son of a bitch. Let's go!"

Fifteen feet, twenty—Harding's left eye measured the beast's retreat in the coming wisps of fog such altitude brings. Harding felt as though he were still, docked, watching a boat drift from the shore and his shaky grasp.

"That's cops-and-robbers crap, man," Stone said. "That's not procedure, and you—"

"Shit," Harding said, and yanked the gun from the holster on his right hip with his left hand and started to roll down the window, but with the sudden motion, his right hand slipped the wheel and the car skidded sideways about six feet up an embankment. Stone dove sideways and threw the wheel left; Harding's foot hit the brake, and the car spun loose, wagging itself like a tail without a dog, and screeched when its tires touched the fog-slicked pavement and bolted down the highway again.

Stone's face flushed. His breath, frosted from the cooler air, was forced out in scattered little puffs. His voice was low. "Damn you, Jonathan."

The Buick had them by two car lengths now. Harding, too, breathed heavy, shaken by the car's rebellion and near-successful grasp for control. Stone kept staring at him, shaking his head. You didn't shoot your .38 from a speeding cop car window, especially on a curve-ridden road such as this. You might miss your fleeing target and hit a motorist. Or a pedestrian. Even on a deserted road, on a foggy, godforsaken night like this. You didn't shoot your .38 into the fog and the darkness and hope to hit an outline, a green ghost disguised as an animal.

Then Harding's voice came out of the silence, beyond anger, resigned, almost sad. "We're out here, Stone," Harding said, "out in space, man. We're cut off." Harding shook his head three times. "Cut off. . . ." Then he said nothing. His pistol sat on the floor between his feet.

Maybe it was the vacuumlike void speed becomes: the sound of air *swoosh*ing. Maybe it was the fog, the condensation dripping on the windows like streaks of rain. Maybe it was the white noise static from the crackling radio buzzing in Stone's ears. Or what Harding just said. Or didn't say. Or the painful feeling that they had definitely gone beyond some point together, crossed over a borderline some time back, and it wasn't the one that lay between San Marco and Winston Beach. Whatever it was, Stone exhaled and slowly withdrew the pistol from his holster.

He was a good shot, a target master, second-place marksman at the state regionals. The trophy made his father smile. On the practice range Officer Van Dam always supplied the needle: "Why you such a good shot, Stone? I mean, for such an old hippie peacenik."

Stone would half smile and shrug, a little annoyed. "I don't know," he answered once. "At demonstrations I was a lot better at conking a cop at a hundred feet with a rock than I am with a pistol." Van Dam didn't bother with him much that day after that answer, even in joking, though the whole story was a lie. Stone had never heaved a rock at anything more serious than the still plane of pond water that stretched out past his parents' backyard at woods' end, let alone a cop's head. It would have been like hitting family.

Stone smiled to himself, then his eyes refocused and fixed themselves past the fog onto the two red beams that glowed up ahead; his jowls slowly fell, then tensed. His left hand started to crank down the side window. His right hand readied the gun.

Harding fidgeted and leaned forward as if his body weight could push the car through the curves any faster, push the gas pedal closer to the engine. A wider bend made its appearance, and the patrol car gained half a car length and that was all.

"Now or never, man," Harding said. Stone stuck his head out into the wind, his arm extended straight, the gun jittering from the air pressure and the cold. He shot one round toward the Buick, and nothing. It was as if it were a phantom, the bullet passing through it. Harding growled, and now even Stone was irked by what had happened. Not even the *ting* of metal, a ricochet off the trunk, nothing. The Buick drifted another five feet farther away as the curve started to straighten.

Stone quickly reaimed and fired. In a pop of glass exploding, one of the red taillights burst, leaving only one red eye ahead in an unlit, fog-packed road to follow.

"Don't blind the son of a bitch!" Harding shouted, though he knew that wasn't what he meant, knew that it was *he* that was turning blind, that the beast was about to disappear from sight, the killer beast, this verdant speeding cyclops of an eight-cylinder motherfucking ghost machine.

Just as feared, the coastal highway straightened; only one sharp, blind turn lay ahead, then for the most part a road that might as well be a runway: the Buick would take flight and soar.

Harding's eyes brightened, flashed toward Stone. "Reach over and can the lights right after the Buick makes the blind turn up ahead."

"What?"

"Can the lights," Harding shouted. "Everything—the headlights, the flashers. No siren."

"Why?" Stone said, disoriented.

"Just *do it*, man!" Harding said, gripping the wheel,

watching the single red bulb fade right and vanish half a dozen car lengths ahead. "Now!"

Stone reacted quickly, flicking the siren switch, the flasher switch, and banging in the headlight knob with his fist. They watched their vision grow dark. The last thing Harding saw was a yellow diamond sign, its bent arrow telling him to veer right immediately or be airborne above ocean rock. Harding yanked hard at the wheel, and the car responded with a piercing screech like a baby being pulled from its womb, hugging the road for security.

Harding spotted the single red light up ahead, and as if by will, it grew larger, closer. Stone looked amazed. Stone had failed to understand what Harding instinctively knew: that the way to beat a phantom is to be a phantom, the way to beat darkness, be darkness.

The Buick had heard the screech, saw no car, no lights, slowed in that split second of curiosity. And in that split second, Harding gunned his engines, drove the car almost by the sheer force of his shoulders swelling. Stone's head reentered the night's gusts, and his arm shot out, his gun cocked.

"Stone, baby!" Harding yelled.

"Yeah!" Stone cried out, his mouth wind-filled. Harding moved swiftly, and the patrol car's lights burst on like the first flash of an explosion. They struck the Buick flush ahead, only ten feet ahead, exposed and vulnerable for maybe the last time. Stone trained his sights down, down at the roadway, just past the border of the taillight's red glow, down at the rear tire. He had never seen anything so suddenly, so clearly, in his life. He cracked a big smile, and two shots flew and penetrated rubber.

The right rear tire flattened instantly, and the Buick became an imbalanced chunk of green metal flying into a backside spin. As it swerved a full half-circle, its headlights found Harding's eyes and filled them with penetrating light. He swung right; the patrol car bucked over a bumper rail and landed on a bushy slope. Stone smacked his collarbone on the dashboard; Harding's head snapped back. The Buick's whirl ended when its left side smashed up against two sloped trees and some overhanging branches fell over the roof and down its other side. Both cars lay dead and swallowed by fog.

The dotted line cut across his eyes like a four-inch scar with his name on it. The Devil had stuck the contract through the bars and into Longo's face close enough so he could smell his own dried blood on the document.

"So? Yeah! So?" Longo was retreating now, stumbling back. "What's the deal? No big deal. We have a deal. Okay. We're here now, so tomorrow we're maybe out and doing again and we'll see you sometime lat—"

"Nix tomorrow, Tommy," the Devil said.

"What?"

The Devil sighed and rolled his eyes and hated having to say it, but: "There is no tomorrow, Tommy." The Devil looked at the befuddled little man in the overpriced suit.

"What are you talking?" Longo said, shaking his head.

"No tomorrow," the Devil repeated. "The time's up. My end of the deal is done with. Yours is now up to bat." The Devil unfolded the contract again. "Seven years, remember? That getting through the shit you packed into your skull, Tom boy? You got seven real good years, seven party years, seven roll-the-dice-and-come-up-seven years, and they're all used up, babe." The Devil's eyebrow raised up. "Not unlike yourself."

Longo's hand flashed through the bars and snatched the contract from the Devil's hand. "What kind of— Piece of bullshit, this is!" he said, looking at the paper, not really reading much of anything, just seeing his name, his blood right there, his soul right there on the fucking paper—

"Shit!" he cried out, and started tearing at the paper, but it wouldn't tear. He pulled at it. He stuck it between his teeth and pulled at it some more like a dog trying to pull off a piece of tough leather.

The Devil started to laugh. "Heavy bond paper," the Devil said, and he laughed some more, watching this wild man in a suit biting, pulling, tearing his heart out before him.

Longo's screams brought Rick Hernandez to life, or as close to it as possible after the night of drink and pills he'd had. Longo jumped at his waking, mumbling friend as though he were the answer, or had it, or might get it.

"Rick! Rick! Get the fuck up! Come on! Rick! Shit!" Longo pounded on his friend. Hernandez sat up dazed and feeling sick.

"What the fuck you yelling for, asshole?"

Longo shot the paper at him, almost crying. "Look, man, he's here. The motherfucker's here!" Hernandez focused in on the contract, and his head cleared like a gust of wind shooting through a smoke-filled room. He slapped the paper down on the cot and stared at the Devil across the way.

"He wants our ass, man," Longo said, crying now.

The Devil stared at Hernandez and pointed his finger at him like a cocked pistol. He bent his thumb and fired.

A bullet flew out from the foliage and whistled by Harding's brow. He ducked beneath the window's edge, picking his gun up from the floor.

"Stone, you okay?" Harding said.

"Yeah," Stone replied, rubbing his bruised bones. "Barely, man."

"Stay down and back out your door." Harding raised his head slightly so his eye rested just above the window like a marble on a ledge.

The Buick was quiet. Stone swung his door free and, butt first, shimmied down to the damp, leafy ground. "Okay," Stone whispered from a squat.

Harding hunched at the window another few seconds, his stillness matched only by the uneasy one that grew across the darkened distance between. Harding's weight just so slightly shifted back, his eye just so slowly rolled right, and the Buick's passenger door blew open as though pressurized; a shadowed figure leaped out, firing red bursts—one, two, three rounds that cracked and shattered Harding's side window, its shards spraying the top of his head.

Stone jumped up, slapped the roof with stiffened arms, and fired. The figure dodged his bullets in a body roll, then sprang up, shooting behind him once, before he dove into the thicket. He shot again from the dark. Then came a click. Harding's head bounced up like the sun on a new summer's day. An angry cry rose from the trees, and an empty gun clanged against the Buick's fender in a fit of disgust.

Stone placed another shot into the trees and bushes, but the figure was running now, his footsteps tearing into the tangled branches and cracking them like dried bones. Harding and Stone sprang into the dark after him, hungry now, hungrier than ever, their prey without claws now. They hoped.

Through the bushes they found themselves on what was an overgrown private driveway, pebbled; a distant crunching meant the killer had discovered it up ahead as well. They ran awkwardly, fighting the slope and the fog, Harding hating the damn "gunboats," the bulky, black oxfords that came with every set of blues. It was like running with your feet sunk into two blocks of wood.

Stone, the faster of the two, stopped and stuck his left

hand out and against Harding's heaving chest in resistance. "Lookit there," he said, pointing upward.

Harding squinted and saw the top outline of an old, gabled house resting above a short set of trees. "The hell's that doing here?" Harding said.

Stone shrugged. "Didn't think they built anything past Point Sampson four miles back."

A sharp bang, board slapping board, made Harding flinch. It came from the house. Stone squeezed his face in an effort to hear better. Footfalls and another muted slap of wood, and Harding knew the house was now the killer's sanctuary.

They quickly approached the dilapidated building's front porch; the years' wear and moist ocean breeze had made the wood pungent and droop in fatigue. The house was small but in the light of youth must have been a comfortable retreat, cozied up to the shoreline trees and tucked away. But Harding looked beyond its present sadness and sensed its danger, its killer, its cancer roaming its wooden viscera.

"I'll check the back," Stone said, "see if he's got an escape hatch."

Harding nodded and watched his partner fade, blue into black. Harding quickly looked up, up to a window, gable-framed, and thought he saw something gleam—one eye, a blade, something for him. The wind had shifted, and the fog was being torn in slow, cottony wads of moisture, spread apart, revealing a sliver of yellow moon; its glow filtered down a soft spray of light that outlined the south side of the ancient house.

Harding moved to the illuminated side and saw the windows boarded up just as they were on the north and west sides; the door then creaked aside with a swift breeze, announcing its uniqueness: the only way in. Harding swung wide of the house toward the sole entrance, fearing the doorway, watching it, when he suddenly tripped and lost his balance, broke through a brittle shrub, and crashed up against somebody or something.

He whirled and stuck out his gun. The barrel was two inches from a five-foot statue crouched over—a cherub with its face chiseled off, the gun aimed at where a closed-lip smile of heavenly peace was once plastered. Harding teetered still from his collision and grabbed the cherub's wings to steady his balance, his heart, while his next impulse was to tear the stone feathers off the statue's back.

"Jonathan," a voice whispered loudly from nearer the house. Harding spotted the heavy-breathing cop a few yards away and drawing near. Stone glanced at the angelic statuary, its fingers clutching a granite flower by its stem, its face flat and empty, and he felt a sadness wash over him.

"What about the back?" Harding asked. "Any doors?"

Stone rubbed his eyes and looked grim. "No. I mean, the back door's boarded up solid. There's a cellar hatch, but that's all nailed up, too." Stone's gaze drifted toward the house. "No. He's in there. Front door's the only way."

Harding half smiled and said, "Dead-end street."

"He could still bust through the boards. On the windows and all," Stone said. "I mean, the place is rotted out. You could crack the beams with your bare hands."

Harding shook his head. "Yeah, but we'd hear it a mile off and nab him."

"Yeah," Stone said. "Well, enough of the bullshit, man. I'll hold the front, keep my ears open for the back, and you go to the car and radio in for the assist."

Harding didn't move, and Stone felt his partner turn indistinguishable from the sculpture beside him.

"Let's play it safe, Jonathan," Stone added. "Okay?"

"Let's *play* it, man!" Harding leaned into his partner,

arms wide. "He's in there, no gun, no way out. We yank him out of there like a bad tooth."

"The sarge—"

"Fuck the sarge, Stone," Harding said. "You see the sarge here? You see his belly taking the shots from that thing inside the house? His fat butt chasing Sherry's green machine in the dark for fifteen miles?" Harding's stomach felt empty and afraid, but somewhere he was grabbing on to it, clutching it, embracing it. It all led to the house. "This house, man, is ours. We were taken here. *We* are taking *it*."

Harding's stare was as crazed as Stone had ever seen it; Stone countered with an even softer tone. "I'm here, too, Jonathan. I want him. I want him for Gardenhire's sake, you know?"

Stone took Harding by the shoulders and squeezed them more in affection than restraint. "But how do you know that bastard doesn't have another gun in there? That he doesn't have another *bastard* in there, huh?"

Harding tried to talk, but Stone interrupted.

"You feel led here, man, and if you're right, that's scary because maybe it's his hideout we got led to, so who knows what's waiting for us in there?"

During the few seconds of silence, Stone's gaze remained strong. Then Harding's gun slowly rose up, aimed up, came parallel to his ear, his taut jaw, and he said, "You coming?"

Stone tried to remember the last time he had won a fight with Harding. Or with his own father. Or with anyone, for that matter. He hated his partner for that instant, that sudden exposure, that self-disgust, and now he was no longer afraid. Disgust destroys fear, not bravery. Stone raised his gun up, too, yet not in so dramatic a stance, nor with such rigid determination.

"A coupla jerks," Stone muttered.

Harding's lips bent up at the edges in a solemn smile. "Down these mean streets . . ."

"And up my ass, Jonathan," Stone replied, and Harding laughed.

They crouched toward the moonlit structure, its decay almost noble in translucence. Harding glanced toward the second-story window again. Nothing this time. No gleam, just a cracked window in a dead stare. As Stone climbed to the porch, his foot fell through the third step, and he nearly sunk to his thigh, but Harding snatched him by the forearm and yanked him forward in one smooth movement. Stone spun up against the open doorway, back against the frame, gun poised. Harding ducked into the house under Stone's cover and stood stiffly in the foyer; the close, damp air nearly smothered him. The house felt wet like a moist mouth.

Although almost completely devoid of furniture and decoration, the few items left behind—the puffy armchair, soiled and gushing its stuffing from volcanic cushion holes; the wallpaper, a discolored rainbow with isolated tongues curled down looking parched and thirsty even in the moisture-laden atmosphere; the squares of rat-eaten rug—all stank with rot as though laid out for decades in this creaky wooden mausoleum. Harding felt a part of the house's death; Stone wanted to vomit.

They both glanced at what was supposed to be the stairs leading to the second floor, but minus a banister and every third or fourth step, it looked more like thick rungs to a precarious ladder. They stopped at the basement door, which lay swung open, off one hinge. Harding looked into the dark below, felt a sweep of damp, cold air embrace his face and tighten the muscular cords of his neck.

The moon gradually brightened and found a dirt-spattered cellar window. Some light filtered through, sending bright fingers into the dark, pointing fingers of moonlight, until one finger spread to become a gleam, and the gleam hardened to become a blade. The blade turned and only a sharp-edged gray outline remained, seven inches long at least.

Harding lifted his chin toward the glowing basement window, and Stone nodded. He backed out of the doorway and trotted outside; Stone would circle to the window.

Harding watched the sharp outline move below and transform into a blade again. Then a bulbous circle of black eclipsed the blade, a head of thick blackness blotted out the gleam, hid the dangerous light. Its figure crouched beneath the cellar steps. Harding listened for its breath, tried to hear beyond the stillness.

He looked at the dilapidated steps, then, after holstering his gun, braced his hands on either side of the doorway. He waited until the crouched shadow slowly glided forward, until the black roundness moved beneath a cellar step unseen as the moonlight once again faded. Harding sprang upward in a standing jump, his arms outstretched, his feet together—an exhilarating sensation, suspended, dangling in the dark, thrusting out, a force directed into nothing, then the sudden driving jolt.

Harding struck the middle of one wooden step like a wildly flung ax. It split apart with a soggy crack as his whole rigid body sliced through the stairs and landed on the killer shadow, his heels catching the back half of the shadow's darkened skull. In that careening moment, Harding felt happy wearing gunboats, using them like black leather sledgehammers, driving the invisible mass down to the cellar floor.

The gleam spun from fingers, out of control, and clattered against the corner of a crumbling foundation wall. The two bodies entwined and rolled, grappling at each other's necks and shoulders. Harding threw an elbow and heard the soft crack you hear when stepping on a hard black beetle: his blow had caught the killer's nose. Harding followed with a flick of his knee, and the seemingly parasitic being released him.

Stumbling to his feet, Harding pulled his .38. Then he felt a breeze brush by, and suddenly his forearm stung and the .38 was gone. He heard it land a few feet away, then felt a boot sink into his underbelly. He groaned and buckled. Two sets of meshed knuckles in a double-fisted arc swung wide and smashed his left cheek, and Harding thought he was flying once more. He was—both sideways and down —toward the cellar floorboards.

On impact they collapsed beneath him, and he fell again, this time landing five feet down in a trench of eroded soil. Harding's face hurt; it was red and half buried in worm-infested dirt. He turned on his back much like a landed tortoise and squinted to see above him. He could barely move.

Then the moonlight slowly reentered the cellar depths and touched what little it could. Even Harding's strained vision could not miss the killer's outline above, standing at the trench's brink and, even more so, the gleam reasserting itself in the killer's hand. It pointed downward toward Harding's supine body.

Harding felt his stomach fire up and wanted to unleash a cry, a scream—he was naked and to be sacrificed, his heart cut out and swallowed. His mouth wide, he couldn't utter a sound.

The blade flashed and rose up ready to fly when in the silence, in the dark, above and somewhere to the right, came a click. And the penetrating words, "Freeze, motherfucker!" Harding closed his eyes and listened to his own blood rush back to his heart, listened for Stone once again.

"I said, *Freeze* your *bod*, man," Stone yelled in a

pounding rhythm. "I mean *solid!*" Two footsteps came closer to the hole. Harding opened his eyes and saw a gun up above with two hands wrapped around it and pointed at the shadow, which stood rigid, arm still raised, blade still readied.

"Now . . . drop the toothpick," Stone said, normal voice now, almost nice. "And not into my partner down there, either. Drop it real slow, like ketchup."

Nothing moved above Harding for what seemed like three months. Finally, the shadow lowered his arm in surrender, yet at the same instant flicked the knife downward; it stuck in a loose floorboard. The sudden motion made Stone act fast and rough. He yanked the killer's arm up, twisted, behind his back until the pain made a knee buckle, then jerked the dark figure straight up so his ear met Stone's lips, his back became Stone's front, both locked in a pose from some perverse tango.

"I guess you don't use Heinz, man," Stone whispered through clenched teeth to the head beside his. Its reply, after a second arm jerk of no more than another inch up the shoulder blade, was a stifled grunt.

Feeling he had his prey secured, Stone looked down into the eroded trench. "You okay, Jonathan?" Stone saw Harding's body but not his head, saw his burgeoning belly heave up and down. Harding surprised himself by hearing his own voice.

"Yeah," he said, "I think so." His belly made one long, last heave like an ailing furnace bellows. "I'm okay."

Harding's face came into the moonlight when he raised his head. Stone smiled at him.

"Shit, man," Stone said, chuckling, "looks like they laid you out and you're waitin' for the headstone."

Harding half smiled and tried to chuckle, too, but as he braced himself to rise, his left hand touched something hard, strange, disturbing. He neither looked nor turned his head, yet he raised the hard, now slimy thing up from the earth out of reluctant curiosity. When he finally looked, he was holding the fragmented hand of a skeleton, its bony fingers entwined in his, fingers brittle and eaten away, all of them deformed except for the one that wore a golden band.

Harding stiffened at the sight and felt a presence suddenly to his left. Falling back flat, he jerked his head sideways and saw an entire spread of human bones lying next to him. A skeletal head faced his, only inches away. Its mouth gaped open, its jaw out wide in a laughing grimace only death can perform, our cheeks living muscle, offering too much resistance for such a cavernous expression.

Still, Harding's face contorted, almost mimicking the fleshless one before him, and he screamed. As he began to lose consciousness from the killer's earlier blow, fragmented images flashed past, delirious images—a burning newspaper photo, the smiling sunglasses at the station house, an X-ray of his own head—for in that instant, skull to skull, had come the terror not from sudden, overwhelming danger, but from the flicker of recognition. The blood now drained from his head, his pupils capsizing. Harding slowly fell into the flood of unconsciousness, but on the way down, he thought he reached into his own bones and set free another bottomless scream.

His feet stuck up in the air, nestled between an intersection of iron bars, the Devil sat comfortably in his cell watching the mirror reflection from the black, shell-like polish of his imported leather shoes. He had consciously decided to ignore the echoing screams, though no doubt they pleased him by the way he puffed on the brown cigarette that hung from his lips; tight, little balls of smoke in a steady rhythm like the Little Engine That Could and knew damn well it could the week after next, too, blindfolded. He nodded at the commotion of twin images projecting from his feet, fuzzy images, clamoring images; nothing behind him was really clear to see, except the desperation.

Sergeant Fowler had ignored the screams, too; his thoughts were huddled over a college football pool from the *San Marco Express*, a weekly exercise in precise guesswork and the only form of exercise practiced by the precinct's oldest veteran. That is, Fowler *tried* to ignore the screams—they seemed far off, at first, as from a distant, stone cavern; they weren't the vibrant screams that pleaded for a team to score so as to at least make the point spread. But as Fowler raised his head, the screams became those of a bleacher crowd whose collective faces were being torn off.

The sergeant gave a sharp look to Officer Fanelli, who heard them as well yet sat motionless, brow furrowed, chewing gum slowly, almost cautiously, as though he might find a bone.

"Damn, Fanelli, check out the racket already," Fowler said, smoothing out the newspaper he unfolded and shaking his head. Then the sergeant noticed the slight hesitation in Fanelli's movement; the officer got up all right; however, while his feet took one step forward toward the commotion in the holding cells, his body appeared as though it were taking two bigger steps back.

Fowler grumbled and pushed himself up from the table. "Let's go tend to the zoo, huh?"

Fanelli only slightly showed his sense of relief at getting Fowler's company, not wanting to disrupt the sergeant's scowl.

"Right, Sarge," Fanelli said, hitching his pants.

"Shit! Come on! Hey!"
"Get us outta here, you friggin' pigs!"

"Help us! Please—God! Help us!"

"Let us out! *God damn you!!*"

The two policemen had stopped abruptly the instant they entered the holding cell area and watched, somewhat at a loss, Rick Hernandez and Tommy Longo climbing the iron bars, trying to get a footing on nonexistent notches in the metal, sliding to the floor, writhing, rolling, skittering across the concrete, banging against another row of bars, squeezing their flesh, their faces, their heads, trying to spread themselves through the bars like so much dough, all while yelling and crying and screaming their throats raw.

They reminded Fowler of large monkeys in heat, only wearing suits by Dior and cologne that came in bottles of cut glass. Their self-generated sweat had for the most part cut through any oily layer of perfume that might have lingered, and now the cell area stank with animal smells, even defecation.

The sergeant looked at Officer Fanelli, whose slow chew had become still, like setting cement, his face washed white. "Never seen a doper flush himself out, did you, Fanelli?" Fowler squinted and puckered his lips. "Not pretty, that's straight."

Rick Hernandez flung his arm out through the cell bars, his fingers shaking. "Hey, man! Fat man! You gotta *move* us—now! Hey—no shit! You gotta *do it!*"

Fowler moved just out of the arm's grasp. Fanelli, farther back, lingered. Fowler scowled. "What's the goddamn racket for? Huh?"

The dope dealer's arm rolled back like the withered tongue of a party favor. His chest caved in; his voice cracked. "We ain't shittin' around here," Hernandez said almost in a whisper. His eyes popped for emphasis. "We ain't." He swallowed hard. "The dude's got the power, man." Then Hernandez started to cry as his trembling hands rose and covered his face, black onyx cuff links where his eyes once were.

Fowler bristled. "What the fuck are you shits talking about? What's your stinkin' drugs trying to say to me? Hah—you slugs."

Tommy Longo pushed his shriveled friend aside and jammed his face between two bars hard so it hurt. His eyes flew up at the pain, but it brought him to, made him feel the coldness of the steel, the peril in his blood.

"*That* man," he said, jutting out his bottom row of teeth, "that man there's the Devil." His head still, his eyes shot to the right. "Satan, man."

For a few seconds Fowler stared at the face stuck between the bars like a glob of clay. He looked at Ralphie Moranis, the strutting cock of cell block eight an hour ago, now lying on his back, jaw slack, nodding toward the ceiling, oblivious to the ruckus. Then Fowler turned to the adjoining cell.

The sergeant's puffy face soon appeared on the buffed leather toes of the Devil's raised shoes. Seeing him, the Devil turned, smoothly, as if on a pivot, feet back on the floor, and faced Fowler. He took the cigarette from his lips and flicked the ash with his thumb.

"Hey," the sergeant said to him, "you the bad-ass Devil talking hellfire to these sweethearts over here?"

The Devil shook his head. "Officer, I asked if they wanted to smoke with me," he said in a flat tone of voice. "I had no idea they would take me so literally."

Fowler flexed his nostrils twice. "Wise-ass," he muttered, squinting at the Devil's face. Like trying to look through a rock. "A wise-ass and dopers," Fowler said. "Nice package." He shifted his stomach back toward Fanelli.

"They really sound kinda scared, you think?" Fanelli said.

"Nice fuckin' package," Fowler said. "All kinds it takes. And we get 'em."

"Don't leave, man!!" Longo shouted as he lunged at the retreating officers, only the bars keeping his bones from hurling themselves into Fowler's back like a squadron of flung hammers.

Fowler swung out his nightstick, a short blunt sword withdrawn, and broad-swiped the bars above Longo's twitching, pleading arms. As the club clattered against the iron, bar by bar, the noise made his arm jerk and lose purpose and fall. The Devil mused silently: the music of hell's harp—black club on cold metal.

The staccato tune played again as Fowler brought the club back along the bars, only this time for emphasis, for lasting effect, as the first swipe had already done its job. Hernandez and Longo sat together in a pile; Longo whimpered.

"Now pipe *down!*" Fowler shouted, sticking his club back alongside his thigh like an extra-large beef jerky. "Or I'll send Fanelli in there to gag the bunch of you hopheads."

Fanelli squirmed, as Fowler knew he would. "Come on, Fanelli."

As the two policemen passed out of the holding area, a groan came up from behind them, a communal groan from a single, deep desperate letting-go, the fingers no longer feeling the rope, the intestinal groan that comes before the long fall. Sergeant Fowler heard that groan, and like no other, it sent a cold fist through his spine, long immune in the folds of protective fat.

"They gonna be all right, you figure," Fanelli half stated, but really asked.

"Just strung-out hopheads, Fanelli," Fowler said numbly. "You see my friggin' pencil?"

* * *

Stone never quite understood why, but he always liked it when an ambulance, maybe two, and a few prowl cars clustered together like a nestled herd and flashed their lights about the night, each flash and turn out of sync with the next yet together producing a kaleidoscopic swirl of red and white that danced along a crime scene, along Stone's own rubber face, and making glow the sterner faces that traced and dusted, and opened their bottom vest buttons, and flipped pad paper and questioned, then questioned some more. All these wrinkled detectives with pusses to match, and Stone still felt good somehow. Maybe it was the sense of gathering, the sense that it was the one time the force merged and became a true, purposeful "force" and not departments butting heads.

Sometimes Stone felt ashamed, that he was being perverse, glowing at such times that usually meant death or, at the very least, injury. Still, just the lights flickering on these homicide boys absurdly placed them in some dour disco, and Stone would snicker.

Besides, tonight was different: a successful collar, at last. He touched the gun on his hip out of habit and let out a long breath. It became a small cloud before him, the fog having grown denser, almost like a hovering rain. It was like walking through seltzer water as the drops burst on your face and made your nose itch. "It's God giving us the Bronx cheer," Harding would say when in such weather, "right straight in our mugs." And he would demonstrate by sliding his tongue out and giving Stone the raspberry.

"Why would He do that?" Stone once asked out of nowhere.

Harding felt unprepared for the question and shrugged. "For a life well done," he said. "As a goof . . . maybe as a way of saying, 'Lighten up already!'"

Stone walked past a somber lab man, who pointed toward the openmouthed ambulance for the attendants;

evidently Harding had damaged a few ribs on the blade-wielding bastard before Stone appeared. When Stone finally reached Harding, he saw his partner slouched in the front seat of their patrol car like a child caught in the womb.

"Well, I gave Lieutenant Hoskins the whole rap. *You* know," Stone said.

The car door was open, so Stone leaned back against the window as the hinges protested.

"Oh, yeah?" Harding said.

"Yeah—and you should have seen the tie on him. He must've laid some scissors on one of my old paisley shirts—man!"

"Yeah," Harding said. "Ties got more expression than his sour puss."

"I told him you'd give him—whatever—later on. I covered your part, too, but they want you—too—you know. Your story."

Harding looked up at Stone. "I know . . . thanks."

Stone shrugged. "The docs look you over?"

Harding nodded. "Oh, yeah. Nothing new. They pointed at all the bruises they found, and I told them I knew where they were 'cause that's where it hurt a lot. Said my ass would hurt the longest since I got it bounced like a basketball a few times tonight, so I shouldn't let anyone kick me hard or anything the next few days."

Stone said, "That include yourself?" Harding wet his lips with his tongue and said nothing.

Stone shifted his weight, unburdening the door. "You sure you're okay? I mean, you looked pretty freaked out before. I never saw—"

But Stone stopped, having almost said, "I never saw you scream before," or "a *man* scream before," or something that he felt would have made Harding feel even more naked.

"I'm okay," Harding said quietly; he touched the vulnerable spot in himself that forced out words. "I just didn't expect the skull face. It was like—" Harding shook his head. He had lost the touch; the spot felt hidden again.

"Yeah," Stone said to fill up the voided sentence. "Listen, Jonathan." Stone scanned the commotion for the wrinkled suits. "Why don't I stay here and take care of the homicide guys. The joker we nabbed'll be downtown soon; you go on ahead and start the forms up and rest it. I'll catch a ride with Neery, no sweat."

Harding straightened up, allowing the moist ocean air to fill and cleanse his lungs. "You sure?" he said, eyes showing a flicker of life.

"Yeah, no sweat," Stone said. "I'll be in and help in no time. What say?"

Harding nodded and smiled. "Yeah, hey . . . thanks." Harding shut the door, and the car pulled away from the ramshackle house and its imposing guests slowly, uncharacteristically, not with the short, girlish squeal from its tires, but with a phantom air: Harding didn't want to be seen, didn't want to be heard. He slipped away, not feeling he was *there* at all.

Stone watched the car leave and watched a bigger car arrive, one that looked officious yet without the need of red flashers or a badge decal blown up twenty times and stuck on the side of its door. The gleam and black bulk of the car was officious enough, as were the faces on its passengers. Two men calmly got out of the car, and Stone was impressed and a little worried. They walked toward Lt. Hoskins, who was just inside the house; they had better, grayer, well-pressed suits—they were in charge.

Stone wondered who the hell they were. He took a few steps backward, still watching the new arrivals, then turned and almost toppled Detective Lieutenant Neery, one of the better "upstairs" cops at the precinct; he at least still remembered and respected the beat cop and the car patrolman, maybe because one of his fingers had been shot off during a quiet night tour, a sniper's bullet, skinning his cap and striking his left hand, which lay on the steering wheel. His pinkie dropped into his pants cuff. They never found the gunman and had no reason to believe he had ever struck again. Neery had taken the sergeant's test the next month.

"So what's happening, Lieutenant? Do I get to tell you my ghost story, too?" Stone looked at Neery sorting through a plastic trash bag.

"What are you talking ghost? . . . Oh!" Neery smiled and coughed on his cigarette. "You mean, the bone heap—yeah. There's your ghost." He pointed to a larger plastic bag ten feet away near the assistant coroner's shoes.

"Got anything yet?" Stone asked.

Neery shrugged, tired. "Yeah, well, just from what's been dug up, doc's determined it's a Caucasian male . . . uh, was." Neery put the small sack down and arched his back, producing a small crack. "He's got a nice dent in the back of his skull, your skeleton friend. Got a real crack back there, back of the head. Split wide."

"You talkin' murder?" Stone asked.

"Could be," Neery said, then yawned. "Brother! . . . You know, hard to tell. The ground musta been eroding under the cellar floorboards for a long time, and if he's been buried there all these years . . ." Neery shrugged again, then nodded. "Sure smells like one."

Stone picked up the smaller sack. "Can I?"

"Sure. No prints. Not after all that time," Neery said as Stone stuck his hand in, rummaging.

"You gettin' any sleep, Neery?" Stone asked.

"With a new baby? You kiddin'?" Neery laughed.

Stone smiled at the baggy-eyed, baggy-pants lieutenant.

"That's right. I forgot." Stone stuck his nose back in the sack.

Neery said, "Not much there. Just a belt buckle, coins from his pants—"

Stone pulled out a ring and held it tenuously as though it were an actual piece of the skeleton itself. He examined it in the misty moonlight, barely making out the intricately etched design inscribed inside the gold band. It was a five-pointed star with a number 1 at its center.

Stone looked away for an instant, somewhere between the busy lieutenant and where the ocean rumbled behind the foliage beyond the bluffs. He grew cold and thought of Jonathan. He thought of letters Jonathan had showed him from his father's company, First Star Chemicals, letters Jonathan had taken from his mother's "secret place," he had said, letters his father had written to famous men like Secretary of Defense James Forrestal and Edward Teller, letters shown to Stone with Jonathan's face flushed with pride and hunger for more, letters with the company symbol on it, a symbol (as best he could recall) very much like the one on the ring.

"What's up?" Neery said.

Stone looked perturbed, momentarily unsettled.

"Wait a sec," he said, verbally pushing Neery off. He squinted down again along the ring's inner band. Following the star ran the inscription:

N. H. & D. H.—1947

Stone felt the fog penetrate his neck, dampen his back. His throat ached as though he had swallowed a cue ball. He knew for a fact Jonathan's father's name was Nathaniel. His mother was . . . Doris? Dolores? They were married when? After the war, maybe. Jonathan was born in 1949 or 1950, just after his father died in the accident.

Jonathan always said his father died in an accident, a chemical fire at his plant.

Stone held the ring tightly in his hand now, and Neery looked at him with concern. If the ring were Jonathan's mother's . . . She must have been wearing it all these years, he would guess. How could it get . . . ? If the ring were Nathaniel Harding's, then the skeleton was really . . . ? Stone shook his head and looked at Neery. He gave him a tight-lipped smile. "Can I keep this a while?"

Neery shrugged. "Sure," he said. "Don't let me catch you hockin' it or giving it to your best girl." Neery chuckled.

Stone nodded, and the crumpled detective turned away. On a night of fiery shopping bags, and bleeding cops, and decaying houses with skeletons rising up like bad dreams, the gold ring in Stone's hand held the most fear for him, even though it made as much sense as everything else that night, which was no sense at all.

Stone placed the gold band in his pocket. He would show the ring later as a boy would show his friend a found object—a multicolored stone or a foreign coin—as though it possessed something neither understood, like a charm or a curse. He would show the ring to Jonathan.

Harding's left hand held his head, his right a pencil; his eyes watched the clock. The words he had formed were no more connected to what had really happened at the old house than was the fog to the dark sky: you grabbed at it, tried to see through it—all you got was wet and lost. The report needed facts—time of arrest, procedure, pursuit, laws violated—is that what these scribbles signified? Harding rubbed the pencil with his thumb grazing over the "No. 2," feeling its relief on his fingertip. His shoulders hurt. His eyes fell back on the clock.

The rest of the station house passed by the long Formica

table Harding hung over and made a small racket for so few in number and so late in the night. Officers Burton and Costa were squabbling over an old pizza tab; a couple of drunk drivers were cursing Van Dam for all eternity plus fifty years; though Van Dam listened sternly, odds were he was taking mental notes for use in his own future tirades; and Sgt. "Beans" Fowler was laughing out loud at nothing Officer Fanelli could figure out. Fowler's mouth was wide open and full of his half-chewed namesake.

Many a midnight snack saw Sgt. Fowler forking up another cold mouthful of pork 'n' beans straight from the mother can. Some had claimed Fowler even spread Crisco on his sandwich bread when he sprung for cold cuts, but no one came close enough to verify the report.

Harding rubbed his eyes, and when they refocused his head jerked back a notch. Precinct Captain Horace Schulman marched into the station house, his face tired and pale, his eyes bagged as though underlined three times for emphasis. He walked in his customary tilt: his back straight but angled down from his lumbar and getting progressively worse because of a degenerative problem, some suspected. Others said that as Schulman got further and further promoted, his posture became more and more acute. When he became chief of San Marco Police, Van Dam figured, he'd be the only man to be able to look behind himself and kiss his own balls at the same time.

Harding also recognized a few of the cops with Schulman as being from the investigation team at the ancient house. The captain was never at the precinct this late unless an arrest tied into something larger, something a patrolman only glimpsed a piece of, like sticking the first screw in the first cog of something that was going to become a train engine . . . a Cadillac . . . a nuclear missile . . . something he'd never see the whole of.

As the captain's door swung open, Schulman stopped before it and turned to Harding.

"Officer Harding," he said softly and with a tone that usually meant he was going to say something else but never did. He simply walked into his office, leaving the door open for the seated patrolman.

Harding's face averted Sgt. Fowler's and looked to the clock. Mimicking Captain Schulman's posture, the hands read two-thirty. Harding shoved his chair back and marched into Schulman's office with his eyes down as though following seeds through a dense forest.

The captain looked up from his desk, a perpetual mess of papers and sandwich wrappers that never floated toward the wastebasket because it was stolen one night and he just didn't care anymore. He twirled his index finger downward. Harding took the cue and eased the door shut behind him. Schulman hadn't bothered to take off his coat, and as his hands mindlessly moved from pocket to pocket, he sniffed loudly.

"Officer Harding," he said calmly, "tell me why you didn't bother to radio in for assistance on the code eighteen tonight."

Harding cleared his throat. "I did, Captain. I was informed during our pursuit that help was scarce because of the fire in East Hills."

"Don't play coy, Patrolman," Schulman said, his face changing color from pale white to pink. "Two in the morning is not my finest hour. Cute loses a lot when my clock reads A.M. in single digits. When the feds come to call to gripe about procedures and the deal we made with them. When the chief loses a cop, a bust, sleep, and his temper all in one night: cute goes damn little distance." Schulman rapped his knuckles on the top of his desk. His other hand found its destination—a bottle of nasal spray.

"I'm not trying to be cute, Captain," Harding said

numbly, watching Schulman's hand rise up, spin the cap off the spray with its index finger and thumb, and hold it, spray once in each nostril, replace the cap and spin it shut, and shove it back into a coat pocket, all with robotlike efficiency and detachment. Schulman never noticed what his hand did, Harding couldn't help but. Captain Schulman did not have a cold; the fact was Captain Schulman was an addict, only his daily toot came from the nozzle of an analgesic.

Schulman gazed at Harding more intently. "I'm not talking about the pursuit, Officer Harding. I'm talking about the capture. The suspect's apprehension at the house. No radio contact was reported."

"We shut our portables off, seeing as we were trying to sneak up on the—"

Schulman took an overpowering breath through half-swollen sinuses, a whining, sucking inhale that stretched his sinuses taut as a rubber sheet. "Crap!" he shouted. "You botched procedure!"

"The suspect killed a cop, *sir!*" Harding tried to tie down his feelings, rope them before they bucked loose. "Officer Stone and I saw it, radioed in, and gave chase." Then he added, "We got *no* help, and expected none."

Schulman rose, ready to throw the insolent officer out of his office, but, having stood too quickly, his back forced him down as though kicked in the belly. His eyes rose, though, almost out of his head. "Suppose I told you that that was the point, *Officer*," he snarled under his breath. "And if you so graciously had radioed in at said house, as procedures instruct, you might have been told so, and not fucked . . . up . . . royally."

Harding felt weaker all of a sudden. "I don't understand."

Schulman laughed once and shook his head. "Officer, do you know where your suspect is now?"

"Northside precinct ja—"

"On the streets," Schulman spat. Harding stiffened. "Just where we wanted him." The captain rose successfully this time and stood nose to nose with Harding. "Only *not* roaming free to relocate, set up new headquarters, or be up for a murder trial."

Harding looked into the captain's face as though it possessed all knowledge and he was using it like a bludgeon.

"We're working with the feds on this one, Harding. They told us about this guy. He works small-potato coke deals, like the one you walked in on, but he also recently got his hooks in on some cross-country smack routes via Miami and New York. The feds wanted us to sit on this guy. Let him breathe free. Let him score a few rounds." Schulman sniffed straight in Harding's face. "Yeah, even let him kill a cop in cold blood . . . for now."

Schulman moved back around his desk and looked out the window. "It didn't matter. We *had* his ass; the feds, too. Murder will lock him up good. But we wanted the bigger connection, the coast-to-coast line this punk was tapping." Schulman looked at Harding again, Harding's face aimed toward the sticky floor.

"We knew about the house. His H.Q. Maybe it even would have been the place of final contact with the bigger fish. Some heavyweight lawyer showed up at northside about three minutes after he was brought in, obviously a gift from the East Coast connection. The judge let the lawyer put on his legal show, let him think it was his razzle-dazzle that got his client immediate bail, when it was the feds whispering in the judge's ear to let him go." Schulman sat, calmed down to a degree, feeling a sense of failure. "But now, things are jeopardized. The lawyer sent may be the punk's death warrant, getting him released to knock him off since now he's an assigned risk to the East

Coast big boys, murder charge and all. The house is no good to him or us, so now double the manpower has to keep track of his whereabouts until he settles in again, some other house, some other town. Then he wouldn't be our bother . . . except for the murder." The last words weighed Schulman down in his chair; even gravity felt heavy.

Harding tightened his jaw. "He killed Gardenhire," he said quietly. "It's not my job to run around mazes like a dumb fucking rat trying to figure out dead ends and bump my head on walls and smell my way to some big cheese I'll never see." Harding raised his head and stared at the slumped captain. "I responded to a crime; I did my duty as an officer and a human being."

The captain snapped, "Your duty was to radio in at the house before capture for backup. There you would have been told to back off and return to duty."

"And would I have gotten a reason?" Harding asked.

"You're not here to get reasons. You get orders. I didn't even have to tell you anything about it all now if I didn't want to."

Harding almost said "Thanks" under his breath but held back.

"But I thought," Schulman continued, then paused. "I thought you should understand why you're being put on report." Harding dropped his hands to his sides like two sandbags. "You were senior officer," Schulman continued. "Officer Stone is looking at a reprimand."

Harding's chest ached. "And what about the body?"

The captain looked at Harding as though he spoke Chinese.

"The body we discovered at the house, in the cellar. . . ."

The captain let out a breath and sniffed hard again. "Just what we needed around here: a forty-year-old stiff and more work." He turned to Harding and gave him a mock wink. "Good job, Officer."

Captain Schulman seated himself and stuck his head in the storm of paperwork on his desk while Harding stood before him shaking. Then, his eyes burning as though cast toward a fiery sun, he spun around and left the stuffy office. He marched to the table where the reports sat quietly, a neat little pile of words, a record of events that were surface gestures hiding great sweeps of motion underneath. He stood at the table looking at the pile for a full minute until his hand swept down in a shoveling swipe and sent the sheets flying, swooping off, then drifting down like dead leaves to the station house floor.

Sgt. Fowler among others watched the sudden display. Harding shut his eyes and knew he blew it. It was the first time in years he showed Fowler his feelings, *any* feelings, and he already regretted the lapse. Sorrowfully, he also felt that nothing could be done, not willpower or drink, to hold them back any longer. They tore at his chest; he looked at Fowler, his face full of spoon and cold beans, and Harding waited for the needle, the prick, the excuse to explode into thousands of pieces over everything and everybody.

Fowler swallowed the mound of beans barely chewed that had settled in his left cheek like a wad of tobacco and set the can down before the red-faced Harding. The sergeant leaned up against the patrolman and smacked his lips. " 'S'matter, Harding? Work cutting in on your depression? Aren't you happy being sad no more?"

Harding turned sharply toward the smirky face that breathed foul pork air on him. Fowler straightened up as much as he could to gain some height on the taller Harding and broadened his chest in defiance. Fowler's fat pulled at his shirt so the buttons that arched his belly became a vertical row of squinted eyes.

The assembly area in the station house was quiet now, waiting; the cops and a few scattered suspects watched from handcuffs or adjacent desks, from water coolers. Some even listened through cracks in open doors, doors that led to nearby holding cells where sounds quite by accident drifted in from the assembly area and echoed among the iron and brick. The audience for such random noise proved apathetic for the most part; except in this case, one prisoner was neither too drunk, too bitter, nor too caught up in his own plight to listen: the Devil took another drag on his cigarette and was all ears.

"Fuck the paperwork!" Harding said loudly, too loudly to convince anyone that he was in control. "Fuck the badge! . . . And fuck *you*, Sarge!"

Harding was shaking. He looked up and noticed himself, felt the ever-present, hovering silence. Then came the singular sound of Sgt. Fowler scraping the bottom of the can with his spoon. Harding was in for major detention now for sure, maybe even a short suspension, and the sergeant didn't even have to say it or make a scene. He just looked up from his empty can, stuck the last clump in his mouth, and smiled a spoon-filled smile at the pathetic officer. Fowler finally broke his fist through that damn wall.

The tension dissipated; Harding fell back on an adjacent desk, looking down. The precinct went back into motion, as though it had taken a short nap and was stretching its muscles.

Harding felt a hand on his side and looked up. Officer Hall nodded in a way that asked if Harding was okay. Harding half smiled a reply and nodded back.

Harding leaned there a while, feeling flush and especially vulnerable, not sure what he would or could do next, trying to get a fix on his teeter-totter mind. . . .

Then Stone walked in the assembly area, his cap in

hand, his eyes blank. Harding watched him approach almost in wonder.

"Stone . . . hey. Just missed the nervous breakdown by seconds," Harding said, still shaking.

Stone didn't hear him. "I have to show you something."

Harding looked puzzled and was afraid of Stone's tone of voice. Stone slid Harding along the wall and farther into a corner that went unused because of the broken fluorescent light above. He stopped just shy of the door to the holding cells where ribs of light shot through the slight opening and striped Harding's pale face.

Stone avoided Harding's eyes as he pulled the ring from his pocket and held it up to his partner's face, letting the meager fingers of light shine on the inscription and help support the weight of the ring in his hand. Harding didn't touch the ring; he leaned in, still relying on the wall for balance, his eyes inspecting the gold band as though it were a rare and perishable artifact.

Stone saw the jolt of recognition in Harding's gaze and felt Harding's hand snatch his, steadying the ring's shimmer.

"The hell you get this?"

"Tell me what it is first," Stone said.

"What's the game, man? Where'd you . . . ?"

"Come on, Jonathan, man, just humor me. What is it?"

Harding's grip softened, and he blinked a few times to clear the film in his eyes. "It's my mother's wedding ring—"

"Shit," Stone said, dropping his arm, but Harding pulled it back up.

"Hey, how'd you get it? What gives?"

Stone knew where this was leading, and he hated leading. "She still wear it?"

"Sure, of course she still wears it. What do you think, she threw it out when he—"

"Did your father still wear it when he died?"

Harding let go of Stone's hand now, needing both hands for the wall behind him, giving in. "Stone, man, please, huh?"

Stone placed the ring in Harding's hand as though it were a gift so personal no one else should see. "The skeleton we found, at the house . . ."

Stone's words and the touch of the shiny metal in his palm put Harding back into the grip of damp earth, his face alongside bone, his hand caressing fleshless fingers . . . one of which held a ring. This ring. Harding looked again at the star, the symbol, the date. His father's ring. His father's bones.

"Could that really be your father down there?" Stone asked, still hoping Harding would think of something to make this improbable ghost go away, leave them to a few tokes at home with a late horror movie to laugh at.

Harding kept shaking his head, trying not to look at Stone, at anything. "How can that be? . . . He died . . . my mother told me. . . ." Harding felt dizzy. "My father died in a fire. . . ."

Before he had even finished saying it, Harding could not believe he *was* saying it, a blush filling his cheeks. As if trained, or worse, robotic, these words became a wearisome litany, not of a pain released, but of a nerve exposed, the string of words a strip of flesh peeled off. The more he heard himself let out his hurt, the more he was skinning himself alive.

How many times now had he confessed his father's death? How many times had he told Stone that Nathaniel Harding's chemical factory exploded with his father in it? And that Jonathan himself hadn't even been born yet, was protected from fires and death and ashes in his mother's dark womb, newly formed?

"A hundred times?" Harding had once pressed Stone. "More?"

Stone had smiled and said, "Not *that* bad."

"Only fifty times, right?"

It had become a joke. It was all a fucking joke. And Stone just delivered the punch line.

"Yeah," Harding said, totally dazed. "*You* know. Factory fire. Chemicals. My mother said the accident . . ." The words caught in his throat like rocks. He wanted to vomit.

Stone clutched him harder, but Harding nodded. "Okay, okay . . . I don't understand here. How could he be in the cellar? How . . . ?" Harding focused his eyes on Stone's. "They have cause of death?"

Stone shook his head, which didn't mean "no" but that he knew and wished to God he didn't have to say. "I was coming to that. I didn't want to see you until Neery confirmed it with me again. . . . The skull was cracked. A split in the back caused by a blunt object."

"He was murdered?" Harding said, his jaw tensing.

Stone shook his head again. "I don't know. Probably, considering, you know, where we found him. They think it happened maybe thirty-five, forty years ago. Hard to tell exact, Neery said. Like the late forties."

"The factory fire was in forty-nine," Harding said. "Doesn't look like he was in it, though, does it?" Harding's chest was starting to work hard again, getting tight.

"Guess not, man. Listen—"

"Neery find anything else?" Harding asked.

"Nothing worth anything," Stone replied in a whisper.

"What about the investigation?"

Stone gave a little shrug, a little tilt of the head.

"Well?" Harding said.

"Well, you know," Stone said. "They'll give it the once-over, sure, but—"

"They like fresh meat, those boys."

Stone got defensive. "Neery didn't say that. He's okay. He just said . . . the case is forty years old. . . ."

"So they'll sit on it," Harding snapped.

"It's policy, ma—"

"Hey!" Harding snatched Stone's shirt. "Don't give me fucking policy. Not now, man."

"Come on, Jonathan, ease up. I'm not saying it's right. It's what they got. No leads. No manpower—"

"It's history. Yeah. So forget it, right?" Harding let go in disgust.

"Really not much to go on, Jonathan," Stone said quietly, putting his hand back on Harding's shoulder. Harding looked up and nodded at his friend.

"Yeah. Just my daddy's bones. . . ."

Stone pulled at the muscular shoulder. "Come on, man. Let's go back to my place. Blow some weed. Or go to Nero's, huh? And have a few." Harding stayed silent. "Let it lay. Let the bones lay. At least for now. I can snoop around, talk to Neery, maybe . . . but—"

"I gotta go see somebody," Harding mumbled.

"Who the hell you gonna see now? It's late, man. Let's—"

"I'll be by," Harding said. He slapped Stone on the arm in assurance. "Nero's, man, I promise."

Stone looked at Harding skeptically. "You're not there in an hour, I'm putting out an all points."

Harding saluted and Stone laughed, then looked serious. "I mean it." He turned and walked away.

With his friend gone Harding's face dropped another foot, and the air was getting thin. He stuck his head back on the darkened wall, and as he looked at the sputtering fluorescent light, he pulled a key from his pants pocket. It was a house key, his mother's house, and he wondered how many locks it would open, assuming you could ever find all her damn locks.

"Fucking night," he said to himself.

Harding's face grew red and his eyes watered as he also pulled out his wallet and carefully extracted a damp, pressed picture of his father from a wartime newspaper. It was at best an adequate picture, black and white, a sober picture shoulders up, one that could easily have been used on a hundred-dollar bill; the face was that strong and that distant. This was probably the fullest physical incarnation of his father that could be—two-dimensional and in tones of gray. The early stages were but stories told by his mother (though only when pressed), stories that blurred with all the other stories in a boy's mind: Robin Hood, the Lone Ranger, Father as saint, Flash Gordon. With age, all but his father faded from Jonathan Harding's personal mythology, but like all surviving myth, it was beset with mystery, the tale both powerful and wanting in its simplicity, its sketchiness. His father embodied Jonathan's spiritual paradox of having something, yet never really having it; of feeling as if you are holding something in your hands, until you look at it, and you are holding nothing at all.

Harding brought his hands up to his eyes and began to weep, keeping the hurt within his grasp. He contained the sobs as best he could from the far end of the room where cops and trash tugged at the law from different ends of the same greasy rope. Only through the opening of the holding cell door, through the barred light from its depths, through the sleeping cells, could the sobs be heard, as could the whole, amazing, absurd conversation between the two officers, a conversation that brought a buzz to the Devil's ears like a pesky fly that keeps you up and half-crazy.

The Devil laughed and his eyebrow arched up, humpbacked, like the slope of a steep roller coaster whose riders shriek and fling their arms up in surrender as they plummet, then when they hit bottom stiffen, fearful and laughing, fearful as they hit bottom, of the next steep plunge. The Devil peered through the crack in the door and smiled at Jonathan Harding. He smiled at the rider, limp and dazed, having hit bottom and just waiting, waiting for his next fall.

The Devil was ready to oblige.

• four •

His face was blurred, yet the dark line that made up his middle-aged, sober smile was unmistakable: his father never showed his teeth. He wore a white smock, the kind in which mad scientists brought monsters to life or mixed flasks of multicolored chemicals. The latter was probably not far from the truth in his father's case. He was standing in front of his company, First Star Chemicals, with his partner, Clifford W. Snell. Stocky, goateed, dressed in wide tie and loose-fitting suit, Snell looked like a dishonest Turk next to his father's straight-backed frame. Snell had his hand hanging on his father's shoulder, unreciprocated. Snell handled the accounting; his father, the projects. So said the article, "A Chemical Balance." Overall, they looked confident together even tinged in yellow, as the newspaper had faded badly in its frame.

"Jonathan?"

Just two feet to the left and Nathaniel Harding was thirty years younger. The photo was almost all white now; the brown that remained outlined a boy of maybe eighteen or even less in full army uniform. The helmet, like an oversize metal cereal bowl dumped over his father's head, was straight from everybody's picture-book memory of World War I and the only comical image Mr. Harding's history afforded Jonathan.

Below the photo came the Virgin Mary, her helmet a halo, and next to her Jesus Christ, uncrucified, and next to him a few other mass cards taped up on the wall. The centerpiece among the scattered photographs and newspaper articles was a wooden crucifix below which sat a large trunk, covered with fine white lace.

"Jonathan?"

In the middle of the snowy lace, a large framed photo sat up, a wedding picture of Mr. and Mrs. Nathaniel Harding from 1947. A fresh rose in a thin, tall, crystal vase fronted the picture; a Bible and a cross flanked it. The black-and-white photo showed his mother in a lace bridal gown, and only now did Jonathan realize it was cut from the same finery that covered the trunk. He touched the lace and looked at the picture, as though actually touching the bride's hem. His mother looked unaffected, glassy-eyed, all of thirty-four, and beautiful. His father looked like his father, that is, a bit uncomfortable, stiff, holding hands and yet detached. Maybe his father hated having his picture taken. Isn't that what his mother said about him once?

Harding leaned back on his haunches, giving his knees a rest, and looked over the wall and the trunk and the darkly lit attic room they all rested in. The memorabilia, the rose, the pictures, the crucifix, all combined looked less like an altar and more like a shrine, as though if you pried up these boards, his father's skeleton would—should—

Harding sat up quickly, hunching his tense shoulders. He removed the Bible, the cross, the rose, from the top of the trunk. He lingered for another moment over the wedding picture; their hands were below the frame, so he removed that, too. He slid off the white lace and pulled at the trunk lid, which creaked but opened. His head disappearing into the darkness within, Harding's hands discovered an old fedora, a pair of gloves, a lab coat, black shoes, and discarded them outside. When his head reappeared, his hands held out a photo album with "Happy Honeymoon" embossed in gold on its ivory cover.

Harding flipped through the photos, the lake shots, the boat shots, the I'm-holding-a-fish-as-big-as-my-leg shots, looking for a close-up. Then his father appeared holding up his hand to the camera as he is splashed with mud on his bare chest and trunks and wants no part of posterity. Harding pulled the book closer and inspected the ring on his father's finger.

"Jonathan!"

Harding jumped as though "caught." The voice that seemed distant and went unheard now filled the small upstairs room with its anger. His mother's shadow loomed from the doorway, three times her real size, and Harding was unsure whether he was thirty-six or six. But the shadow was deceiving, its power but a shadow, because as Harding squinted to see his mother, the bare bulb from the hallway that lit her from behind illuminated her dressing gown like a cheap Chinese lantern. The stark light revealed a frail, skeletal outline—something dark and bony and withering sheathed in thin cloth.

Then a strange memory, yet not; a childhood flash, something other, loomed, briefly—a tree-shadow, man-shadow towered in the doorway instead of his mother, a darkness growing toward him, about to engulf him as it had in the past. Then gone.

"What are you doing up—" Harding started to say.

"What am I doing up? What are *you* doing scaring me half to death? Why don't you answer me? What do I know, who's in my house? I figured it was you, but—God forbid—"

"I'm sorry. I didn't hear you. I meant, what are you doing up *here?* You know you're not supposed to be climbing stairs. The doctor said."

The bony outline could barely lift its pained arm while the shadow raised its large hand accusingly. "I should ask *you* that. What are you doing? You know I never want you in here. You're not a kid anymore that I have to yell at you. Why do you make me still yell at you?"

Harding rose up off his knees to at least lessen the shadow's comparative size. "Mom. Mom. I needed to see some things, that's all. I didn't mean to wake you. Go back to bed. I'm sorry. Please go downstairs and—"

"You shouldn't be in here."

"Mom, please!" Harding forced himself to stay calm. "Please. Do as I say."

There was a small sigh. "I'll make you some coffee."

"I don't need any coffee right now."

"I'll make some coffee . . . then you can come to see *me.*" Harding couldn't see her face but knew she was hurt. Part of Harding, a part he always hated, didn't even care.

"I did . . . I will. I just had to come up here. I'll be down . . . please."

Mrs. Harding said nothing. The shadow disappeared, and the light shone once again on the open trunk with its dark, black, unfathomable hole. Harding stared at the hole, then, like the uncertain lion tamer, stuck his head inside.

Harding walked into the dark living room from the kitchen cradling the fresh coffee in his hands. There were no lights on in the living room; only the television's glow showed him where his mother was. Harding kicked aside an empty grocery bag sitting in his way and took a long gulp from his cup.

His mother sat about three feet from the twenty-inch color screen, nestled in a soiled armchair that never went with the room, fiddling with the remote-control unit in her hand. Mrs. Harding looked twenty pounds too thin; having always been trim, it all seemed to come from her face. Her hair was in a scarf, like a pirate, so as not to see the clumps, and the brown robe was tangled on her. Harding wished his mother would shut off the TV. Its light gave her hands and face a blue tint that made him feel as if he were about to speak to a spirit beyond the grave, to the little that was left behind after her death years ago.

"Had double shifts this week," Harding said from nearly behind the chair. He wasn't about to tell her he was about to be suspended. "Sorry I haven't been around. I'll get . . . the kid, what's-his-name, to do the lawn. Jimmy. It's looking ragged."

Mrs. Harding stared at the television, its sound way down.

"Heard from your mother-in-law?" she said.

Harding shifted his feet. She never said her name. "Not since last time. She took the kids to San Jose with her. They sent a postcard with grapes on it. Kids send you one?"

His mother nodded. Harding knew when June divorced him that the custody of David and Suzanne would go to her, that their care would be neglected in the hands of a cop. At least being a cop was the excuse. He also knew that June's mother would ultimately be living with the children more than June, even before she got the new job upstate and started taking week-long organizational trips for the national consumer group for at least half the year. June had barely been home without the kids, and with them, Harding had always thought most of his salary went to child care with him on day shifts and her leading the charge downtown against some San Marco County board decision. That his own mother could never care for his children needed no reasons, needed only a walk past the run-down house or a glance at her own decaying frame. Still, such evidence made the idea of June's mother supervising the children no easier, no less touchy.

Funny, it was only recently that Harding realized that June's leaving him was one of the least traumatic mysteries of his life. Her departure barely fazed him. And maybe that was exactly why she departed in the first place. But the kids, their loss . . . he felt as though he had surrendered two small, vulnerable pieces of his soul.

Harding touched his mother's hair. "How do you feel?" he asked.

His mother shrugged, her eyes still on the set.

"Chemotherapy any good?"

"They wear me out," she said. "I don't like treatments when you can't tell if you feel lousy from the disease or lousy from the medicine—it's lousy just the same."

"Maybe you should be in the hospital like they say."

"Don't start with me," Mrs. Harding snapped. She started flipping through the channels, tapping the remote button, never staying on one program for longer than a few seconds.

Harding exhaled through his nose and put his coffee down on the lamp table. The house didn't look like the one he grew up in, looked like some cave. He had warm memories, though he couldn't remember anything before the age of eight, really. His mother was supposedly put away for a while when he was about three, a residual effect of his father's now uncertain death at the factory, a burning internal powder keg that took years to finally explode. Harding stayed with his grandmother; though again, he didn't remember a face. Maybe a kind of embrace, but no more.

Harding finally squatted next to the chair's puffy arm,

looked at her watching the flashing tube.

"I have to ask you something."

"You shouldn't upset things," she said distantly. "Being up there. That's his place. My place. I made it for him and me. It's private."

"He's my father," Harding protested.

"You were always digging around up there as a kid. Always asking questions. You stole a picture from there once, I know. From one of my albums and kept it under your comics."

Harding was amazed. "You knew about that?"

His mother didn't say, "Of course." She didn't say, "I'm your mother. I know things." She didn't have to.

"Must have kept you satisfied most of the time, that picture. The questions weren't so many anymore."

"I keep it in my wallet now," Harding said.

"I was wondering when you'd hit that certain time again, and the digging would start all over." Her fingers still worked the remote, her eyes fixed on the tube. "Television really stinks, doesn't it?"

"I only wanted to get closer to him," Harding said. "Like you were once."

Harding waited a few seconds, then said: "I need to nail down a few things with you."

Mrs. Harding shrugged slightly. "Nothing you don't know."

Harding flinched. "How can you say that? There's everything I don't know."

"You read the articles, seen the pictures. A hundred times. He was big in the war effort. He was a great man."

"Yeah, I know all that. 'He was a saint.' I've heard it."

"What's more to say?" Mrs. Harding shouted, getting agitated. She squirmed in her robe, then added, "He's dead. There. That's another. Your father's dead."

Harding gripped the fat arm of her chair. "Look. I need to know some things, that's all . . . to make sure of something. Something important. He died in a fire at his factory, right?"

"Yes. An accident. You *know* this!" Mrs. Harding's voice was starting to shake. Harding pressed on.

"The cops and coroner were *sure* he was there? You said there were no remains."

Mrs. Harding turned sharply and looked at Jonathan for the first time since he arrived, looked coldly at him, both mother and son bathed in the television's icy glow. She said nothing.

"I need to be sure," Harding continued, face to face. "I need to know about his wedding ring." Unconsciously, he glanced down at hers. Mrs. Harding fingered it for protection.

Harding's voice was getting louder, stronger.

"Did he always wear it? I mean, would there be *any* reason he would give it to someone without you knowing? Or did you know of a time he ever did? Did he ever hock it, or sell it, or throw it out the damn window? Did he have it on the last time you saw him? Did he have it on the day he died?"

Harding stopped. He finally saw his mother's dead eyes looking through him and heard only the sound of the muffled TV. She turned back to the television set and started changing channels again, pressing buttons again.

"Remote control," she said. "Just push a button. Doesn't really change what you see, though. Go from one piece of crap to another. Doesn't change a damn thing."

Harding's face turned crimson and he stood up. He looked away, ashamed, angry. He cleared his throat, not to regain his mother's attention, but to cut off the tears he felt surging. Putting his officer's cap back on, Harding walked from the room. There was something lodged deeper than in that dark hole in the trunk upstairs or in the vacant hurt look in his mother's eyes. Something that made him the way he was, that lay like sediment in his gene pool. Something deeper he was ready to take a crowbar to, use his .38 on, or sell his own soul for. Something deeper he simply had to know, his mother be damned.

Fowler held the drunk by the armpit and pulled him along like a shabby coat rack. "Come on, let's go." He waved his free arm. "Fanelli, get the door to the lockup, huh?"

Fanelli jumped from his paper stack and led the way for the sarge and the new customer.

Fowler talked into the all-too-young wino's ear. "Gonna get some rest now. So you can sober up and we can book your ass for assault." The wino didn't understand much being dragged along.

Fowler looked to Fanelli, a bit surprised. "At least the punks stopped their racket."

Fanelli pushed open the door to the lockup. "Yeah, you're right. Didn't even notice, you know?"

"Just strung-out punks, like I said bef—"

The sergeant stopped dead, his cheek twitched, and he threw the wino off him like a worn and heavy overcoat that made him far too hot. "What the . . . ?" Fowler started breathing heavy, fast.

Fanelli finally looked at the first few cells, and his face contracted as though exposed to a bright, piercing light. He could barely look, but he had to. He couldn't believe. . . .

"Oh, Jesus," he said, almost in prayer.

Ralphie Moranis, Tommy Longo, and Rick Hernandez all hung by their silken ties, stiff and white, like grotesque mannequins swinging from their necks and displaying the latest in men's wear. Only their faces were far from any dummylike blankness; each face was frozen in horror, their mouths open, drooling. Their eyes were open, wide open, as though unlidded. They swung there quietly two feet above the floor, and in between the half-dozen floating Italian leather shoes, Fowler saw the Devil reclining in his cell, cross-legged, smoking another cigarette.

"It was a horrible thing to witness, Sergeant," the Devil said, shaking his head at the tragedy.

Fowler's face grew redder and redder. He was speechless, scared, crazy. "You *what!* You son of a bitch!" Fowler grabbed Fanelli by his shirt. "Get the doc—quick! Get the captain, too. Go!" He had to shove Fanelli from the scene, the young officer's face having been fixed on the three dead men.

Fowler turned back to the Devil's cell. "You fucking bas—" The cell was empty. Fowler slammed his body up against the bars if for no other reason than just to hold on to something real, grab something hard and sure. His eyes circled the empty cell foolishly, he knew, as though the prisoner might be sitting on the ceiling. Fowler's face registered fear and pain.

He mumbled to himself: "What the fuck's going on?"

"Ever give your mother the third degree?"

Stone watched his partner as he spoke across the table, watched him stirring his drink, staring at the swirling whirlpool he created, feeling the whirlpool drawing him in. Jonathan was at the brink, Stone thought.

"There she is dying on me, and I'm grilling the shit out of her." Harding was bleary-eyed from all the crying and the alcohol and skeletons and the dope. He looked up at Stone while underneath the table his hand was passing a joint to Stone's waiting fingers. They had been sitting at Nero's now for almost an hour, drinking and smoking grass on the sly like a couple of local toughs lighting up in the boys' room because they could.

"She knows something, though," Harding continued. "She's always known something. I think I've felt it for years but never saw a connection until tonight. I always felt like I was some kind of penance for my father's death, like I was her punishment. She was always so damn quiet. I wanted to know. I was a kid."

Stone took a quick toke and dropped his hand back to his lap.

"She didn't say anything much tonight?"

"Just her standard line," Harding said.

"How long were they married?"

"Not long. About two, three years." Harding shook his head; he felt anger kicking through the cloud of marijuana. "Two weeks after the accident, she found out she was pregnant with yours truly. As if the burden of my father's death wasn't enough . . ."

"Don't play guilt trips, man," Stone said.

"I know my father was well off for a while, but definitely on the decline. I got that sense from the stuff I read, anyway. Sure as hell, *we* weren't well off, my mother and I."

Harding watched Stone suddenly stop midtoke and wave his hand around his face and in the barroom booth. Stone stuck the joint back under the table, while Harding turned his head and looked up.

"Hey, Pete," he said.

Pete put fresh drinks down and stuck his fingers in the empty glasses to lift them. "How you boys doin'?" Stone held his breath and nodded at the paunchy bartender, who stroked his bald head and leaned in to the two cops. "Listen, I know you guys said you got off duty early tonight, you're not in uniform or nothing, but I think those kids over there, I think they're smoking some funny stuff."

Stone and Harding looked to where Pete had discreetly jerked his thumb and saw a booth packed with animated teenagers. Harding looked a little farther to the next booth and saw a man who looked familiar, and although he wore mirrored sunglasses, he felt the man was gazing at him.

"I smell *something* funny," Pete said.

Harding nodded. "We'll check it out, Pete. Don't worry." Stone nodded, too.

Pete started to look worried. "Don't scare 'em out, but. They ain't paid yet."

"Don't worry," Harding said, and Pete walked away. Stone gasped, and the smoke spewed from his mouth as though he were a rocket being propelled at takeoff. He started to laugh.

"You bozo," Harding muttered, and they both started to laugh. Harding took his fresh glass of gin and tonic and gulped down half. "You know," he said, suddenly embarrassed at his own selfish obsession. "I don't know anything about *your* family. Your father. I've talked so much about mine all the time. . . ."

Stone quieted down, almost sober. "My old man was a cop."

"You're kidding."

Stone shrugged. "Detective Lieutenant Butch Stone, homicide."

"Where?"

"Here. San Marco. Real tough cop, they say, and I believe 'em." Stone sniffed and rubbed his nose. "Had a hippie for a son, though. A freak. Man . . . those years . . ." Stone's face expressed the pain his tongue didn't want to. "Think I joined the force just so we'd have something to finally talk about. It still winds up being a rap about how much better it was way back when."

"It was," Harding said. "Cops had a freer hand. None of this bullshit about—" He stopped himself from being boring. "So he's still alive, then?"

"Yeah, retired. He and Mom live in Long Beach. Not far."

Harding felt himself drifting off, his head burning. "I don't know. Everything seems far to me. Unreachable. The job's a joke—"

"Hey, Jonathan—"

"It is!" Harding yelled. "My wife and kids are gone. My mom . . . well." He took another drink. "Then today I find out I lost something I never even had." Stone touched Harding's arm. "I'm going to find out, though."

"Find out what? Who killed your old man? How?"

"I'll do some of my own digging. Be my own private investigator—"

"You dumb . . ." Stone was squirming, his fists were locked on his knees as he leaned over to Harding. "You gonna deal with the Internal Affairs Board when they find you poking around in files and shit? You gonna deal with the D.A.'s office?"

"I'll deal with who I fucking have to, man. I want some answers."

"Jonathan, homicide finds out, it's your badge, straight off. Don't blow everything. You ain't fucking Philip Marlowe, man."

"I can try," Harding said.

Stone was beside himself. He felt he was not only losing yet another fight, but losing a partner, losing a friend, losing a man to another force, something that pulled Harding farther and farther away from him.

"Where are you coming from? Jonathan, whoever killed your father is probably dead. That was forty years ago. You can't go back. You can't change what happened."

Harding's rage came out rationally, calmly, through blank eyes and a stiff mouth. "It's *my* past, damn it. *Yours* is all cozy in some Long Beach bungalow. Mine's been murdered on me. I never got to live it or touch it. I've got nothing to lose, man, so fuck it."

Harding's head reeled, and he raised it slowly to see Stone standing.

"Great, *man*," Stone said, wobbling. "It's six A.M. and all I hear's the weed and booze and shit talking. You come outside, you'll see the big fucking sun rise and realize what the hell year it is."

Stone pulled some bills from his pocket and flung them on the table. "Come on, let's hit the air, man."

"I'm going to sit a while," Harding said. Stone looked at him suspiciously. "I'll be okay, I swear. I gotta go bust those kids for Pete anyway, remember?"

Stone backed off. "Okay. Okay, you do that. But call me later and we'll settle this crap with Fowler and maybe get some tickets for a Dodger game or something."

"Okay, man. Take it slow."

Stone gave Harding a last long look and pushed the swinging wooden door to the street. It was daylight, and there was the big fucking sun rising. Stone guarded his eyes as though in a salute and headed home.

Harding fingered his glass, dabbing the water beads that sprouted on its side, and sensed something. He turned his head and nonchalantly took a look over his shoulder— nothing—bar, kids, Pete. He turned back and tensed. A man with mirrored sunglasses sat before him in the booth. Again, Harding recognized him from somewhere, had seen him in some nighttime vision or car chase, maybe more than once, maybe even tonight.

"I hear you," the Devil said, lifting off his silvered shades and folding them neatly in his palm.

"Who the hell are you?" Harding asked. He felt shaken —by the man's sudden presence, certainly—did he leap silently in the booth like a cunning cat?—but also a bit just by the man's presence, period.

"Is that the kind of thing you say to someone who hears your pain and answers the call?"

Harding looked confused. "No, that's what I say to some jerk who sits in my face uninvited at a bar. Now take off."

The Devil didn't move, unless you counted his voice, which seemed to slither up Harding's forearm and into his ear.

"I can help you, Jonathan."

Harding shifted back, his shoulders pressed against the booth. "The fuck you talking about, man?" Then the realization: "How did you . . . ?"

"Okay, so I know your name, sure. Jonathan Harding. You're a cop, etcetera, etcetera, but hey, I'm no sideshow trickster here to sell you tickets to see the fat lady. I'm here to fulfill your wishes, Jonathan. I'm a striker of bargains, a maker of deals. My clients get what they want. They pay me my standard fee."

Harding felt trapped, angry. Why was this slick-looking piece of slime talking to him? More so, why did he keep listening, want to keep listening? He slammed his fist to the table to break this spell, this bullshit artist's web of words . . .

"Hold it! Back up—look. I don't know you. I don't want to know you. Get lost!"

The Devil took the cigarette from his lips and shook his head. "Whoa, hey. Listen . . . I don't know you from Adam, either." The Devil raised an eyebrow. "Wait—I shouldn't say that. Him I knew. For a while we were like this." And the Devil crossed his fingers and smiled. "But let's lay our cards on the table. You found the father you lost taking the Big Snooze in somebody's basement. So, believe me, Jonathan, I can relate to the anxiety mode you're in. But, you see, I have the power to help you find the person responsible for your old man's premature nap. . . ."

Harding sat as though naked, stripped of his clothes, mind, his past, and all in front of a man who talked matter-of-factly about death and fathers and business deals as though they were all interconnected in some sleazy universe outside the one Harding held securely to him but was fast decaying. Harding's hand slipped into his jacket and pulled out his gun so nobody would see him put it beneath the table.

"All right, you son of a bitch," Harding said quietly, threateningly. "I don't know how you know all of this. But I got a thirty-eight slug under here that says your belly button is looking for company. Now . . . who are you?"

The Devil nodded. "The tough lingo is good, Jonathan, but ease up on the heater, okay? We don't want to disturb the locals. I was getting to that. My name is Berner. With an 'e.' Sol Berner. At least for now. You'd know me better as the Devil."

Harding looked at the Devil somberly and blinked once, twice. And a small, dark part of him almost nodded, almost laughed and said, Yes, it all fits, I believe you would be, you'd look like this, you'd feel my desires, feed off my weakness, my need to die and re-create, to redo, to relive, to be born again through hellfire . . .

The Devil sighed and squinted as though he were trying to look through to Harding's mind. "You know . . . Satan, Lucifer, Beelzebub—"

"Yeah, well, '*bub*,'" Harding said, "I think you're a loony case. I'm taking you in."

The Devil's brow furrowed in analytical thought, then an admiring smile. " 'Bub.' I like that. It plays. Hard-boiled all the way for you, Jonathan. I put you back in the 1940s. Forty-nine, to be exact?" the Devil asked rhetorically. Harding was getting scared now. Tried to let the irrational fears and beliefs be overcome by the concrete, solid, real world—Fowler! Sgt. Fowler must have sent one of the undercover boys to . . . to . . . what? Scare the crap out of him? Torment him? Lure him into a deal? What deal?

"I can give you the power to go back to 1949. I can give you the independence to make your own rules. Follow your own leads. Play private eye." The Devil stubbed out his cigarette and folded his hands in front of him. He looked straight into Jonathan's eyes. "I can give you the past, Jonathan. I can give you your father."

Jonathan felt hypnotized, looked comatose, stared back

at the Devil and thought he saw flashes of red break through the otherwise placid brown pupils that were gazing back. Harding swallowed, his throat felt swollen.

"I don't"—he almost said "won't"—"believe you. Now get up—slow." Harding's heart raced, made him say something he knew was wrong. "I'll shoot you if I have to."

The Devil sat back in the booth, still looking at Jonathan's bloodshot eyes blinking a little faster now, just enough fear and belief coming through, just another push . . .

The Devil raised his meshed hands to his mouth and leaned back onto the table, his elbows fixed onto the surface. "Threats don't mean a horse's fat behind to me, Jonathan . . . especially with an empty gun."

Puzzled, Jonathan's eyes glanced to the side, just long enough to concentrate his sense of feel onto the gun beneath the table. Ridiculously, it felt lighter.

Then the Devil's meshed fist opened a crack, like a furrowed rock being split by lightning, and a bullet fell onto the table, bouncing and rolling in a wobbling arc up against Harding's glass. Harding didn't move, just stared at the shell, its head, its .38-caliber thickness, and before he could acknowledge it as police-issue ammunition, a second bullet from the Devil's fisted hands plummeted and bounced. Frightened, Harding shot a look to the Devil, who wore a knowing expression. Then he released a third bullet, a fourth, a fifth, and a sixth, and after the last bullet rolled to a stop, the Devil opened his hands like a performing magician and wiggled his fingers in exercise; then, placing his hands flat on the table, he leaned in to Harding and said, "Can we talk deal now?"

Harding yanked his gun out from under the table. His fingers stumbled, then flipped the barrel out and spun the chambers like a tiny wheel of fortune that came up zero, house wins. Harding flicked his wrist and let the empty barrel return to its home. He placed the gun to his side on the vinyl booth seat. The revolver no longer had any meaning to him. Nothing much did anymore. He gazed at the table, through it, as though staring through space, through time. Then he stood up.

"Don't deny my powers, Jonathan," the Devil said. "I know you believe in me. I know what you want. I can send you back. You can find out who killed your father. I can do that for you, Jonathan. You *know* I can."

Harding began to shake his head slowly as though underwater, his fingertips brushing the table for balance.

"Mainly, Jonathan," the Devil said bluntly, "I can give you a life. Bottom line: you're a loser. You're a loser of a cop who'll never get his Dick Tracy badge and decoder ring. You're a loser of a husband whose wife went that-away with the family gene pool. And tonight, to nobody's surprise, especially your own, you're a loser of a son whose dad got stiffed before you could wave him bye-bye and whose mom plays mum for forty years 'cause she doesn't know better . . . or does she? Either way, you're on the outs in all departments, J. H., and I'm the only ride you got left outta here."

Harding reeled at this cascade of truths, felt his ego mashed into a tight, hard ball and in self-disgust kicked through the gutter, bounding away, lost down the sewer. The Devil was always thought of as being the relentless pitchman, the eternal, infernal salesman; in fact, he thought he never got enough credit for being the consummate shrink instead: shock therapy, no couch, instantaneous results and screw Freud.

Harding backed away from the booth slowly like a trapped animal, his jaw locked, his eyes darting around suspiciously. He moved toward the door. Maybe in the sun, the bright sun . . .

The Devil no longer looked at the slowly retreating shadow but, lighting up another cigarette, leaned back into the darkness, allowing the red tip to be the only remaining sign of his presence.

When Harding moved through the barroom door, his stomach dropped and vibrated, his skin grew cold as though he'd stepped into a butcher's freezer; he felt indescribably altered. Then the sunlight struck him, almost like a blow, his eyes shutting down, his body arching back as though pushed by heat and light. His body sensed the buzz of street life and traffic before his eyes could refocus. He breathed hard, then, adjusting to the sun's rays, stood there, just stood there. His eyes couldn't take it all in: cars motored past him, but instead of scooty Hondas and Chevy station wagons, there were Packard coupes and Mercury convertibles and a swarm of big, dark humpbacked cars with grilles like clenched teeth and headlights the size of sewer caps. People passed wearing floppy fedoras and baggy-legged, striped trousers and wide ties and pillbox hats and white gloves and nylons with a long, dark line running down the calves. The Blue Bonnet Hotel, knocked down two years ago for being an abandoned firetrap, stood across the street, gleaming white, little banners flying from poles across its entrance, where a brown-capped doorman tipped his hat to a slinky blonde in a tight-fitting velvet dress and red pumps. Street lamps were short, straight, and had double branches up top with two lights looping down. The streets looked cleaner. The air was brighter; never had the sun felt so strong on Harding, who by now had fallen back on the barroom doorway, his face contorted, stricken, the pedestrians making a small arc as they passed him, thinking him an unpleasant morning drunkard.

Having regained his footing, Harding scrambled up the doorway and pushed, pushed to find his vision again, his sane vision. The darkness enveloped him, as did the stomach vibrations, the chill to his skin, but it was all welcomed. He staggered into Pete's bar and spun around to make sure it looked the same. The teenagers wore tight jeans and had the latest haircut. The calendar alongside the jukebox said 1986. The booth he had sat in before still had his half-finished drink and six slugs gathered together on the table. However, the booth was empty. Harding turned his head, left and right, searching, then finally lighting on a corner of the bar, a dim corner where a stool was being occupied by a patient man smoking a Camel and drinking a rum and Coke.

Harding felt he had his senses in check now. Knew what he was capable of doing and what he was about to do. He walked over to the Devil and stiffly sat beside him at the next stool. The Devil shoved a hidden gin and tonic in front of him. Harding dazedly looked at the Devil through the large mirror behind the bar and said, "What do you want?"

The Devil wrinkled his brow, then fell into quiet laughter. "What do *I* want?" He took another gulp from his glass and shook his head, laughing again.

Harding felt ready, felt angry. "I mean, how does it work? The deal."

"You like what you saw outside?" the Devil asked.

"I saw . . ." Harding was unsure what the hell he saw. He just knew he'd stepped into another world, another time.

"It was 1949, Jonathan. Like I said. Simple as that. You believe in me now?"

Harding released a long breath. "I guess I've always believed in you. My upbringing and all."

"All from the Other Guy's point of view, I'm sure. Two sides to every story, Jonathan."

"I've seen a lot of you in my police work, too. The scum, the trash of the world—"

"Hey," the Devil said, "I admit, I'm not too choosy about who I do business with. No offense. But let's face facts: lots of people come cheap."

Harding didn't want to hear any more. "What about the deal? *My* deal."

The Devil put out his cigarette and smiled. He liked it when they came back hungry.

The Devil handed Harding the contract, six pages long, cleanly typed and bound in a red vinyl folder. Harding placed it on the bar in front of him and drank down more of a third gin and tonic as his eyes ran over the document.

"So the deal is simple," the Devil said. "I set you up back in 1949 so you fit in. Get you an office to work from. Give you an investigator's license. I lay you out as a private dick with all the trimmings—no more police manual, right? You play it your own way. And as a bonus—we're talking freebie here—you'll be able to go back and forth in time at will. It's 1949 one minute, 1986 the next. Up to you. I think it's a beautiful package."

Harding looked up from the contract and into the Devil's eyes. "And you want . . . ?"

"My standard fee," the Devil said.

"My soul."

The Devil shrugged. "For what it's worth. I figure if you can't eat it, spend it, or screw it . . . you're getting the fat end of the zucchini."

Harding tried to ignore the Devil's remarks and said, "Let's get this time travel business straight. I just say 'Presto-chango!' and I'm there?"

"No gimmicks, Johnny. No cheap stunts like magic words or contraptions to get into. It's the modern age. You want it, you get it. Talk about your instant gratification, this is it. At will you wind up in the past or present . . . in roughly the same location you were in before, give or take a few feet." The Devil took a long drag on his cigarette. "There is one hitch, though."

Harding looked at the Devil suspiciously as though waiting for a hard-breaking curveball.

"No big deal. You just can't do it in front of anybody; you can only do it when flying solo. Seeing some clown popping in and out of time freaks people out a little. Even puts the fear of God in some, and the competition I don't need. Not that a few scares couldn't be fun . . ." The Devil threw a quick smile at Jonathan and thought of how far Sgt. Fowler's jowls must have bounced off the floor when he himself departed his jail cell with nary a "poof!"

"That's why doorways are a good prop to use," the Devil continued, pointing toward the wooden barroom door to the street. Harding nodded. "This way the people on either side don't know how far you're going or how far you've come."

The Devil didn't like the look on Harding's face. "What's biting your buns here? What's the face?"

"I was thinking, what if you decide to take the power away from me?" Harding said.

"The time travel bit?"

"Right. What if you suddenly decide to keep me stuck in 1949 or whatever? Just take it all back as easy as you gave it to me?"

"No can do, J. H. Once I give somebody something, anything—the power to hit the ponies on every race, or to snap your fingers to bed any babe in town—or hunk—got enough women under contract, believe me—that's it. I can't take anything back until the contract is up or a client croaks early . . . like from too much of a good thing." The Devil raised a salacious eyebrow, though his face re-mained deadpan. "So till death do you part. You got it. You keep it."

Harding pushed the contract along the bar into the Devil's chest. "So how is it this page says the deal's good for only seven years?"

The Devil cocked his head. "Standard arrangement. What can I say?"

"Well, I say, bullshit on that. What good's a lifetime

power when your lifetime's only seven years? I want to see your puss again only after I'm dead and gone, and no sooner."

Harding was flexing his muscles, feeling a little more powerful now that something new and important was almost for the taking. But the Devil looked at this tightly wound, sweaty, drunken cop as someone whose lifetime would probably be more like maybe seven months. Maybe.

"Sure, John-boy," the Devil said. "Why not? Drop the seven years. You got it for life."

Harding nodded, then glanced at the document. It was already changed to his specifications. Harding kept looking at the contract now and feeling his heart drop, his legs wobble, not wanting to look back up at the Devil, who waited, sipped more rum and Coke, and waited some more.

"So," Harding finally said. He got up the courage to look the Devil in the face. "I want it."

"I know," said the Devil. "That's why I'm here."

Harding looked at his own reflection, his own woozy self in the mirror across the way. He felt almost tearful. "Funny," he said quietly. "My mother . . . when I was bad . . . or even in one of her moods . . . my mother used to call me 'the Devil's son.' 'What else should I expect from the Devil's son?' she'd say. She'd be damned serious about it, too. . . . Now look at me. . . ."

The Devil picked his teeth with the cardboard tip of a Chinese restaurant's matchbook cover. "I'm here to be your business partner, John-boy. Not your old man."

Harding looked at the Devil with contempt. "Right." He shot down the last inch of his drink. "I suppose I sign in blood."

"Yesterday's news," the Devil said. Harding's face looked puzzled, but the Devil only used those dramatic traditional remnants when he wanted to keep the level of fear high, to keep the drowning level right below the nostrils, to keep punks like Ralphie and the boys in line. Harding didn't need such leashes; the Devil wanted him free, cocky, and careless. Short life, quick payoff.

The Devil pulled out a pen from his jacket and handed it to Harding, who was almost reluctant to take it. The Devil said, "Hey—writes red."

Harding pulled the pen from the Devil's hand and started to write his name. "You don't take people's souls very seriously, do you?"

"My clients say that a lot," the Devil mused. Harding finished writing, and the Devil inspected his signature. "I always wonder why when they've just signed theirs away." He raised his head, smiling. Harding wasn't.

"Okay. Done. Deal's closed." The contract was no longer in the Devil's hands. "And I'll tell you right now, Johnny-boy, I think you're going to be terrific."

"I bet you say that to all the damned."

"See?"

Harding grew impatient, the drinks wearing him out. "Do we start now?"

The Devil motioned behind him. "We've already started."

Harding turned and saw no teenagers or flashing juke-box. The dark oak booths were the same, though not as worn, but now filled with three Joes who looked like the Bowery Boys all grown up wearing oversize caps and baggy pants. A woman with a red hat and a black veil had her cigarette lit in the next booth by a gent who had hair as shiny and black as a polished bowling ball.

"Want another drink over here?" a voice said. Harding turned back to the bar and stared at a guy in his late twenties, full head of red hair, though receding fast, and an apron wrapped around him that showed no sign of bulging from the middle. Still, the same gravel voice.

"Pete?" Harding said incredulously.

The bartender took one step back. "Yeah. So what are

you gawking at, buster? Want a drink or no?"

Harding almost laughed but couldn't help staring. "Uh . . . no. Sorry."

Pete shook his head at the faggot and walked away.

"Would you look at Pete?" Harding said, still wondering at the sight as he turned to the Devil, who now wore a dapper pin-striped gray suit, red tie, and black wing-tip shoes. His hair was slicked down, short and parted just off center. His upper lip sported a mustache, thin as though drawn with black crayon. Overall, he looked, as they say, dangerously handsome.

The Devil said, "Catch yourself in the looking glass, Alice."

Harding's eyes shot left. There he was looking at himself as though he were spying on a stranger, half over the shoulder, head tilted down, the stranger looking a bit scared and mean in a dark blue suit cut as sharp and straight as his jawline, his tie matching; his hat, charcoal gray and wide-brimmed, hovered over his relentless stare. The thick, slanted mustache, the kind stamped on every other patrol cop from San Marco to Boston like a club membership badge, had vanished. Harding was clean-shaven, which made his nose dominant and strong and his mouth bigger.

"That's you, Johnny. Clean and sharp as a crisp C note," the Devil said.

Harding couldn't stop looking in the mirror. "I gotta be drunk, dreaming, or fucking insane."

"Johnny?"

Harding responded to the Devil's call by turning his head and was met with a burst of light that whitened his vision as though somebody threw a bright sheet in front of his face.

"Hey!" Harding yelled.

He raised his arm to block his eyes. A few prolonged blinks, and Harding saw the Devil holding a large box camera that had a flash gun attached with a bulb the size of a bald man's head.

"What was that for?"

The Devil pulled the film casing from the back of the camera. "Reality check, Johnny. You're awake, sane, and sober enough to know better. A few publicity shots won't hurt, either."

"Publicity shots?"

"Sure. Get your picture in the paper maybe, cracking a few big cases. Get your clientele rolling. I already got you listed in the phone book."

Harding slid off the stool and approached the Devil. "I *got* a case—my father's killer. So cut the crap. Where's my gun?"

The Devil corrected him. "Your *heater*. Don't lose the lingo. All part of the charm. Look inside your jacket."

Harding stuck his hand under his wide-lapeled jacket and fingered a shoulder holster that felt like a part of his rib cage. He drew out the Colt .38 Special, not unlike his police issue, a few inches from its cavity, then set it back inside. It was loaded.

The Devil hit Harding on the shoulder with the back of his hand. "Let's blow. The car's outside."

"What car?"

"*Your* car. What do you think?"

Harding went into his back pocket and pulled out some change. He threw some on the bar and, as he left, realized in 1940s money he probably left Pete a tip double the cost of the drinks.

Harding and the Devil walked into the day's bright sunlight, as strong as Harding remembered it an hour ago, the scene just as before, Thurston Boulevard, San Marco, 1949.

As my dogs met the pavement, the hot California sun stung my eyes and glared at me as if on a dare.

Harding spun on his heels, confused. "What the hell was that?"

"That was you," the Devil said, putting on his fedora to block out the light.

"I know, but I didn't say anything."

"Look," the Devil explained. "I thought some narrative voice-over would heighten the effect a little. Give it that real feel of fantasy. Get you hooked and involved."

"You're nuts. I suppose no one else hears that."

"Not a soul. Pardon the expression."

The Devil swiveled around, looking, and spotted an old man standing outside his sandwich shop two doors down, sweeping the sidewalk vigorously, while holding a soiled hankerchief to his nose.

"There," said the Devil, pointing.

Outside some deli an old geezer was slapping dust silly with his broom. He'd stick a hanky to his snoot on account of the dirt he kicked up with each swipe.

Harding walked up to the old man and tapped him on the back. "Hey, did you hear that?"

The old guy's face wrinkled like a Polish accordion . . .

"Hear what? Watch, don't step in my pile."

. . . he said, and went back to his private dustbowl.

"What did I tell you?" the Devil said as Harding returned to the curbside.

"I'll tell *you*," Harding said bluntly. "Can it . . . now!"

The Devil shrugged and pulled a stray piece of tobacco from his tongue with his cigarette hand. Harding started to feel uneasy about the whole deal. "This is all a friggin' lark to you, isn't it?" When the Devil didn't answer, Harding turned and walked away. The Devil sucked on his cigarette and looked on, eyebrow arched.

The gray Buick coupe moved through the comparatively light downtown traffic. At the wheel the Devil looked placid, a Camel drooping from his lips like a poor soul hanging by his fingernails from a fleshy precipice. Harding sat alongside looking out the side window, a familiar position in even somewhat familiar surroundings, except that the feel, the sense of place, was something other. Scenes of San Marco history were racing by like pages in a historical picture book. Buildings, if having still survived in·the 1980s, were brighter, fresher now. It might have seemed so because of the lighter air. That Harding could actually see the Hostos Mountains, which distantly surrounded the Vera Vista Valley, and their green, rugged detail, amazed him. Only after a day's rain had washed away the smoggy blanket would the mountains' fuzzy outline appear and give Harding a sense of majestic blue-gray walls encircling the city. The San Marco before him now was wearing a perpetually young face, unlined and innocent and nothing like his own.

They were on their way to his office, to set him up, to get him rolling. The Devil's lingering presence kept him tight; his stomach gurgled.

"Something is eating me about this deal," Harding said. The Devil drove on silently. "Working on this case—it might be dangerous. What if I get plugged here? In the forties. Do I die? I mean, do I die *here*, but still exist in 1986?"

"Good question," the Devil said, eyes on the road.

Harding cocked his head. "So?"

The Devil shrugged. "You got me, buddy."

"What?"

"I don't know."

Harding swung his body toward the driver's seat. "What do you mean, you don't know?"

The Devil jerked the car to a stop in front of a red light, both he and Harding nearly slamming into the dashboard.

"Hey, pal," the Devil said, looking to his passenger. "I'm not the Omnipotent One here. You want omnipotence, talk to the G-man uptown." He pointed upward with his thumb. "I paid dues for the little pull I got. I started from the top and worked my way down—remember?"

Harding thought he saw a lick of flame flare up in the Devil's pupils. "Okay, okay," he said, no less angry, but less agitated.

"You die here—I don't know." The Devil gunned the Buick, which roared loudly and squealed through the intersection, pressing him and Harding to their seats. He jerked his arms, and the car swerved into the oncoming lane. "Want to experiment?"

Harding pushed the wheel back quickly, the Buick slipping back into the right lane. "Just skip it, okay?" he said, still holding the wheel for a few more seconds, then letting go. The Devil looked straight ahead.

"Wise up, Johnny, and play the game loose."

"And the name's Jonathan to you," Harding said. "Not 'pal,' 'buddy,' 'John-boy,' or 'Johnny.' "

"Not so sure about that," the Devil said.

"What's that supposed to mean?"

"How far you think a name like Jonathan Harding is going to get you? Doesn't play. You need a moniker with some muscle."

Harding's jaw tightened. "So what's the punch line?"

"Your card," the Devil said, flipping out a small printed calling card from nowhere and into his fingers. Harding took it and read: *Johnny Hard, Private Investigator.*

He growled his response. "Johnny Hard . . . I'm supposed to be a private dick, not a porno star."

The Devil smirked. "Part of the package. I accept no substitutions."

"This deal is starting to have a hell of a lot of loopholes."

"What loopholes?" the Devil said. "I give you some old wheels, a new handle, a gat that goes *ker-chow!* when you pull the trigger . . . and all you can do is project hostility."

"I'm forever grateful," Harding said.

"'Forever' is the key word there," the Devil replied.

They looked at each other challengingly.

The Buick pulled up in front of a large twelve-story office building made from stucco and painted that pale, pale blue that even looks faded with a fresh coat. Harding thought he recognized the building, though he wasn't all that familiar with the southeast side of San Marco, the side that slowly drifted into decay and general dishevelment— vacant lots of grass like unkempt hair with garbage piles, small wood-frame bungalows where the Mexicans found a home to hold numberless relatives or "friends" in hiding. The first signs of its decline were evident to Harding even now as he got out of the Buick and hitched his pants. They felt like a belted blue parachute with legs.

The Devil pointed the way inside the Helmsley Building, which was named after a city councilman who helped build up the area with cheaper housing. Harding knew his son, Robb Helmsley, a real estate salesman, an asshole.

Two steps toward the door and the location became fully realized as though suddenly a vague memory were formed and hardened into swirling plaster. The Helmsley Building, shit. Harding's wife, June, helped to demolish the decaying structure and to secure a new hospital in that very spot, a place of "hope for the have-nots." At least that's what part of her speech had said to the San Marco County Board of Estimate. While married, June Harding was a mother, a housewife, and a restless public servant, the orator for the Community Improvement Group of San Marco County. Once a corporate promotion writer, her later, more altruistic job gave her life, always revved her up, even when the bureaucracy threatened to strangle her and her plans the most. Harding envied her that but distanced the feeling by jokingly calling her "Saint June." Unfortunately, his wife was a poor winner. She hated his job more than he did. "I can do more for people with one five-minute hearing than you can in five years on the streets," she had said. So it was: her little speeches gave San Marco a shelter for battered wives, a community "lunch pail" for needy families, and the San Marco County Hospital.

"Saint June the Divorced," Harding muttered. The Devil looked at him questioningly, but Harding just shook his head, thinking of his kids and ghosts of fathers.

The Spanish-tiled entranceway led to an elevator that looked like a moving cage for gorillas. A short, pointy-nosed elevator operator in a too tight, shark-skinned jacket gave the Devil a three-finger salute and a greasy smile. "Mr. Berner."

"Scooter!" The Devil nodded and grinned. "What's the buzz, pal?"

"Found me a horse who's finally treating me right," Scooter said. "Now if I can get a filly with two legs do me the same thing, I score a daily double, if you get the picture." Scooter leered, then cackled like a sweaty gnome.

Harding wondered if this little creep had a deal of his own, or maybe his deal was already up and hell was riding this cage up and down for all eternity. It was certainly hot as hell.

Harding pulled at his tie and took off his hat, wiping his brow. Scooter yanked open the elevator door at the third floor and shot a glance at Harding. Scooter nodded curtly and eyed him like a wary weasel. Harding smelled something foul on his breath and spotted a brown paper bag on the elevator stool with a bottlelike shape to it.

Harding stepped off the elevator behind the Devil, who acknowledged Scooter with a fiver. Harding figured to take the stairs from now on. The hallway had three smoky-glassed doors on each side, all of them dark except the one on the end, which was open. Harding and the

Devil walked into a dreary little reception room that had a shabby couch holding up one wall and a wooden desk jutting out from the other. In front of the desk stood a tall, buxom blonde with piled-up hair and lipstick the color of a freshly painted fireplug. She chewed gum like a horse at its fodder.

"Hi, Mr. H., Mr. B." Harding just knew her voice would sound like what comes out of a squeak toy when you squeeze it.

"Hi, sweet-stuff," the Devil said. "Any messages?"

She wiggled her way to the back of the desk and jiggled as she sat and looked over her notepad. Any body movement made her jiggle. Even when she just sat there and smiled, she jiggled. "Nope. Nothing."

The Devil winked. "Thanks, baby."

Harding's face grew red. He pushed past the Devil and, opening the door to the back office, marched in.

The main room was no less dreary except that it had two windows that let in reflected sunlight off of another faded blue building an alley away. Harding figured if you squinted hard or had drunk enough booze, the pale color and plaster swirls might even look like a view of the sky. But he had drunk plenty, smoked dope, too, and it still looked like cheap stucco. Everything in the room looked cheap: the two desks, scratched and bulky; a sofa, the shabbier twin of the one in the reception room; a fold-down bed with a mattress that looked soggy; pale colored pin-ups of bosomy bathing beauties holding beach balls and stroking car hoods, all for Rosie's Mechanic's Shop on Waverly Street; and, finally, him. He felt cheap, felt his mission, his drive, cheapened by the events so far.

He saw a door that led to an adjacent bathroom the size of a cupboard, then walked to a standing coat rack, its branching crown missing one of the four hat hooks. A light gray trench coat hung from the rack. He lifted its sleeve and shook his head; the sound of footsteps behind him made him turn.

The Devil leaned on one desk, thumbs hooked in his pockets, hat pushed up off his forehead. "So what do you think?"

Harding wiped his lips with the back of his hand. "For one—I don't think I need some gum-popping broad with an IQ you can count on the thumb of one hand working here." Harding threw his hat on the other desk, then spun toward the Devil again. "What's her name? No, let me guess . . . Mazie."

"You peeked," the Devil said.

"I would've tried 'Dumbo,' but her ears weren't big enough."

Harding strode past the Devil and into the reception room, swinging around to the front of the desk, leaning into Mazie's startled face and oscillating chest. "Mazie—baby—dollface—sweet-stuff—you're fired. Turn in your wiggle and beat it."

Mazie's eyes widened. "Huh?"

Harding marched back into the main office as quickly as he left it, the Devil passing him to console the shocked and crying secretary. "Okay, honey, listen," the Devil said, handing Mazie his pocket handkerchief. "Here . . . and take this, too." The Devil handed Mazie twenty dollars, which she grabbed with her left hand and shoved down her dress in one quick motion. "He's all worked up," the Devil explained. "One of those days, baby. He just—"

Harding slammed the back office door shut, hearing now only muffled whines and low tones of consolation. He tried to think of his purpose, his first step. Maybe buying a newspaper, which would at least give him the exact date. Maybe he could call the house, his father's house, talk to his mother on some pretense about the death, be an insurance agent from some obscure company: "Your husband had a secret policy as extra protection for you, ma'am, only we need to settle a few questions. . . ."

Harding started pulling drawers from the one desk, looking for a phone book, not knowing his father's home number, not even sure he remembered exactly where his parents used to live before the accident forced his mother to find the more meager house in which she'd raised Harding as a child.

The Devil came back into the main room. Harding looked up, then around past the Devil, and seeing the reception area empty, kept searching the drawers. "She'd better be history."

The Devil didn't answer, so Harding looked up again. The Devil nodded and strolled slowly to the other desk and fell onto the chair, allowing its wheels to take the blow and roll back to the wall a foot away. He propped his feet up on the blotter. Harding put his hands on his hips.

"She was only part of the 'feel' of things, Johnny," the Devil said. "I figured a secretary like Mazie gave the setup some texture. Like having some good hootch stashed away in the top desk drawer. Right side." The Devil pulled a bottle of Scotch from the predicted drawer and stood it up on the desk.

Harding went back to his own drawer pulling. "I'm here on a murder—remember? Where's a damn phone book?"

"'Course I remember," the Devil said, uncorking the Scotch. "I never forget storylines or due dates."

"You sound like an agent," Harding said.

The Devil swung his feet back on the floor and poured a shot. "I am *the* agent, kiddo. The agent of evil." With that, he opened his hands sideways, palms out, in a gesture that said, ta-da. Then he drank the Scotch with a swift jerk of the head.

"Ah!" Harding said, finally holding a San Marco directory. He sat down with it on the desk in front of him and started flipping through it. "Well, I remember the contract saying you get your ten percent when I'm croaked." He looked up from his task. "In the meantime, I can run this case on my own steam here on in. 'Thanks loads, babe.' Now scram!"

The Devil watched Harding move his finger down a column on a page. "Muscularity you got, Johnny. You ooze the stuff. But, you know, it takes more than rippling your pecs to be a good P.I. Takes other kinds of power, too."

Harding's nose was still following his index finger. "Is it okay if I don't take notes, or will there be a pop quiz?"

"The power of observation, for a start." The Devil got up and walked to the outer door to the hallway, which was closed. "Observe," he said, and opened the door wide, all the way to the inner wall, revealing the hand-painted black printing that formed an arc on the smoky glass: BERNER & HARD, PRIVATE INVESTIGATIONS.

A card appeared in the Devil's hand, and he held it out to Harding. "See? I got a card, too . . . partner."

Harding was standing in the inner doorway to the back office. He turned and stormed back into the main room, throwing the phone book up against the wall, knocking a half-dollar-a-night motel room painting off its nail, the wall looking the better for it. The Devil followed him inside and closed the inner glass door behind him.

Harding screamed, "That wasn't part of the deal!"

"That wasn't *not* part of the deal, either," the Devil replied, even-toned. "I like to keep an eye on my business arrangements."

"What am I? Your only client? Business slow in this dirt-bag of a world?"

"No," the Devil said. "You just got more interesting possibilities than the average. Most guys want dames or dough. But you, you want . . . justice? the truth?" The Devil shook his head and started to laugh, then stopped.

"I'm like everybody else. I like a good story."

Harding walked up to the Devil slowly, his muscles tightening. He spoke sharply. "You just stay out of my face, you hear me! You're just trouble."

Harding felt like he was back on the beat, in the mall parking lots, on the case of some restless punks hanging around cars, looking for something to happen or something they can make happen. He grabbed for the Devil's collar and jerked it to him. "Just keep your ass clear!"

The Devil hung there by his own lapel, unruffled. "You're thinking with your triceps again, Hard-boy."

Nose to nose, both turned to the sound outside, the door opening and a shadow falling on the inner smoky glass. Still in his clutches, the Devil turned back to Harding, who was almost close enough to kiss.

"You have a client," he said matter-of-factly.

"*You* have a client!" Harding said, throwing the Devil aside and against the wall. "Not me. I've *got* a case! I didn't sell my ass to take on goddamn clients."

"I got your soul," the Devil said, straightening out his suit. "Your ass is still marketable."

"Don't crack wise to me, Mr. Bub." Harding bent down and picked up the mangled phone directory from the dusty floor. "Not now. I'm here for one purpose—to solve my father's murder and zilch else."

"So what should I say to our waiting customer?" the Devil asked, indicating the shadow on the inner door.

Harding's hands were back pushing pages, a bit more frenetic than before. "How about 'Buzz off!'"

The shadow knocked on the glass.

"Let's show a class act, at least," the Devil said, buttoning his jacket as he approached the door. "We'll explain we're not interested." He swung open the door and stuck out his hand. "Hi. I'm Sol Berner. Come on in, Mr. . . . ?"

A large, well-dressed man in his early fifties entered and hesitatingly shook hands with the Devil.

"Harding," the man said. "Nathaniel Harding."

Jonathan Harding's arms went limp; the phone book tumbled and fell to his shoes. His mouth slackened. Harding gazed up and saw his father, saw his father turn to him, offering his hand, nodding curtly, formally, his look troubled, his bearing authoritative. Harding's blood shot up through his head like a capped geyser, then was forced down, straight down to the bottom of his stomach, dragging everything with it, including his eyes. His vision grew spotty, faint. However, his stomach gave way first, *whoosh*ing up the booze inside. Clutching at his shirt, Jonathan felt the sickness overtake him, and he staggered quickly to the bathroom.

Mr. Harding looked to the Devil with concern as the hollow echo from the toilet kept ringing each time Jonathan vomited.

"He'll be okay," the Devil reassured him. "Told him not to put all that kraut on his jumbo dog. Got a sour belly." The Devil pulled a chair around. "Take a load off."

Mr. Harding exhaled and sat his large frame down, folding his hands in front of him as though waiting for punishment. Harding emerged from the small bathroom sweating, leaning up against its door frame, dabbing his face and neck with a damp towel. He looked at his father again, peering out from behind the towel that covered his mouth and nose, wiping them, allowing his eyes to stay above his protective wall of fuzzy cloth and just stare.

The shock of his father's appearance was only second to his sudden arrival. Not that he didn't look like his father, like the pictures of the hefty, well-developed man whose face was a register of precision and whose expression seemed to demand the same. His features were cut cleanly, his wrinkles chiseled in, his jawline fine-edged, chopped from a larger chunk. His outline, his shape, did not shock him; that he finally appeared in color, and not in smudges of inky gray and black, did. His skin was pale, a man who kept indoors even in these southern climes, and surprisingly spotty, as though ragged areas of skin flaked off to reveal a marble-white foundation beneath. The effect of chemical research, the lab pollution, accidents, all were part of his father's facial features, a rough history revealed.

"Are you all right?" his father said with some feeling and a hint of impatience, discomfort.

"I'm very sorry about this. I—" Harding felt inadequate.

"Well, you should watch those street vendors," his father said accusingly. "It is obvious to me that they're professional poisoners."

Harding stopped wiping himself. "What?"

"So . . ." the Devil said quickly. "Mr. Harding. What's your beef?"

His father's back arched on his chair, and he pulled his shoulders back as though prodded; he appeared uncomfortable.

"Are you always this direct?" he said in a defensive tone of voice.

Harding flung the towel aside. "Ease up, Sol!" He stepped up to his father and extended his hand. "Please. I apologize for my actions . . . Mr. Harding."

His father looked up and shook Jonathan's hand. Harding felt the different layers of skin on his father's hand, the smooth parts, the scaly bumps, the patchy white areas, having the same texture as his face, like holding his face. Harding flushed as he realized he'd held his father's handshake too long and then let go too quickly, nervously, as though pulling away from a flame. His father didn't notice, though, his mind distracted.

Harding moved back to his desk. "Please, relax. Do you want a little Scotch?"

"Is that my choice of glasses?" his father said, indicating the Devil's used one and its squat, smudgy mate. "I'll pass."

"Well, mind if I . . . ?" Harding said, lifting the latter. He needed a Scotch like he needed a knife in his gut, but he didn't have a knife handy.

"Go right ahead," his father said. "Your stomach might refuse."

Harding sensed his father's disapproval yet pushed the drink down his throat just the same. His heart was at top speed, and his senses were all too alive; he needed to dull things a little, take the points off the needles. "So, how is it you came here? Someone recommend me?"

"Us," the Devil interjected.

Harding glared at the Devil.

"No," his father said. "Luck of the draw. Really, your large ad in the Yellow Pages"—Mr. Harding's eyes took another quick tour of the unappealing room—"a bit deceptive. As you know, my social circle doesn't promote the practice of hiring peepers."

The Devil smirked. "At least they don't like to publicize it."

"That's what they call you, correct? Peepers?" His father directed his question at Harding and with an obvious tone of disdain.

"Among other things." Harding nodded. "Some are even nice."

Mr. Harding saw the slight rise of challenge in the young man's eyes. "Sorry," he said, his manner tight. "But if you have any perception at all, you see that I don't really wish to be here. I don't find 'spilling one's guts,' as they call it, an ennobling process. For me, it is more like what occurred in your bathroom a few moments ago. I find it difficult explaining my personal life to anyone." Mr. Harding stared at his lap.

The Devil stuck his feet back up on his desk. "Shrink's office is one floor up, three doors down on the right."

Mr. Harding began to stand up. "Maybe I should go."

"Please!" Jonathan cried out, grabbing his father's shoulder, holding him. "Please." His father looked him in the eyes, and Jonathan felt contact, slight, like a bird lighting onto a small branch. "Trust me," he said to his father.

Looking away, Mr. Harding sat down again. Jonathan stuck himself in front of the Devil and said in a harsh whisper, "One more squawk and I give the Devil his due."

Harding turned back to his somber guest. "Just tell me about yourself—your job, your family. We'll get to why you're here. I got nothing but time."

His father nodded. "I'm a respected businessman. A chemical researcher. I started out small, poor, and alone. Now I have part ownership in a chemical corporation—"

"First Star Chemicals," Harding said almost to himself.

His father stopped. "Yes. How did you know?"

Caught off guard, Harding fell silent and blinked like a toy doll.

"We seen your mug spread all over the society pages a few years back. Splashy wedding, huh?" the Devil said to Jonathan.

"Right," Jonathan said, recovering. "Go on. 'Part ownership . . .'"

"Yes," his father continued. "Clifford Snell and I. He's really more the business end of things—investments, the books, contracts. About that I know next to nothing. My end is the research. I've gained a high reputation. Won awards . . ." Mr. Harding was starting to fade out.

Harding threw him a line. "You must be proud," he said, feeling a little proud himself.

"I *am* proud!" his father declared as though suddenly charged. "I am proud of my work and my country. It was the government war contract, in fact, that boosted our company. I didn't like my end of the research, the idea of my work going toward weaponry and death, but with Hitler around . . . there are some things you *have* to do. Since the war, the business has been going progressively less well." Mr. Harding's chest deflated. "Much less . . . but . . ."

Jonathan again tried to help. "So that's why you're here, then. Funds are down, maybe too fast—you suspect something criminal within the company."

His father looked up slowly, and Harding saw a look unlike any he'd seen in the snapshots he snuck midnight peeks at in the darkened upstairs room, a look of total sadness and betrayal.

"No," he said. "It's my wife."

Jonathan reached for the bottle of Scotch, almost knocking it over. He poured a healthy glassful and stared at it for a time as though it had something to say to all this. He drank it down in one gulp and walked to the window, dizzy, alone. Very alone.

"Your wife," he said.

"Yes," said his father.

Jonathan peered at the billboard that fronted the alleyway: a woman's hat, wide-brimmed, tilted over one eye that peeked over her bare shoulder, which had written on it, "Something—something—perfume."

"What about her?" Jonathan said, still facing the sooty panes.

"She's a fine woman," Mr. Harding said. Jonathan turned back toward his father and bit the edge of his glass. "I still want to believe she is, anyway. She came from New York and, soon after, was my personal secretary for a year . . . before I married her."

"Any children?" Harding asked.

His father looked depressed. "No. What does that have to do with anything?" he said angrily.

"Nothing," Harding said. "Just asking. Please . . . what has your wife done?"

His father shifted in his chair, feeling put upon, disclosing everything when nothing made sense. "Wait—let me backtrack. Over a year ago our house was robbed. Much of my wife's jewelry was stolen. We were well insured, so that was no problem. But last week I did something unpardonable." His father looked to the floor. "I pried into her personal locker. It's her little area in the basement. I never go there. But when I did, last week, I found many of the stolen jewels in a small box within the trunk."

Harding asked, "Are you sure they're the same ones and not jewels from some past . . . person?"

"I bought them myself," his father said, perturbed. "Besides, she had no one seriously before me . . . and vice versa."

Harding started to pace, shaking his head. "Why would she rob herself? Or even hire somebody to?"

When his father didn't answer, Harding stopped pacing. "And what made you break into the trunk in the first place?"

Harding's father remained silent.

"There's more," Jonathan said.

His father nodded, and Harding made sure he sat down.

Mr. Harding tapped his finger on the arm of the chair as though waiting for something, maybe something inside him, to stifle the details about his wife, but words started to spill from his lips as though he were a barrel too filled with runoff, unemptied for too long to quell the overflow.

"Dolores—my wife—goes out at night at least twice a week. I often work late at the lab. She's very active in social clubs, charity groups. Last week at breakfast we talked about her involvement at one club, the Vera Vista group. She said that during the previous night at the club, the group decided on a benefit cooking contest. After breakfast she left for some morning shopping . . . that's when I went to her trunk."

Harding shook his head, so his father explained.

"You see, the social club she said she had attended had a fire that same night and had burned to the ground. I saw it in the morning paper on my way to the breakfast table. She was never there. I couldn't believe she was lying to me. I even asked if the club was redecorated yet, and she went on to say how they had found time after the meeting to hang a few flowered curtains purchased by Mrs. Hart..

"Dolores had been edgy of late, acting peculiarly, but lying . . . this was inexcusable. I researched further. She wasn't at a few other places on various nights."

Jonathan didn't realize his father had stopped talking until Mr. Harding looked to him in expectation of a response. He straightened up and rubbed his forehead, massaging in the Scotch to all corners of his brain.

He asked, "Have you mentioned anything to her? The fire?"

"No," his father replied, "I'm sure she knows now, though. I can tell."

"Any theories?" Harding asked.

"Of course. She's seeing another man."

Harding pushed the thought away like a chop served up raw. "Wh—"

"Why?" his father said. "Come now, Mr. Hard. Naiveté in a private eye is bad business. Use the eyes God gave you. I'm an old man. I'm also, you can say, a 'proper' sort. Not the easiest to play with." Mr. Harding gave Jonathan a knowing look. "I went to her trunk that morning, Mr. Hard, to look for love letters. Instead, I found jewels."

Harding kept playing the role, numbly, barely, but

playing it out with whatever strength he had.

"Do you think this other man she's seeing . . . you think he had something to do with the robbery?"

His father looked askance. "I think we've now come to *your* job, haven't we?"

"You want me to find out if your wife has a lover and if it maybe connects with the stolen jewelry." Harding tried to speak as businesslike as possible, as though discussing with Sgt. Fowler whether to look into a report about a cat up a tree.

Mr. Harding appeared despondent, used up. "I suppose so," he muttered. "I suppose I need this outside confirmation of things I know in my heart." His body was bowed, but his head rose up and his eyes hardened. "I play life clean, Mr. Hard. I play it straight. I don't allow for corruption of values. Hitler corrupted my world. I want to know what corrupts my house. Like a cancer, once it's in, it spreads quickly unless you stop it. . . ." His voice grew hoarse; he was tired of talking. "Is your fee as advertised?"

Harding was still numb and had no idea what the ad said. Could be in dead fish for all he knew. He just nodded.

"Do you require an advance?" his father asked.

Harding shook his head.

"Then I guess that's it." His father rose stiffly and handed Harding a business card. "Company address and phone on the front, home on the back. And be discreet, please."

"When did you say your wife was going out again?"

"I didn't," his father replied. "But it's tonight."

Harding stood and nodded, tight-lipped, as his father shook the hand of his son and then of the Devil, who didn't bother to get up. His father almost through the doorway, Harding called to him, "Mr. Harding?" The gray-haired man turned. "I do require one thing."

His father didn't like the sound of this. "What is that?"

"I know this is going to sound unorthodox to you—

loony, really—but . . ." Harding stared at his father's wedding ring, trying to see if it was the same one he'd found in the basement. Aside from the stark light from Harding's desk flashing off the young yellow gold on his father's fleshy finger as opposed to the dulled, oily grime pasted on the ring from his father's fleshless one, the rings looked identical.

"Do you have any friends or business associates living in the Winston Beach area?" Harding asked.

"No," his father said.

"Ever drive up Primrose Road or might have reason to in the near future?"

His father grew impatient. "No."

"Good. Don't go anywhere near there."

"What?"

"That's the deal," Harding said.

His father almost had to laugh. "I don't understand."

"I don't blame you," Harding said. "I told you it would sound loony. Just swear you won't even think about going to Winston Beach."

His father shook his head and wondered whether this request belonged to that hidden power all good private eyes were supposed to have, the innate instinct for trouble, the patented "hunch." But his own instinct, the one based in empirical science, told him otherwise.

"It's ridiculous," he said, looking to the Devil, who just shrugged and made a face. Mr. Harding exhaled. "Fine. I won't go to Winston Beach, drive up Primrose Road, whatever you like. I had no intention to in the first place. Is there something you suspect already?"

Jonathan kept silent.

"You won't tell me," his father said.

"That's part of the deal, too," Harding said. "Let's leave it at that." His father felt he had heard enough sincerity in the detective's last appeal; he accepted the condition with a nod.

"Thank you," Jonathan said.

"Report when you can and as soon as possible, preferably at my place of business. Good day." Mr. Harding swiveled briskly, left quickly; the second his large frame moved out of sight, Jonathan wondered whether his father was ever there at all. He sat down again with a plop like a sack of garbage somebody dropped in a can waiting to be dumped. He rubbed his sore eyes.

My old man was in a prize pinch and needed help pronto, but I felt as low as an earthworm diggin' for China.

"I told you to can that voice-over crap!" Harding screamed, his body suddenly primed, leaning straight and taut, ready to spring.

Unfazed, the Devil said, "Part of the pack—"

"Screw the package!" Harding shouted. "I want out of the package! My life's no joke, you son of a bitch!"

"You want to dump some more texture? Okay." The Devil shook his head in disappointment. "But you're losing your style, J. H."

Harding laughed. "Losing my style, he says . . . I'm losing my fucking *mind!!*" Rising from the chair, he kicked it over behind him with a short jerk of his leg like a bolting mare. He started to pace. "I thought I was supposed to find out who killed my father. Instead I find him walking through my goddamn door! Our contract—"

The Devil dropped his feet from the desk to the floor with the force of two phone books. "Our contract, Hardboy, says I give you the power to play private eye and to shuttle between the forties and the eighties. Finis. And now you're flapping your lips about how you'd rather see your old man dead than alive. I've given you the chance to meet him. I'd call that a bonus."

Harding quieted quickly, his head buzzing, confused. "You could have warned me," he said quietly.

"You'd like to squeeze the surprises right out of life, wouldn't you? Hey, I'm no pooper, pal. I don't know how things turn out. I just throw in all the ingredients and shake well."

Harding wasn't paying any attention to the Devil's protestations, leaning his head against the dirty windowpane, letting the cool, shaded portion of the glass calm the pulse in his head. He spoke in a low voice, a defeated voice.

"When I was growing up, I always felt that I had to find my father in *things*. I'd sit in the biggest chair in the house to maybe feel how he sat, or I'd take chemistry in college and try like hell to care about it beyond somehow wanting to know what he knew. I think even my becoming a cop was trying to find his sense of right and wrong, something my mother would keep shoving in my face every time something inside me sprung loose and made me wild.

"Now I've found him—here—not a thing, but real flesh and blood—*mine*—and I don't know what to do with him. How do I save him? How do I get to keep him in my life this time, this way?"

"You sound bad, partner," the Devil said.

Harding kept muttering, watching the dead alleyway lead to the back of a shirt factory. "I expected—I don't know—something else. Not having to stop my father from being murdered or having to nail my mother for theft and adultery. I don't know what I'm doing here anymore. . . ."

"Yeah, real bad," the Devil commented. "You know, maybe you want to dump the whole number. Nix the deal cold." The Devil was pouring himself another pony of Scotch. "Why go through the aggravation? Life's a bitch without finding out your mother is, too." The bottle gave up its last drop, so the Devil tossed it in the wastebasket and stuck his nose into the second drawer down. "We could end our agreement right now. On your word, of course. And I'd have to get reimbursed for my end of the deal: payment of one soul due immediately upon termination of contract, but maybe it's time to cut free the noose, hmm? . . . Ah!" His hand found the bottle of gin shoved to the back of the drawer and pulled it out with a short-lived smile. Short-lived because as he held the bottle out for Harding to see, it fell in direct line with a .38-caliber bullet's possible trajectory. Harding stood there sweating, his right arm rigid, the gun gripped tightly, aimed directly at the tip of the Devil's steep nose. A second of silence passed as Harding stood there, his face stern, while the Devil actually looked stunned, his brow a row of crevices.

Harding slowly squeezed the trigger. The bullet burst the bottle and shot through the Devil's head.

Lowering the ragged remnant of glass in his hand, the Devil opened up a smile toward the stiffened assassin. "You didn't really expect to kill the Devil, did you?"

Harding lowered his arm. "Just checking," he said somberly. As he put the pistol back into his arm holster, he grabbed the towel and wiped his face.

The Devil lit a cigarette. "So what about it?"

Harding flung the towel at the Devil's head, and it caught him right between the eyes, covering his face and knocking his hat and cigarette to the floor.

"The contract holds, horn-head." The Devil flipped the towel off his face and acted unruffled, though Harding noted a touch of anger—a jerk of the arm, a flash of fire red flitting in and out of his eyes—just enough to give Harding the extra push, the kick and pulse of movement and determination. Harding picked up the fallen cigarette and stuck it in his own mouth, taking a long, lingering drag.

"If I'm stuck with this deal," Harding said, "then the dealer is stuck with me. I'm getting my soul's worth and maybe pulling a few down in the bargain." He glanced at the card his father gave him, thought a second, and shoved it in his breast pocket. The Devil watched him put on his fedora and reload the one bullet that had been fired. "Your old lady in for a stakeout tonight, Johnny?"

Harding just looked up from his .38 toward the Devil, paused, and, flipping the barrel back in the body, said, "Speaking of out, I want your cloven hooves off this desk and out the door before I get back. I've had enough of your personal texture, too."

Johnny didn't wait for a reply as he passed the Devil glaring and slammed both doors in his wake. The Devil took out another cigarette and placed the tip near his mouth.

"Sure thing, pal," he said belatedly, then blew on the end of the cigarette. It sparked and popped into flame, glowing steadily, as the Devil sat, drawing the burning smoke into his throat.

• five •

Harding thought of burning the house down for one, letting fire cleanse his mind, rid it of the Victorian gravesite his father would soon lay in. But then such a dramatic act would not remove the danger or incinerate the murderer's will; it would merely decompose one crime scene to give birth to another, some other house, some other floorboard. In 1986, the skull would still have the same ugly rent from the same blunt object, only a different set of feeding worms.

In spite of his rejection of such an idea, Harding still aimed his gray Buick toward the ancient house in Winston Beach, determined to find out who lived there and if there existed any link between it, its inhabitants, and the disturbing story his father had detailed to him that morning.

If not torching the house, then what? Lock his father up in a closet? Put a watch on him twenty-four hours a day?

Harding didn't have the manpower or skill to pull that off, nor would his father put up with it. Harding was certain his father would discover the shadow, would sense his being tailed constantly. Surely the police would be no help, finding the tale impossible; Harding would have, too, had he heard it while on duty, easily a potential topic during a late boozy roundup at the Palm Tree Lounge.

The newspaper Harding saw a ruddy-faced kid hawking on his way out of town had been no help. The date on it confirmed it was 1949 all right, and a few days before the supposed fire at the First Star Chemicals plant, but what good did that information do him? His father was to be buried miles away, killed at some future date Harding had no control over. Then did his father hide out after the fire and pretend to be dead? If so, why? Could he get the answer out of him in time? Would he come up with any answers at all?

Harding felt embarrassed by all of these weak solutions, reembarrassed at asking his father not to go to Winston Beach. The blow could be struck just as easily in San Marco and the broken remains brought to Winston Beach. Unlikely, dangerously stupid on the murderer's part, but possible.

The only path Harding saw he could take was the one that would root out the source, would penetrate the riddle to the basis of the act: Why should his father be killed at all? And the only way to gather the possible answers was to investigate every part of his father's life, to immerse himself in his father's concerns, and, certainly, to take his father's case. That his mother might be the center of some murderous, deadly spiral of events—but Harding caught the welling pain in time and washed his mind free of such an image upon seeing the ocean a few blocks away, its waves moving up fiercely, then in retreat, pulling the sand away, smoothing the surface, keeping everything even, in check.

Harding would find his parents' house later in order to watch his mother's movements, but it was early afternoon, and the entrance to the coastal highway, Primrose Road, lay at the next turn and a few miles farther, the ancient house.

Harding pulled the Buick onto the ramp and up the hill, though he was fighting the gearshift, having to yank the arm up and over, missing second and bucking, then catching it, causing the car to jerk, then pull away. Not used to driving such an old-model heap, Harding hoped he never had to count on it in a chase, especially a reenactment of the one last night that was and seemed forty years away.

In comparison, this daylight drive felt slow and was taking forever. Around one steep bend a roadster convertible leaned on its horn behind him, then roared its way around his lane, weaving across the double lines, its driver yelling indistinguishable invectives as he passed. Watching the roadster pull ahead and away made Harding's fingers move but an inch toward nonexistent flashers and stop; his cop instincts needed to be suppressed almost completely and for more serious spots than witnessing a reckless motorist.

Suddenly Harding jolted the car to a dead stop. In spite of his gear problems and puttering motor, the entrance to the old, gabled house had sprung upon him so quickly that he hit the brake pedal too fast and was now thankful the roadster had shot by him seconds earlier or else they would have collided. Harding realized that the entrance surprised him because of its changed appearance. No longer did the foliage devour most of the slope and almost hide the driveway like two massive green doors almost closing. The bushes and trees were trimmed and well kept, the driveway exposed, although now a locked metal gate barred easy access and a tall stone wall, attractive and strong, surrounded the property like an English fortress.

Harding drove the car a half mile farther up Primrose to where he could pull off on an overlook that afforded ocean picture taking for most, and then he walked back toward the metal gate. The iron rails were narrowly spaced and solid, so he examined the perimeter of stone, seeking loose parts, footholds. He tried one segment and struggled to the top, then over. He avoided the pebbled driveway, not wanting its crunch to announce his arrival.

When the house finally reappeared, it was as though little elves had stolen in at night and banged and hammered and sawed and painted and left the afternoon sun something to beam upon. The old house was now a fine old house, polished and maintained, its turrets like fingers on a muscular hand, its gables no longer somber but pointing toward the sky. The porch was screened in and newly painted.

Harding stopped walking and listened. He heard feet, little feet, many little feet, running, cutting through leaves, panting, coming his way. Harding's only refuge was the house, the gate being too far back. He ran, turned his head back once and thought he saw the head of one dog emerge from a bank of bushes, turned and ran harder, passing the stone cherub with heavenly smile restored, hoping to reach the screen door in time. He took both steps up with one stride and pulled at the handle. It was locked. He banged at the white wood: "Hey! Somebody—let me in!"

Two dogs, Dobermans, black except for mouths of shiny white, came racing and snapping out from the west, and a third followed. Harding pulled again on the door handle, then thought briefly about shooting the dogs, until his eyes fell upon the screen door lock.

Its bolt operated backward: it didn't keep anybody out, but would keep somebody in. Harding had no time to wonder why or care. He flipped the knob to the left, whipped open the door, and closed it behind him as one dog threw its two front paws at the screen and bared a pointed smile.

With the dogs outside, Harding turned to the inner door, the door leading into the house. He knocked loudly as though to outdo the barking Dobermans, then he stopped. He thought he sensed somebody behind the door, just behind the curtained panes.

"Hey, somebody there? Could I speak to you?" Harding shouted.

A set of wrinkled fingers pulled a small part of the white curtain back, spotty fingers, then a pair of old eyes came into view. They belonged to a woman past seventy easily, but how far past was hard to say about most people who pass that certain age where a hundred and one would be as good a guess as eighty. The woman looked at Harding with the light of some expectation, but then it flickered, and her eyes looked as useless as her withered hand. She looked unsure of why she was there, possibly even where she was.

"Where you going?" said a hoarse voice behind Harding. Harding looked around and saw a middle-aged man in a pair of weathered overalls carrying a small rifle. He had a shock of white hair on his head and a tan even most Beverly Hills residents didn't get enough vacation time to acquire. Harding could tell by the roughness to his skin, though, he didn't get it in a beach veranda; hard outdoor work, more like it. Some might have said he was a retired executive finally living the natural life, if he didn't have quite so dumb a look on his face, one that he had to carry with him wherever he went.

The man shut the dogs up with a small bark of his own,

then said: "I said, where you going?"

Harding came to the screen door. "I was just trying to find somebody home. No need for the gun."

The man cocked his head and said, "Well, this gun is for a gopher I've been chasing awhile . . . and whatever else might show up."

Becoming uneasy, Harding pointed back toward the curtained door. "Anybody home? You live here?"

"I work here," the man said, "I tend the place. I live over by the other side of the trees there." He pointed with the rifle. "Same property."

"Well, I was looking for the owner. He or she around?"

"How'd you get in here?" the man said as the dogs circled his legs restlessly like a black whirlpool at his feet.

"I'm a real estate broker. I have a client interested in buying some land. Good proposition, I swear, if I can talk to the owner."

The man sniffed. "How'd you get in here?"

Harding took a deep breath. "I climbed the wall."

"You must wanna do business awful bad."

"I had to get in touch somehow. I had no phone number. The gate was locked, and nobody answered when I called out. I thought I'd climb in and talk straight to the owner." Harding threw up his hands. "I'm no crook."

"Too bad you got all dirtied on the wall 'cause the owner's not here."

Harding turned back to the curtained door and saw the lady's eyes again, her plaintive, lost face; then an arm came around her body, a dark arm in a white uniform. A nurse, possibly. Then a Mexican woman stared at him, her white cap on crookedly, and shut the curtains closed.

"Who was that?"

"What?" the man said, acting dumb. When you are dumb and you act dumb, you do it badly.

"The old woman," Harding said.

"She lives here like me, but the owner's not here."

"How do I get in touch with him?" Harding thought he saw the man move the rifle from having it point toward the ground up twenty degrees toward Harding's feet.

"I don't know. He's not here."

"What's his name?" Harding was pushing it as far as he could without the gun raising any farther.

"What's yours?"

"Sol Berner. With an 'e,'" Harding said.

"A Jew, huh?" the man replied, nodding his head slowly.

"Look, I just want—"

The rifle raised up another ten degrees, kneecaps for targets. "'Look,' yourself. I think I call the cops. I think this is trespassing."

"Hey, no cops, okay?" Harding slowly opened the screen door. With that, the dogs stopped revolving around their personal sun and stared at Harding.

The gun barrel elevated and pointed at his stomach. "Maybe you could convince me otherwise."

Harding felt dense. Did this guy want a fight?

"You must get a good piece of moolah for doing some guy's legwork, I mean, jumping walls and all. You get a commission from your boss?"

Harding thought, *Now* who's dumb?

"Sure," he said, already sticking his hands in his pockets, having no idea whether he even had two pennies to put on his own dead eyes.

"How much?" the man said, smiling now, getting the hang of this game he'd learned somewhere.

Harding's eyes widened as he felt a wad of bills in his pouchlike pants pocket. He pulled out a few and counted. "Thirty bucks?"

"Pretty good wages," the man said, lowering his rifle and holding out his hand. "I'll take that—since you didn't trespass, then you never came here. But if you never came here, then you don't deserve the commission neither."

Harding was too amazed that the Devil had actually supplied his pants with money to pay much attention to the man's logic. He just forked over the three tens and started walking back toward the gate.

"I'll tell the owner you weren't here," the man shouted to Harding's back, and chuckled.

Harding walked slowly through the brush and trees back to the segment of the wall he had scaled before. When he was ten yards from the spot, he turned quickly. "Son of a bitch!" he said to himself, leaping the last few feet as far as he could, jumping as high as he could to get a good handful of jutting stone. He pulled his right foot up in time before one Doberman bit all the way into the heel of his well-polished shoe. Harding fell over the other side without grace.

Harding stuck his hand in the paper bag, pulled out the corned-beef sandwich, and tried not to get any of the pickle juice on the business card. He flipped the card over on the car seat with his unsoiled pinkie. The address read: 443 Sampson Blvd. He took a large bite from the sandwich and shoved it back into the bag. Sticking the car into first gear, he nodded. Old-timers were right: corned beef was better back then. Harding had spent all of forty cents for a sandwich thicker than the Buick's seat cushions, and it was delicious.

He pulled into traffic, which at rush hour was the modern-day equivalent to a Sunday morning when everybody sleeps in, forgetting church and hopefully the previous night's entertainment. The bite of sandwich tasted fine but dropped heavily into his tender stomach. Harding was anticipating, at least his belly told him he was, anticipating the stakeout and whatever followed.

Sampson Boulevard wasn't far from the deli and wound through an upper-class neighborhood where the people weren't so rich that you couldn't see their houses, but rich enough so that you could see just how elegant they were and wish you had the money to afford one, too.

Harding slowed at a line of sculptured hedges, cut like giant teardrops, and peered at a house just beyond them: number 443, his parents' home. It was a large house in the Spanish style with pristine-white walls and a bright clay shingled roof. The windows were latticed and round-topped, the upper set capped handsomely by burgundy awnings. Flowers were abundant, including bright red azaleas that were interlaced and climbing up the walls between the shaded windows like fresh petals and grass sprouting between your toes on a hillside. The driveway led up to the house, encircled a multicolored flower bed, and came out the other side of the towering hedges.

Harding made sure the house number was correct, not used to seeing such grandeur associated with his family. He turned the car around, looking for the best angle to the front door. Luckily the house was near enough to a corner so that he could park on a cross street straight on and view from a distance those who entered or left his parents' home. Lucky, too, that on this cross street sat a few cars he could hide among, the neighbors having company of some sort.

Harding reopened the brown bag and took a few more nervous bites of his corned beef. Twilight had nearly passed; the red sun teetering at the horizon was dropping quickly, being rushed by low sea-blown clouds, mostly dark and threatening rain.

Two hours later, the partially eaten sandwich on the seat, his stomach unsettled, Harding checked his watch by the ornate street lamp. He took a long breath and wanted to go to the bathroom. This pause had allowed his fatigue, as well as the gravity of the moment, to catch up with his hectic pace. He needed movement. Sitting, waiting, made his mind spin dark thoughts, his restlessness almost causing him to bolt from the car, bang on the door, rush inside and say, "I am your son. I deserve a reason for my life. I deserve another chance."

A light came on adjacent to the front door. Harding sat up straight and wished he were closer. A beautiful dark-haired woman in a short white jacket and tight white skirt came out, and not even in the instant the porch light glowed on the woman's delicate, pale face, highlighting her well-formed cheeks and nose, did Harding realize it was, in fact, his mother. But as she lingered in that soft light thinking, her eyes looking up and away in thought as though searching the sky, not until her lips parted and formed a perfect, red O, did Harding see his own expression of forgetfulness in hers, his own wandering eye and rounded lips, and understood their origins. Only then did he feel in awe, his mother's youthful, lovely face astonishing him.

Harding clearly remembered her face during his adolescence, a face unravaged by her current illness, though still troubled, vexed with day-to-day life. But the face that glowed this night was a face before memory, as though antediluvian. Her hair was a thick black crown, which shook and disappeared back into the doorway as his mother balanced herself on one foot to say something to someone inside, her right leg rising straight back, her curved, seamed leg leading to a white spiked heel. Harding dropped his eyes and squeezed the steering wheel, anticipating.

Dolores Harding brought her head back out, though now a hat adorned it, the brim sloped enough to darken her face, transforming the chiseled relief of her features into just another patch of night.

Harding saw her walk out of sight but heard her heels click on the driveway, a car door slam, and a car whine, then start. A blue Ford convertible with its top up emerged from the hedges and turned south. Harding flipped his ignition key and, finally finding first gear, followed. He followed her all the way into the center of downtown San Marco, where people still lingered after work, cars drifting along the closing shops. The blue Ford dipped right at Bayford, which meant she was headed toward the older section of downtown.

Harding passed her without looking when she parked the convertible in front of the YWCA, and he swung around the bend just far enough to sit ten feet from the corner and see if she went inside. She didn't. His mother was walking up the block, toward him, having possibly seen him, possibly confronting him. Snatching the corned beef from the seat, he jammed the bread in his mouth, trying to look like a man who had to eat and run. His mother crossed the front of the car, and Harding watched her swish by. She held her purse high, crushed to the side of her bosom, but her head was more down than level as she walked. It was a determined walk, knowing where it was going and how to get there without really looking. A passing man with a skewed tie and a few under his belt smiled and said something to her, leering. Perturbed, he moved on.

When his mother broke into a light trot near the far corner, Harding threw his sandwich to the floor and wasn't sure whether to use the car or jump out and give chase. He even gave the tipsy pickup artist a second look, wondering if he had said something more meaningful than "Nice ass."

Before Harding could get halfway out of the car, he saw what his mother was running toward: a city bus had pulled up to the curb, and she just made the closing doors.

Harding jumped back into his seat and, ignoring a symphony of horns, made a fast illegal U-turn right into the departing bus's exhaust.

The bus headed deeper into the poorer sections of San Marco, not far from where Harding and Stone had bounced around last night with the green Buick, ricocheting off curbs and bums like an automotive pinball game.

On a corner where junk shops met a clot of charred and abandoned three-story walk-ups, his mother left the bus and marched into the official slums of San Marco. Harding saw the same drifters and punks he saw when his patrol car used to pass through, only the color of their skin had changed, more poor whites, lots of blacks—the Chicanos would come later. Also, a scattering of well-tailored men moved through the neighborhood, just as they did in the 1980s and for the same reason: the train station. San Marco Terminal sat in the middle of decay, and the few train commuters who could not afford a cab to the station would rub tailored elbows with the street life. This was why his mother, dressed in summer whites, did not look too conspicuous in such an area, only hurried.

Harding quickly decided that motoring around in this boat called a Buick was cumbersome when tracking somebody who was on foot and maneuvering the way his mother was through people and cars. He pulled the coupe in front of a butcher shop that smelled as if its freezer had blown a fuse for a few days.

Trotting across the street, he stayed half a block behind his mother, whom he kept in the right-hand corner of his eye, her white hat bobbing across the way, an easy target for his strong peripheral vision. Then the hat stopped bobbing and vanished. Harding looked toward the store where it disappeared and found it wasn't a store at all, but Ridley's Pawn Shop; so said the wooden sign next to three large balls skewered on a three-pronged hook like metallic fish bait.

Harding stationed himself next to a beat-up Packard just beyond the perimeter of light spilling on the sidewalk from a nearby street lamp, where he began worrying about back alley exits and back room rapes and anything else that the pawnshop offered as trouble. He checked his watch: six minutes, going on six years. He pulled out a cigarette and tried to think what he could go hock as cover should time and his mother slip away from him. Maybe he could pawn his soul, then hand the Devil a claim ticket when he died.

Harding flicked the cigarette away as soon as he lit it. His mother had stepped out of the pawnshop, hitting the same stride as before, a vision of white as before, only tucked under her arm next to her purse was a small package, rectangular, tied with string. She was walking faster now, and Harding matched the pace. He noticed she wasn't backtracking; the bus route was the other way.

When Harding turned the next corner with his mother up ahead, he saw the San Marco Terminal dead on. He moved up closer, not wanting to lose her among the commuters as she entered the barnlike terminal. The terminal was the second-oldest building in San Marco, but the City Building Supervisory Board never let it show its age. His mother click-clacked along the highly polished floor and without breaking stride dumped the brown package into a trash bin, then kept her straight-line path toward the 4th St. exit.

As though the dropped package were a signal at a track meet, two men, stationary objects in the foreground, suddenly shot into motion the moment the trash barrel shook with its new arrival. Harding veered to a candy counter and watched.

One man had a hangdog face and mean eyes; his neck

was massive. He wore a brown suit two sizes too large for him, which was deceptive. It made the big man look smaller, as though you could take him in a bar fight, until he removed the tent he wore and you saw how large he really was and you handed him your wallet and your wife so he wouldn't hurt you. This man reached into the trash bin with his long right arm.

The other man had a shiny blue suit and worn straw hat that made him look too much like a racetrack tout who bet plenty and owed plenty more. His hands were lively, and their every fifth movement became a squeeze, then pull, at his crotch. The man's expression was as hard and as penetrating as Harding had ever seen, only his hands were having a nervous breakdown. This man used his icy stare to play lookout for his partner, at which time Harding showed him his back and fingered a Hershey bar.

The brown package virtually smothered under his arm, the large brown suit walked away as though he had never stopped, and the blue suit followed a few steps back. Harding had no choice now. His mother was gone—she'd hopped on the bus heading back to her car. He had to shadow these two, at least find out where the package's final nesting place was to be.

The streets outside offered steady rain since the clouds had made good their dark and windy promise. Harding hunched his shoulders as the drops felt surprisingly cold on his back, and puddles formed quickly in the sudden downpour. He peered through the waterfall that cascaded over his hat brim. The two men ran to a canary-yellow Ford, the one with the hands sliding behind the wheel. Splashing water with each long stride, Harding raced to a cab about to circle the station toward the taxi stand.

"Cabbie, hey!" Harding yelled, and smacked the back fin as the car passed him within inches, then squealed to a stop. Harding leaped into the backseat, then, weaving back and forth, tried to locate the Ford through the misty window and sweeping wipers.

"There!" Harding shouted into the cabbie's ear, pointing his arm past the cabbie's cheekbone. "The yellow car. Keep it in sight." The cabbie turned to look at Harding; his face was craggy and his hairline was nonexistent, but he threw the five strands he had left across his dome, inky fingers smearing from the rain. Harding stared back and let the driver give him the once-over.

Harding thought the cabbie nodded, but it didn't matter either way because the instant the driver turned back around, his foot kicked the gas pedal and the cab sped within two cars of the Ford, which had stopped at the corner light.

Shadowing the yellow sedan was easy in spite of the rain and not just because of its loud color—the Ford was in no hurry; after all, it wasn't a heist and this was no getaway, just a pickup, maybe special delivery, maybe daily mail service. Harding wondered if his mother made up that circuitous route herself or if somebody showed her how.

A few miles south into the more industrial end of San Marco, the yellow Ford pulled into a large car lot that housed a concrete-and-brick structure, long rectangular box on top of longer rectangular box. The visibility was very poor, and Harding had to rub hard at his window and squint to see the dark figures run around the bend from their parked car among several others.

"Follow them," Harding ordered, and as the cab also rounded the bend, Harding tried to make out the painted, cracked lettering on the top brickface—ROME CO. was the best he could do. Then came the turn in the bend, and Harding leaned over the front seat and doused the headlights.

"Hey!" the cabbie protested.

Harding held the driver's shoulder and said, "Relax.

Stop here." He watched the black rectangle suddenly sprout a lighted doorway, allow two shadows to enter, then turn to black again.

"You know what this place is?" Harding asked the cabbie, noticing more than a few parked cars in what looked like a warehouse lot. The cabbie shrugged.

Harding clicked his tongue. "Thanks a lot." He pulled out the loose bills from his pocket. "What's the tab say?"

"Ten bucks," the cabbie muttered.

"Ten bucks?" Harding gave the meter a good look. It read two and change. "That doesn't say any ten bucks."

"No, *I* said ten bucks." The cabbie turned his head, his lower lip eclipsing his upper. "I don't like playing Joe Law."

"Yeah, well, I'm not the law," Harding said.

"Yeah, and I'm not the duke of Flatbush, neither, but I can spot a cop even with his shield pinned under his balls. Ten bucks." The cabbie raised his hand to check any immediate response. "And if I don't get the ten spot, I knock on that door and yell copper."

Harding slapped two fives in the cabbie's palm and bolted out of the car and into the rain. As the cab sped off, Harding popped open the umbrella he took from the backseat; it cost him too much, he thought, but maybe the balding son of a bitch dissolves in water.

Harding approached the doorway where he saw the package with the two bruiser escorts disappear. Uncertain whether to knock or not, he swung the door open, prepared for anything. Anything except a well-built blond with a rock jaw and bulging chest wearing a tight-fitting white tux that could have been skin he shed only come winter. The man was good-looking, especially for a bouncer.

Harding had entered a small foyer that was painted

white with gold trim; curlicue designs tried to hide the factory plasterwork. The only door belonged to an elevator, again white and gold, and fronted by the handsome bouncer, who looked at the rain-soaked man with the knowledge that he wasn't dealing with a regular.

Harding smiled at the watchdog. "This the Waldorf?"

The bouncer's tanned face showed no emotion. "Okay, Joe, heat inspection." With that, his hands flipped Harding around like a throw rug and gave him a shove against the wall.

"Guess not," Harding said, more to himself than to the man who ran his hands down his chest, throwing the umbrella aside, pawing him like a bear climbing a tree. Harding had been involved in more than one frisk in his life, but all from the other end, and he didn't like being its roughed-up recipient.

"Best not squeeze too hard," Harding murmured. "I might stick my shoe up your nose."

"Oh, yeah? Well, my nostril's a size nine," the bouncer said, flipping Harding back around to face him.

"I wear nine and a half," Harding said. "Tight fit."

The bouncer looked into Harding's face and jerked the gun from under Harding's shoulder. Lifting the weapon to his face, the bouncer said, "Pick this up later, hotshot."

Backing off, the bouncer pushed the elevator button and the doors squeaked open. Harding walked inside and said, "Maybe we'll play footsie then, too," and the doors closed automatically.

Harding joked to himself that he probably didn't need a claim ticket, but he felt uneasy without his gun. Even off duty, he would carry his firearm, a practice that upset his wife, especially at movie theaters or supermarkets. June always thought he was preparing for the tragic, fatal shoot-out, but he continually denied it. Doctors carry their medical bags in their trunks, writers carry pens or pencils in their pockets . . . cops carry guns; the uniform was for public display; the gun had the law behind it and was what Harding privately felt clothed him.

Naked, Harding watched the elevator door open up on a factory floor of white with gold, shaded lamps dropped down and highlighting the green felt of blackjack tables, crap games, roulette wheels, and keno. A small band whose leader was a horn player blew a tune Harding couldn't place except on one of his mother's seventy-eights. The trouble was that outside of one good-size group at a blackjack table, the band made up the bulk of the crowd. The casino had a few low rollers here and there, a lot of somber faces, and waitresses with their arms folded looking for the glass that wasn't being nursed to death.

To the side of the band shell, Harding saw the brown suit with the package talking to a tuxedoed man with a thick gray mustache. Then the package and Brown Suit moved behind the shell. Harding moved along the tables, ostensibly watching the games or picking out a lucky seat, but really trying to see behind the trombone section. Swinging around the side, he spotted a hallway behind the band that had a few wooden doors along it. A door popped open the moment Harding stepped inside the hallway entrance, so he ducked back behind a beam that supported the band shell's foundation. The brown suit came out from the hallway and passed him, heading for the casino area.

Harding cautiously moved down the row of doors, fairly certain it was the third one on the right. The trumpet music was echoing as in a sound chamber, so he stuck his ear next to the door to hear if anybody was inside.

"Hear anything interestin'?"

Having been leaning on the wooden door, Harding flinched upright, then, seeing the blue-suited man with the icy stare and fiddling hands behind him, quickly leaned the other way, up against the man's lapels, in a tipsy sway. Harding blinked into the tiny eyes that waited for an answer and acted as though he had worn out more than one shot glass this night.

"Hey!" Harding said, deliberately a little louder than necessary. "This the can?"

The blue suit just pushed Harding off him by leaning back hard with his chest. "This door say it's the can?"

Harding looked at the door, then back at the man squeezing his hands. "I can't see so good," he slurred. "That's why I was listening for the flush."

The man's thumb aimed down the hall past the band shell. "Other way, jerk."

Harding hit the man's shoulder twice. "Thanks, bud." He moved slowly away, wobbling just a little. Some of the biggest drunks he had ever snatched off the highway could walk a straight line easy as long as they stared at the line under their feet at each step. They just couldn't see five feet ahead of them, which was why Harding had used the broken line whenever possible, would watch them veer the moment the white paint became lost underfoot and head toward the grassy embankments and eventually the drunk tank. Harding's drunk arched just right, he thought; a smooth straight line when pie-eyed and unguided was a graceful, unsure semicircle, perfect for circumscribing the band shell and circumventing the man's lingering stare.

Harding sat himself down at a small cluster of tables where losers were having a few to ponder a way to recoup, to find another game, better odds. Harding felt he fit right in. He waved his hand to a girl who had heavily made-up eyes as dark as the serving tray she balanced on four fingers.

She fell into her spiel rapidly. "We got two sizes of drinks. A two-bit size and a dollar special. That's a jumbo."

"What do you get for a little information?" Harding asked, his eyes falling to a long set of legs that led to a sequined bodice. Her eyes narrowed and her tongue circled her lips. She looked around cautiously. Her voice lowered and was minus the bounce of salesmanship. "Well . . . I got ten-dollar information, twenty-dollar information, and privileged information like my phone number, if that's what you're getting at."

Harding smiled. "Relax." He pulled two bills from his fist. "Here's twenty. And ten more to drop the comedy and play straight."

She palmed the bills smoothly. "For an extra ten, I'd play Vegas. Shoot."

"This place always so popular?"

The girl stuck out her lower lip. "It's a little slow."

"A little slow?" Harding said. "I've seen busier churches on New Year's Eve."

Annoyed, the girl looked away. "Okay, so it's in trouble." She gave Harding an up-from-under look. "I just don't like thinking about the breadline, okay? I can't exactly move into the vice presidency at General Motors from cigarette girl."

"Who runs the place?"

"Guy named Gunther. Harlen Gunther." She jerked her head as inconspicuously as she could. "Over there near the phony pillar."

Harding looked and saw the man with the gray mustache again. The tuxedo suited him well and contrasted nicely with the salt-and-pepper hair that showed no sign of dwindling although he must have been in his mid- to late forties. He smoked a cigarette confidently, blowing the smoke out his nostrils like two divergent faucets, talking with the two men Harding had been tailing. All three were overlooking the one crowded blackjack table and its subdued commotion.

"The guys with Gunther?" Harding asked the waitress.

"The dog-faced guy in brown is Thick Dunbar—"

"I believe it," Harding said, figuring his name applied not to his constant lack of understanding, but to the redwood tree he had for a neck.

"The other guy . . . don't know his real name. They just call him Frisky."

"Gunther own the club?"

"Nah. Just runs it."

"Who owns it, then?"

"Who knows?" The girl turned her head to the blackjack table and another wave of murmurs. "Whoever it is, though, can't afford what that Harding dame is doing tonight."

"Who?"

"I said I didn't know who owns . . . ?"

Harding grabbed the girl's arm. "No. The woman—"

The waitress pulled her elbow away from Harding's grasp. "Paws off, mister!"

Harding raised his hand in surrender. "Sorry. The girl."

The waitress gave him a second look, making sure this guy wasn't some crazy. "Carla Harding," she said. "You know, that Harding fella who owns the chemical what's-it. Across town."

Harding fell back in his chair and pushed the hat brim off his forehead. "Yeah," he said.

"You okay?" the waitress said, quickly feeling sorry for this guy whose face looked pasty all of a sudden.

"Yeah," Harding said again. "Carla?"

"Yeah, that's his daughter. She's been cleaning up tonight. Ain't it always like that, though. Moolah goes to moolah every time."

Harding kept mum, so the waitress adjusted her bodice

and left. Staring at the buzzing blackjack table, he leaned forward trying to see the center of the action, but the onlookers were two deep and the only face he could make out was that of the Mexican dealer. He got up and started toward the group when his gaze fell on another table, on a familiar set of shoulders from the rear. Harding's face reddened as he marched toward the nodding figure at the nearby crap game and jerked its arm from behind. The Devil turned and faced his attacker, unsurprised.

"Johnny, yeah." The Devil threw Harding's hand off his jacket. "Watch the suit."

Harding spoke loud enough for a few bettors to take notice. "I have a sister!"

"That's real swell for you, kid," the Devil said. "I have a customer." The Devil tried to turn back to the bouncing dice, but Harding prevented him with another pull at his jacket.

"How did I get a sister?"

"Easy," the Devil replied. "Your father screwed your mother more than once. You'll excuse me."

Harding's hand still did not allow the Devil to turn. "That's not what I mean."

"Hey, I don't keep track of your family's reproductive organs, baby-face. I'm not even keeping tabs on *you* right now. I thought I'd follow you to see what developed, but when I got here . . ." The Devil moved closer to Harding and whispered, "This place is loaded with losers. I can sign up five, ten plus, in a dunghole like this. Catch this one."

Harding looked to a man hanging over the edge of the crap table as though he were hanging on to a ledge with a forty-foot drop. A human ball of sweat, he let go one hand to kick back a highball and then fling the dice down the felt runway.

"Twelve. Craps," said the pit man, raking in the double sixes and three tall columns of chips.

The Devil leaned back into Harding's ear, chuckling, as he gazed at the man whose face sagged yet another three feet into the table. "The stiff is ready to deal."

Harding could care less. "So you don't know from sisters."

The Devil poked his finger into Harding's tie. "It's your family tree, pal, and you're up it. Get some other sucker to hand you a ladder."

The Devil slithered away, his eye on the sagging face up ahead. Harding rubbed his jaw and walked to the blackjack table. Manhandling a few onlookers to get closer, he saw the stacks of red and blue chips in a neat and growing rectangle sitting in front of a woman no more than twenty-one. She was a redhead whose hair was pulled tight and wound into a bun on top that looked like a crimson circle of cheese. Her face was a gathering of mannish features—a strong jawline, a wider forehead with eyes far apart, big teeth—yet she was attractive, her lips thick with red, her lashes long and black, her sneer sexy without giving an inch. She sat holding the table with her left hand, gripping it as though it steadied her, rubbing her thumb on the felt and flashing an odd smile to some of the male witnesses. The other hand pushed a cigarette in and out of her mouth. She enjoyed it, lingering on the exhale, tasting the sweet tobacco and her constant victory over the cards and the casino. However, she would occasionally laugh, droopy-eyed, and speak a few words to herself out of nowhere and as though alone. Then the sexy sneer and another twenty to the house's eighteen.

Harding tried to make sense of his mother having a child, a daughter, at the age of what? About fifteen? And with whom? He saw little relationship between the woman called his sister and himself. No expression matched his, no movement except perhaps the arching of her back as a sign of being in control, the same straightened-back reflex he used when confronting suspects. A relationship he *did* see, or sense, really, was one between Carla and the dealer. Although his expression was placid, businesslike, the handsome Mexican's eyes would show a fraction more white to contrast with his brightly dark skin each time he flipped a card to his redheaded player. Maybe it was a suppressed display of sexual attraction; maybe it was something else.

Dunbar and Frisky drew closer to the table themselves with Gunther just behind them, which meant the hallway was free for browsing. Harding took a step back, bowed his head, and strolled behind the band shell. The horns cried out a Dorsey melody as he slipped over to the third door again. He tried the knob. Locked. He peered into the keyhole to see if he could maybe jam a pen inside, pick it open like in the movies, though he hadn't any idea how to do it precisely.

Harding stuck his hand into his inner jacket pocket for a pen, but it was forced out quick and empty by a large, tanned set of fingers. They pulled and twisted in such a way that Harding could feel his own fingertips almost tickle the back of his neck. The blond bouncer turned Harding toward Frisky, whose hands looked for another weapon, flapping across Harding's body like large, panicky birds.

"Hey," the bouncer said to Frisky, "I remember now. This is the guy with the big shoes. Yeah. That's it."

Finding Harding clean, Frisky pulled at his own trousers and went along with the fun. "You sure?" He put his nose a fraction of an inch from Harding's head, which was shivering from the pain of his twisted arm. "When I met him, he had big ears. And they were right up against this door, you know?"

The bouncer pulled up another notch on the arm, causing Harding to grimace and bite his lip hard enough to draw blood. "You're kidding?" the bouncer answered as though his neighbor just told him from the next yard that his socks were whiter now using a new detergent. "You know . . . maybe he's just got big trouble."

Frisky performed an exaggerated nod. "You're right. Sure. Big trouble. Now I recognize him." Frisky punched Harding in the gut once, fast and deep, his body buckling as the bouncer let him go. Harding dropped to the floor, smashing his head on the tile.

Harding gurgled in his dream state, feeling flat and wet, and only when the puddle reached his nose did he snort and jerk his head up, until the pain in his stomach and neck forced his head back down. He blew air out of his mouth and made foam on the slick, watery tar. Cranking open one eye, he slowly recognized the parking lot and the rectangular structure that housed the gambling casino. He lifted himself from the ground, trying to shake the blows and the water from his head. Drizzle was ever present; he reached over for his fedora, mashed in like a bent trumpet. Putting it on his head, he realized he'd never worn hats before, always hated the policeman's cap (made him feel too much the little boy in dress-up blues), but he liked this crushed piece of felt. He stuck it on his head and looked for his gun. Didn't think they'd return it—they didn't.

Harding got to his feet, his pants soaked, and felt lucky his nose didn't fall where his ankles had or else he'd have possibly drowned in three inches of water. He marched uncomfortably under a short overhang that was within spying distance of the door he hoped was the only way in and out of the casino. He also hoped that his newly discovered sister hadn't left yet. He looked at his watch; he had been unconscious but a few minutes.

Harding waited nearly an hour, his arms folded, his pants, if not drying, at least not absorbing more water. Then the door opened and out sashayed Carla. Her heel clicks were heavy, directed; her movements abrupt—her hips were like oil pumps in the dark moving in opposite directions. The light rain did not affect her; she wore no hat, and her red hair gleamed as she passed a parking lot lamppost on her way to the far corner of the lot where Harding glimpsed a car obscured by darkness.

Harding moved away from his shelter toward the curvaceous shadow. As he did, he noticed another shadow whose only curve belonged to an extended back-flung arm that suddenly jumped toward the girl from a black Buick.

Harding shouted, "Watch out!"

Carla turned and, spotting her assailant only a foot away now, shifted her weight on her high heels enough so that his blow only caught her just below the shoulder. She toppled over, and a leg kicked at her, then a hand grabbed at her purse and pulled it from her grip.

The purse fell back on Carla's lap as Harding lodged a choke hold on the assailant from behind. He pulled at the man's neck, adding a knee to the small of his back, but immediately a slow burning pain built up on his forearm, and Harding saw that in spite of this strangulating vise, the man had retained his massive cigar and, using his mouth, had stuck its lit end into Harding's sleeve. Harding shouted and released his hold. The man quickly swung his elbow back, driving it into Harding's tender stomach.

Harding bent double, then swerved to avoid the man's kick to the head. He took it on the shoulder and went down sideways. The attacker mumbled something that never got past his stogie, then struck out again with his shoe. It was a weak blow because Carla's wasn't. The man spun to the floor like a pile of empty clothes. Through the drizzle Harding saw Carla brandishing a section of pipe evidently drawn from her open purse.

Harding sat up rubbing his belly, looking up at the redhead, who stood with her legs wide and shoulders back. "Thanks," he said.

"Yeah," Carla replied. "Thanks yourself."

Carla turned and started to walk away, but Harding got up as quickly as he could and grabbed the pipe from her hands before she could drop it back into her handbag.

"Hey!" Carla said as she tried once to retrieve the pipe, only to come up with an empty snatch.

Harding inspected the piece of lead in his hand, feeling its heft. "On your way to plumbing school?" he said.

Carla cocked one hip, her drooping eyelids rising to get a good look at her hero.

"A trick I learned from my old lady," Carla said. "She carries one, too."

"You mean . . . your mother?" Harding said, frowning.

"Yeah. She knows lots of tricks." Carla smirked.

"I guess she must," Harding said, starting to drift, his eyes wandering.

Carla whistled, bringing Harding's attention to her. Then she snapped her fingers and pointed to the pipe in his hands. Harding stared at her a moment, then nodded, holding out the weapon. Taking it, Carla placed the pipe back in her handbag with a click.

Harding jerked his head toward the unconscious thug. "Know this guy?"

Carla frowned like a sad clown made more so by her thick, red lips. "No friend of mine," she said.

Harding walked to the body and turned him over. "Yeah," he said. "But do you *know* him?"

Carla shrugged—vanilla, chocolate, whatever flavor you like—such was her concern.

Harding examined the mug's face, happy to see his teeth had finally set free the cigar, though only after a lead cylinder loosened his jaw. It was a round face, an unfamiliar face, a face that didn't belong to the Harlen Gunther gang of hoods, assuming he'd seen the full complement inside. Harding frisked the man's jacket and pants, pulling out his wallet finally. He read the driver's license.

" 'Dooley Manson,' " Harding said, then looked up to Carla for a reaction. She stood there, arms folded, lips pursed. "No bells ring?"

"Not a clang," she said curtly. "Look, I have to blow."

Harding trotted ahead of her, blocking her way. "Hold on, slow down. I just helped you out of a tight spot."

Carla cocked her head. "Funny. I thought *I* was the one with the pipe."

Harding showed half a smile, but Carla's face stayed placid with only a slight playfulness in her stance. "What's your name?"

Carla looked into Harding's eyes, then down at her purse. "Carla Harding. And what's yours?" She looked up now; she pulled her green eyes open, which meant they only drooped one-quarter of the way, but still the effect was one of flipping a shade too quickly, losing control of it, so that the glare suddenly blinds you. Harding peered through her glare.

"John—" He stopped, pulled back, then succumbed. "Johnny Hard."

Carla shut one eye then, cackling, inspected him with the other. "Give me a break."

"Business name," Harding said flatly.

"You some kind of actor?" she said.

"I feel like one."

"So what's the business?" Carla asked, actually curious.

Harding worked through his initial embarrassment and tried to gain an advantage. He smiled at her coyly.

"I save people," he said.

"Mmm." Carla nodded. "Innocent dames in distress and like that, that it?"

"Sometimes. Sometimes even not-so-innocent dames on the take . . . and like that."

Carla's face hardened, her cheekbones rising sharply out of nowhere like bulging daggers just under the bedsheets. "What's that supposed to mean?"

"I mean, you sure had a good run of luck tonight on the table."

Carla further widened her eyes so that Harding would concern himself with what was hidden beneath her awninglike lids; meanwhile, her fingers would dip into her purse. But Harding put a lock on her wrist.

"Stow the pipe, muscles," he said. "I'm not after your dough."

Harding released Carla when Carla released her tension. She started stroking her necklace with her thumb and forefinger, manipulating the large white charm at the end.

"So what's it to you?" she said. "I get lucky at cards. Tonight real lucky. I got a good-luck piece. See?"

Carla pulled her necklace forward, showing Harding a white, triangular charm that looked as though it were ivory. "A tiger's tooth," she said meaningfully, rubbing the sharp tip with the fleshy part of her finger.

"I thought it was one of yours," Harding said.

Carla dropped the tooth, letting it fall to her chest; in fact, she dropped the charm twofold:

"Get to the point, funny man."

"That Mexican dealer. Got nice hands. Nice and fast. Takes a man with fast hands to appreciate them. I played some fast cards myself in 'Nam."

"Where?"

Harding made a face. "A lousy Oriental place."

Carla wasn't impressed. "Bad chink food and cards?"

Harding laughed to himself. "That sums it up pretty good."

"So?" The edge in her voice grew sharper; she felt a squeeze coming.

"So . . . a little eye contact . . . aces up . . . picture cards from nowhere . . . blackjack!"

Carla got the pipe completely out of the purse this time before Harding barely managed to prove how fast his hands really were by clamping down on her forearm as she tried to poke a hole into his stomach, thrusting forward as though wielding a foot-and-a-half blunt sword. As Harding held her arm down and watched her face dissolve into humiliation, he spoke quickly, jabbing her with words.

"How long you two working at it—two, three months? They take inventory, you know. Gunther didn't look like some sap fresh from the tree."

"So we got a system!" Carla licked her lips, her eyes mournful. "I thought you came to help me."

Harding let her go and, taking her purse, put the pipe back into its resting place where it didn't seem to nap much.

"I did," he said, giving Carla the handbag. She took it and straightened up. Her humiliation had vanished as though meaningless and unaffecting, just a passing affliction like a case of minor heartburn.

"Let's go somewhere and talk," Harding said.

Carla arched her back, Harding recognizing the sign of regaining control. He tried not to notice her bosom jutting forward in the process.

"Where?" she said suspiciously.

"How about your place? You don't live at home, do you?" Harding envisioned walking into his parents' house on Sampson Boulevard behind Carla announcing she'd brought home a date: "your son."

"That a joke?" Carla snapped. Harding didn't get it, losing sight of the conversation. "Are we going? I have a place."

"Good," Harding said, then looked to the wet, prone body. The drizzle had stopped, but Dooley Manson still looked the victim of a shipwreck. "First, let me get Mr. Manson over here behind this car to buy us some more time should anybody care there's a guy laid out in the parking lot. Then you can drive me to my car. It's not that far. From there I'll tail you, and no games."

Carla watched as Harding stuck his hands under Manson's shoulder blades and pulled, dragging him along the slick surface. She said, "Hey!"

Harding looked up from his task and saw Carla's stance, the legs spread again, pulling her dress tight across her thighs, making taut ripples across the fabric.

"Am I inviting you to my place because you came to my rescue or because you know my gambling scheme?"

Harding continued pulling the burden beneath him as he gazed at the more challenging one above:

"Your pick, sister."

It finally came to him: jalapeño peppers.

Harding said, "Your place smells like jalapeño peppers."

"Is that right?" Carla answered, kicking off her shoes and dropping about as ungracefully as she could into a battered armchair. "Who invented pumps? You tell me." She stretched out her nyloned toes and moved them up and back slowly like a feathered fan. Harding sat across from her on another armchair, this one green as opposed to the blue one Carla languished in, both colors as incompatible as their occupants seemed to be.

"Something wrong?" Carla said to her guest.

Harding's eyes had moved from nylons hung over a peeling radiator that looked like a pair of brown legs that melted with the heat, to a wall both gray and brown and somewhere in between depending on what patch of faded paint you concentrated on, to a few malingering pieces of furniture, the crippled loiterers of the living room, so he guessed there must have been a funny look on his face.

"I would think," he said, "that Nathaniel Harding's daughter would have ritzier surroundings."

Carla sat up, dropping her hands between her legs, allowing her cleavage to extend beyond her kneecaps as she leaned forward. "You would, huh?"

"Doesn't Daddy send you an allowance?"

"I don't need an allowance from Daddy," Carla said sharply. "I do okay."

"No dough from Mommy, either?"

Carla sucked on her teeth, showing the underside of her tongue. "Daddy's got the green stuff. Mommy's got Daddy." She said it as though she were laying out a mathematical logic problem.

"Envy goes real good with your eyes," Harding said.

Carla stood up, not so imposing without the heels, her shortened stature making her appear more vulnerable than she really was. "I hate people with money," she declared. "So when I get rich, I'll at least hate myself for a reason. You want a drink?"

Carla turned away without waiting for an answer and padded to a makeshift shelf that stuck out in the middle of the wall and looked good for nothing except maybe keeping an open bottle or two of whiskey handy. Such use was evident here based on the various bottle rings absorbed in the unstained wood. She turned on her bare heel and raised the bottle to Harding, who shook his head.

"You're a barrel of laughs," Carla muttered, and poured herself a few inches in a coffee mug.

Harding almost felt sorry for the woman who drank her cup down as though thirsty from a climb, reaching the top—the big casino swindle, money in her handbag held down by leaden bodyguard—strutting in her grubby nest, swigging two-dollar booze in celebration.

Harding looked at his own hands fumbling with themselves.

"When I asked your father if he had any children," Harding said softly, "he looked depressed and said no."

Carla was concentrating on the bottom of her mug. "Wouldn't you be depressed if I was your kid?" But before she could raise the cup to her lips once more, she slapped it down on the nearby folding table. "Hey, since when did *you* speak to my father? What gives? I thought—"

Harding raised his hand. "Sure, yeah, I know your father. At least, I just met him."

Carla poured another quarter cup of whiskey and looked at Harding from the corner of her eyes. "So you're maybe working for him?"

"Maybe."

Carla smiled to herself and took a gulp of hootch. She left some to play with in her cheeks as she walked back to her armchair and sat. She swallowed before she laughed so she wouldn't choke.

"He get you to protect me? That would be a hoot. He doesn't give a damn and a half about me."

"Then what about protecting your name?" Harding said.

"My name?" Carla laughed so sharply a swirl of whiskey

splashed out of the cup onto the wooden floor. She didn't notice. "You're a real screwball. Next you'll be throwing around words like family honor, apple pie, Mom—"

"What about Mom?" Harding said, leaning forward a little.

"What about her?"

Harding tried to gauge Carla's reaction, but all he saw was a tense woman sipping booze noisily. He said, "I don't know. She seem . . . different to you lately? I mean, the last few weeks or so."

Carla shook her head and snickered. "Different, huh? You mean bleach her hair blond to get Daddy hot?" She stuck out her lower lip, full and shiny from the whiskey. "Roots always show, baby, and they're black as sin." She made the last remark through the echo of the coffee mug, having held it to her lips, now tipping it up, licking the final sweet drops.

"No," Harding said, "I mean, strange different."

Carla shrugged. "Couldn't tell you."

"How often do you see her?"

Carla put her cup on the floor and got up. "Not much," she said, moving languidly to a walnut chest of drawers, probably the best piece of furniture in the place, as it at least had a shine on it, although somewhat dulled and spotty. What also gave it character, though, was a large porcelain elephant, jade green with black swatches, its trunk raised above its head in an elongated S.

Carla leaned over the dresser top and touched the animal affectionately. "You like my elephant? I've had him for a long time. He's a good-luck piece, too," she said, referring back to her tiger's tooth.

"I don't get it," Harding said. "All this luck business and you still needed a dime-store scam to rip off a casino."

"That's right, Mr. Hard. That's 'cause you gotta know

what luck is and what it's good for." Carla began stroking the smooth arc of the elephant's back. "Luck is tripping over somebody's lost bus ticket while walking to work so your dogs get a day off from smacking the cement. Luck is catching the eye of some good-looking Joe in the park and he happens to have dough he likes to spend only on top-heavy redheads. Casinos got nothing whatsoever to do with luck except to use it as a drawing card. Luck's the come-on. But it's the house that sits there with all the game odds. So . . . instead of changing the odds, I changed the game. That wasn't luck, Mr. Johnny Hard, that was what you have to do to win—make believe you're playing the sucker's game, when he's really playing yours."

Harding was impressed with the speech but didn't show it. "And what do you call me running into you and your game winnings getting mugged in the parking lot?" he asked.

Carla smiled and put her head alongside the elephant's. *"Dumb* luck."

Harding let out a short laugh. "You still sound superstitious."

"Sez you," Carla said, pouting. "For your info, elephants mean good luck in places all over the world. But only if the trunk is raised." She worked her hands toward the long, curved porcelain snout and began to stroke it delicately. "Yeah. No good if the trunk is down—bad luck. Only raised."

Carla smiled and giggled, parting her lips as she let her hand slip under to the root of the trunk, then let her fingers lie downward and trailed her rising palm up the length of it, a lingering stroke, until the long, painted nail on her thumb tickled its tip.

Harding shifted in his seat.

"Got a problem, Mr. Hard?" Carla said, almost sing-song.

"You always rub the trunk like that for luck?" Harding said, watching her hands sliding on the shiny porcelain surface as though it were oiled and slippery.

"I need to if I want to keep winning," Carla said matter-of-factly. "What do you think keeps it up?"

"Your winning?"

"No, the trunk."

Carla burst out laughing. Harding meanwhile took out a cigarette and lit it.

"I can see what a loss you are to the Harding social circle," he said, shaking out the match. "Dinner parties always call for a good rubdown."

Carla stopped her massage and jerked herself up, the booze sloshing up to her head as she rose. She felt her veins open and take in the alcoholic rush.

"You got some nerve, buster, throwing my family up at me every two seconds. My father send you to be my bodyguard or my personal nun?" Carla stood with her hands fisted and flexing.

Harding was fed up. "Look, I'm here to get a line on you and your family. Your mother, for one, and—"

"And I don't know a damn thing about her!" Carla shouted. "I've only known the slut for maybe two years."

Harding cocked his head. "What's that?"

"I'm her stepdaughter!" Carla said the word as though she were cursing. "That's right. And she's my stepmother. And we know the reputation stepmothers have, don't we, Prince Charming?"

She glanced at Harding, who was trying to put this last piece somewhere but, like all the other pieces, had to set it aside, so many pieces set aside, the complete picture a mystery, even the value of seeing the whole damn picture becoming a mystery; Harding just wanted to find a corner for a start, something with two straight lines intersecting, to grab on to for support, for an edge.

Carla kept talking. "My real old lady disappeared when Daddy was just into nickel-and-dime research at some college. She missed out on the big bucks, stupid bitch. Daddy couldn't handle me all alone." Carla posed suggestively, her breasts jutting out. "Maybe he'd like to handle me now, what do you think?"

Harding stubbed out the cigarette barely burned; he was still not used to the harsher smoke of these unfiltered brands with every bit of tar and nicotine tearing at his throat. He was less used to women like Carla, aggressive in everything she did or said, from waving her curves like a pornographic flag to laying pipe.

He got up out of the chair. "I want to see the Mexican," he said.

"What?" Just a tilt of the neck, a shift of the shoulder and head, turned Carla's pose from sexy to threatening.

"I want to see what's-his-name, your dealer friend."

"What do you want with him?"

Harding got up to explain. "Number one: I want to find what he knows about the casino's money sources. Since he's so willing to pocket a bundle of it so freely, he might know whose trousers he slipped his hands down. Number two: I want to get you both out of this sleight-of-hand bullshit you're pulling."

"For Daddy's sake," Carla said, answering her own question why.

"In part."

Carla looked defiantly at Harding. "What if I don't let you see him?"

Harding flattened his lips in disappointment. "I squeal to Harlen Gunther and the cops like a fat, friggin' pig."

"You son of a bitch!" Carla shouted, and lunged at Harding with both fists, more in frustration than as a real threat to Harding's health.

Subduing her, Harding stood over her fiery face, breathing heavily. "Shut up and get ready."

Carla held her bosom; it hurt more from the inside than from Harding's rough handling. Struggling up to her feet, she said, "Let me change, at least."

"Hurry it up," Harding said as Carla walked into the bedroom, angry, her jaw three feet ahead of her as she marched.

Harding let out a breath, stuck his head into the kitchen. Bleak and tiny, it offered the strongest scent of jalapeño pepper in the apartment. The open window displayed a strong reason; the building sat across from Los Gatos, a Mexican spot Harding remembered some of the old-timers yakking about when he was a rookie, how even Mexican food went downhill over the years—"Chicano chit," as they called the modern cuisine with the assumption Chicanos were a step down from Mexicans, as though they weren't really Mexicans, at least not like the sombre-roed guitar players at Los Gatos who never would have the balls to try taking over union jobs; such was precinct logic.

Harding knew this neighborhood as completely Chicano, but here in 1949 it was like a border town area, a mix of American goods and Spanish markets. The poorer whites lived here, the ones who worked construction on the new power plant rising up in Kingsfield. The ones who had Mexican boyfriends, too, Harding surmised.

Harding didn't like the murmur he heard from the bedroom. He darted out of the kitchen, almost ran through the green armchair, and slapped the bedroom door open. Carla was on the phone looking at him through her vanity mirror, her voice dropping down an octave as the door swung wide.

"I'll explain when we get there, Romero," she said, her eyes fixed on the figure approaching her angrily. "Okay, honey, bye."

Carla hung up quickly before Harding had a chance to do it for her, only harder and with her hand coming along for the ride.

"What are you pulling?" Harding said, yanking her up from her stool.

"I had to call—so he wouldn't think I was double-crossing him. I couldn't just bring you there cold."

Harding spoke between his clenched teeth. "Well, he'd better be there and minus any loaded artillery."

Carla saw a glint of fear show itself for only an instant in Harding's gaze, but she snatched at it quickly, used it like a pickax, and laughed sharply into Harding's face.

"Romero wouldn't need a gun for you," she said, turning back toward the vanity, adding the finishing touch of perfume to her neck. "He could spit and knock you over."

Harding struck the small glass bottle out of her hand. "Your talk is almost as cheap as your perfume. Let's move!" He pulled her arm and pushed her to the door.

Harding followed Carla by car for maybe half a mile through her neighborhood when he broke into a sweat, suddenly doubting, suddenly feeling he was playing this meeting too fast and easy. The setup was less than ideal and not by anybody's book: Romero might be waiting to throw a few distractions his way, be they bullets or some neighborhood *cholos*. Meanwhile, Harding's gun sat across town, a permanent resident of the casino's armory.

By instinct, his hand dove into the glove compartment and moved about like an antic spider. His face flushed as he pulled out a clean black .38 revolver. He flipped it open; a bullet filled each chamber. It wasn't the same gun, was just an extra, and just where an extra was supposed to be. Harding barked out a laugh: the Devil was his friggin' fairy godmother.

Harding followed Carla up a short stoop into a brick apartment building about five stories high. She walked quickly as though alone, letting doors go behind her after she'd opened them, making Harding feel like little brother trying to keep up, scurrying.

Carla finally stopped at a door marked 3C and was about to knock when Harding in a quick final dash caught up and held her arm back. He positioned himself close behind her and pulled the new gun from his holster; her rounded body covered his, Harding feeling the heat radiate from her in this partial eclipse.

"Now," he said softly. Carla tightened her jaw and knocked.

A voice behind the door spoke cautiously, "*¿Quién es?*"

"It's me, Romero," Carla said in a normal tone. "Open up. It's okay."

As the door just began to open, Harding used Carla as the knob and swung her forward, following the arc of the door, moving inside quickly, sending Romero back on his heels, almost stumbling over a stack of newspapers.

"What is *this?*" Romero said, his arms out, not knowing what to do, his eyes wide and puzzled.

"Big surprise, right?" Harding said sarcastically.

Carla fell to Romero, her hands flat on his solid chest, covering it like a section of territory she knew well, territory she owned and protected.

"Let me explain the whole thing to him, okay?" she said immediately, pushing Romero back into a far corner of the living room before the Mexican could utter a word, though his mouth remained half-open.

Harding watched as Carla talked in a low murmur to Romero, his large, egg-shaped eyes never veering from

Harding. But after a few moments they shrank, less fearful, almost playful as they danced toward Carla and her chest-roaming hands. Romero did not look much different from the way he had at the casino, less polished, perhaps, since he wasn't in dealer's garb—the red vest, the blousy shirt, the tight black pants—but still he proved handsome, even in a worn, wide pin-striped shirt hanging out of his pants like part of an incomplete baseball uniform.

His short sleeves showed hard brown arms, a shade of brown Stone always lamented never reaching, always complaining about having Eskimo skin in sunny California. Harding moved about the room, edgy, unsure. He wished Stone were there with him, his other life becoming more and more dreamlike than the present past, which unfolded yet uncountable layers.

Romero stroked Carla's arm and nodded. An orange cat loudly mewed at Harding's side and jumped to a window ledge, out the open casement, and onto a fire escape. Harding flinched and pointed his gun at the cat in the window, then took a step back, lowering the barrel.

"Why you no put the gun away, huh? Before you kill something." Romero approached Harding chuckling. Romero seemed at ease now; Harding wished he felt the same. Romero held out his rough, blistered hand as part of his plea, a hand that confused Harding since the only hard labor it had seen lately was the tossing of kings and jacks on their heads. Harding holstered his .38.

"So you know the plan we do?" Romero said, raising his eyebrow and shrugging.

"Hard to believe the casino hasn't caught on yet, too," Harding said. "They usually spot these things in a hurry."

"Many things are hard in believing them," Romero said, struggling a bit for the pieces of English in his grasp. "But they get done, eh? I see no *problema*."

"Not yet," Harding said.

"Hey, if they no catch on to us—what? It is a few months now. They know *nada*—nothing." Romero drew closer to Harding, nodding, sizing him up. "But we talk some more. We talk about your business here."

Harding said, "Fine." Then he found himself stuck in a pregnant pause as Romero moved about the room and glanced at Carla, who was biting one of her longer red nails.

Standing quickly, she said: "I'll go get some smokes." Harding wasn't sure if she was leaving because she felt uncomfortable with him there, getting her to come here, not wanting to hear the details spilling out to a third party, or maybe the pause was for her in the first place.

"Good," Romero said. "We the men. We talk."

Carla almost let loose a sneer but roped it back in as she threw the door open and left. Harding caught himself reviewing her exit and perfume trail in his mind's eye: "Tough stuff."

"What?"

Harding straightened up. "Tough stuff."

Romero smiled. "Real cojones." He too stepped into Carla's scented trail, then turned to Harding. "So what you do? Carla, she say you no want money from us."

"That's right."

Romero smiled wider now, but the wider grin produced an overt malevolence not seen in his tamer smile. It also produced two yellow-stained teeth farther back in his mouth, the only blemishes to an otherwise perfect latino face.

"Like someone just say: Hard to believe," Romero replied.

Harding made a face. "Like someone else say: Many things are hard in believing them. . . ."

Romero kept smiling and nodded. "Your English stinks, señor."

Harding tipped the brim of his hat in response.

Romero laughed, and like a demon exorcised, the malevolence disappeared from his expression.

Then Harding added: "If I wanted to blow the whistle on you two, I could have done it tonight easy. Maybe even in the middle of the action. And whether they believed me or not, they'd have put a sharper eye on you, and maybe slipped me a nice piece of change for the tip. Maybe even put me on the job as the sharper eye."

Romero leaned up against the bedroom doorway. "How we know you not doing that job now?"

Harding shrugged. "You don't . . . but I'd be a jerk to confront you two and spit the whole deal out. Look, I just want some information about the casino's operation."

"That is what Carla tell me."

Harding was losing patience. "Well, that's it! Are we talking or jerking around?"

"You want talk on casino. Information."

"Whatever you got."

"Well, my friend, I can tell you what the casino she got. The casino got much trouble."

"My eyes told me that," Harding snapped. "What can *you* tell me?"

"The mob, they put much heat on casino, much pressure, it doing so bad."

"On Gunther?" Harding asked.

"*Sí,*" Romero said, tucking in his shirt. "Gunther get pressure, but not from mob. From boss. Boss get it from mob."

Harding sat on a straight-back chair that fronted the open window, leaning forward, getting somewhere. "Just who is this boss?"

Romero shook his head as he reached for a pair of blue suspenders slung over a lamp. "One with money, amigo."

"That knocks out you, me, and the cat," Harding said. "How about narrowing down the rest of the population?"

Romero either ignored or did not understand the sarcasm. He said, "Mr. Gunther, he my boss. His boss . . . *his* problem."

"And you're helping out his problem real good by skimming at the tables."

Gunther smiled, hunching over, clipping the suspenders to his pants. "When the ship sinking, you get the lifeboat, eh?"

Looking over Romero's lowered head, Harding briefly saw a calendar and what appeared to be a big H filling every other box on the weekend. He blinked and thought the letters surrounding that H became "Mr. Harding," then Romero looked up and only a brunette's disembodied head remained, a calendar girl's tiny face sitting on top of the Mexican's like an apple, winking one eye. Harding tried to look around Romero, who stood even taller now, flexing the suspenders, testing their elasticity.

"Carla say too you want us stop cheating casino."

Harding said, "That's right."

"Why? You no know me, her." Romero shook his head.

"I have personal reasons."

"Well, amigo, already we finished." Romero smacked his hands together. "Tonight last big kill."

"That was it tonight?"

"But sure. We no so *estúpido* like you think." Romero laid open his right hand and worked his left as a five-prong steam shovel snatching invisible money from his palm. "See? Every week or so we take little bit, little bit. Things look very bad for casino. Last legs, no? So tonight— *aboom!*" Romero's crane hand swallowed his right whole. "We take the rest. Now we stop. We have enough. We wait." Romero scratched his chest with both hands, up and down, his personal way of preening. "We leave maybe two, three month. No hurry. Money still good."

Romero laughed at his joke and padded into the bathroom in his bare feet.

"Honeymoon money?" Harding said in a raised voice. He squinted to make sure. Every other Saturday box on the wall calendar definitely had the name "Mr. Harding" printed in it.

"Sí," Carlos echoed from the bathroom. "Why not, eh? It is beautiful in Méjico."

The cat screeched and jumped over Harding's shoulder and onto his lap, forcing him to jump as well. Romero bolted into the room and stopped. His face, although partially covered with shaving cream, vividly radiated his sudden fright. He dropped the foamy mug, spilling the soap along the carpet near the cat, making it screech and leap again. Romero's gaze had focused at a point just behind Harding, but before Harding could swivel around, a blow struck him alongside his face, a roundhouse of a blow aided by something hard and cold, and he and the chair toppled over. When his head bounced once on the wooden floor, Harding blacked out. He didn't feel the second, slighter bounce.

Harding rose slowly, balancing his upper body with a stiff left arm, swinging his heels under his buttocks, then pushing off as though he were turning underwater at the side of a pool. He drifted over to the lamp for support but, knocking it over, reached for the door frame to the bathroom. He clung to it and took a deep breath. His head started to allow his legs to regain their strength, so he locked his knees, pulled back his shoulders. Another breath and his eyes focused sharply, too sharply. His immediate view of the bathroom was one of yellow and red, the red coming from splattered tiles and a floor covered with a blood-soaked towel. Romero was lying on his face; the bullet hole at the rear of his head was an exit wound, a hairy crater of scalp and thickened blood. Harding started to black out again, stumbled back, and allowed the wall to slam him in the back for support.

He rushed toward the window, but as he braced one foot on its ledge and began to hoist himself up, a gun appeared before him on the fire escape.

"Going somewhere?"

Harding backed off and raised his hands, though the blood was rushing from his head to the center of his stomach; his arms wavered, weak as dead branches. The policeman crawled through the window and into the living room, his revolver still aimed at Harding. He was young, thick-lipped, and moved ungracefully off the sill. His dress uniform looked ancient, the large buttons of polished brass struck diagonally across his chest as though he were upholstered in dark blue.

The front door swung open and another cop crashed into the room, bringing with him a commotion from the hallway. He turned back through the door and shouted, "Keep them out, Tommy! Tell the boys in fifteen to help."

Walking back into the room, the cop strutted in bow-legged, older; he looked like his back hurt him when he walked. "Who's this?" he asked the younger patrolman.

The first cop frisked Harding down as his elder took a glance inside the bathroom. "Oh, yeah," he said, stooping over Romero's body. The younger cop walked over to the bathroom, reading the investigator's license he took from Harding's wallet.

" 'Johnny Hard,' " he read. "Private dick."

The older cop moved his head back as though he suddenly smelled something worse than the corpse in the bathroom.

"Johnny Hard?" he said to Jonathan. "You—"

"Yeah, I know," Harding said woozily. "I gotta be kidding."

The young cop smelled the barrel of the gun he pulled from Harding's holster. "Gun smells fresh. Bet it's your slug in this wetback."

Harding didn't answer. The older cop slapped his right arm, a signal for him to lower them both. As the policeman snapped on the cuffs and pushed him outside, the rumbling crowd of people in the hallway raised their level of commotion, the two hallway cops trying to exhort them to return to bed. Harding remembered he could escape into the future only if he were alone, which at this point meant only after a report, only after an interrogation, only after a lockup, and only then if he didn't get a cellmate. It was going to be a long night.

"Yeah, but I still don't get how come we ain't never heard of you."

The homicide detective kept flipping Harding's investigator's license over as though the back side were anything but blank. Harding found it hard to turn his palms up in a "what do you want from me?" gesture since both wrists were cuffed to the arms of the wooden chair he sat on. "Am I supposed to be on billboards or something?"

The detective's fuzzy face floated out of the darkness and into the harsh light, where his displeasure appeared even greater. "No—we just figure if you solved something, anything, since . . . uh"—he looked at the license again—"1945, you'da come up on our books. You follow?"

Harding saw the door to the interrogation room open at the opposite end and a tall shadow enter. The other detectives quieted, and it almost sounded as though they stood to attention. Harding heard one back crack; the owner sighed in relief.

"I'll take over here," the new arrival said. And though his words were unthreatening, his voice coursed through Harding with the jolt of a cattle prod. His head snapped and tilted; his muscles flinched. The man's outline in the dark was like looking at a vapor trail, the faint familiar remains of someone left in time and space and yet materializing before your eyes. The lanky figure moved slowly into the light, tossing off its floppy gray fedora on the table in front of Harding, sitting alongside it. Harding's head struck the back of his chair: it was his partner, Dale Stone. At least, the man bore his face—same sunken cheeks, same receding hairline and pale skin, only the mustache was gone, as was the little girl's mouth. This face had two straight lines for lips that ran parallel with the two lines tracing its forehead. Still, the likeness, his presence, was startling.

"Stone!" Harding said, unsure whether he meant it as a question or not.

The man dipped his hand below his thigh, then swung it around like an anvil and smacked Harding across the face with a *whoosh*ing follow-through.

"That's *Lieutenant* Stone to you, shamus."

Harding felt his right cheek flare up and burn with pain, but the image of Stone's face turned sour still left him more stunned than the blow. He stared at Lt. Stone numbly.

"He got a record?" Lt. Stone said to the darkness.

"No sign," a voice replied.

Lt. Stone shriveled his face up at Harding. "Quit gawkin' funny at me."

Harding kept staring. When Lt. Stone raised his hand again, Harding quickly forced his eyes away from the homicide lieutenant. Harding was sweating now, breathing irregularly.

"What about my rights?" Harding said in a low voice,

more to the table and Lt. Stone's propped-up knee than to anyone.

"You got one of *my* rights," Lt. Stone said. "How about one of my lefts this time?"

Harding heard some closed-mouth laughs out of the dark like the rumbling of a coming storm.

Harding started to laugh at himself, realizing the only Miranda this forties dick would know wore big hats with fruit on top. "So much for the good ol' days," he murmured.

Lt. Stone squinted. "What? You feel like yakking? So come on and tell me about Romero."

"I told your friends here three times already."

"I know," Lt. Stone said, lighting up a cigarette and putting the spent match in his suit pocket. "But this time sprinkle a few facts in there, so when I go home for once, I can tell my old lady I seen the truth. It'd make her day."

Harding's head sank down wearily, then he raised it up; his voice droned. "One of my street contacts told me about this guy Romero who knew how to get hold of some counterfeit green cards. I had a client who has relatives in Mexico he wanted to bring across. But not like animals through barbed wire, he said. He wanted them walking in like men. My client made enough money in L.A. to afford any means possible of getting his family through, including paying big money for fake green cards. So I went to Romero's—"

"Alone?" Lt. Stone asked.

"Yeah—to make the deal."

"And your client's name?"

Harding shifted his weight back on the chair. "Pancho Villa."

Lt. Stone swatted Harding across his face again, harder than before, but Harding was at least ready for this one.

"It's a nasty reflex, I know," Lt. Stone said. "Some

people laugh. I hit." He slid off the table and with his hand brushed off the invisible dust left by his pants where he'd sat. Harding wondered how far this story was going to take him; how many welts per wisecrack, how many bruises. Stone's father seemed far stronger physically than his son, though their frames were nearly identical. Muscle meant little when anger could power your strength.

Lt. Stone continued: "You were entering into an illegal act—phony green cards."

"My client seemed like a good man. Had a real concern for his family. Their honor. I wanted to help out."

"For a P.I.'s price," Lt. Stone said. Harding said nothing.

"So you shot Romero 'cause he wouldn't sell."

"I didn't shoot Romero," Harding said.

"An innocent man," Lt. Stone said to the surrounding darkness. "What'll they think of next?"

Harding looked around and sensed a huge arena of black surrounding him, black bleachers filled with shadowed spectators cum jurors.

"Look," Harding said as steadily as he could. "Somebody slugged me, and when I woke up Romero was dead. Somebody came up behind me. They used the fire escape to do it."

Harding glanced up for a response, but his interrogator had stepped into the unlit void and become headless, a gray suit pulling up its sleeves, rubbing its reddened knuckles; it even straightened its tie.

"Look at my head, goddamn it!" Harding shouted. "Look at the wound!"

"Yeah, I seen," the eyeless voice said above a pair of hands that pointed at Harding's bruise. "It ain't neat and tidy like one of my shots. Then again . . . maybe you're just clumsy. You look clumsy."

"Yeah," said a sly voice somewhere to his left, laughing. "Maybe he bumped his head on a bed frame, huh? When he was hiding under the mattress of some poor Joe he was tryin' to catch cheatin'!"

"Yeah, that's it," Harding heard Lt. Stone say. "Occupational hazard for a peeper. Bed-frame bumps from all that crawlin' around."

A general laughter rose, Harding making out maybe four distinct voices, maybe forty.

"Maybe we'll get a demonstration of some of that crawlin' here, too, pretty soon," Lt. Stone added, and the laughter died out faster than usual. The darkness held a tension; something expected, seen before, not looked forward to. A scuffle of feet to Harding's left, a clearing of a throat behind.

Lt. Stone's head finally rejoined his body in the light. It moved in close to Harding. Harding smelled Sen-Sen mixed with cigarette smoke on his breath:

"And what about the girl?"

Harding answered unthinking. "What girl?"

Lt. Stone came over the top this time, and like some brutish magician there appeared a rubber sap in his hand from empty air striking down on top of Harding's skull. The blow forced Harding's eyes shut and almost sent him floating out and into that darkness from his little island of light. But he pressed open his eyes and mouth and remained conscious.

"*That* girl," Lt. Stone said.

Harding shook his head. "No girl I know feels like that."

Lt. Stone moved the sap up to his chest just to see Harding flinch, but then he nodded to somebody in the room.

Harding heard pad paper being flipped and a voice, the old cop with the bad back at Romero's, he thought. "Landlady said she heard high heels clopping around along with a man's footsteps, and they was both headed to the Mex's room. She says she took a peek and seen a man with a gray suit and fitting this guy's description. She said the girl was a redhead built on top like the Chrysler Building gone sideways. . . . Well, maybe not them exact words."

A pad was flipped shut, and Lt. Stone once again leaned into Harding's face. *"That* girl," he said.

Harding couldn't see if Lt. Stone had the sap in his hand or not, but he couldn't see it last time, either, so the difference it made was none.

"I picked her up at a dive near my office. Had this Romero business to do, so I took her along. I didn't want to lose her company for the night. She came up, then I sent her for some cigarettes when business started."

Lt. Stone pointed his sap to the left. Another voice responded as though directed to in a cloistered choir. "Landlady said she heard the high heels leave alone and not come back. Then the shot came ten minutes later."

Lt. Stone turned back to Harding, his brows raised in mock astonishment. "Well, whattaya know . . . a corroborated fact. Yeah. One lousy truth in a fat pack of lies."

"Hey, I didn't know this jerk, Romero!" Harding shouted, watching the sap and its movements in and out of sight.

"How about a hood name of Turley?" Lt. Stone asked flatly.

"Who?"

"You know him? Heard of him?"

"Turley?"

"That's right. Max Turley. New York City. Delancey Street. How dumb can you play?" Lt. Stone's voice was rising, gathering momentum.

"I don't know any Turley."

"How about a Gunther?" Lt. Stone shouted.

"Harlen Gunther?" Harding said, immediately wishing he hadn't.

"Bingo! Finally some paydirt." Lt. Stone stuck the end of the sap into Harding's throat. "I was going to try Harry Truman next to see if you were playing fair. Tell me about Gunther."

Harding took a deep breath. "I just heard the name. Never met him. I got an underworld source who mentioned him. Think he said he was running a casino for some rich guy who was into the mob for money. That's all."

"That's all, huh?"

"That's it. That's all I know." Harding was getting testy. He was tired and hurt in too many places.

"You know what I think *I* know. I think I know you're lying. I think I know you're probably one of Turley's boys come west to plug Gunther and his pals. And you started with Romero."

"I don't know a Turley! I don't know Gunther! I had no reason to kill Romero, damn it!"

"Sure, but somebody who *had* a reason decided to pop by, saw you through the window, and figured you'd make a swell fall guy."

Harding nodded. "Maybe."

Lt. Stone's veins began to dominate his forehead like blue worms dug in just under the surface. "Tell me another fairy tale, Mother Goose."

Lt. Stone almost leaped into Harding's lap and pulled his hair, yanking his head back to the chair support. He spoke straight down at Harding as though force-feeding the words down his throat. "Only skip the tale, and I hate fairies. So try the truth. One more time—what happened?"

Harding felt as though his Adam's apple were about to pop out like a Ping-Pong ball, his neck bent back in an inverted U. "I told you," he rasped.

Still holding Harding's hair back with his left hand, Lt.

Stone drove one, two, three punches into Harding's gut, not allowing him to bend with the blows, restraining him by his roots. A blue arm came out of the blackness and placed a hand on Lt. Stone's shoulder. Lt. Stone shrugged it off but at the same time let go of Harding. He backed off, sweating, and in retreat backhanded a shot to Harding's temple with his sap.

"Again!" he screamed at Harding.

Harding was near vomiting, shaking his head, his teeth incongruously aching from the hair pull. Something was growing larger and more painful on the left side of his forehead, weighing him down, pushing him down through the chair, the floor, the dark.

Lt. Stone rushed at him again, a blur of sweat and gray. "Stay awake, you bastard, and tell me the story again!"

Then the door to the interrogation room opened. "Lieutenant?" said the beam of light from the hallway as it spread across the table but fell short of the limp Harding. Lt. Stone backed off and walked to the doorway. Harding heard buzzing, mumbling, ringing, his own heart beating —somewhere near his bowels at this point.

He squinted at the lieutenant's silhouette; it nodded in the bright door frame, then cursed. Then the shadow play ended, and Lt. Stone became whole again and full in Harding's face.

"Guess what, fella? I'm puttin' you back in the street. In your case, the gutter. But listen—you and I ain't finished up here, I can tell that."

Lt. Stone raised Harding's head with his thumb and let his eyes light up in a way that made Harding's gaze intensify.

"You look at me like you know me from somewhere," he said. "I musta been a nightmare you had. I'm that kinda guy."

Lt. Stone struck up another cigarette, shook his wrist

once, and stuck the dead match in his jacket pocket with the others. He walked over to the door and flicked on the room light. Harding thought he'd entered the center of an explosion, his pupils contracting like hardened rubber bands.

The old cop lifted Harding up. "Let's go now."

Lt. Stone's voice trailed off. "Throw him in the can for a few hours, then dump him."

Harding looked around. Nobody but the brass-buttoned cop and him in a small brown room barely bigger than the table. The cop held him up by his right armpit, Harding's body having sagged off his left leg. "You got off easy," the old cop said.

"Yeah," Harding mumbled. "What's today? Xmas?"

"You can walk, can't you?"

Harding took baby steps forward, feeling his balance return.

"See?" the old cop said. "Most guys we gotta pour into a cell."

Harding licked his lips and turned to the cop who was his human crutch. "Hey, what did that detective say to Lt. Stone just now?"

The cop looked at his prisoner with the eyes of a father to a naughty boy and laughed. "You really wanna know?"

"Sure."

"He said that Romero's wristwatch was missing offa his wrist."

Harding's face went blank.

· SIX ·

Bang, banging: Harding's head re-echoed—did he actually hear the shot that killed Romero? From above, far off, the sound came round again, cavernous and white. Harding felt the texture of the sheets encircling him, wrapping him up like a scratchy cocoon, or was he a mummy, numbed, dead? As he flipped over, tightening the binding linen, the pillow felt like a sack of coarse sand to his swollen eye and he yelped somewhere, possibly aloud, possibly in his woozy state, feeling the banging in his eye, hearing it *through* his eye.

Harding finally released his leaden lids to what he hoped would alleviate the sound, the shot, the something in his brain that flashed in the darkness. The sunlight from the bedroom window met him halfway up the blanket, warming his sheet-bound legs. He blinked twice, and the sight of the silver radio alarm clock and the growl of some kid gunning his turbo engine and screeching across the nearby intersection combined to precisely locate his body: it was his apartment, his bedroom, his bed; it was 1986.

He reached behind for the edge of the pine headboard to pull himself up, prop himself back, his stomach sore, feeling punctured still by the fists from last night. No dream that, he thought; 1949 really happened, and it hurt like a son of a bitch.

Harding took deep breaths in spite of the pain his stomach and ribs offered with each expansion. He wanted a clear head. Last night only offered up a wide, spiraling journey that never seemed to overlap itself and offer connections, crisscross points of knowledge. His mother led him to a pawnshop which led to a package delivered which brought him to a dying casino, his first beating of the night, and the discovery of a stepsister. Maybe that was one place the dizzying road finally merged with itself—his mother, his stepsister, the same casino where the package changed hands. From this tenuous intersection the circle widened farther, the arc expanded, flattening out to encompass a Mexican dealer, his scheme, and his death. And somehow his calendar. Another crossing: Why would his father's name be on Romero's calendar? But the insidious circle swept farther still—there was Harding's arrest, his brutal grilling, then the mention of a mysterious Turley gang and an unknown motive for wanting to eliminate Harlen Gunther and his associates. The final oblique turn came with Harding's subsequent release because the Mexican's watch was missing.

Jonathan took one last deep breath, half wishing it *were* his last, and felt the mattress grow softer beneath him. Here was the true intersection, the completed circle: his bed. He woke up in it the day before yesterday, and he woke up in it today, but nothing in between that he had held as solid remained so now: the floor might be a tract of swallowing dust, the sunlight a streak of garish yellow paint. Harding suddenly burned with emptiness, with wanting to fill his bed with his children, June, something tangible, close, his. What the hell year did he say it was again?

The banging became hollowed out, wooden, transformed from gunshots to a violent knock on his front door. He sat up, too quickly; so, steadying himself on the nightstand, then lamp, he walked through his apartment, his furniture offering bent arms and curved backs for support. He shuffled his feet and felt a bit more at ease in the rooms' familiarity, this converted motel, the Sundeck Apartments, which had no sundeck, just the stench of an abused pool.

"All right!" Harding yelled toward the final bang. He swung the door open, and Stone stared at him from the doorstep. Harding flinched. When Stone's face re-formed into the concerned features of his longtime friend, Harding pushed out a short breath and relaxed.

"Hey, it's me!" Stone said. "What the hell is wrong with you?"

Harding shook his head and turned, shuffling back toward the kitchen. He checked himself: he had his underwear on, at least.

Stone threw the door shut behind him and, following Harding's slumped shape, kicked aside the footstool that sat in front of the portable television. "I was knocking like crazy out there. You don't answer your phone. Where were you yesterday?"

Harding held his two arms straight out, supporting himself on the kitchen counter like a buckling bridge, his head dropping down beneath his shoulders. Then his face peeked over his back, through his tousled hair, and he said, "Did your father beat you as a kid?"

"What? Where did that come from?"

Harding didn't answer, but his frozen position kept the question alive.

Stone threw out his hands. "Yeah—he beat the crap out of me. So?"

"No surprise there," Harding said. His attention returned to the counter and his search for coffee.

"What are you talking about, man?"

"Nothing," Harding said, swirling the remains of two-day-old brown liquid in a Pyrex pot and judging it drinkable. He stuck it on a burner and turned on the gas. Facing Stone, he looked with affection into his partner's eyes and half smiled. "All I know, man, is that God must have given you your father's face and your mother's heart."

"Will you tell me what the crap you're talking about? I tried calling you all day yesterday. I was at your door a hundred times." Stone's tirade quickly ended when the sun from the kitchen window intensified and lit the left side of Harding's battered face.

"Look at you," Stone said. "You look like you got stepped on. What happened?"

"I can't say."

Stone straightened up. "Give it a shot."

"Go with me on this," Harding said, a calm plea in his voice. "I'd tell you it was a bad dream if my ribs weren't bent the other way, but as it is—let it ride, okay?"

"'Let it ride' . . . shit." Stone flung his officer's cap on the small Formica table, folded his arms, and leaned back on the refrigerator. "You don't trust me?"

Harding stopped pouring his boiling coffee and shot an angry look at Stone.

"Okay." Stone raised his hands in mock surrender. "Let it ride."

"You want?" Harding said, raising the coffeepot.

Stone shook his head and watched Harding wince as he

gingerly sipped from the steaming cup, his left eye swollen to the size of a blue billiard ball. Opening the refrigerator door behind him, Stone broke out a tray of ice cubes, then cracked them on the crumb-covered counter. He scooped a handful into a dishrag and bundled it up like a hobo's lunch.

"Here," he said, slapping the ice pack in Harding's hand. "Lay some of this on that eye. Might shake people up seeing a patrol cop tooling around looking like Quasimodo, man. Doesn't build up the confidence factor . . . especially in me."

Harding placed the cold compact on the faded blue hills that made up his left cheek and temple. "Patrol today, huh?"

"Eight A.M. You coming?"

Harding slugged down the remainder of the coffee and walked to the sink. He slapped the water open fast, the only way anything over four drops would shoot out the faucet, and rinsed the cup. He looked outside at the sickly green outdoor walls of the two-level converted motel, a moldy green that matched the smell of the stale pool water ten feet from his window.

"We got room for the records office on our tour?" Harding asked quietly.

Stone tilted his head. "Yeah?"

"I may have to make a bank run, too. Need extra money."

"You're not hurting for cash, are you? Just tell me that. No hoods are bouncing you around for—"

Harding spun around. "No, no. Just ease up, huh? No loan sharks, no hoods—it's . . . it's a case I'm on."

Stone dropped onto the small kitchen chair, nicking his elbow on the Formica table. He didn't know which way to look. He spotted a familiar Polaroid clinging to the refrigerator with a pineapple magnet. Jonathan's two children

—David, maybe nine; Suzy, about three—hugging, squeezing smiles out of each other. Stone always wished that he had a son or two, a wife—funny how he always thought of her second—a family, like Jonathan's, only Stone wouldn't let it all drain away, become kitchen still lifes. Stone never understood why, instead of being able to love the living, Jonathan wanted to embrace the dead.

"This is about your old man, isn't it?" Stone said finally. He looked up at the man in the bikini briefs, his face full of welts, a pack of ice stuck to the side of his head.

Harding said: "I need your help, Stone."

"And you're playing fucking Dick Tracy, aren't you?"

"Fucking Philip Marlowe."

"Asshole!"

"I'm playing that part pretty good, too, right now. That's why I need your help."

Stone stood up and adjusted his gun belt out of habit. "Isn't it enough you pulled detention, got an F-4 report stuck in your file, got me a reprimand? What are you working on, a sure suspension?"

"I'm working on myself," Harding said. "I'm working out my history."

"So how come somebody worked out on your face?" Stone said mockingly. Harding stayed quiet and moved to the police uniform that lay crumpled on the couch.

Stone continued: "You won't let this go, will you?"

"At this point," Harding said, "it won't let go of me. Too much at stake."

Harding and Stone stared at each other, both knowing there was something inside Jonathan he needed to purge or accept. What that something was had buried itself within a hidden core, some insoluble genetic code, something to do with his father.

Stone shook his head, allowing his anger to dissolve, letting it dissipate. He always thought doing so was a sign of good health, rather than a sign of weakness, though some had told him otherwise. "Man, you must be into something if you look like that after one day."

Harding smiled. "So you helping? I need a crack researcher . . . okay?"

Stone nodded. "Yeah, sure. Fuck."

"Okay," Harding confirmed. He tucked the blues under his arm and began searching for his gunboats. "I need to know about a Rome Company. The history of the place. It was around in 1949. See if it still is around. Maybe it was a spaghetti company or something, I don't know. I need an owner."

"What are you doing?" Stone asked.

Harding found his shoes under the television stand and walked toward the bedroom. "Getting dressed."

"I mean, while I'm doing your leg work, jerk-off."

Harding stopped and winced in pain. He was moving too fast for his tender stomach muscles, and they yanked him over. His eye level was sinking, approaching Captain Schulman's eye level and subsequent worldview. No wonder Schulman felt like the small cog in the commissioner's big wheel.

"Yeah," Harding said, drifting. "I'll be looking into things. Shit."

He threw the ice pack down on the coffee table and touched his face. It felt forty feet away and just as many times as sensitive. He slowly headed for the bedroom to change.

"I just better not catch up with the guy who did that to you," Stone said. Harding paused thoughtfully, but cared too much for his friend, so he just nodded.

"Right," he said.

Then the half-naked cop closed the bedroom door behind him in an act of unconscious modesty.

* * *

Harding moved in and out of the station house almost unnoticed and without scene, partly due to the surprising fact of Sgt. Fowler's absence. "Took a day," said Sgt. Dooley, his replacement, checking off Stone and Harding on the duty roster. "The man deserves time. He's put enough in." But further investigation by Stone in the locker room broke through Dooley's overly defensive speech and unearthed the real reason, though still vague. It seemed there was an escape the other night while Fowler was on duty with no evidence of resistance or cell damage. Although the sergeant wasn't actually suspected of aiding the escapee, Captain Schulman thought it best Fowler take a short leave. Besides, Fowler looked like he needed it, Van Dam told Stone. The sarge was pale, like his blood was sucked out, he said. Maybe it was from seeing the Three Stooges swaying in the breeze by their Ralph Lauren ties over in the next cell. The press guys only got the report on the hangings; the escape story never saw the columns. The warrant's out, but the guy's not dangerous.

"Got the report copy here," Stone said to Harding as he drove the patrol car down Lennox Avenue. "Guy named Berner. Sol, I think it is. First name."

Harding laughed and picked up the report from the seat space between them.

"What's funny?" Stone asked. "You laughing at the sarge?"

Fowler meets the Devil and bails out, Harding thought. "No," he said, but not explaining anything further.

Then the car swerved onto Bucker Road, and the San Marco County Hospital shot into view on their left. Harding almost said something like "There's where my office used to be," then suddenly stopped, and for an instant the balance tipped in his head, the blood swelled up and flushed through his skull; he was sure he was completely insane.

"Three suicides and an escapee in one night." Stone shook his head. "Who said things are quiet? Poor Sarge. Wait till I tell my old man."

Harding, more somber now, thought about the possible relationship of Berner and the three hangings. His chest ached as though his own soul felt a sudden tug, the squeeze of a noose, the clutch of Sol's hot hand.

Harding sank down a few inches in his seat and for the first time wondered if there was any way out when this was all over. Any way at all.

The county clerk's office was a monument of dilapidation. That the government building was donated by a woolen mill gone bust fifty years ago explained part of its collapsed state: cracked walls the color of oatmeal with the lumps included, the ceiling fans creaking out a rusty song at a speed that stirred neither your soul nor the air surrounding.

Harding strolled up to the counter, which acted as a barricade to the desk area. Five women, looking as run-down as the room they worked in, were milling around, directionless, it seemed, in and out of the paper-filled tables and file cabinets, talking. Words like "picnic yesterday" and "no way the TV goes" sounded out between the squeaks from the fans' rotations. Incongruously, a personal computer sat at each of seven desks, technology among the rubble, and the only sign that clued Harding he didn't walk through the doorway and accidentally trip himself back to 1949.

Two women were seated just beyond the cast-iron barrier; both were elderly and looked passively angry, even though they were talking about the best wedding they ever went to. The closer clerk with red hair dyed just this side of orange sipped her coffee and had a sandwich lying atop her computer keyboard. The other clerk left her hair gray and her smile in the drawer as she sniffled and nodded at whatever was said. Both women ignored Harding completely.

Harding's first impulse was to pull the revolver from his holster and shot one into the ceiling. Instead, he removed his cap and leaned over the barrier, pointing to the errant sandwich.

"I don't think these gizmos run on mayonnaise," he said.

The orange head turned and revealed a pasty face and looping eyebrows drawn in as though by thick felt-tip pen. Harding gave her a second look momentarily, thinking she was Sol Berner in drag. Her hand removed the sandwich and placed it beside her paper coffee cup, then she stared at the wounds on Harding's face because they were there.

"The computer's down," she said.

"Sorry to hear it," Harding said. "When is it up?"

"On," the clerk muttered.

"What?"

"On line," the clerk said, louder.

Harding stopped leaning and stood up. "Lady, I *am* the line." He waved his hand as though to prove the existence of empty air behind him.

The clerk forced herself to explain. " 'On line,' not 'up.' The computer right now is down."

Harding pushed on: "Well, I need information on a deed to some property in Winston Beach. I'm thinking of buying the—"

"Fine." The clerk put down her coffee and looked at her friend as she tried again. "The computer is down. When it is on line and running, you'll be serviced as long as you have your section, block, and lot number."

"For what?"

"The property."

Harding showed her a piece of pad paper. "I've got an address."

The clerk shook her head. "We don't take addresses. We need to know what side of the street the said property is on and how far it is from the nearest cross street—"

"How about longitude and latitude?"

"—but for now, the computer is down." The clerk took another sip from the paper cup and turned away, reaching down for her purse.

Harding jammed the paper back into his breast pocket and waited until her orange hair reappeared above her curved shoulders.

"This badge used to mean something," Harding said as the clerk pulled out a matted tissue.

Her eyes touched his for an instant, then returned to the task of unfolding Kleenex. "My brother-in-law is a cop," she said. "I know your type."

The clerk blew her nose sharply and stuck the tissue remains into her purse.

Harding was leaning against the trunk of the patrol car that they'd parked behind the government building in a handicapped zone, when Stone trotted up.

"You got anything?"

"Yeah," Harding said, "a fat headache courtesy of modern bureaucracy."

"I got a warehouseload of zeros," Stone said, pulling out his yellow notepaper.

"No Rome Company registered?"

"Plenty of Rome Companies registered. Here." Stone gave Harding the sheet. "All from 1945 on with lots of warehouses. See? Two Italian food companies. Pasta makers, I guess. Sauce. Here's an appliance distributor. Nothing in downtown where you said."

"Doesn't sound right."

Harding folded the yellow paper at off angles and put the awkward piece in his pants pocket.

"Your lead cold?" Stone asked.

"The lead's still hot. The *clerk* is cold. Besides, the computer is busted for a while." Harding's hands supported him from behind; they enjoyed the heat from the trunk, the dark blue sheen absorbing light. He looked at his feet, thinking.

Stone moved toward the driver's door. "Let's get back on the road."

Harding didn't move.

"What's doing?" Stone said.

"I want you to call in for me. I'm taking sick time."

Stone came around to look at his partner more closely. "You okay? You hurting bad? Those lumps look—"

"That's not it," Harding said, turning away from Stone's maternal scrutiny, feeling freakish. "I need to find out who owns the house my father was found in."

"I know who," Stone said matter-of-factly.

"What?"

"Is that the mystery?" Stone said. "Neery told me that night, the night we found your dad. It's the county, man. The county took it over years ago. There's been lots of political disputes over what to do with the area, so *nothing* gets done with it."

"What about previous owners, then?" Harding asked excitedly.

"They're looking into it."

"Yeah," Harding said. "Real hard, I bet. Means I got to find out past owners somehow, but I can't hang around for the computers to kick in."

Harding stared at Stone, and Stone shook his head. "What do you want me to do?"

"Okay," Harding said. "I want you to stay on Neery

should he get any names. Otherwise, get the bitch at the county clerk's to get you the owners' names for the house. You might have to get a survey map with all sorts of block-lot bullshit on it. Just stay on her case for me. And you better go in civvies."

Stone made a face that Harding ignored. "Where are you going to be?"

"Call me in on sick time. Tell them I got stomach cramps. Tell 'em I fell on my face—I mean, look at it. They'll buy it with the shape my mug's in. . . . I need time."

Stone latched on to Harding's arm. "I'll take some, too."

Harding shook his head. "No, man, I'm going somewhere you can't."

"Same place you got your head looking like a mashed potato?"

"That's the one," Harding said.

"Nice vacation spot," Stone said wearily. Harding barked out a quick laugh. He could have told Stone the truth; he wanted to. At least the part about seeing relatives, because that's what he was going to do: visit suspicious stepsisters, thieving mothers, secretive fathers. What he wouldn't have mentioned, however, was his intention of seeing one of Stone's relatives, of his having decided that morning to drive to a restful retirement cottage in sunny Long Beach, far more neutral ground, to visit Lt. Butch Stone, retired.

The uniform would help, Harding thought, would carry more weight, like knowing a lodge's secret handshake. For the first time, he looked down at his badge, 329, just to see if the sun bounced off it. He couldn't believe the apprehension that built up inside him. The man must be seventy by now, but every time Harding flinched when accidentally touching his swollen face, Stone's father regained his youth.

The cottage held no surprises for Harding. He was familiar with the surroundings and this section of Long Beach. Lots of cops farmed themselves out to this community, which the precinct called the Faded Blues, where tracts went cheap to retirees through some political favors handed down years before Harding joined the force.

He walked past the chain-link fence that connected a series of similar fences down the curving block. There was no shade in sight—not even a palm tree hovered in anybody's yard—so Harding sweated all the more as he marched on the barren stretch of grass up toward the front porch.

He rapped on the rust-pocked screen door. A woman appeared, wiping her hands slowly on her apron. She had gray hair that was bundled up above her forehead, but she had to swat at a few strands dancing at her nose like pesky flies. "Oh, well, hello!" she said, opening the door. Harding felt instantly comfortable, removed his hat, and nodded to the smiling woman. "Officer?" she said, almost bowing.

"Mrs. Stone?" Harding asked, though one glance at her vibrant eyes and he realized the phone book had led him to the right address.

"Yes, of course," she said. "Please come in. I have a full pot on." Her head shook ever so slightly when she spoke, which caused people not to think of her palsy but of an inner excitement over what she was saying; it was the swagger of joy. Harding was sitting in a country kitchen nook before he could form his thoughts, a mug of coffee at his side. Mrs. Stone sat down quickly across the way, spry for a woman in her sixties. She noticed the young officer's swollen temple but chose to ignore it. Then her face turned sour for an instant: "It's not about Dale, is it? Oh, God, he's all right? . . ."

Harding instinctively wanted to reach out and touch her fragile hand, but he kept his professional distance. "Oh, no, it's not that. I'm his partner." Mrs. Stone's dour expression slipped off her face. "I'm Jonathan Harding. I don't know if—"

"Of course he's mentioned you." Mrs. Stone blushed as though she should have known it was Jonathan without ever having met him. "It's amazing." She got up and looked at him. Harding thought maybe he looked better at a downward angle.

"What is?" Harding said.

"That you should come here," Mrs. Stone said. "It's certainly about time. Are you on duty? Where's Dale?"

"Mrs. Stone, I'm here to see your husband, if I could. Dale is on duty. I'm on sort of a special assignment."

A trace of coolness passed over Mrs. Stone's demeanor. "My husband? He's retired, you know."

"Right," Harding said. "I'm not here to take him back or anything." He didn't know what he meant by that, making Stone's father sound like a stray mutt being returned to its owner. "I'm looking into an old case, and I need someone to remember the details better than the reports do." Harding smiled, maybe a bit too hard, a common practice when he'd lied as a kid. He wasn't going to mention that he couldn't get near the report files on the Turley gang, which were entrenched with homicide and had no business in a patrolman's hands.

"I see," Mrs. Stone said quietly. "He loves old times, I can tell you that much." She sighed and said, "Follow me."

They walked to a short landing down which dark stairs

led to what must have been a small basement considering the size of the cottage. "Teddy?" she called into the dark. Mrs. Stone always used her husband's middle name, finding "Butch" improper for anything with less than four legs.

"Hah?" came a loud gargle from below.

"I'm sending down a visitor, an officer who works with Dale," she yelled, though in a conversational tone. There was no response. She looked at Harding. "You can go down. He heard me."

Harding took a few unsure steps as Mrs. Stone closed the basement door behind him without turning on the cellar light. He felt his way down the banister. He stopped when he thought he saw a glint of something, something shiny like a ring.

"Yeah?" came a voice from behind the stairs.

"Mr. Stone?" Harding said, his eyes adjusting to the semidark now as some light spilled near his feet onto the concrete floor. He saw a workbench cloaked in darkness except for a bright, hard light that dangled above it and shone on a bald head. The hunched shape was spiny, thin, but recognizable. The light formed a harsh but perfect spot of white on Lt. Stone's scalp as though a section of his skullbone were exposed.

The old man turned and tilted his metal lamp shade toward Harding, scorching his eyes with brilliance, forcing his hands up as shields. Lt. Stone inspected the center of the spotlight's attention. "Oh . . . a copper!" He laughed and let the lamp shade down.

"Mr. Stone," Harding said, recovering from the glare, "I'm Dale's partner at the precinct."

"Oh, yeah?" Lt. Stone said. He filed down the last bit of jagged edge on a piece of heavy copper tubing. He picked it up like a metal club and said, "Bathroom sink rotted out. Piece of crap. 'Least my hands still work good." He dropped the pipe on the workbench with a loud thud, forcing the lingering tools and nail jars into a small hop to attention. Harding noticed Lt. Stone's taut yet pliant hands, seemingly his center of strength in spite of his thin frame.

"Is he a good partner?" Lt. Stone looked up at Harding.

"Even better. He's a good friend."

Stone nodded; his jaw played with his ill-fitting dentures before he could respond. "You're right. That is better. You're Harding." Jonathan seemed surprised. "I heard the name from him. Memory's still jake. Nobody can bullshit me that way. Not yet. So what gives?"

Harding inspected the old face, his friend's face in another thirty-plus years, only (he hoped) without the bitter lines, the traces of brutality—there were at least four inch-long scars cutting their separate angular paths about his head. Lt. Stone was wearing a ratty sport coat, was filing metal in a stained blue serge, Harding thinking maybe it was the same one worn the night of the interrogation. Last night. Then Harding realized he'd never shaken Lt. Stone's hand, that the lieutenant had never extended his, that it was a little too late either way.

"Dale said you were a walking criminal file. I need to dip inside. Get a handle on some old times."

"Take a shot here," Lt. Stone said, reaching over his workbench toward the picture-window-size corkboard filled with papers and woodcraft diagrams; some headlines, all urine yellow, obviously aged and not helped much by the basement damp, announced quick arrests and not-so-quick deaths of thugs and mobsters and were spread across the board like crooked captions among fuzzy Polaroids and an old badge. Unlike his mother's makeshift altar where memories lay pristine and guarded, here was a cop's collage: you cut open his guts, throw them up on a board, and try to read them as you would in a ritual sacrifice.

Lt. Stone leaned over with some effort and pulled a tack from the board. It held a bundling of dark brown hair, at least six inches long and tied at both ends with white string. Harding didn't think the lieutenant was the keepsake-locket type, though this lock Harding was now handed was more than a fistful. He could only nod and thought of Mrs. Stone and what she must have looked like younger with earth-brown hair and the same hopeful eyes she gave her son.

"That's Dale's," Lt. Stone said.

"What is?" Harding said, shaking his head.

"That hair you got there. It's your partner's." The lieutenant laughed and pointed to a gray square on the wall with wavy borders: a Brownie black-and-white picture. "Dale after I scalped him and got myself rid of a daughter." Harding peered into the shiny blur and saw Dale in his patrolman trainee uniform, cap level, held to his chest, hair trimmed, and, uncharacteristically, not smiling.

"So what's this 'old times' business?" Lt. Stone said, suddenly brusque.

Harding straightened up. "It's a case I'm looking into. It goes way back, so I could use something firsthand."

The lieutenant stuck his son's hair back on the wall like a donkey's tail. "What about?"

"The Turley gang," Harding said.

Lt. Stone sneered, which pulled his wrinkled skin like a dried-out rubber mask to its elastic limit. He moved himself off the work stool and once again grabbed the metal tubing, only this time he raised it high above his head. Harding's first instinct was to duck. Then Lt. Stone jabbed the pipe upward—two solid pokes—on the cellar ceiling. A quick scuffle from the floor above and the cellar door opened. "Teddy?"

"Put out some lunch," Lt. Stone shouted. "You eat yet?" Harding shook his head stiffly.

At the kitchen table Mrs. Stone helped to remove Lt. Stone's jacket. Her vibrancy had become muted in her husband's presence; she was all business, and the business at hand was eggs and liver for lunch.

"Don't worry," she said quietly to Harding as if she were telling a family secret. "No liver for you." Harding nodded a thank-you. "Scrambled good?" she said.

"Fine," Harding said, removing his gun belt. He laid it across the empty chair beside him. Lt. Stone stared at the holstered revolver, his hands meshed in a knot of fingers, his cheek rested on the knot. The police issue that preoccupied his vision kindled no nostalgic sparks; it was a piece of strength from which to talk. "Alvin Maxwell Turley. Smooth Al. Max Turley, the Devil of Delancey Street. That's what they called him. All them names for the same piece of scum."

Harding noticed Lt. Stone's voice turn to gravel, his words like shredded flakes of metal coughed up from his throat. He took a drink of club soda. "I hate this shit," he said more to the glass than to Stone. Then his eyes glazed over in recollection.

"I was in New York for a little while, call it like an exchange, whatever. I worked with an old pal, another detective who jumped to the East Coast a coupla years earlier and took a post on the city cops. He fills me in on the kinda trouble he's got on his side of the world, and its name is Max Turley. He ran the heavy rackets back then, Turley did. Lotsa gambling, lotsa prostitution. And I don't mean two-dollar hookers—"

He quickly lowered his voice, his eyes rolling behind

him to make sure Mrs. Stone wasn't there. "I mean the big-money dames they call escort or whatever bullshit today." He sat back again, his voice no longer secretive. "My buddy could handle that kinda dirt, at least get it controlled, clamp it down. Right? But he says this Turley louse, he's a killer, too. Mean like some sewer rat. This joker knocks off as many in his own organization as he does in his enemy's. Kills cops who don't want to take a cut. . . ." Lt. Stone's pallor grew blank, sickly, and he looked back to the hanging revolver. "Killed my pal's boy for that. . . ."

Mrs. Stone entered with two plates and placed them in front of the two quiet men. She stood a moment and bowed her head, as though respectful of the silence. "Excuse me, Jonathan." She glanced at the motionless lieutenant. "Sorry." She somberly retreated through the doorway at her husband's back and lingered in the kitchen. Harding watched her shuffle pans and sponge her sink as though dazed.

"Turley killed your friend's son, a cop," Harding said.

"Yeah, I don't know if he pulled the trigger. Not that he didn't squeeze a few," Lt. Stone said. "But I was still in town when it happened. Went to the funeral. They shot the boy in his car, then torched the car. It was a message hit. Better than Western Union."

The lieutenant dropped his head inches from his steamy eggs and liver and started eating rapidly. Harding looked down into his plate and forked up a yellow bloom of egg, then set it back down.

"Turley married one of his hookers, believe that crap?" Lt. Stone's mouth was full and noisy. "Had a kid and everything. Slime goes middle class. That was the joke, anyway. Some people laughed at first. Some people died laughing."

"Harlen Gunther find it funny?" Harding said.

Lt. Stone stopped eating, a piece of egg caught between his lips. He sucked it into his mouth and sent his tongue out for final clean-up. "You know about Gunther?"

"I know that for some reason Turley might have wanted him dead."

"Yeah, you could say that." Lt. Stone almost started to laugh as he slugged down the rest of his club soda. "You could say maybe he wanted Gunther to join him sitting in his grave." Harding didn't understand and shook his head.

"You don't know much of anything," Lt. Stone said with an edge to his voice, suspicious. "The files woulda told you this much. Gunther was Turley's top boy in New York. But Gunther got tired of playing second banana to him. He set some of his personal goon squad out for Turley, and they iced him while his ex-hooker wife was out pushing a baby carriage. Gunther took a big slice of the gang's loot, and he and his pals come to San Marco to set up shop. I was back by then, so that was my inheritance from Turley's getting nailed—Harlen Gunther. Lucky me."

"Any of Turley's boys ever catch up to Gunther?"

Lt. Stone pushed his plate away and wiped his nose with his napkin. "Maybe. Who knows?"

"Whatever happened to Gunther?"

"What are you asking me for? What's the report say? He won the Irish Sweepstakes. He dropped dead in a bowling alley. What do I know?"

Mrs. Stone heard her husband's voice raise and looked toward the dining room from the kitchen, her eyebrows lifted, wondering, holding her husband's jacket by the collar. Harding lingered at the table and took a few bites from his plate.

"Max Turley," Lt. Stone muttered. "Hadn't thought of him in a long time." He cleared his voice; the junkpile in his throat rattled. "We all got bodies buried," he rasped. "I just wish I buried his."

Harding heard the words but watched Mrs. Stone behind, bending down over a metal trash can, looking toward the dining room, pulling out burned matchsticks and shaking out ashes from her husband's jacket pockets.

· seven ·

Carla Harding marched out of her apartment building, her padded shoulders seesawing with each long stride. The sun was bright, the sky high: her red hair glowed orange this afternoon, but her eyes and skin could not adjust; her pace was as much to get out of the sunlight as it was to get out of her flat.

Jonathan watched for a while, the sloped gray brim of his hat letting his shaded eyes cool while the rest of him burned in the desert sizzle. The heat helped his lumps, though; he thought he felt his cheek bake and shrivel, pull back his bruises. Harding stepped out of the short alleyway just before Carla was to pass. When she almost ran into him, the sight of his somber face made her jump.

"Christ!" she said gruffly. Her masculine tone made it sound like a curse. Then she showed fear and tried to cross the street, but Harding had her by the upper arm and started pulling her toward the alleyway.

A middle-aged, paunchy passerby in short sleeves and a crewcut quickly moved in. His unlit cigarette flailed in his mouth like a blameful finger as he spoke: "Hey, buddy, what gives?" Before his wide frame could step between Carla and her attacker, Harding applied one forceful shove, his fingers spread on the sweating man's damp chest, and sent the stranger four steps backward, nearly flipping over a fireplug.

"Butt out!" Harding said, and he continued to pull Carla into the alley as the man quickly crossed the street, looking back warily, both pride and cigarette lost in the brief exchange.

In the shade of the alley, Carla eyed Harding coldly, though a hint of fear still lingered in her lips. "You are a piece of work, you know that?" she finally growled. "Are you nuts? Get your two-bit gumshoe license out of here, will ya?"

Harding made sure he was fronting the entrance to this short ravine that cut through two tenement walk-ups, his back to the busy street. "Why?" he said, raising his head and eyebrows. "You think I murdered your boyfriend?"

Carla backed off, looked down at her yellow dress. She pulled part of it up to inspect a possible tear, revealing more leg than any slit evening gown would ever allow. Her concern seemed ridiculous since the dress was soiled, as were the thin white gloves she wore with which she rubbed the cotton folds.

"I don't know," she said, still looking down. "Probably not." She threw her dress back to her calves, the full span of her legs disappearing. "I hope you didn't expect me to stick my neck out for you, did you? When I saw those black-and-whites pull up . . . brother, I blew fast."

"You sure did that," Harding said, pacing now.

"You kept me out of it with the law?"

"Not to save *your* skin," Harding snapped.

The left half of Carla's mouth slipped up in a smile. "I figured you did. No coppers called."

"Only they know I had a girl with me. Those pumps you curse about telegraphed you to the landlady."

Carla spread her gloved hands wide, a snake oil salesman's gesture, a preacher's imploring. "Then what the hell are you doing here? Don't you know whoever knocked Romero off, they might be looking for me, too?"

"That's your problem," Harding said. "Mine is that someone sapped me at Romero's—from behind—hard—then used my gun on him."

"So?"

Harding stopped pacing. "I've seen lead pipes in action before, remember?"

"News flash, kiddo—I'm not the only one in San Marco carrying protection or with access to a handful of two-by-four."

"I know."

"Or lead pipes, either." Carla's lids lowered apropos to the blow.

Harding saw a flash of white, his mother's body filling it, what she wore last night, and the bundle held tight. Was there another bundle tonight?

"I know," Harding repeated. His tone indicated he wouldn't say it again. "Is dressing like a canary traditional mourning wear where you come from?"

Carla's head fell back; her neck made sure it didn't come off.

"You don't get it, do you? You got this 'apple pie' business stuck on the brain. You shoulda been a priest, hotshot." Harding just looked at her, so Carla let out a stale breath. "I had a thing for that sap Romero. But I didn't marry him, and I can't afford to let anybody know I had anything to do with him seeing he's dead and I might be, get it?"

Harding nodded. "Right."

Carla pointed directly at Harding's nose. "Try being more of a detective and less of a dick. Check out my story. I was in the drugstore the whole time."

Harding blinked slowly for effect. "I did. You were." Carla's mouth shifted, then opened. "That make me less of a dick?"

Carla's fist wasn't nearly fast enough, and Harding grabbed it and smashed it back on the alley wall, then he pinned her other hand and laid his knee to her belly, pressing. The bricks behind her were damp, and the smell of the alley's scattered garbage lingered there.

"You're a bigger one than I thought," Carla hissed. She didn't bother to squirm.

"Now that I got your attention—tell me who would want to kill Romero. Any friends? Enemies?"

"All his friends and relatives are in Mexico."

"So who at the casino? Gunther? Tell me about him."

Carla didn't want to look at the taut face stuck in hers, so she talked to her right shoulder. "Big-shot manager. Second-stringer all the way. Loser. Comes from New York—the Turley gang. All I know."

"How is it you know about the Turley gang?"

"If you know about the casino and you know about Gunther, you know about the Turley gang, okay?" Carla quickly shot her eyes into Harding's. "Romero and I dug deep before we sank our hooks into the joint's money bags. We did groundwork. We knew what we were doing. They didn't know nothing. It wasn't Gunther that got to Romero. Or his watchdogs, either."

"But Romero told me he didn't know who owned the casino. All he knew was the West Coast mob who ran things were unhappy the place was nosediving."

Carla shrugged. "Got me. We only got so deep. Gunther was there. He was the Joe we had to duck. Who cares who his boss is? We knew the casino money was dirty with someone else's hands; who cared which mud puddle it came from?"

Harding's weight slowly moved more and more into his knee, more and more into Carla's soft belly. "How did my—how did your father's name wind up on Romero's calendar?"

Carla was finding it harder to breathe. The breakfast dry toast in her stomach was caught in her lungs. "Why don't you ask him yourself? He's *your* client, right?"

"Your mother know Romero? Or Gunther?"

"I wouldn't know who that slut knows. Or care."

"Why do you always call your mother a slut?"

Without Harding's realizing, the last question was asked with the slightest tone of someone being lost, the almost imperceptible hint of unknown lingering hurt. To Carla, it tipped off a sure shift of power even with a knee bone pressuring her groin like a pestle ground in her womb. "Why are you always so interested in my *step*mother, anyway?" she purred.

Harding opened his mouth, then shut it, tense.

Carla pulled her neck farther out, stretching her head to Harding's, while her body remained pinned. She whispered: "Hey . . . is it you're gettin' some or want some?"

Harding hauled Carla from the wall and swung her around, letting go, sending her into a pair of open trash cans, which toppled and clattered and echoed like tin cymbals. Carla slipped finally, and her knee buckled into a grease-stained brown bag. She clutched the rolling can and fell sideways into the strewn trash.

Harding waited until she looked up, looked up with ice-hard anger at his pointing finger. "Stay available and stay low or your name goes to the cops and your ass goes to the casino boys."

"You wouldn't dare," Carla growled.

Harding raised one eyebrow and cocked his head. Then Carla's stern face raised a knowing smile, sitting up like a bright and dangerous yellow flower sprung from the compost. "The Harding name," she said. "Wouldn't want that dumped in the garbage, too, would you?"

Harding turned sharply, trying to hit the sounds of street traffic before the alley allowed the cave-hollow laughter to reach him.

Harding had little patience for another bout with déjà-vu. The sensation had become a pervading malady as past and present sections of San Marco would overlap and be one, old section—the public library with its sloping park alongside, street corners whose buildings looked younger in 1986, restored under the Preservation League (Saint June had a partial hand in those fund-raisers, of course), than they did through his Buick's thick, imperfect windshield in 1949. The recurrent feeling had evolved from wonder and strangeness to a sense of bad connections, evil links in a chain of time, heavy, weighed down with personal history. Déjà-vu made him say: It's all the same. Past, present—the lead pipe that feeds him water for his morning toothbrush is stained with forty-year-old blood; the Devil kicks up his feet at an old bar in the future, a new office in the past—the dirt, the dust, piles up from body ashes, alley garbage smells the same no matter what time frame you're in.

And so appeared the county clerk's office. Like a picture puzzle—"What's wrong here?"—Harding stopped inside the doorway and said to himself aloud: "No computers." That's all that differed there in the past; its dilapidation was still retrospectively intact. The oatmeal color lingered, though its lumps had shifted. The wall cracks worked their way through the plaster at the precise angles and splits as would a tributary map of the Mississippi. The fans' rotating sang the same old song of rust and thirst for oil.

Harding dropped the upper half of his body over the wooden barrier as he let out a sour breath in the process. He dropped his hat on the desk before him where a skinny, precise man sat, a burgundy bowtie at his neck, a sandwich before him cut in fours on a napkin—ham and cheese, hold the mayo. Harding's hat almost covered it like the felt top to a serving platter.

When the man looked up, he pushed his brown-shell glasses to the top of his nose and gave Harding a quick scan. "John is on the right, two doors down," he said, "and keep the empties out of there."

Harding had thought his face was healing; he knew his spirit wasn't. Though tired, he stood upright to improve his appearance. "I want information on a house."

"Oh," the man said, his eyes widening, though Harding couldn't tell if in interest or mockery. "You'll have to wait."

Harding leaned back over the low barrier, all weight on his fists, which pressed down upon two of the many stacks of paper that covered the man's desk. "What's the problem? Your file drawer 'down'?"

The clerk shook his oblong head disapprovingly. "Please remove your hand from the Sawyer district," he said in as stern a voice as he had.

"What?"

"Those papers . . ." The clerk began tugging a stack out from under Harding's left fist. Harding released the other pile voluntarily. "Good," the clerk said emphatically, inspecting the top sheet closely. Then he spoke, mumbling to himself. "You smudged the Colby Building?"

"I want information on a house," Harding said, his

voice robotic, a bit crazed. He stepped farther outside himself, thought he probably wore the same useless, withered look as the old lady behind the door window at the house he was trying to get a handle on.

The clerk appeared flustered. Shaking the handful of documents in his hand, he said, "I happen to be responsible for every piece of property from East Hills to the Pacific. Not a light responsibility, I may add, even over lunch—"

Harding shook his head; eyes closed, then opened: "Tell me something—you need mutated genes to sit at this desk? You got a ten-year-old daughter? 'Cause I think I met her about thirty-seven years from here."

The clerk finally stopped fingering the wad of papers and listened. "I don't understand."

"Here's another one you won't get," Harding replied.

The man tucked the fist-imprinted sheets under another pile, the one farthest from Harding. "I don't have time for riddles."

"How many twerps does it take to fill an ink bottle?"

"I wouldn't know," the man answered, not looking up.

"Me neither." Harding grabbed the clerk's bowtie like the handle to a dresser drawer that was jammed. "What say we find out?" Then he pulled. Instinctively turning his face away, the man let his ear take the blow as it landed hard on the open bottle of ink near his blotter. It overturned and spilled, slowly seeping blue down Harding's lingering grip, the clerk's red tie, the Sawyer district.

The man didn't cry out or cause commotion; Harding's fisted knuckles were framing his Adam's apple as would wooden stocks a sinner's head. All he could do was rasp: "What do you want?"

Harding tightened his grip. Wasn't he just here? Fucking déjà—"I want information on a house!" he barked into the clerk's ear. "Now—do I need section—block—lot number crapola?"

The clerk added confusion to the pain that took over his face. He had no idea what Harding was talking about. "You got an address?"

Stunned, Harding relaxed his grip. "That's all?"

The clerk let out some air built up by a tensed-up body. "An address—yes," the clerk said, still shaking. "What *else* would you need, for God's sake?"

Harding straightened. "Look at that," he said in mock shock. "Go backward and experience progress."

Harding stared at the name he had jotted down at the county clerk's office—Frank DeMonte—whose address was also in Winston Beach, but he could not associate the name with either the old house that DeMonte was on record as owning or any other facet of this case. "This case." This case was his life, his family life, its history, and somehow he sensed his mind pushing it away, abstracting it: he was falling into the Devil's movie, seeing it as though flashing through sprockets from out his eyes, not actually living it. Whose *case* was it, anyway? A part of him deliberately watched events turn as though from a screening room; another part, the tender, hidden underbelly, pulled it all in like a pincushion that could accommodate not one needle more.

Harding turned the knob to the inner office, and the swinging door revealed the Devil lying across the ratty couch, a newspaper splayed over his face. Harding slammed the door behind him, rattling the framed glass. The Devil didn't move at first, then his hand peeled back a corner and an eye peered out; it shone, red-hued, like a fizzled comet.

"You look like you're in a swell mood," the Devil said.

"It's 'cause I'm so loved." Harding dropped his hat on his desk and his stiff torso into the wooden chair. Its arms caught him, while the springs, which tilted him back, kept him from falling, though not without a squealed protest.

The Devil curled up like the end of an unbottled genie's shoe. "You mean you're not even going to *try* to give me the heave-ho?"

"I need a gun," Harding said, rubbing his eyes.

The Devil almost laughed through his wattled nose. "You're really gonna waste good lead trying to plug me again?"

"Too tired for this," Harding muttered, then said loudly: "I need a gun. The casino we were in last night kept the one you gave me, and the one I found in the glove compartment, the cops got."

"Busy boy. Good thing you had that spare I gave you in the car, I bet."

"Yeah."

"You're welcome," the Devil sneered.

"You got another gun or what?" Harding brought his chair forward, planting his forearms crossbones on his blotter.

"Where do you think a P.I. hides his heater, Johnny, if he needs an office spare?"

Harding thumped his fist to the desk. "I'm not playing your damn games, Sol!"

The Devil's feet swiveled and flew to the floor, his head jerking upward in challenge. "You want a gun, friend— well, it's my fucking football."

Harding spun to the window and watched the crimson globe of a sun waver and bend as it fell, ready to bury itself below the horizon and let the night slide over it like a black, secret panel and keep it down, extinguished.

"Under the carpet," Harding said quietly.

The Devil studied his partner, wondering how long he himself would think this game fun, how long this "special" client would be worth his evil wonder. He slowly rubbed his hands together, two smooth pieces of flint, warming up. "What? And trip on the lump? Use your noodle, Hard-boy. It's a heater, not a bedbug."

Harding rose slowly and stepped to the crusty metal radiator under the warping windowsill. He sent his hand down into the dark space behind and, along with a brushing tickle from a spider's well-established web, brought up a .38 Special, heavy with dust and definitely loaded.

The Devil nodded, all business. "Bingo. Better take care of it like it was your only child, Johnny. It's the last you get from me." Harding ignored the threat. "So . . . you figure yet how your newfound sister ties in with your mother stealing from your old man?"

Harding shook his head, securing the gun under his jacket.

"Are you even sure your old man is clean? Just because I haven't made any deals with him doesn't mean he's sprouting wing-shaped feathers and taking harp lessons, either."

"I don't know, Sol. The amount I don't know could fill three city blocks right now." Harding searched his pockets, found a pack of cigarettes, and threw it on the desk. He wished he had a joint. He plunked himself, dead weight, down on the swivel chair.

"And what I *do* know—I'm getting more scared the deeper I get into this thing."

The Devil twitched an ear from his supine position.

"Scared? What for? The deal's aces. You got what you wanted."

Harding laughed from the gut, a forceful, singular

burst. " 'What I wanted'?" he said, feeling his throat thicken. "I thought what I wanted—no, what I needed—was to get to the root of my father's death. To find out what's driving me, pulling me down . . ."

Harding looked toward the late afternoon sky and drifted into it, allowing himself this release into thin air—somehow even talking this way to Stone, he felt vulnerable; to Sol, he realized he had nothing to lose. He had already bargained the most essential piece of himself away.

"All my life I've been so damned fucked up with my having lost my father. But all I've managed to do is lose *being* a father. Now I'm passing down this damned legacy to my own kids. They'll wonder what killed *their* father. Where'd *he* go? Who the fuck was *he?* Only the fire my kids lose their father to won't be from some chemical accident, but from you, your fire. The one that's been inside me all my life."

Harding looked at the Devil; the Devil stared back, listening with what Harding thought almost passed for sympathy.

"It's kept me alone and violent. It's kept me from ever feeling a part of my family. It's made me deny my kids. My wife, too, I suppose—" Harding shook his head.

"Well," the Devil said quietly, "maybe that's why I stick around, Johnny. You and I got a few things in common. We both lost our heavenly homes, you know."

Harding kept looking at the Devil, and maybe it was the watery glaze in Jonathan's eyes, but Sol almost looked sad and, for an instant, like a fellow sufferer. But the Devil quickly pulled away from their shared pain and shut Harding out with a quick shrug.

"Anyway . . . I go for pity like I go for castor oil on the rocks." The Devil lay back down on the couch and stared at the white ceiling. Harding sat up, pulling back his jacket and his emotions, keeping both tightly buttoned from now on.

"You make your own future," the Devil said thoughtfully, then glanced at Harding. "Only you, strange boy—you made your future the past. And you wonder why your fuse box is scrambled."

Harding didn't respond. The Devil watched him march to the small bathroom and heard the water run, the sound of face-splashing. He took his lit cigarette from the stained coffee table beside the couch and breathed in the hot smoke. "You getting ready to tail your old lady again?"

Harding marched back out, his hands shiny, streaked as though melting. "What do you think?"

"I think you should talk to her. I mean, if a boy can't talk to his mom, who can he talk to?"

Harding wiped his hands on his pants and rechecked the pawnbroker's address in his pad.

The Devil spoke to the ceiling, cigarette smoke drifting and hanging to his arm's orchestrations; as to children clouds form whales and grotesque giant faces, so to Harding the smoke shaped itself into parallel bars, cagelike, then gradually grew points like wispy daggers. "Tell her you caught on to her scam. Pin her up—see if she squirms. Maybe she lets you in for a piece of the action."

The Devil crushed the cigarette out in the ashtray, all smoky shapes dissolving with it, then pulled the newspaper that sat on his chest back over his face.

Harding shook his head. "I pull that stunt and my father drops me. He'd trust me as far as I trust you."

The Devil's voice seemed to come from a place far deeper than three thin sheets of inky paper. "With the story today, he may see the resemblance."

"What story?"

"The newspapers, J. H. . . . Tell me you only read Joe Palooka."

Harding snapped the newspaper off the Devil's face, which now wore a dead man's smile, eyelids shut. Harding noisily shifted the large sheets as he scanned them.

"Page four, big shot," the Devil said. "You're not head-line material yet. Icing a Mex won't do it."

Harding flipped through two sheets, folded once, then punched the floating page down and ironed it with a stroke of his flattened palm. Third column over, a small headline read SLUM SHOOTING—DEATH PROBE. His eyes shot through the copy, seeing words like "Romero," "un-known means of employment," "murder," "bullet matches weapon," "suspects," and of course, "Johnny Hard." But nothing written upset Jonathan as much as the grainy four-by-four photo of himself adjacent to the arti-cle, a ghostlike, smudgy image, behatted and frozen with a look of baby-faced astonishment. The caption read "Local Private Investigator Involved."

The Devil flipped open his eyes and shrugged, his voice laconic, accepting. "Don't sweat it, Johnny. Any kind of P.R. is good P.R. The Eleventh Commandment in the trade."

Harding's expression registered both fear and anger, neither overcoming the other. "How the hell—this pic-ture, the one you took at Pete's—"

"In the bar, that's the one," the Devil replied.

"How did they get it? You give it to them?"

"They called looking for you. Comments, pictures, anything for their deadline." The Devil glanced sideways when Harding didn't respond. "That's what P.R.'s about, kiddo, getting your mug spread in ink so the workaday slob can spot you in a crowd of workaday slobs. Natch, I didn't think you were shooting for the top rung, murder one. I thought maybe they found out you caught a bad guy like you always wanted."

"Didn't you ask what the damn story was about?"

"You're right," the Devil said. "I'm lousy with details."

Harding stared at the Devil's deadpan face not knowing what to believe, not sure the paper was even real, not sure it was a prankster's mock or a dangerous turn.

The Devil pursed his lips, his grayed eyebrows slanting away from each other like raised stone drawbridges. "Better learn fast, Johnny. What you *do* in this world doesn't count spit. Doing it in the daily rags—now that's the trick. Notoriety. It gives you a name besides John Doe, whatever you do. Even murder one. Gives you power. People respect that filly and want to jump on for the ride. And if your old man knows what power is all about, he'll respect it, too."

"You dumb ass! My father sees this, he'll think I'm no better than dirt."

The Devil shrugged, closed his eyes. "What's the diff? He already thinks it of your mom. Maybe he'll see the family resemblance."

Anger lifted Harding from his chair and drew him an arm's length away from the couch and the body laid out on it. "You've got a bullshit answer for everything, don't you?" he said, making a fist not quite as tight nor as primed as his nerves. He snatched the Devil's throat. The Devil's eyes flashed open, a harsh crimson ball in each socket. His voice rose like the stench from a sewer.

"You can throw lead my way all you want, Hard-boy, but don't—even—*think* about hitting me."

Harding felt the front of his body swell and sweat with heat as though facing a coal fire swept by a sudden gust and stirred white hot; his back by comparison drew a chill from the contrast in temperatures, a chill also sprung from fear, from confronting his own fiery eternity someday. He wondered whether the contract would be foreshortened with the blow through an undiscovered loophole. He lifted his heavy fist, prepared to find out.

"Oh! Oops, sorry, fellas—"

Harding's body suddenly cooled as the female voice drifted in from behind. The Devil's face had shifted masks; his welcoming-the-world, miles-of-smile countenance shone like a well-waxed figurine. Harding turned, his ruddy fist unknowingly held like a stemmed rosebud, and saw a short, delicate blonde with a pixie face. She stood in the back office doorway with large, liquid, soda-pop eyes growing wide and wondering if they were ready to witness a fight.

"No—come on in, come on in!" the Devil shouted, bouncing off the sofa, effortlessly breaking Harding's hold. "Dames beat fisticuffs any day. What can we do you, doll? Need to find a missing boyfriend?"

"No, I need a boyfriend. I mean—" The blonde blushed and shook her head. "I mean, I need a job." She looked at the Devil and hesitated, then turning to Harding, she let her gaze linger a second, then fall to the floor, and she smiled. All Harding could see now was her hair bunched toward her forehead in a large curlicue like a G clef reclining to one side.

"There was some fella out there. . . ." She looked up at Harding and pointed behind her. "Your elevator guy?" She swiveled her short, trim nose as though it caught a foul whiff of air. "Kind of rat-faced and shrimpy . . ."

"You don't mean good ol' Scooter?" the Devil asked.

"Yeah, that's the handle he gave, anyway," she said, unknowingly showing disbelief.

Harding snickered, "Got him to a T." The blonde's face still angled downward, but her green eyes peered up from under her fanciful swirls, emeralds hiding beneath a house of gold. "Well, you know, he was an okay Joe, but he talks a little too close and touchy for my money."

Harding just nodded, but the Devil smacked his lips, slightly miffed. "So? What's your business here?"

"So"—she shrugged—"he said a couple of P.I.'s upstairs canned their secretary, and me looking for work—" The blonde shrugged again and stuck her neck out.

"Well, doll," the Devil said, moving toward the girl, "I'm really sorry. Mr. Hard here has no use for your skills and even less use for your gender, so you can't—"

Harding grabbed the Devil by his shoulder before he shoveled the blonde out the office door. "Hold on, Sol, baby," he said. "Somebody's got to answer phones around here. Responsibly, anyway."

Harding smiled at the girl, who stood somewhat awkwardly in the doorway, her weight on one leg, her hip cocked, not in defiance, but in relaxation, forming an angular shelf. She was wearing powder blue with thin white stripes, and though a good size too small on her, and torn at one pocket, you could tell it was the best dress she had. Harding almost fit his hand on her protruding hip as he led her into the front office.

"Let's go in here and talk a sec," he said, hearing the Devil snort hot air at his back. The blonde said, "Okay," and tottered a bit on her high heels as she turned. She was no more than twenty, twenty-one at the outside, and in spite of a little girl's face and size, her body roamed around in her dress restlessly as she moved with innocent inhibition.

"So what's your name?" Harding said, sitting sideways on the reception desk.

"You mean my moniker? See, I know that talk." The blonde beamed, then flushed; a deferential chuckle. "Anyway . . . Laura Gabriel."

Jonathan nodded once. "Are you hard?" she asked.

Harding pulled his head back a notch and wasn't sure if he burned red or not, or even whether she could see his face that well in this light to tell, and what the hell kind of question was—

Laura pointed to the backward writing on the smoky pane of glass. "Are you Hard or Berner?"

"Oh! Well, I'm—yeah—Johnny Hard." He wished he had his hat on so he could tip it and raise a thin wall of formality to hide his overall embarrassment.

"Johnny Hard," Laura said, shaking her head. "Great name!"

"Yeah."

"That Mr. Berner inside?"

"That's right."

"And that creep *was* Scooter, then?"

"In the flesh. Sorry about him, if he came on—you know—"

Laura puffed up her cheeks, pulling up one shoulder. Then she released the air as though her mouth became a ruby-red puncture. "No big deal. 'The cheaper the crook, the gaudier the patter.'"

She paused and smiled. Harding's smile looked vacant.

"Don't you guys ever get to the movie house?" Laura tsked. "Bogey. *The Maltese Falcon.* You missed it."

Harding felt she was accusing him of something. "No, saw it on TV once."

"Where?" Laura thought she misheard him.

Harding looked puzzled, then understood. "I mean, yeah, somewhere. But I saw it, sure."

Laura looked at the broad-shouldered man in front of her, bobbing his head in affirmation like a puppy, and she laughed. "That's a line from the movie. That's what he says. That's what I like. I like that private eye jazz." Her little smile revealed a slight overbite. "I'm going to night school now, you see. I been doing odd jobs for the college, secretarial things, but forget it—they're really dull." Laura quickly shook her hand as though trying to scatter the words before they reached Harding's ear. "No, no, I don't mean the secretarial work is dull or anything, I mean some of the people, what it's all about; the papers you type, it's not . . . *real*"—her fingers enclosed an invisible but tangible object—"like the movies."

Harding understood her excitement, liked her excitement, even understood what she meant. His life felt real lately, very real—like the movies.

"I got good secretarial skills, honest. I do shorthand just okay, but I type like crazy. I got jitterbug fingers on the keyboard." Laura let her fingers loose, and they danced in the air, kicking around, fluttering like fronds in a nightwind's gust.

"Sounds good," Harding said. "You do research. You answer phones."

"I do research. I answer phones. . . ." Laura nodded expectantly.

"You know the alphabet, so you can take messages. . . ."

Laura's jawline drew rigid, but her eyes dipped with hurt. "I don't like being talked down to."

Harding smiled to himself. "And you don't take shit. You're hired."

"You mean it?" Laura said, hopping once, her hands clasped. Then she frowned. "And it's jake with Mr. Berner, too, you figure?"

Harding looked deep into Laura's worried eyes. "What's jake with me is what counts."

Laura laughed, grabbed Harding's forearm, and pulled; her body glided toward him as though she were on skates and he a supporting pole along the way. She pressed against him quickly and bounced away like a runaway rubber ball. Swiveling back his way, she said, "Okay, boss, when do I start?"

"How about right now?" Harding said.

"That's swell by me. What case you working on? Can you tell me?"

Laura watched Harding's face gradually sour, as though she reminded him of something he shouldn't have eaten for lunch. "Not right now, Laura. I need you to dig into something for me."

Feeling a little repentant, Laura sat down behind the desk and stuck her hands between her legs. "Sure thing," she said in as businesslike a tone as she'd used since coming into the office.

"I want you to locate and call a Frank DeMonte. He should be in the Winston Beach area. At least that's where he lives. See if you can make an appointment with him for me, maybe during the day where he works. Tell him I'm interested in buying the old house he owns up on the coastal highway. Don't take no for an answer, and don't tell him I'm a private eye, whatever you do."

Laura looked at Harding, feeling a little insulted.

"I'm doing it again, huh?" Harding said, his eyes getting big and sorrowful as he leaned over the desk.

Laura leaned over to Harding. "You keep forgetting. I seen the movies."

Harding nodded. "I seen da light."

Laura chuckled and rolled her chair sideways to the phone. "I'm on the job, boss."

Harding got up and smiled at her, watched her cradle the mouthpiece under her chin and wink at him.

"Sure thing, angel," he said. He got up and walked into the back office. Did he just call her "angel"?

"Johnny Hard, boy hero." Harding heard the Devil's

voice from across the room, but was too busy locating his fedora to inspect the smirk he was sure to find under Sol's seedy mustache.

"Job's got to have some benefits," Harding said, "besides you sticking your pitchfork up my ass."

"Question is," the Devil replied, "where you sticking yours?"

Harding looked up at that one and saw the Devil sitting on the couch removing his jewelry and placing each heavy piece on the coffee table before him. He flexed his now ringless fingers like small tentacles, then kneaded his eyes and face.

"You're becoming a little dull, J. H.," he said, rising out of the worn cushion and strolling into the bathroom. "A little too predictable. This babe up front, for instance . . ." The Devil shook his head in disappointment and turned on the water in the sink. Harding walked near the doorway behind him, but his eyes seemed fixed by the shiny metallic pile the Devil had left on the shabby table.

"I got business elsewhere," the Devil said above the sound from the streaming tap. He washed his hands and slapped his face. "I hope you pick up the ball, get more movement." He snapped his fingers twice. "You know, action. Of course, I'll try and help it along when I can," he said, grinning to himself.

Harding was no longer paying him much attention, his vision having focused in on the Devil's booty—a few elaborate rings, a charm bracelet of polished silver, a watch (the Devil ruled by time, too?) with a diamond-studded dial, double rubies for midnight.

Harding moved quietly to the table and snatched up a ring. It was weighty, gold, and emerging in relief from its surface was the grotesque face of a woman, a banshee whose eyes were round sapphires, whose perfect oval mouth wailed in spite of an emerald stuffing it full. Harding donned his hat and turned toward the door in hurried steps.

The faucet jerked closed. "Hey!" the Devil shouted.

Caught, Harding froze, then, angry with himself, bowed his head and peered over his shoulder somberly. The Devil was still in the bathroom, a crescent of his back visible and turned toward the doorway. Harding heard him wiping his hands with his handkerchief.

"Where to?" the Devil asked as a matter of information.

Harding took in a deep breath, though not so loud that the Devil would wonder what was worth feeling relieved about.

"Pawnbroker," Harding said.

The Devil chuckled. "Out of scratch already?"

"Got something to make do," said Harding with a sly smile. He flipped the ring in the air and snatched it at its zenith, fist down as you would a fat, bothersome moth, then strode out the door.

They all hung there and hovered over him like a junkyard about to collapse in upon itself: snake-shaped saxophones with brassy, dented mouths, three-legged chairs, ancient firearms, dusty blankets with American Indians dancing on them, shovels, handsaws, toy train engines, lots of photos, framed and dog-eared, displaying people who, if they weren't already dead, looked it.

Only a cage—sitting in the middle of these piles, these objects hanging, dangling, drooping, these curving stacks and shaky pillars of junk surrounding—would protect you from the imminent implosion. But that cage was already occupied in Ridley's Pawn Shop by a calm black man who sat rubbing his nose methodically, his large belly bisected by the jutting platform that ran through the squared-off hole in the wire and supported Harding's elbow at the other end.

The black man's eyes finally rose up from under the bill of his red cap, pretty eyes for a man, and they opened up like the window to a friendly neighbor. "Good day ta ya, uh—I wuz gonna say 'gent,' but even these mean ol' eyes sees you been slept in. So let's say 'mister.'" The cage vibrated a bit under Harding's elbow with the black man's belly laugh. "Don't means to catch a laugh at yo' expense, there."

Harding shook his head and smiled at the joke. "You the night man here, too?"

"Heh-ha. Night man. Day man. I'm the man, son. State yo' business."

Harding took the Devil's ornate ring from his breast pocket and laid it in the cage hole. "I need someone to fence this."

The black man's belly jogged the plank again, only not from any laughter; if anything, the man suddenly became nonchalant, as though Harding could have put somebody's freshly cut ear in front of him and he would have worn the same passive expression. He frowned slightly, squinting at the piece of jewelry in a nearsighted pose, then stared at Harding.

There was an edge to his voice: "So why come here, Jack?"

Harding poked his hat up on his forehead and acted conspiratorial. "Because . . . a lady I know sent me. Good-looking brunette with gams to die for. You know her. I doubt she uses her real name, so let's just say she deals with you in baubles, the kind rich 'gents' sprinkle on dames like so much fairy dust. In fact, she made a drop here last night. You gave her a bagful of bills tied up nice. *That's* a lady to remember, am I right?"

The black man squished up his nose as though he were fingering putty and snorted. "Maybe." He smiled, but not the neighborly smile. "'N' maybe yo' the heat."

"Squint your peepers at me again, pops," Harding said. "Do I look like the law? Besides, I know the whole setup. The lady laid it all out straight. What would I need with this sideshow? I'd bust you flat right now from her say-so."

"Well, there . . . Jack, you know . . . I needs time to tap the source and get the dough—not that I *can* gets the dough." The black man waved his fingers with an open palm. "Let's see the rock noseways."

Harding pushed the ring farther into the cage hole until it sat clearly on the other side of the wire, where the black man picked it up like a stray peanut and rolled it around his fingertips delicately, amazingly so for such a meaty stump of hand. When he brought the ring near his dilating nostrils, Harding couldn't tell if he was inspecting it carefully or smelling it to see if it was edible.

"I got more," Harding said.

"Take it slow, speedo," the black man intoned. "One stone a throw."

"You're kidding me. How many the lady get to you?"

The black man stopped his myopic examination. "Plenty. But only one load a month, maybe. We needs to work slow this first time 'round, son. 'Sides, the drop last night—that's it fo' July."

"Are you saying she doesn't come here anymore?"

"Not 'til August, nope." Putting the ring down, the black man worked up a smile. "I'll give my source a rundown on this kind of merchandise you got here, good 'nuff? You come see me in a week maybe and we'll cook us up a deal."

The black man tapped the ring with his fingertips back under and through the cage hole, and Harding pocketed it.

"Next week," Harding said, giving him a two-finger

salute off his hat brim. The instant Harding closed the door behind him, the black man reached over to his left blindly while his remaining fingers dug into his weary eyes. He always knew exactly where among the rubble like a junkyard mongrel the telephone sat.

Harding waited in the vestibule, his hat hanging over his groin, flapping against it in impatience, when he thought he heard his mother's laugh—a laugh, though, ringing with jaded youth. He walked a few steps toward the sound, down the first hallway in a house that was deceptive. From the front and certainly from his vantage point the other night, his parents' home had appeared stately but modest in size; however, the thick trees and plants that hid its side yard also hid much more. The house went back farther than he imagined, had a depth unrealized to the casual passerby. The dark-skinned servant who had let him in sauntered away and down a central corridor that seemed dark and endless, though obviously just a trick of light, or lack of it, really. She faded to black with just the sound of her slowly clicking heels diminishing.

The laughter had replaced that retreating echo, and he now moved slowly though hesitatingly toward the source, drawn somehow. Soon music, slow band music—maybe the Dorseys, Harding wasn't sure—replaced the laughter, or at least lingered beyond it. Reaching an archway where both the music and a golden light from the waning sun wafted through, Harding dipped his head into the glow.

Three women sat on various stuffed chairs, one on an embroidered love seat, in a sitting room that had rhapsodic trombones and clarinets on the turntable, and a woman stood among them in a dark blue blouse and pants outfit lifting her thickly bunched black hair up above her head and laughing; it was Harding's mother. The women responded with chuckles, and one almost blew tea from her cup back into her face as she was in the middle of a sip. Mrs. Harding swayed in time to the slow, soft horns, and what struck Jonathan most by the sight was his mother's bare arms. He had never remembered seeing his mother's arms so free, so smooth, so exposed. The house was warm, even as the sun set, warmer than most, and he wiped his brow with his sleeve. Even with San Marco's fickle climate—quick coastal chills on August nights, sudden flushes of heat in February—Harding's standard childhood image was one of his mother in a completely buttoned kelly-green sweater, a larger-than-she sweater, quite possibly his father's, though he had never thought to ask, one she kept for years through his adolescence and well past normal wear. Woolly green arms chastised him, cursed him, hugged him, bore him up to her breast as though he were the heaviest burden ever to be laid upon her soul. So what were these dancing, rocking arms doing here so free?

Suddenly the arms stopped swaying and performed a lifting gesture toward the woman in the love seat. The woman rose, and the two of them started to dance in each other's arms, slowly swaying to the beat, Harding able to hear his mother's voice talking to her partner as they moved along the rug. The other women watched their feet; Harding watched his mother's hips.

Then she saw him. She didn't misstep or halt in any way, nor did Harding pull back into the vestibule like the little kid not allowed in the parlor with the grown-ups. Discretion here might have been wise, since Harding intended to follow his mother in the near future, and any recognition, any hint of her suspicion, would jeopardize his tail. Still, he just watched his mother watching him as she danced and talked, her dark eyes drifting into his with a faraway look at first, then one that held fast and diminished the distance between them. She shifted her weight constantly, effortlessly, so that the curves of her body shifted, too, and flowed into yet another smooth series of silken, melodic arcs. Harding remained fixed and staring in the doorway: he never knew his mother could dance.

"Mr. Hard?"

Harding turned quickly to the short servant who had let him in and was now pointing down the same hallway she had vanished into moments before. He didn't look back at his mother as he started toward what he was told was the laboratory. The end of the corridor was as dark as he thought it would be from when he was at the other end, but a quick right and a well-lit room nestled in the rear of the house led his way.

The windowless room was overly bright and overly hot, but nothing like the fantasy laboratory—no rows of vials with rainbow-colored chemicals filling each and smoking; nothing bubbled; no tubes twisted their way through the air, corkscrewed, and dipped, just to place one drop of a dark condensing liquid into an oversize, mysteriously empty beaker. There was a noxious smell, more irritating to the nose and eyes than odorous, and brown fluid dominated most of the test tubes, thick like syrup or low-grade oil. Harding's father was pouring such a liquid with gloved hands when Jonathan entered. Placing the two beakers down quickly, Mr. Harding pivoted on his heel. He wore a stern expression and an over-the-shoulders, tie-back white apron, amazingly unstained, which made him look like a businesslike asylum keeper or a plumb-line-backed butcher working far beneath his station, and most especially like his father, the research chemist.

Harding spoke before his father did. "I told your servant I was sent from the plant with important data which needed your immediate look-over. But I figured my name would clue you in on what I was really here for."

"What *are* you doing here?" Mr. Harding quelled his anger in as low a voice as he could under the circumstances.

"Your office said you work at home sometimes."

Mr. Harding pulled his gloves off quickly. "I mean, what kind of fool are you to come to my home like this? My wife could see you."

Harding decided to skip the confessional. "What kind of a fool do you take me for?"

"A rather big one at this juncture," Mr. Harding said, slapping his gloves down on the lab table.

"So it seems," Harding said with a trace of resistance. "What do you mean?"

Harding drew closer. "I mean, you have to answer me some questions so I know that you and I are being straight with each other. Like what's your connection with a guy named Romero? Right now a murder rap could be pinning me to the wall."

Mr. Harding grimaced. "I know, sir; I read newspapers."

"And I read dead men's calendars. How is it your name was scribbled on Romero's?"

Mr. Harding took a breath as though it were the one that almost got away. Dropping his head, he walked to a small, shielded box that looked like a stand-alone oven. "It's unfortunate about Romero. But considering his alleged other job—which I knew nothing about, by the way, until I saw the latest edition, this suspected card dealer business . . ." Mr. Harding faced Jonathan from across the room. "He was my gardener. Part-time. We haven't all that much land that isn't taken up by this house, so . . . He'd come every other weekend. The police know all this. I told them already. That's *all* I know of the man. He was my part-time gardener."

Harding nodded as his father looked at his watch, either in a gesture to open the oven at the right moment or one to signify it was time for Harding to leave.

"That how he met your daughter?" Harding said. "Pruning the begonias?"

His father's face grew pale, and his motions ceased all pretense of being in the middle of virtual chemical history.

"Yeah, I met her," Harding continued. "Sweet girl. Like meeting a blunt object head on."

His father wasn't looking at him when he decided to speak; he wasn't looking at anything in particular except perhaps a fuzzy mental picture of the past.

"Carla is the end product of a broken home. Her mother was no good . . . so too the daughter. Carla stayed here a while with Dolores and me. She was desperate; I was being charitable. She met Romero one weekend and they got along, I would imagine. She always liked the greasy types with their hands in dirt. Like her mother."

"You were married before?"

Mr. Harding looked at Jonathan as though he had asked a stupid question, which in fact he had.

"I meant," Harding said quickly, "how could you say that if you were married, if she married *you?*" There was a compliment in there somewhere but far too buried to matter.

"Just lucky, I guess." A flash of a smile? Harding thought he saw one, thought he just heard a small joke, one his father told with himself as its butt. "The first Mrs. Harding isn't talked about in this house. She wasn't . . . true . . . ultimately."

"Meaning when you finally found out." Jonathan didn't

want it to come out that hard. His father moved toward the oven again.

"It's enough to know that she took Carla and died somewhere in Chicago, I believe, and Carla showed up on the proverbial doorstep one night, only not swaddled in bunting, but as a full-grown, foul-mouthed twenty-one-year-old—"

"Her desperate, you charitable."

"That's correct." Mr. Harding nodded curtly.

"Then what?"

"Family fights, what have you. . . ." Mr. Harding shook his head, remorse seeping in, lining his brow. "Too many arguments, raised voices—ridiculous of me to even let her stay two minutes, let alone—let's just say there is no love lost between Dolores and Carla. So good riddance."

Harding felt sad because he felt sadness coming from his father, although the proud head remained level, eyes remained stern.

Then Harding said, "So when somebody asks you, like I did, if you have any children, you say 'no.' You just make like things don't exist."

Harding watched his father's head shake a little, then his jaw level drop. "Not the best way to forget mistakes," he said quietly. "But it's one way."

Mr. Harding walked to the back door, an exit hidden from Jonathan when he'd walked in, and opened it up. The red sun shed its weakened light on his father, and the faintest hint of music entered the room. Harding walked closer and noticed his father could see into the sitting room window from the doorway where it was very dim in the twilight, could see shadows move to the whisper of harmonious trombones. Harding thought of his mother possibly being pregnant with him at this very moment.

The question came out of the faint music: "Ever wanted a son?"

His father turned his head to Jonathan, wrinkling his forehead at first, then producing a waning, sad smile.

"No," he said flatly. Mr. Harding turned back to the dimly rocking shadows.

Then he spoke: "You see, Mr. Hard, this world has very little security, a vast number of moral criminals, and far too many risks. Birth is a crapshoot, if I may use the vernacular, a throw of the dice, and in my lifetime they've been loaded too many times. Your son could become the next Mussolini, Stalin. You never know."

Harding nodded. "Could become the next Einstein or Gandhi, too."

His father laughed.

"Or maybe," Harding continued, "just a good, honest man."

There was a silence before his father turned to Harding and allowed a small smile to appear, a locking of stares.

"Maybe," his father said. Harding looked into his father's face, and although he saw little if any of his own features, he felt his mutual trust.

Mr. Harding quickly closed the back door and moved away, toward the gloves he had removed in anger before. "Please," he said, grabbing the idle pair. "Leave. The women will be going soon, and I don't want you here."

Harding realized he had shifted to business and his own wasn't settled yet. "A few quick questions, please. You know a man named Gunther. Harlen Gunther."

His father shook his head. "No, I don't."

"Have any investments in a Rome Company, downtown somewhere, a big storehouse . . ."

"No."

"How about your partner, Mr. Snell?"

"I doubt it. Never heard of a Rome Company."

"Okay . . . now the jewels—"

Mr. Harding lifted his mind from his work, wearing an

expression of discovery. "Yes—listen—a few more jewels are missing from Dolores's little hiding place. I checked this morning while she was bathing."

"I know," Harding said. "I followed her to a fence last night."

"A fence?" his father almost shouted. "How could that be? She can't need the money! I—"

"I don't know," Harding interrupted. "But you said she goes out a *few* times a week. And I know it's not to make a drop. At least that's the pawnbroker's story. She only makes a drop maybe once a month."

"She does go out a few times a week still," Mr. Harding said. He paced now, unsure of his movements. "As I said before, probably to her lover. I didn't realize a fence—"

"You still going with that lover theory?" Harding asked.

"You have any others, Mr. Hard?" his father replied rhetorically.

"How about *real* club meetings and what-have-you?"

His father looked at him with sadness, either because his own perceived truth was overwhelming him again or because in looking at Harding he was looking at the last remnant of naiveté in the world.

Jonathan bowed his head. "She going out tonight?"

"Late, she says. Console a friend about something. I don't even listen to the reason anymore. Eight, nine o'clock."

Harding sighed. "Okay, then. I'll tail her."

"Fine. Thank you," Mr. Harding said. "Now please go." He spun around and lifted a beaker, already lost in thought.

Harding backed up a step, started to swivel away, but stopped. "Mr. Harding?"

Harding saw the beaker immediately lower as though its engines failed. "Yes—what?" his father barked.

"Could we have lunch sometime?" Harding said. His

thoughts flashed to Stone's father, the buttery eggs, the ashes, but he wiped his mind clean when his father turned to him, puzzled.

"No business," Harding added.

His father asked, "Then why?"

"I think I'd enjoy it," Harding said as straightforwardly as he knew how.

His father nodded. "Of course." No less puzzled, his father turned back to his chemistry; Harding, no less determined, to the hallway, when he suddenly thought of his own two children, their tender faces clearer to him in the hallway's darkness than they had been in the past year.

The sitting room was empty as he passed it, though the record was still playing. He backed up a step to look in again, saw his mother's white handbag, her companion on last night's detour, sitting within reach on the mahogany table that was stationed just inside beneath a gold-leaf mirror. Some actions must be executed without the precautions or hindrance of thought; Harding grabbed the bag, his body hovering over it, as though hiding it from what little crimson-hued light was left in the day, and snuck his hand inside. Tissue remnants were fought through; a set of keys he dared not pocket jingled slightly and were silenced. A wallet would help. Makeup kit, two makeup kits, some sucking candy, a sudden cold piece of metal. He shook his head, half laughed (although he had no reason to) as his fingers encircled a shaft of pipe that lay below like the cold foundation to a bright new house.

A blur of movement in the mirror and Harding snapped the handbag shut, just as his mother walked into the sitting room from the french doors adjacent to the patio. He sweated that timeless, instantaneous sweat whenever he rummaged his mother's handbag for chewing gum or a stray nickel.

Harding adjusted his hat in order to give the mirror a reasonable function, so too his presence in the room. His mother's reflection smiled at him, then moved to the Victrola and lifted the tonearm. The quiet disturbed him, not to mention her ignoring his obvious snooping. Or was he finally getting good at it twenty-five years past childhood?

"You wanted some dance lessons?" his mother asked coyly.

Harding faced her, cocking his head. "Is that what I was watching before?"

"Women around here are born with silver spoons in their mouths and lead in their feet."

Harding thought she was going to say "handbags." Mrs. Harding smirked to herself. "Twice a week, keeps me busy . . . Mr. Hard, right?"

Harding was struck by the voice. Most voices don't really change over the years, but it was as if the mother who sat before the glowing television, withering in angry denial at his questions, was throwing her voice across time to this beautiful likeness, her young and wizened puppet whose brow was now raised inquisitively. "That's not it?"

"No," Harding said finally. "That's it. I just came by to give your husband some research material from—"

"I know your story, Mr. Hard," his mother said, lifting her chin. Harding figured the maid as the source. "I also know a lot of people from the lab, and you're not one of them. I don't know where you're from, and I don't think you'd tell me if I asked, but tell me—please—is my husband in trouble?"

"Do I look like trouble?" Harding asked.

"Yes," his mother answered.

"Thanks," Harding said.

He took a peek into the mirror and saw a man who looked better than he had that morning but not much.

"Would he have reason to *be* in trouble?" Harding said.

"I don't know. I know he wouldn't be seeing a man who looks like you if there wasn't some reason, a good reason." His mother opened her arms slightly and approached him. "I'm sorry. I don't mean to insult you. Really." She smiled and touched his arm. "I didn't mean to say you weren't attractive." Harding stiffened his arm as if it had gone numb. "I just know with my husband's standing"— she was searching for words—"you're just not the kind my husband—"

"He wouldn't be caught dead with a bum like me," Harding said with a vindictive edge. His mother let go his arm and retreated.

"I wouldn't put it that way," she said. "He has his standards, that's all. In friends, workers, in his business dealings—"

"In a wife," Harding said with no hint of expression. His mother let the statement settle, unsure whether it was meant as a compliment or not.

"I would hope so," she said almost in defiance.

"And in his family in general, I assume," Harding said. "I'm starting to know him a little."

This statement registered a small flicker of pain. "This isn't about Carla, is it?"

Harding furrowed his forehead innocently but said, shrugging, "You'd have to ask him."

After a short, awkward silence, he nodded. "I should get back to the lab."

Mrs. Harding, who had been staring into the intricately vined green wallpaper pattern on the far wall, looked at him and said mechanically, "Drink?"

Hesitating, Harding wondered if she wasn't ready to reveal something, something she saw tangled in the clutch of vines within the wallpaper.

"Sure," he said.

Her voice grew harsh. *"I don't.* And nobody who works for Nat does, either. He wouldn't allow it."

Harding looked at Mrs. Harding's imperious face. It was almost totally dark now, and without any gracing lamplight, her expression showed a youthful decline, a gray, icy edge. Another one of his mother's stupid traps, Harding thought, hating her for it.

"I should get back to the lab just the same," Harding said, and started out of the room.

His mother walked up behind him at the front door, this time showing far more despair on her face. "We're a religious family, Mr. Hard."

Harding shook his head. "I don't know what that means," he said, and shut the door behind him.

"Berner and Hard."

Laura put on her sexy phone voice without realizing the connection in Harding's corner booth still made her sound almost like the static-filled Mary Gates coming over his patrol car radio.

"That's Hard and Berner, no matter what he says," Harding replied.

Laura recognized his dry, ironic voice and laughed. "Hey, boss, how's tricks?"

"Enough lingo, Laura," Harding said. "Tell me what you got from Frank DeMonte. Anything?"

"I got his home number and gave it a buzz. Lots of commotion, like kids were busting up the place, but the woman who answered—Mrs. DeMonte—said her husband would be home soon, but didn't think he'd be selling the house right now, but she said she didn't have a head for business, so you'd have to talk to her husband. I told her you were representing some rich fella who loves to restore old houses, who's on some rich preservation board. I made up a name."

Harding barked out a laugh for his phantom association with his ex-wife.

"What's the gag?" Laura asked. "She was impressed."

"Hey, *I'm* impressed," Harding said. "It's on me, kiddo. The gag was on me. You think quick and work fast."

"Thanks." Laura beamed over the phone lines.

"What about getting him on the job?"

"He does door to door. You know, sells-gadgets-nobody-wants kinda guy. No way to nail him down."

"I'll hit his house. Nice going, angel."

"You wanna get a bite when you get back? I mean, you know—"

Harding chuckled. "You work fast all right."

The Devil bolted into the reception room from the back office and glared at Laura.

"Is that our darling dick?"

Laura nodded.

"Shovel it here, sister!" The Devil pulled the phone from Laura's hand almost before she could let it go. "Say, J. H.," he intoned, "you quittin' the peeper biz and takin' up jewel heists?"

"You mean the ring," Harding said.

"I mean the missing ring, Hard-boy!"

"Hold your horns, Sol," Harding said, taunting. "It's snug in my coat pocket and on its way home."

"Now," the Devil growled.

"Soon," Harding said.

"Now!"

Harding's heart was pounding and almost slipped and fell off his rib cage with the Devil's resonant cry.

"Why don't you come and get it, Sol. You're so damn good at popping yourself in and out of places like a regular spook in a funhouse. Do it now, you want it so bad."

The Devil stood erect and simmered, slowly calming himself.

"No, Johnny. You bring it to *me*." His voice was precise; each word branded itself in the air. Like parents to babies, like tyrants to foes, when you want them to come to your bidding, you do not jump to them and use force; you wait and make them crawl.

The line went dead. The Devil held the buzzing phone to his ear for another few seconds, then lowered it to its carriage.

Oblivious to the Devil's growing ire, Laura freely spoke aloud. "Johnny's okay—Mr. Hard, I mean. He just likes doing things his way, I can tell." The Devil wasn't paying much attention, inhaling deeply into the nub of a cigarette. "I like him," she continued, nodding, her eyes scooting upward, a gesture suggesting somebody sitting up very close to the big screen. "I like his looks. His moxie, too. His devil-may-care . . ."

The Devil stared at Laura, wondering if she was talking about the same person. "Then again, doll," he said, flicking the spent butt to the floor, "He—may—*not*."

Laura didn't understand; the Devil didn't see that she had to. But most certainly, Johnny would.

The five kids swarmed around Mrs. DeMonte as though she were being circled by fifty. They moved as she moved like little billows of dust she was consistently kicking up, covering her legs.

"Want a coffee?" she asked with a not unfriendly tone, though a weary one, one belonging more to a waitress at an all-night diner.

"No thanks," Harding said, a response that made her smile and nod her head as she walked away, her clamoring whirlwind to follow.

"So you're the guy who met my cousin Lionel?" Frank DeMonte said, wedged into a overly soft lounge chair. DeMonte fingered his suspenders as many wearers do, just out of their being there; his tie was mostly undone, the knot somewhere down his chest, off center, like a hangman's noose; his wide-striped pants led to bare feet, airing out on a hassock, his soles reddened, many toes encircled in tiny Band-Aids, looking like capped electrical wires.

Harding realized DeMonte was referring to the gun-toting hick with the Dobermans who'd skimmed him for thirty bucks. "You mean at the house?"

"Yeah," DeMonte said, and he started to laugh, then coughed a phlegm-rattling cough. "Yeah, chased you off." He laughed again, shrugging off the episode.

Harding didn't think he was young enough to wait for an apology, so he continued. "There gold on that property? Felt like I was storming Fort Knox."

DeMonte reached for his beer. "Nah. Just what used to be my mother. A nurse. A good piece of property." He took a drag off a damp cigarette with his other hand. "I figure, I mean, I was taught that a good piece of property is worth protecting."

"That's all who live there?" Harding asked.

"That's it. I let Lionel live there. You know. He does a job. Anyway . . ." DeMonte adjusted himself, pulled himself from the cushioned wedge, and brought his shoulders forward in a business huddle. "About the house and all. My hands are tied right now. No way I can sell it 'cause of my S.O.B. of a brother."

Harding looked inquisitive, so DeMonte kept going. "My brother, my 'big' brother, the oldest—you know what I mean?—he acts like he's still in the army. You in the war?"

Harding was taken off guard. "Yeah."

"Where? Europe?"

Harding shook his head. "The Pacific." Vietnam was around the Pacific, he thought.

"Ouch," DeMonte said. "Wouldn't have wanted a piece of those bastards. The Nazis were bad enough. My brother was bad enough. Big-shot first lieutenant. Me, I was a G.I. By the book, my brother. Got my family doing dances by the book, too."

Harding wondered whether DeMonte was ever going to get to the point. "The house?" he said.

"Yeah," DeMonte said, getting testy. "The house. My mother signed the house over to me 'cause I got kids, a family. My brother's single. What's *he* need? But then she gets crazy like she's senile or something but she's only fifty-five so it can't be that. The doctors don't know jack, but I say, if she's nuts, put her in a home."

Harding noticed Mrs. DeMonte's head had dipped into the doorway and she glared at her husband. DeMonte suddenly noticed, too. He looked at her directly and spoke a little louder. "If she's nuts, put her in a home," he repeated. Mrs. DeMonte's head disappeared. "So what's my brother do?" DeMonte continued feverishly. "He gets my mother to do some legal hootchie-cootchie where I can't get the house, sell it, do nothing with it, so she can still live there with rotating nurses for a wad of dough every day you wouldn't believe if I told you."

DeMonte's voice ran out of breath with that sentence, and he hacked again. Then his callous tone suddenly softened. "She's worse than a vegetable. At least a vegetable don't talk to herself in the mirror like it's another person she's scared of. Or she thinks she's somewhere in Virginia when she was a kid. Or she'll have fits. . . . Doesn't even know who the fuck *I* am anymore. Haven't been there in over a year now." DeMonte pulled in another stream of smoke from his cigarette. "Dumping the joint the minute she dies," he said more to himself than to Harding. "Get another house. Move."

Harding saw the old woman's face again in his mind's

eye and couldn't believe she was only in her fifties, the dull, lost stare of a cruel disease. Possibly it was Alzheimer's, living in an era that didn't know its name. DeMonte stirred. Harding must have been wearing a sad but accusing expression, one that pointed and said, "But it's your mother."

DeMonte slowly shook his head at his houseguest, disgust in his voice. "That's not my mother."

Denial hung in the dewy night air, everywhere; you felt it in your bones. Harding squirmed in his seat, fatigued and achy, as he drove back down from Winston Beach. Although DeMonte expressed bitter feelings, Harding concluded, he appeared honest. When questioned about knowing Harding's father or mother, or having anything to do with casinos or pawnshops, DeMonte shook his head as if to say he had enough to do with underhanded brothers and nonexistent mothers, not to mention the five squawking dust clouds he had to feed on a commission basis. He complained, but it was straightforward; DeMonte wouldn't have anything to do with Nathaniel Harding's death. For that matter, Nathaniel Harding wouldn't have anything to do with DeMonte's life. If what Harding's mother said was right. If anything Harding believed was right anymore. Yet somehow his father winds up slugged and dead in that dying lady's basement. Maybe years from now after the old lady has died, after the house has been sold. When *is* now, anyway?

Harding looked at the time—half-past seven. He pushed the accelerator a bit farther. He wanted to stop at the office, then back out to his parents' home well before nine and his mother's next leap into the dark.

He first noticed Thick Dunbar's chiseled face a block after he'd parked the car and started walking, maybe two buildings away from Harding's office in the Helmsley

Building. Dunbar tried hiding his granite brow behind a *San Marco Sun-Times*, but Harding spotted his breadth and width and especially his shoes, scuffy brown oxfords the size of hard-shell tortoises, their soles turned up from wear at the toes. Harding remembered them from the floor of the casino after Frisky and the blond bouncer sent him there, Dunbar coming over to join in on the good times. One brown tortoise in the chest would make you remember for a while. He remembered all their shoes that night before he blacked out. What else was there to do down there?

Harding ignored Dunbar as he passed him reading in the doorway of a closed-up barbershop. When he turned into the Helmsley Building, he spotted Scooter across the lobby sitting on his stool just inside the elevator, reading with one hand a paperback as flaccid as a grilled-cheese sandwich, then quickly standing and just as quickly leaning up against the elevator door with his free hand in his pocket as though just passing time until Harding appeared. The awkwardly casual pose froze Harding a moment, then Scooter's head raised, his chin flicking up in a gesture that usually means "hello" but now was the equivalent of setting off a flare.

Harding saw a twisted movement to his right, from just beyond the pillar alongside him. He ducked instinctively, and Frisky's blow sliced the air and only the back half of Harding's scalp. His eyes almost crossed; an instantaneous dizziness subsumed him, then retreated. Harding threw out his right leg, and his foot landed just above Frisky's belt, sending him backward, as well as sending Harding sprawling in the opposite direction from the off-balance thrust.

Harding slapped the marble floor with both hands and lifted himself up quickly, his spinning head almost dragging him back down by its own whirlpooling gravity.

Frisky's head had cracked into the pillar on the way down, so the henchman was on all fours, angry, a pin-striped mongrel trying to remember how to walk like a man.

Staggering to the revolving front door, someone with a quicker mind would have remembered the trailing Dunbar, but Harding was still fuzzy, still operating on a thin line of fear, not just for his own safety, but for possibly missing his stakeout, his mother's nocturnal trail. A glance behind revealed only Scooter's wing tips peeking out from behind the elevator wall and the door closing for a speedy getaway. A glance ahead revealed the approaching Dunbar, the newspaper removed from his face, a hunter's seeking glare its replacement. Harding had pushed the door a quarter turn when Dunbar entered midspin and saw the jerk he was after. He tried to pull the door to a halt, to trap Harding, giving his partner inside a chance to come into the action, but Harding had the momentum, having entered first, and so pushed, actually slid, the straining Dunbar into the lobby while squeezing himself out between the exterior wall and the metal-framed glass door to the street.

Dunbar *whoosh*ed through the door again and out faster than Harding expected, or maybe Harding's brain was running slower; Frisky had tagged him good for a glancing swipe. Harding ran through the sparsely populated street looking for a doorway to run through, one that would allow him safe passage to 1986, at least for now, but all the storefronts stood in darkness, closed for the day.

Dunbar's long, lumbering strides brought Harding within two lengths of his meaty grasp. Harding had to lose Dunbar, at least make Dunbar, people in general, lose sight of him, in order to use the powers given him by the Devil's contract. The heavyset thug drew short of one arm's length by the end of the block.

Running on delirious impulse, Harding turned into an

opening between two apartment houses, hoping the alley would present him with accessible back doors to the future. The alley, two car lengths wide, ran deep and ended not out the other side of the block, but at a dilapidated two-story garage. The large, pull-away door was shut, and patches of bricks were missing around it, like makeshift windows or holes from discreet cannon fire. But a gray metal door was ajar, and its vertical crack became the target of Harding's now even faster pounding feet.

Dunbar lunged. He caught a piece of Harding's shoulder in his grasp and pulled. Still in full stride, Harding's right side was being bent back, tugged down. He stumbled slightly, swerved sideways, and at the last moment dodged a hanging fire escape ladder, forcing Dunbar to release him or strike the metal obstruction head on. Then, near a row of shiny silver garbage cans, standing in file like armored dwarfs watching childlike the large grown men in deadly pursuit, Harding swung back his right arm, toppling a can behind him. Dunbar was too close to his prey to sidestep the rolling, clattering barrel, tried leaping over it, but skidded off its side and fell forward on his left arm with a grunt.

From his prone position, Dunbar, breathing heavily, angrily, pulled his piece and snapped off two shots at Harding. Jonathan thought he felt the paths of angry wasps cross his, buzzing by, then implanting themselves in the garage wall ahead.

Harding drew closer, ran faster, to the side door's dark edge, enlarging, becoming the crack of Time, the crack of Doom. Now was his chance. He pulled at the door, which screamed out from decaying hinges, and stumbled into its unlit interior and into . . .

Harding spun on his heels. Unless this car shack existed in 1986, just as dark and decimated, there wasn't any change at all, no free fall into time, nothing. How? Why didn't—?

Harding heard a snicker. "Got troubles, eh?"

He looked up; the voice came from up left. Blinking through the colored blotches before his eyes, Harding saw a form, a crouching form, up on a ledge that protruded from one of the large holes in the brick wall. A shaggy-faced bum in a dirty yellow shirt was perched like a scraggly parakeet near the window, illuminated by the little alleyway light that drifted through. The tramp must have seen the chase, seen him coming from the window, and watched him stumble in: that was why Harding couldn't jump through the years.

Harding fell on his rump, feeling dizzy, depleted. He pulled his gun out, propped up against the wall in the dark.

"I'll be quiet," the voice said with a slight jitter. Then Harding heard the tramp sobbing. The colored spots started to swirl again; the darkness didn't help; the exertion didn't help; the back of his head thumped steadily. Harding saw a shadow, a large shadow, probably Dunbar's shadow, enter the doorway. It grew, seemingly larger, bigger than the doorway, yet passed through the doorway. The shadow vision, the same one he had had when he saw his mother in the doorway the other day, was again drifting upon him. Harding shivered and blinked his eyes slowly. He felt as though he were dreaming, or had been dreaming, dreamed this somehow and yet at the same time was re-creating it here, living it, though not quite the same way. He gripped his gun tighter, tried to feel the handle as real.

He had dreamed this times before, was dreaming of a shadow, a growing shadow, that was like a big, narrow rock or a thick tree but one with a face, a pair of dark knots for eyes. He heard his mother cry out his name as the ominous tree suddenly shook violently at its base, felt himself yanked back as if by an invisible lasso or a gust of protective wind. The shadow spread itself and fell, fell a long time, and landed at his feet. He felt safe yet captured, put upon by the lasso, which had multiplied and, like snakes, engulfed him. A weight was placed on his head and never left.

Thick Dunbar straightened up from his inspection of the motionless body before him and laughed. He turned to Frisky: "KO'd in the second."

Rubbing his sore stomach, Frisky held in his perfunctory chuckle and grimaced as he swung his foot into the side of the unconscious Harding.

"You up, princess?"

Harding squeezed his eyes open, still a little dizzy, felt his body cushioned, plushly cushioned at that, then saw the face to match the voice: Thick Dunbar's face, with a squared-off smile, then a laugh. Harding propped himself up but felt enclosed. He was in a car, a plush car with leather upholstery wrapped around mattress-thick seats. From the back Harding saw Dunbar's head peering at him over the front passenger seat and Frisky sitting at the wheel, his eyes somberly inspecting him from the rear-view mirror. Harding had a strange sensation that the car wasn't moving. He blinked out the window to his right, and it wasn't. It was parked in the alley just outside the brick garage where he'd passed out. Harding touched his sore rib, a singular pain on his right side he didn't remember having before or getting.

Frisky snorted through his nose, watching Harding. "You awake? You remember us, buddy?"

"Yeah, sure," Harding said, allowing the seat to comfort him while it could. "Tweedle-dum and Tweedle-dumber."

"Mr. Gunther wants you now," Dunbar said, ignoring Harding's crack.

"Oh? In how many pieces?"

"One," Frisky said, "but we can arrange something, maybe."

"Okay, okay, let's drop the funny stuff and conduct our business here, okay, Mr. Hard? Or should I call you Johnny?" said a voice from Harding's left. Jonathan flinched when he saw Harlen Gunther sitting on the opposite side of the backseat all along, leaning against the window, smiling. He held a drink in his hand, which looked like a tumbler of whiskey and water, though there was no apparent bar inside the auto.

"Whatever," Harding said. "It's your show." He looked to the silent duo up front. "Just a word from you, huh? You tame your pets real good, Gunther."

Gunther chuckled, nodding. "Well, you know, a man in my position . . . when I request things, Johnny, people usually honor my requests."

"Bet your muscle-bound messenger boys got something to do with that. What do you think?"

Gunther kept chuckling. "No matter. They get honored, that's what counts." He sipped from his glass, then said seriously, "But you know one thing that's even better than honor, Johnny?" He didn't wait for a reply. "In her."

Dunbar shook out a laugh while Gunther smiled at him in response. Frisky just played with the wheel, drumming it with his restless fingers, as though he were waiting for something to happen, something good.

Harding watched Gunther scratch his gray mustache with the back of his thumbnail while holding the near-empty tumbler in a gesture of control. His head, tan and bobbing, appeared too large for his neck, like an expanding leather football. Harding sensed that the nighttime was Gunther's element, that while the sun baked him asleep in the day, the dark awakened him to get his business done. Gunther was everybody's best friend and nobody's fool. Harding, however, still was in no mood to be approached like a Rotary Club gathering.

"What is it you want, Gunther?"

"Weeell," Gunther said. "Since you bring it up, I can tell you more what I *don't* want than what I want." He grinned.

"I'll bite. What is it you don't want?"

Gunther looked up as though he were just thinking about it, but no doubt he had the list memorized. "Well, I guess what I don't want, and don't particularly like, is a private eye snooping around my casino."

"First off," Harding said, "it's not your casino. Somebody else owns the place, and you're just the overpaid watchdog. Second—that's old news, don't you think? I paid the admission price the hard way, and I didn't buy a return ticket. So I can't believe you threw me in here for that."

Gunther made a face and shrugged. "So maybe also I don't like my dealers getting bumped off on me. How's that?" He smiled and waited for Harding.

Harding laughed this time. "You're telling me you cared about Romero? Cut you open and you bleed guacamole." His voice grew louder, tenser. "Why am I here, Gunther?"

Gunther poked up a finger. "Don't raise your voice, okay?" He almost choked midgulp. "Things get outta hand. 'Cause if I raise mine, the boys get kinda nasty."

Harding sat back in the seat, feeling his impatience welling. Understandably, he would have a rough time telling them he had to leave to tail his mother.

Gunther gave his glass to Dunbar. "So how come the law didn't keep you locked up for Romero's killing? I know you did it. *You* know you did it—"

"I guess you and I don't know a whole hell of a lot, then, after all."

"Yeah, okay," Gunther said, "so you're the prime sus- pect, Johnny. How come they sprung you?"

Harding didn't want to tell them about the missing watch, not that he understood the significance. "How do I know? Maybe they thought I could help find the real killer."

Dunbar laughed, and Gunther smiled at his henchman again in spiritual support. Harding was starting to believe he really liked to keep Thick happy. Frisky was another story.

"You get my setup from the newspapers?" Harding asked.

Gunther wrinkled his brown face like a crushed paper bag. "I don't read newspapers. They're lousy."

"Did a little bird tell you about me?" Harding said. "Or maybe a big black bird. The Maltese Pawnbroker named Ridley?"

Gunther didn't flinch; his smile was the same one he wore to the dance and was going to be the same one he wore when he left. "I don't reveal my sources," he said.

Harding wondered if he should mention Romero's scam, though that would leave Carla wide open to a visit from Dunbar and Frisky.

"What's the story on Carla Harding?" Harding asked.

Gunther looked at Harding quizzically. "You know her?"

"I saw her at the casino last night, that's all. Was filled in on who she was. Won a bundle."

Gunther laughed. "That's the truth. A lucky lady."

"I met her outside," Harding said. "After I got my cheek up off the concrete," he added, not looking at the toughs in the front seat. "She was almost robbed, but I helped break it up."

Gunther nodded. "Like I said, a lucky lady. It's not the best neighborhood. She have anything interesting to say?"

"Some," Harding said. "Just pieces added on to a lot of bits and pieces that don't fit."

"And what pieces do you know about me, Mr. Johnny Hard?" The sudden mix of formality and palsy-walsy swagger put Harding on his guard.

"I don't know. I guess I know you run a warehouse casino, but it's going down for the ten count. You seem pretty at ease about it, so I figure it's your boss that's getting the heat from the controlling mob—"

"Me just being the 'overpriced watchdog' after all," Gunther threw in.

Harding eyed Gunther. "Yeah, that's right. You seem to get employment, your type of employment, pretty easy wherever you go, 'cause you were over with the Max Turley gang in New York City—"

"Wait now. 'Family,'" Gunther corrected. "'Gang' you use for young hooligans." He paused, then started to nod and laugh, his eyes obviously surveying an image from his past. "Okay, yeah—maybe gang is okay. Turley was all hooligan and a bastard to boot." His face, for the first and only time, turned momentarily sour. "Turley was a mean son of a bitch that'd jump up and down on his own mother if he found out she could spit quarters."

"Nice boss," Harding said.

"He died," Gunther said, restoring his one-of-the-boys smile. "I helped. Go on."

Harding decided to bring his mother indirectly to the fore with the hope of picking up a connection. "I also know . . . you or somebody with the casino has some money coming in from stolen jewelry. Nice and steady money. Money maybe needed to keep the sinking casino afloat. Though if you get any more players as lucky as Carla

Harding has been lately, it'll be gone pretty fast, if it's not mostly gone already, and the casino with it."

Harding stopped talking, and there was a silence as Gunther was looking out the side window idly. He turned back toward Harding. "Well, sounds like you know plenty, Johnny. There are a few more things you should know to make your knowledge complete. Important things. Mainly things you should keep away from."

"Like hot stoves," Harding said.

"Exactly, Johnny." Gunther nodded. "Exactly like hot stoves, because these things are all related to personal safety. Keep away from the casino, for one. The daily rags and B.S. reporters, for another. My messenger boys, and especially their messages. And—yeah, finally—big black birds named Ridley."

Thick Dunbar got out of the car quickly and opened the back door for Harding. "That's it," Gunther said, and Harding was immediately pulled out of the car and up against the taller Dunbar.

"Or else . . . okay?" Dunbar said menacingly. Harding smirked and suddenly thought of Laura and bad B-movies and the schoolyard where the tag was "I'll tell my mommy."

"Or else what?" Harding asked, unable to resist.

Thick Dunbar blinked once, then swiveled, his head down searching. He leaned over and picked out a steel shank from a pile of rubble, then waved it in Harding's face.

"Know what this is, cutes?"

Harding nodded. "Yeah, the stuff that beams are made of." The blank look on Dunbar's face told Harding he hadn't seen the movie in a while, either.

"Thick!" Gunther's voice came from the car. Dunbar threw the shaft down. "Get wise and get dead," he spat, then bounced into the car, the car responding with a jolt, the tires spinning, the door slamming, until all that was left was an eddy of dirt and exhaust.

Harding sagged, then stiffened, looking at his watch. Then he ran as fast as he could toward the mouth of the alley.

The smell of exhaust had lingered at the head of the driveway, while a set of brake lights down the block's end had glowed, then dimmed with an accompanying short squeal for the stop sign. Harding's gray Buick coupe sped from his parents' empty driveway and followed the brake lights as they jumped across the intersection. Harding, too, jumped across the intersection, forgoing the stop sign completely, determined to catch up with the car, make sure it was the right one.

Only on nearby Daley Boulevard, a commercial street, did the streetlights bunch up enough for the positive identification: a blue Ford convertible, top down, definitely his parents' car. His mother should be in it, but he wasn't about to pull up alongside to find out. Besides, the route so far was exactly that of the previous night. The Ford again dipped right on Bayford, and the crusty skyline of "old" San Marco fell into view. The Ford parked itself a block away from the same YWCA, and his mother stepped from the car in a royal-blue dress and matching handbag. Her hair dipped to her shoulders, and its tips danced upon them as she strode down the sidewalk, her pumps moving at a somewhat rapid pace yet without the urgency or stiffened, anxious gait.

As Harding recalled, the bus stop was at the next far corner, but how could she be heading for Ridley's Pawn Shop again? Mrs. Harding sat down quietly on the corner bench, smoothed out the tanned nylon on the shank of her left leg, then sat back, staring straight ahead. Harding idled his car a safe distance away and thought about how these actions, her movements, were those of habit, of well-worn routine. This was no monthly, or even twice-monthly, trip. Either she drops jewels at Ridley's like just so many gumballs or—

Harding's answer came when his mother stood up and a bus appeared, a bus with a different route number from the one the other night. She wasn't going to Ridley's after all, but she *was* going somewhere familiar.

Harding moved behind the bus, which after three blocks turned north away from the pawnbroker's side of town toward a more middle-class area of San Marco, one that bordered Romero's, filled with cheaper residential apartment buildings and white immigrant workers, a "safe" neighborhood where already he had to maneuver past two different nighttime punchball games while the boys groaned at the interruptions.

When the bus stopped on Nuart Street, Mrs. Harding stepped off. Jonathan ditched the car next to a fire hydrant, the only available space, and fell in behind her, no more than thirty feet back. She passed a narrow alley and glanced upward, then at the very next apartment building she quickly clacked up three tall steps and turned into its doorway. The building was a five-floor walk-up with elongated windows and was connected with a row of similar buildings until the next corner.

Harding ran up to the short stoop and watched his mother now enter the inner doorway with a key. He shuffled up the steps and tried to time his movement, to see when he could push open the outer door and snatch the inner one before it closed, yet have his mother not see. He waited as she mounted a set of stairs. He watched her calves churn and ascend upward. The black rubber tip to her left blue high heel hopped up the last door-framed step like a bloated tick and she was out of sight. Harding pushed through the outer door and lunged at the inner one. It clicked shut.

Angry, he threw his hands at the mailboxes secured in the plaster wall, his fingers on them, as though he were reading the inky names in braille. He might as well have been scanning a phone book; he recognized nothing. No name drew his attention. Was his mother going to someone else's apartment? Then why the key? If it was her own, why the phony name? And if his mother was covering something up either way, why did she have to be his damn mother?

Harding bounced outside again and ran toward the narrow alley alongside the apartment house. It was only a guess, but maybe his mother had looked up as she passed the alleyway to see if the light in the actual apartment was on or not, which would mean the rooms would be off the alley.

The crevicelike split between the two buildings had two fire escapes rising up across from one another like parallel plants having grown to the same monstrous height and proportions. As he ran, Harding kept looking at the two dozen or so windows, watching if any lit up, signaling his mother's arrival. He climbed the fire escape clinging to the building across the alley and on the way up realized he could see through an oversize, uncurtained window and into the main hallway on the second floor. He climbed another set of creaky, metallic steps and saw the third-floor hallway. Was that a woman's leg that seemingly disappeared into the ceiling at the far end going up one more flight? Harding dashed up yet another dozen steps and turned.

From the far stairs, his mother was walking down the opposite hallway toward him. She moved so quickly, lessening the space between so suddenly, it was as if she would step through the glass window like a ghost and onto the opposite fire escape and meet him. He wanted her to. He wanted then to stretch out his hand from across the alley and she hers and touch each other like errant vines. Once he had hold of her hand, maybe he would know what to do. Maybe he would be able to explain who he was, and maybe she would explain who she was, too.

But instead his mother turned away and stood before a green door just beyond the hallway window. She unlocked it and walked inside. Harding examined the windows adjacent to the door that fronted the alley. They were closed-curtained and lit: somebody was home.

Harding slumped on the edge of his metal balcony, sitting down slowly. He'd wait. For what, he didn't know. His eyelids were heavy, half-lidded. Dry mouth made him want to cough. She had to leave eventually. His father never said she stayed out all night, so she just visited. Or whatever.

Then something irked him; some bug grabbed him by the seat of his pants, and he rose up: he wanted to get closer. He lifted his right leg up and over the low metal railing on the fire escape, secured himself, then made his left leg follow suit. With one hand on the railing, he leaned out and was dangling his fingers no more than six inches from the opposite railing. He looked down, and the dark alley surface was an invisible black, possibly an endless hole, one that would send him past China and into Sol's waiting arms.

Harding pushed off with his feet, and his right hand snatched one of the metal bars that descended from the opposite railing. His body swinging forward in the stale alley air, he slid rapidly down the bar, his grip failing, his weight pulling him downward—then the flash of a final, fiery fall twisted his insides, plunged into his belly, and surfaced as the flush of sweat. What have I done? he thought. What can I do to get out of this deal? To keep my soul? How can I hold on to it now?

Harding dangled there a moment, feeling the pull of darkness. There had to be a way out. He swung himself upward toward the iron landing, toward his mother's secret stronghold. The pendulumlike jolt forced the metal structure to emit a shrill, metallic cry. But after he steadied himself, and no noses poked out any window curtains, Harding pulled himself up and scuttled onto the fire escape adjacent to his mother's hallway window.

No sooner had he risen up to a standing position than he saw a man walking down the hall from the far staircase toward him. Harding spun himself flat against the side of the building next to the window frame, hoping he wasn't spotted. The man's footsteps had stopped, then approached the window quickly. A face pushed itself almost against the glass, searching the darkness for a flicker of movement. Pressed sideways, Harding examined the face to his right, a face breathing hot, moist air onto the glass, a round, puffy face, goateed and glaring. It was a self-important face, and one that lingered in Harding's mind like stale smoke. The man finally pulled back and moved to the same door Mrs. Harding had entered. When Jonathan peered through the window, he saw the back of the stocky man's brown, tailored suit disappear into his mother's doorway.

Harding pressed himself back up against the wall just for the sake of sensation, for the flat, rough brick to shore up his entire body. Then he jogged down the fire escape and out into the street to find his car.

Driving with manic speed, Harding sat behind the wheel, bug-eyed and numb. He pushed at the accelerator and headed for the Burnside Tunnel. The strip was deserted, and after the 1949 Buick coupe blew through the tunnel's yawning mouth, moments later, a 1977 Dodge Charger flew out the other side. Harding checked the rearview mirror, checked his image; his blank stare was the same, only the bill to his blue officer's cap hovered above his eyes like an austere awning. He flung the cap from his head and tried to drive faster.

When he reached the small house his mother lived in, he used his own key. Inside, he flicked on the light and checked his mother's bedroom to see if she was asleep, but she wasn't there. Harding popped in and out of the kitchen and dining room; everything was dark. From the foot of the stairs, the hallway upstairs was dark as well.

"Ma?" Harding called out. Nothing. "Ma!"

The phone rang and made Harding tense.

"Hello!"

"Thank God," Stone said. "Jonathan—"

"Stone, listen, you know where—"

"This afternoon. She's at the county hospital. They think it's a stroke. I tried calling you, man. I looked all over the place—"

"Yeah, wait. Okay, listen. I'll . . . I'll be there. Yeah."

"Where were you, man?"

"I'll explain later. I'm coming now. Bye."

Harding put down the phone and paused. Then he stormed up the stairs, three steps at a time, and went into the tiny room where his mother's memorabilia spread before him like ancient artifacts. He switched on the tiny lamp that threw an orange glow across the sacred corner where he now stared. The rose in the vase seemed to vibrate to life. He walked over to the news photo and peered into it as though it were a hole to the other side of the galaxy. There was his father again; there was the chemical factory again, and there was the arm again coiled about his father's reluctant shoulder, the arm of his partner, Clifford Snell. The bloated, goateed, fat-faced Clifford Snell.

Whirling around, Harding saw his parents standing alongside each other in wedding attire, and he swung. The gold-framed picture flew across the trunk and smashed itself up against the far wall, shattering its glass, and dropped facedown on the floor. Harding winced and held his painful fist, sucking the blood from his bone-white knuckles.

• eight •

This glass was too thick for him to shatter.

He leaned on it as he would a large picture window as a boy, trying to overcome the glare of streetlights behind him and the distracting reflections to see if his mother were inside the beauty parlor or if she had moved on to the bakery. But this particular window thrust him into another world entirely, one wholly present, having nothing to do with the past. His mother was still inside, however, barely seen amid the intestinal explosion of tubes that sprouted from under her bedsheet or up out of her nostrils. Three cubical machines showed their red eyes, not caused from tears or fatigue, blinking occasionally, a trinity of little squat devil dwarves on guard and beeping.

The nurse continued. "The cancer itself and the treatment added to her weakness, of course. So any effects of the stroke are multiplied. She's almost completely paralyzed right now."

"Is she conscious?" That was Stone's voice, a bit hoarse, and to Harding somewhere far away like a voice in his head asking questions through telepathy.

The nurse spoke in a dry whisper. "Oh, yes. Most of the time. You can see her now, but please, Officer, only for a minute."

Harding heard the squeak of the nurse's sneakers fade off and the alternating beeps of the hospital life support systems take over the room's conversation. Stone looked at Harding, his head up against his right forearm, his forearm using the glass for support, his cap waving aimlessly, flapping in his right hand as though affected by the cold exhale from the air conditioners or the slightest of ill winds.

"Guess we should go in, huh? No—maybe you go in alone. She'll be too . . . well. We can't get her excited and all. You know, her heart—" His throat thickening, Stone looked in at Mrs. Harding lying still beyond the glass. Jonathan thought that through the thicket of wires, through the jarring beeps, under the bony bumps in the harsh yellow blanket, the pale white bone shadow of his mother lay, unmistakably, stricken and cancerous.

"Hey, man, go on in," Stone said quietly.

Harding didn't move. "She had her own little love nest, you know. Her own rich lover, too. So what if it was my father's partner."

"What?"

"Maybe when he found out, she killed him . . . maybe she had one of Gunther's thugs do it for her."

"Jonathan, what did you find out about your father?"

Harding lifted himself off the glass and stuck the cap on his head. "I can't go in there," he murmured.

"What?" Stone dropped back a step. "What's that shit?

You gotta go in. Go on." He lightly grabbed Harding by the arm. Harding backed off like a wounded animal. Stone was shocked. "What's wrong with you, man?"

Harding stood there, his shoulders hiked up, his eyes unsure of where to look.

Stone's tone grew angry. "She's your mother."

Harding shook his head, but as a confused means of affirmation. He couldn't deny her the way Frank DeMonte denied his own mother. But he couldn't embrace her, either.

"Give this to her for me." Harding pulled out a foot-long tube of waxed paper from the warmth of his jacket, like pulling out his heart from its hot cave.

"What is it?" Stone asked, taking the tubing without looking.

"It's the part that still cares." With that, Harding turned and walked out of San Marco County Hospital as fast as he could. Stone finally gazed down at what his hand had unraveled from the paper. It was the dark rose from Mrs. Harding's shrine.

His light was still on; in fact, Sergeant Fowler's figure blotted the yellowing shade like a birthmark, then moved away. Harding couldn't say exactly why he was there in front of the shingled two-family house, but he climbed the short stoop and, faced with two white-painted front doors, knocked on the left one, the one with the PBA sticker in its tiny window. Two foot clomps and a pause later, the door opened halfway, and Fowler stood and gazed at his weary visitor. The sergeant in his stocking feet and pajama bottoms was up and alert for the midnight hour, his misshapen body used to any time adjustments the police force shifts had put him through over the years. His white undershirt was sweat-stained and pulled out and over his belly, its cotton ribs pried open like irrigated farmland streaking the expanse of a steep hillside. The brown tinge from settled-in late snacks heightened the effect.

Fowler looked at Harding as if somebody had dumped a wailing baby on his doorstep, though Harding was as silent as the night air. The sarge wiped his damp brow on his forearm and backed off, moving toward the patchwork settee. His left hand had smacked the door as he retreated, allowing it to open fully, a sign to Harding that he could step inside. He closed the door behind him.

Fowler had a girlie magazine splayed open on the settee next to him and a glass of Kahlúa and milk in his hand. He no longer had the stomach for the Palm Tree's gin and tonics or its barroom palaver. After a final gulp, Fowler peered up at the bedraggled officer standing before him.

"Mr. Holdberg's come to see me, huh?"

Harding shook his head. Again: the Holdberg Technicality. Harding had read about it during his first month at Jefferson Law School. Back in 1919 in Illinois, somebody named Goldberg was convicted on fifty criminal counts, but at the appeal a court document was revealed, just one out of fifty court documents, and on that one document the name "Holdberg" had been typed up top and not "Goldberg." As a result, the conviction was reversed, all charges dropped.

When Harding quit law school nine months later and joined the force a year after that, he made two mistakes involving the Holdberg Technicality. The first seemed like a corollary to the case, a perverse addendum that Harding managed to provide. During his first summer he had written up a late-night arrest report on aggravated assault as fast as his hand could move across the form. He wanted to get home for a morning breakfast and some sunshine love, as June was taking a personal day from work and promised pancakes and other "sweets." Back that night for the midnight-to-eight shift, he discovered his suspect, Robert Porrent, had been released. It seemed a Robert Donut had made bail on his pickpocket charge, and when Officer Fanelli found the report he saw Harding's scrawl and read Porrent as Donut; the *P* bloated became a *D*, the double *r*'s became a crooked *n*, a peeled open *n* became a *u*, and a twice convicted felon—who kept mum during the errant procedure—became a free man. (Harding's mother always said he wrote like a Chinaman.) Of course, Fanelli never bothered to look at the differing crimes and physical descriptions detailed on the forms, but, nevertheless, Harding, a rookie, caught the razz.

Harding's second mistake was in telling his fellow officers about the Holdberg Technicality, in using it as an excuse for his actions and as an accusation against the system, a system that let Porrent escape, though Porrent was picked up two days later in a seaside hotel. His audience, which included Sgt. Fowler, listened to the casebook treatise and the youthful railing, then they nodded and laughed their asses off. Later on as a gag, they would scribble Harding's name on the weekly post roster so it looked like Hard-on one week and Half-done the next. For a month they would wave "Bye-bye, Mr. Holdberg" to anybody they set free from the holding cells.

Of course, with time everyone pretty much forgot the whole incident, everyone except Sgt. Fowler. The more Harding grew sullen and complained about the way the system worked its way around the truth like a snake winding through marble pillars, the more he heard "Holdberg" whispered in his ear from the sergeant's thickened lips. Maybe his real mistake involving the Holdberg Technicality wasn't his telling about it at all. It was his caring about it. His letting it become the loss you feel when you reach the bottom of the shot glass and not the joke you tell over the bar at the Palm Tree Lounge. Harding had a heart like flypaper: it tore easy, and everything you threw at it stuck for good.

Fowler lowered his glass between his open legs and leaned back. "Yeah, come to see the sarge who went loony tunes. That it, Holdberg? The night I figure I'll get to see you off my squad roster for a while for your bullshitting antics, they dump *my* ass because I tell them how some prisoner disappeared in his cell like a fucking Houdini. They tell me how maybe *I* need a rest. Maybe they shoulda told me to get some glasses, too. I know what I *seen*, for chriss—"

Fowler stopped himself, stopped his outpouring to the wall he always tried to break down, peer through, many a night. He didn't need Harding's impassive mug now.

Harding sat on a creaking lounge chair across the way. "The fuck you want here?" Fowler said, looking into the empty milk glass in his hand.

"I need your head," Harding said.

"What?"

"I need your friggin' head!" Harding rubbed his roughened mouth with his hand. "You got some water around here?"

"No, I got hot-and-cold running cow-tit juice," Fowler said, raising his glass. "'Course I got water. Glasses in the cupboard."

Harding stuck his mouth under the kitchen sink tap and slurped, then splashed water on his face, his mustache dripping two rivulets along the tile floor as he returned to the living room. Fowler sat grumbling to himself, wondering why he'd let the deadbeat in.

"You were around when Stone's father was a homicide lieutenant, right?" Harding asked, using his uniform sleeve to dam the water flow from his face.

"That was thirty some years ago . . . but sure. I was a

baby. Youngest sergeant in San Marco history. Was on the force six, seven years by then. No college boys then. We were all right outta high school and glad to go, believe me."

Fowler drifted out of his past-evoking trance. "This is what you mean, you want my head?"

"That's right." Harding sat back down.

Fowler shrugged. "What do you care about my career all of a sudden?"

Harding refrained from saying "I don't" but played politic instead. "I need your savvy to tell me about Lt. Stone, what you knew about him. . . ." Fowler looked at him suspiciously. Harding leaned his head back on the chair cushion, trying to stay awake. If he stared at the paisley-printed wallpaper enough, he'd have no trouble. "I'm doing it for Dale's sake. He may be getting himself in trouble about his father. I need the inside line Dale never got." Harding lied as good as he knew how and relied on Fowler's love of telling tales of glory days gone by to override any reticence, even toward him.

"Butch Stone. Jesus Christ." Fowler got up to get more milk. "His son, that Dale, he's twice the cop his father was. 'Cause he's got his hand on the controls. He knows where the walls are. As a cop you got room, but it ain't no ballroom. Today—it's more like closet space." Fowler pointed his finger in spite of the other four digits precariously holding a glass milk bottle by the neck. "But you haveta know your limits." He nodded as if he expected Harding to nod with him. "Doesn't have his father's balls, sure, but he's got the common sense and plays by the book—the job gets done right."

Fowler put the milk back in the fridge and slid his socks back around the half-wall partition that designated where the living room left off and the "kitchen" began. "*You*—you're another story."

"Get off me," Harding said. "Okay? I'm an asshole. Tell me about Lt. Stone and the way he operated."

Fowler eyed Harding as though he felt Harding knew what he was going to say, and in part, Fowler was right. "Let's say it always worked out that he pushed the right buttons, got his suspects to spill most the time."

"Spill what?" Harding asked with an edge.

Fowler laughed. "Whatever needed being spilled." The sergeant blew out his cheeks. "I got no respect for the man whatsoever. It got him out early—"

"Forced retirement?"

"Yeah. All hush-hush." Fowler playacted, putting his index finger straight up perpendicular to his lips. "Some cops still bash people, don't get me wrong, but Butch Stone made a fuckin' Broadway show out of it, you know? Cost him his badge and some extra years of retirement benefits. Cost other people some things, too, but . . ."

Harding looked inquisitive, and Fowler, liking the idea of his misfit cop suddenly attentive, took a slug of milk like it was first-rate Scotch and continued.

"It was his East Coast jaunt, joining his New York friend in homicide for a while, help him nail down a big-time hood—"

Harding mumbled, "Max Turley."

"You heard this story!" Fowler was getting annoyed.

Harding knew why his instinct sent him here now, realized how Beans Fowler was yet another part of this slick towline across time, one he kept shimmying back and forth across, and always bumping into Max Turley at both ends.

"I heard of Turley," Harding said. "A real murderous scumbag. The Devil of Something-or-other."

"Delancey Street, that's right."

"I heard nobody could put a finger on him."

"No—" Fowler belched "—body ever even got a picture of the son of a bitch. Made his rep even scarier."

Harding suddenly thought of Max Turley as a force, some lurking malevolence with no physical substance, like a bad gene.

He leaned forward in his chair, precariously so, for he was overtired and ready to drop. "So didn't Dale's dad go out there and try to help his friend in homicide nail Turley's ass?"

"Sure," Fowler said. "And that's what I'm talking about, the cost. Listen to me. Stone goes and does his punching-bag routine on a bunch of Turley flunkies he picks up here and there in New York. Even roughs up Turley's old lady a little—not in a station house grill room or nothing, just on the street, in public. Like I said, with Butch Stone it was a Broadway fucking musical."

Fowler's face grew flaccid like a rubber inner tube exhaling its last bit of pressurized air.

"A week later one of Turley's boys blows away a cop in his prowl car, then sets fire to it. Nice piece of work . . ."

Harding knew the punch line and tried not to listen.

". . . only this cop, this dead cop, is the New York detective's son, Stone's pal, *his* boy."

"You're saying it was retaliation?"

"Nobody knows nothing for sure. But you figure it out. I heard through upstairs sources that Turley was a butcher, but even when up front he maybe dynamited some Joes who stiffed him for loans or whatever and two other guys, innocent guys, got wasted with them in the blast, the dicks usually found out later, those two innocent Joes weren't so baby fresh, you know what I mean? That they maybe did drug deliveries for Turley's enemies years before. You get me?"

Harding was mum.

"He had reason!" Fowler shouted. "The bastard always had reason. But when the kid patrolman got torched, they couldn't find no reason, no connection."

"Maybe he was offered to be on the take and he refused," Harding said, remembering what the old lieutenant had said at the lunch table.

Fowler grunted, "Maybe. But I heard the kid never said nothing about it before. Look—all I know—and that's the grapevine included—is that Stone shows up in New York, 'helps' his homicide buddy put the heat on that scum Turley, and then his cop son gets fried like an egg. You tell me." Fowler's face became a logjam of wrinkles. "You're not planning to tell your partner about all this crap?"

Harding wondered why Fowler never gave him credit for having a body with even one decent bone in it. "Right. I'm gonna tell him his father was the cause of a cop's son getting hit by a gangland thug. That he got himself booted off the force for grazing his knuckles on one too many jaws in interrogation. I was just about to write him about it, but I ran out of personal stationery. Why'd it take the department so long to catch on to the fucker, anyway?"

"What the hell do I know?" Fowler said. "Times change. Chiefs and commissioners get the heat from the press. Some wide-ties said that after the Turley deal, the lieutenant came back and pulled his shit harder and harder. Like I said before, no control."

Harding laughed through his nose. "So they give him his bungalow and pension anyway. Better than fingering one of their own, that it?"

Fowler didn't answer; he just got up and stretched and belched and breathed in the stale odor of his unvacuumed carpet before he snatched a dish towel off the half partition and wiped the sweat from his face. Fowler's sudden rise might have been a signal for Harding to leave, but if it was, the drooping officer missed it.

"What about Gunther?" Harding asked, almost slurring his words inaudibly. "Know anything about him?"

Fowler reslung the cloth over the short wall. "Who's that?"

"Turley's number two in New York. Got Turley killed."

Fowler rubbed his stomach as though consulting a crystal ball, then he shook his head. "Don't know him. Knew Turley finally got *his* by some gang member, but . . . don't know no Gunther. That his first name or what?"

"Never mind." Harding fell back and closed his eyes, watching the rainbow blotches swirl inside his lids.

"How come you know so damn much about Turley, Lt. Stone, and crap?"

Harding spoke with his eyes shut. "Don't know that much. Just a few clues. Like I said, I think Dale's in trouble."

"Clues, huh?" Fowler stood above Harding now, darkening the lidded backdrop where the colors danced more slowly. "I think you're full of shit 'cause you're always full of shit. But I know your type. You're the type to go private when you quit the force. Notice I didn't say retire. Yeah, you'll get paid to go looking for trouble like cheating wives and missing husbands."

Hiding in the dark shell of his eyes, Harding wondered if it counted when the wife was your mother, the husband your father. And what *was* the payoff anyway?

"And it's a sure bet," Fowler continued, "you'll be bitching about the department to people on the outside, what a joke we are to you."

"I don't find shits like Lieutenant Butch Stone too frigging funny," Harding muttered.

"And what are you, hotshot?" Fowler turned and sat back on the settee. He suddenly looked tired, lumbering, like an aged elephant about to topple sideways, and sad. "You remind me of him," he said quietly to the floor.

"Protect the law by breaking it. Squeezing the shit out of it, anyway. He had some kind of anger driving him, I don't know—you? You're just a depressed son of a bitch. But that'll do it, too. Just as good as being mad all the time. Two sides of the same coin in my book."

Harding opened his eyes and looked at the frowning sergeant, who raised his head and looked back.

"That's right—who are *you* going to get killed?"

Harding was too tired to fight, to care, to disagree. They sat in silence for a while.

"You on duty?" Fowler asked, wondering why Harding was in his blues.

Harding shook his head no.

"Yeah . . . glad *I'm* off. Go in there now, I get the eyes, you know? They all put some imaginary straitjacket on me 'cause I seen what I seen." Fowler took a deep breath. "One more cop shakes his head at me like they just seen a mutt get crippled . . ."

"I don't know if it's worth two cents to you," Harding said in a low, sincere tone, "but I believe your story."

Fowler looked at Harding for a second, then grunted out a laugh. Harding dropped his head backward, pulling his lids back down, interpreting the grumbled laugh as another denial, another assurance he was alone in his dream.

"Need a place to crash," Fowler said hesitatingly, "I got this old cot. . . ."

Harding snickered to himself; as far as he knew, he had crashed days ago. But Fowler heard the snicker as another winging gunshot, felt himself the butt of a gag, of yet another cheap joke. For the next twenty minutes, he gazed warily at the officer opposite him as Harding dropped off in the lounge chair; it was an uneasy watch, like guarding over a sleeping bear.

* * *

Harding stuck the humpbacked Buick anywhere he could, probably a good five feet closer to the corner than it should be, but the haze of the afternoon sun dictated it. It also dictated his agitated, accelerated pace to the Helmsley Building. He couldn't believe that it was almost one-thirty, that he had slept over ten hours. That the entire time was spent comatose and crumpled in a sagging armchair, he could easily believe; his gait featured a hitch in his thigh joint and a lower lumbar region suffering from dull aches one moment to near petrification another. After he had awakened to the alarm of Fowler's neighbor at her son's sudden dumping of his lunch, he hobbled in a fog to find the sergeant laid out on his mattress, the sheets and blankets thrown off toward the bottom of the bed and bunched like discarded paper. He left without a note; what was he going to say? "Thanks for the fucking backache—Holdberg."

In the Helmsley lobby, the stench of ammonia invaded his nose. A rag-ridden scrub lady laid her mop against the wall and bent to lift her dented tin bucket a few more feet to the left of the spreading sheen of wetness that covered the floor. His footfalls made her raise her head, and toothless, she smiled a caved-in smile. Harding nodded, touching the brim of his fedora, then heard a ding. It was the elevator, and the sudden recall of the ambush by Thick Dunbar and Frisky stopped him cold. Not to mention the imminent appearance of good ol' Scooter.

Seeing the bottom platform elevator descending to the first floor and into view, Harding snatched the mop from the scrubwoman's hands. Frightened, she jumped and said something disdainful in what sounded Slavic, but Harding ignored her and ran to the side of the shaft, propping himself and his mop straight up flat against the wall. He heard the gate open, saw nobody come out, but at the first sign of Scooter's shoes poking out, he hitched the mop back and, like a baseball bat, swung it as hard and as level as he could. It was a Ruthian blow, the mop head striking the flaccid-faced elevator man dead in the nose as though smacked with a tangle of dirty gray worms. Scooter flew off his feet at impact. Driven sprawling to the rear of the elevator floor, he landed flush on his spine, sending a shock of pain through his body and his legs up through the air like a rocketed V.

Harding quickly pulled the cage of the elevator shut from the outside and, sticking the mop handle through the diamond-shaped metal grating, poked the control handle to the right, which started the elevator upward. Just before the elevator's floor became as one with the lobby ceiling, Harding jammed the metal mop handle diagonally into the corner opening. The elevator crunched the obstacle as would a punch somebody's belly, but then it jerked to a stop, the bent-up mop handle having had the last word.

Harding handed the bewildered washerwoman a twenty-dollar bill and told her to take a long lunch. He didn't think she understood his English, but his money was comprehended with little trouble, and she left nodding to him, smiling, sloshing her tin bucket beside her as she pushed through the revolving doors. Marching up the stairs, his back stretched sore, Harding heard the elevator alarm ring again and again in the near-deserted building.

When he burst into his private eye office, Laura suddenly stood, startled, her eyes wide and worried.

"What happened to you? I didn't know when you wanted me to leave last night. I was all alone here." She stopped her gesticulating and watched her boss move past her, his limp not as noticeable with speed, and into the back office. Laura followed, scraping her pumps on the floor in her rush. Harding threw down his coat and hat on the sofa with his body coming in third.

"You look plenty awful," Laura said, standing in front of him in the same blue-and-white dress she'd worn yesterday, confirming Harding's thoughts about it being not only her best dress, but maybe her only one.

"I *feel* plenty awful," Harding said. "Any messages?"

"Have some coffee?" Laura asked, nodding yes for him.

Harding gave her a flattened-out little smile. "Sure." All he could scrape up at Fowler's was some cold brew left over in a pot from yesterday, but he didn't have a match to light the stove and couldn't find any, either, which didn't surprise him much: since Fowler liked his beans cold, probably his coffee was guzzled minus the benefits of fire as well. So he'd drunk what he could of the previously overcooked concoction and found a semihard doughnut leaning up against a loaf of rye in the bread bin. The steamy brew that Laura blew on softly and cupped in her hands like a precious chalice bore little resemblance to Fowler's daily morning mud.

"Thanks," he said, sounding civil. "Sorry about yesterday. See? We trust you already." Laura chuckled and sat next to him on the couch with a piece of notepaper.

Harding took a deep gulp of the coffee, still tense. "Where's Berner with an 'e'?"

Laura handed him the notepaper and shrugged, her lower lip a soft, protruding ledge of pink. "Gone. Said he had some foreclosures or something. He a landlord, too? Boy, was he steamed about the ring you swiped."

"Yeah, yeah," Harding said as he winced at a sudden backache, having shifted himself too quickly.

"You hurt your back?" Laura said. "Let me see. I got great fingers, remember? Strong from typing." She moved her hands under his jacket without Harding's consent or protest and began to knead his lower muscles, her fingers long, her nails painted and pinching. Harding jumped at one sudden stab. "Sorry," she said. "Trying to grow them. Got this sore in a fight, I bet."

Yeah, Harding thought, a ten-hour struggle with a soggy cushion.

"I used to do this for my pop when I lived at home. He did construction work with a partner. Got him looking old too soon. Wore out his body."

Harding was silent; he let the cool hands stroke his spine, let the strong hot coffee feed his brain caffeine.

"How old are you, anyway?" Laura said.

"Body age or in spirit?" Harding asked with the spirit of an ageless zombie.

Laura squeezed a handful of shirt and an excess stratum of fat at his side. "This stuff I got a handful of," she said over his right shoulder into his ear.

"Easy to figure," he said. "Just count the rings under my eyes."

She jabbed him with a penknifelike pinkie nail. "I'm being straight now. Level with me."

Harding shook his head. Zero, he thought. It's 1949: he was zero years old. "Thirty-six," he said.

Laura nodded. "Not too old."

"What's that mean?"

"That means you're not too old," Laura said matter-of-factly.

Harding pulled his head around and looked at Laura's coy smile, her arms still elbow deep under his jacket. "But are you old *enough*?" Harding said in a deep tone of voice.

Laura kept her arms under his jacket, her hands flat against his back muscles, heating them like conductors. "Not now if you don't want, but later . . . maybe do something special this afternoon . . . tonight?"

Laura wasn't smiling. She sat in a still seriousness like a

lily seemingly frozen in the center of what was really a warm, placid pond. Harding watched her full, expectant eyes and wondered how much younger she was than his mother, not so much the withered dying mummy in the hospital bed, but the secretive, duplicitous thief and adultress; wondered certainly not so much physically, but spiritually. In spirit, Laura was as unborn as *he* was in body; and he wanted her. He wanted her in anger and in lust. Her breasts were crushed against his shoulder blades and felt hotter than her hands. But the general dullness that shrouded his mind also dulled his physical desire, his limbs like empty tubes. His numbing agitation overcame any arousal. "Maybe," Harding said, smiling sadly. "Sometime." He pecked her on the lips. Then the note, which had been held unnoticed in his hand, passed his gaze and stirred up a harder, truer desire.

"My father called?!"

Laura's eyebrows slid together in puzzlement. "Your father?"

Harding became agitated. "I mean—you know, Mr. Harding." He felt two sources of warmth slip down his back like furry animals fleeing their invaded sanctuary, Laura sticking her hands in the crease of her dress between her legs.

She looked at Jonathan, who let out a long breath. "Johnny?" she said, then realized she was addressing him by his first name. "I mean, Mr. Hard."

He looked at the pretty girl who was more concerned than hurt. "You sure you're okay?" she said.

Harding reached out and touched her right cheek. It was smooth, and he caressed its curving slope. He nodded yes. "I like Johnny . . . now, anyway. When *you* say it."

She nodded in response and watched him walk thoughtfully to the phone, watched him dial as though flinging the holes out of his finger's way. Harding sat on his desk, a leg up, the bum, stiff leg, and spoke into the phone briskly. "Mr. Harding, please."

After a still minute where Jonathan could hear only a murmur of traffic and Laura's breath as though again at his ear, his father answered.

"Mr. Harding. Johnny Hard calling. You have something for me?"

"Yes," his father said. "Bad news. I won't be needing your services any longer. I'm sorry."

Jonathan dropped his leg off the desk free-fall with a thunk, his body standing but slumped. "Wait a minute. What happened?"

"I'm sorry," his father repeated. "I really can't afford a man who is a murder suspect working on my situation."

"That doesn't wash," Harding shot into the phone. "You knew this about me yesterday. You knew about Romero's murder yesterday."

"I'm aware of that, Mr. Hard. And I don't believe you did it . . . necessarily. But I've thought about it a good deal, and I can't afford the risk at the moment. Please understand my position."

"You're lying to me," Harding said almost as a quiet plea.

"Please send me your bill through the company. Not here. Good day, Mr. Hard."

His father then hung up. *"Why are you lying to me?"* Harding yelled, though holding a lifeless receiver. He placed the phone back on the hook without looking, turned, and saw Laura standing up, her hands wrapped around her bosom, her head cocked so that her golden G clef of hair sat nearly upright. "We lost a client, I guess."

Harding shook his head dazedly. "We didn't lose a client. He can't lose me that fast. I just *found* him." What could have happened last night? he thought.

"Found him? Didn't he come to you?" Laura asked, getting confused. Harding grabbed his hat, figuring at some point he would deliver his bill personally, but right now he wanted to meet the other half of First Star Chemicals.

"Where you going now?" Laura asked, making a grab for Harding's sleeve but missing.

"Got to see a man named Snell," Harding said.

"Who?"

"Clifford W. Snell. Why? You know him?"

Laura dropped the corners of her mouth, shaking her head. "Not my type. Sounds too snooty." She noticed Harding wasn't paying much attention as he checked his gun, then moved to the door. "Johnny."

Harding looked back. Laura was leaning on the couch, the curved outline of her dress like two S's staring at their opposite reflection.

"Betcha two bits his middle name is Woodrow." And with her finger she poked up the tip of her nose as a sign of snobbery.

"Yeah," Harding said. His gaze lingered on her fetching posture for a moment.

"See you this afternoon?" Laura said. The door closed; she stared at it, unsure whether Jonathan didn't hear the question or heard it and chose to let his sense of mission ignore it and the soft felt brim of his fedora deflect it like an ancient shield.

The man in the portrait did not exist, of that Harding was sure. This man had a full thatch of black hair, swept up and secure, as forthright as his look. Blue eyes dominated what would have otherwise been called a bloated face; they softened his skin color, smoothed out his cheeks. Harding hadn't noticed such eyes through the dirt-streaked window last night, and certainly the smudge of a newspaper picture with his father held no clue. The beard looked the same: clipped and precise.

The man was stocky as well, the painting squaring off his shoulders with an edge of power and wealth befitting his dark suit and pose. But all this prestige was cut off at the waist by the ornately etched lower frame and the brass nameplate attached that read Clifford Woodrow Snell.

"Son of a bitch," Harding whispered to himself, amazed by the sight of the middle name.

"Mr. Belanger?"

Harding's gaze lingered at the office portrait for a few seconds longer before he realized he was being addressed. He turned to the secretary before she had a chance to say the name again, catching the question in her breath as though she had swallowed a fly. She was a middle-aged woman, unattractive and efficient, both qualities symbolized by the shafts of pencils piercing the bun in her hair.

"Mr. Snell's meeting is over now," she said from her desk.

Harding heard the rumbling of voices from behind her, businesslike tones with the jolt of a laugh here and there, an insider's laugh. Four nondescript men appeared out of the paneled doorway, two pairs of two, passing Harding, not acknowledging his appearance except possibly as the designated marker where they all started to button the top button on their suit jackets before going outside.

A fifth man appeared, unsmiling but talking continually, followed by Clifford Snell, who wore a grin as solid as oak. Still jabbering, the fifth man shook Snell's pliant hand and left.

Harding watched Snell kick out the prop that held his grin aloft and squeeze his palms together as though flexing the muscles under his vest. This was not the puffing, tomato-cheeked face Harding had encountered from the fire escape, which surprised him. In spite of the well-cut gray suit, Snell looked the aging, gypsy bull, a thickset body supporting a waning handsomeness, but handsome just the same, his face full, well fed, and ruddy. The hair was as thin as he recalled, yet he looked half his father's age just by the swagger in his gait.

"Mr. Snell," the secretary twanged, "a Mr. Belanger says he's here to see you."

Snell looked at Harding from across the maroon carpet while still speaking to his secretary. "I haven't the time."

Blue eyes: Harding was struck by Snell's cool gaze. Some paintings don't lie, he thought.

"Mr. Snell," Harding said, rising from the elegant, high-backed armchair, "we had an appointment."

"I remember no such thing," he said sharply. "My secretary will—"

"Dolores Harding made the appointment for me. Remember? She recommended I see you."

Snell dropped his arms to his sides like a tin soldier. Harding smiled and waited while Snell shouldered his grin back into position. An earnest shake of the head and Snell shot out his hand toward Harding. "Of course. My mistake. It's been hectic today. Please come in."

Harding shook his mother's lover's hand. It gave in to his, then pinched down as though driven electrically and held its grip. Snell reminded Harding of all the county board members and industrial gladhands his wife came up against in her fight for the county hospital and all Tweenum district projects in general. Their mutual antipathy for the corporate bureaucrat was one of their early and important common bonds; her ability to deal, to wrestle money from them under the guise of "ethical imperative" (he hated her speeches, he really did), and his inability to sit still for any of the compromising ritual tore at that bond continually.

Harding ripped his hand away from Snell's without looking at him and moved toward the back office. The office was plush, and everything inside swam in beige and brown—a solid front except for a thick red pen that slashed across the tan blotter. Glancing back, Harding noticed Snell conferring with his secretary, so he swung around the doorway and out of his sight. The wall before him displayed in large, dull-gold lettering FIRST STAR CHEMICALS and beneath it a list of subsidiary company names, each etched on a brass strip and screwed to the wall: KLEEN-AID CO., DROMEX CO., DYETRIDE BASE AND GEL, INC.

Harding browsed over the top of Snell's desk: a few inventory reports and a few personal letters he must have brought from home. Harding made note of Snell's address on Canyon Hill Road.

Snell entered and pointed to the dark brown chair in front of his desk. "I asked we not be disturbed."

Harding nodded, then noticed two nameplates on the floor adjacent to the oak desk: SANIFOLD & ASSOC. and RINEHARD GLASS TUBING INC.

"Casualties?" Harding asked.

Snell saw what Harding was referring to and laughed, flipping his hand matter-of-factly. "You could call them that, yes. We're consolidating, in truth. Business is off. A lot of stiff competition after the war." Snell swiveled himself behind the desk, his shoulders forward and in position to land, elbows down, on the blotter. "But that's not your concern, is it—Mr. . . . ?"

"Belanger."

"Mr. Belanger—is it? What is?"

"Mrs. Harding."

Snell picked up the red pen and began to doodle idly on

an empty pad with such a flourish to his strokes as to suggest he was practicing his contract signature.

"You said she recommended you. For what?"

Harding ignored the question. "You know her well?"

"I couldn't say 'well.' We meet, of course. Social gatherings when she and Nat attend and I along with my wife. Why do you ask?"

"No other time," Harding said.

The pen drew in red and ran a sudden straight line for the first time. "Mr. Belanger," Snell said curtly, "state your business."

Harding was ridiculously fascinated by the patterns Snell had weaved onto the pad, an intricate, tight web of red lines curving into each other that made you see shapes that weren't there.

"Okay," Harding said bluntly, "what do you know about an apartment at three twenty-nine Nuart Street?"

"Nothing. Should I?"

"You know anything about Dolores Harding using an apartment, that apartment, on Nuart?"

"For what? What are you talking about? How should I know what Dolores Harding does and about apartments?" Snell stopped drawing altogether now and looked at Harding dead on and motionless.

Harding stared back, then shook his head as though braced by a cold wind and shot out of his chair, turning away quickly, then just as quickly back again. He dropped palms down on Snell's blotter, his face dropping, too, inspecting the somber features of the man before him, almost breathing his breath, almost shoveling his nose under his skin. Snell backed off not an inch.

"You guys," Harding said softly, deeply, "you guys that lie with a straight face and a three-piece suit are the best. Slum people, they always sweat somewhere or twitch a leg once or twice. But with you tweed boys . . . a guy can't tell if it's you or your friggin' oil portraits, even when crap runs out of your mouth."

Snell spoke calmly. "Is that it, Mr. Belanger?"

"Is that it?" Harding raised himself to his full height. "I'll tell you what 'it' is. 'It' is what you and Dolores Harding do on Nuart Street a few times a week."

Snell nodded with understanding. "So . . . you think I'm seeing Mrs. Harding on the side? Is that what you're saying? If you came in with your little trick just to accuse me of that, you're—"

"How do you explain your visit there last night, then?"

Snell laughed. "I didn't see Mrs. Harding last night, or any other night. So you can leave now." He put his head down and shoved aside the doodle sheet for business documents, his pen hovering above the print in review.

"I saw you there myself, you lying fuck!" Harding shouted.

Snell looked up nonchalantly. "Then you have very poor vision, Mr. Hard." Jonathan cocked his head as though his ear had maybe failed to catch the word. "Yes, I know who you are. I saw your picture in the newspaper yesterday."

"That mug shot gets around," Harding grumbled.

"And I don't talk to ridiculous private eyes or possible murder suspects."

"Oh, but you do," Harding said, squinting his eyes like a mask of Wisdom. "Why the hell you let me in here in the first place if you already knew who I was? What made 'Dolores Harding' the magic words? What do you think I know that you wanted to find out?"

Snell dotted an *i* as though he were poking one out. "Nothing," he said flatly as two security men entered and stood readied.

"We're being disturbed," Harding said to Snell.

"No, *you're* the one who's disturbed, Mr. Hard," Snell said, pointing his red pen at him, "if you think I'm having this drummed-up affair. Don't come here again. Take him away."

Harding threw a heated look at the guard to his left, whose arm reached halfway between them and hung there frozen. Untouched, Harding moved through the doorway and, knowing it had not been closed behind him, stopped cold five feet past and took a fast but clear look over his shoulder before four meaty hands moved him along. It was a stale trick learned from his mother, who would catch him with his tongue stuck ten feet out of his head at her when she left the room after a beating or with his hand inches from where he *did* hide the one good steak knife he wanted to use for cutting rope and whittling sticks into arrows. He used the same trick on his own children, and it worked on Snell, too.

Only Harding didn't catch Snell shoveling pistols under his blotter or secreting perfume bottles in his drawers. He caught Snell without the prop of an easy smile, without the fluid stroke of a pen, without the dried veneer of business and authority—amazingly Harding caught a glimpse of the red-faced, fearful man from last night who stood just inside the hallway window, a lost man who was now looking just beyond his desk as though he had stepped out onto a dark and slippery ledge.

Harding bit on a hot dog he had bought quickly through his car window and kept his foot steady on the gas pedal with the image of Clifford Snell's ashen, anguished look filtering itself through the hazy, gray horizon. The twilight grew dreary, with a shaft or two of yellow spotlighting dried-out palms or the dull crowd that moved underneath them in rush-hour tedium.

If anything, Harding, in comparison with the listless, surrounding throng, had speed infused within him. His car swiveled in and out of potential traffic knots, and blood skidded throughout his body in a similar fashion, all prompted by anxiety and Snell's fading face on the darkening horizon.

Harding churned over and over why Snell let him in the office in the first place. Did he want to confirm whether Harding knew about the lovers' nest and now he knows Harding knows? If so, does that mean a shift of plans? A good-riddance motive for his father's murder? And how does it fit in with his father's phone call, which, in effect, fired him? *Does* it fit in? Maybe his mother revealed everything last night to his father—the thefts, the adultery —and her confession was enough to drop the "gumshoe" from his seedy duties. Not likely would his father tell a man such as Harding he was forgiving his wife, forgetting her past sins: that would be showing his heart too fully. But what if he were not forgiving her at all? What if such a disclosure prompted anger, action, something she would reveal to Snell, to Gunther, even, and ask for lethal help?

Harding's mind closed in on itself as the dusk on the day. He was speeding to his father's house, hoping for truth, willing to settle for less if thrown a shallow beam of light. The office was on the way, and he wanted to stop in to pick up any messages (maybe his father already reconsidered?) and to tell Laura to go home for the night.

The "Out of Order" placard strung up on the elevator's closed doors briefly and paradoxically reassured Harding that some order could be made of things even if it meant swinging dirty mops in everybody's faces.

"Hey, Laura, I owe you two bits," Harding said sardonically, walking into the reception room expecting Laura's bounce and coming up empty. The front desk was deserted, and the door to his back office lay half-open and led to darkness.

"Laura?" Harding pushed open the door with the heel of his palm. The blinds had been snapped shut, so the only available light hovered over Harding's muscular shoulders, wrapping around him, pushing his shadow before him, and highlighting the right side of the couch. Breathing, the sound of a woman's breathing, Laura's breathing, steady, readied, came from the left side cloaked in black, then Harding stumbled: he looked down and saw he'd stepped on a blue high-heeled shoe, its mate dead on its side, two steps ahead. Farther still, the bottom of a dress, of indiscriminate color because of the dimness, was outlined in the light and draped on the floor, most of it having been pulled into the dark.

Then Laura's legs slowly appeared, toes first, from the left half of the couch and into the glowing right half as though brought on stage by cue. They were nyloned legs, firm legs, barefoot and restless legs. They sidled up against each other, the sibilant sound of nylon on nylon luring the mind into thinking that somewhere beyond the hiss, through the darkness, hips were shifting with dynamic purpose. While the yellowish light was absorbed by the tanned, curved calves, it was reflecting brightly off of ten hard red nails as toes rubbed the bump of an ankle or massaged the weary, upholstered couch arm.

Harding stood still, watching.

"Laura? Listen . . . I know you wanted to do something special. I'm not sure this is the right time."

Then the thick smell of rose-scented perfume overcame him, spun his head, gagged him: he knew it wasn't Laura.

"I didn't think there was a *wrong* time, Mr. Hard." His mother's face appeared in the light above her arms, which wrapped themselves about her legs as if she were cuddling two children come in from the rain. She was expressionless, her eyes were lidded blue, she was naked except for a strapless bra and a shiny, silken half-slip that rode up her dark thighs as she sat up.

"Your Laura said she had to go on an errand." She

smirked. "I guess I sent her on one. Made her go to my special druggist. Fainting spells, I said." She struck an ersatz Garbo pose, the back of her hand touching her forehead; her right bosom surged upward and nearly mounded over its cup. Then she shrugged with a half smile. "She's a gullible girl . . . she'll be a while."

Harding turned his head away, found himself staring at the kicked-in waste can, locking his vision and revulsion there. His throat had a rock in it. "What are you doing here?"

His mother raised her shoulder, licked her lips, her eyes shooting left, away from Harding toward the same battered can. "Things that need doing." She looked at the stiff detective. "Do private eyes always ask dumb questions?"

She slid off the couch and rose up slowly and quietly like candle smoke, then moved toward Harding. "Last night. When we talked . . . when you were watching me dance . . . I felt something move between us. Something deep. The way you looked at me . . . you felt it, too." The voice was calm, barely, but the words sounded rehearsed.

His mother was almost against him; the tip of her brassiere gently poked his chest. Harding took a step back, still looking away, his lower jaw straining, his blood shot to his head.

"Look at me," she said in a pleading but commanding voice.

Harding turned his gaze toward her.

"See?" she said, her eyes darting, searching his eyes as though she were looking in and around a maze of walls and doorways. "I wanted to come here and feel that bond again. Feel closer. Have something to share . . . an exchange of favors."

Harding nodded, his voice raspy, constricted. "Now we get to it."

"What do you mean?" his mother said, her eyes drifting in the intensity of his gaze.

He kept nodding. "I mean, you were always a lousy actress."

"What?"

"Exchange of favors—that's the point."

Her breathing became heavier, a sign of slippage, but her body automatically undulated in compensation. "Sure . . . that's part of it."

"All of it."

"No. Sure. We could do things for each other." She reached out and touched his arm. Her fingers were chilled, damp; her fire-red nails impressed his skin. "We need each other, Johnny."

"You do me, I do you."

"Something like that."

"I don't tell your hubby about the apartment you got set up on Nuart, that it?" He watched her face try to stay frozen in the mask of cold seduction. He suddenly snatched her by the shoulders and shook her in short, hard jolts, so that maybe this facade of youth, this soft husk of flesh, would expose its fissure points and crumble off her, would reveal the decrepit, dying, cancerous woman from behind the hospital glass. "I lay off you and Snell, or you and the racket you run on the jewels, or you and who-the-hell-knows . . . Who told you about me, my operation here, what I might know . . . Snell? That'd be pretty damn quick. Or maybe you two had it all planned out last night. Gunther tell you? My pictures in the damn papers tell you? Who? What?"

Fear swept over his mother's face now, her pale blush reddened. "Does it matter?"

"Yes, it matters! Goddamn right it matters. 'Cause laying off—that's what I do you. And you do me?"

His mother reciprocated, grabbing Harding by the shoulders; she squeezed. "Look," she said, eyes welling. "They'll kill you. They're on to you. I'm saving your life. I can't say . . ."

"And *you—do—me?*"

His mother was against him now, thigh to thigh, chest to chest; she held on to him as she would a treacherous mountainside. Black mascara circled her eyes, ran together in droplets on the crests of her cheeks. "And I do you," she said in a whispery voice, shaky, scared, but determined to try. "Now . . . any time, anywhere—here, later. You can call me." She tried not to shake up against him. "I know you want me. I know we can work something out . . . please. . . ."

Harding stared as his mother raised her chin, licked her lips, parted them for his taking. Harding struck her across the mouth with his open hand, catching her with more palm than fingers. The smack made her reel to the left, and snatching her, he shoved her near the couch and smacked her again. His mother screamed and struck out herself, hitting him once hard in a sore rib, then slashing his face with her nails. But only after Harding yanked her flailing arm and felt his other hand fly up and form itself into a tightly wound fist did he think of what Gunther had said about beating mothers until they spit quarters, did he suddenly start to cry himself, start to lower his fisted hand in shame and push his mother up against the sofa's arm, making her fall back into the cushions, where she cried hysterically, covering her face.

Then Harding moved deliberately toward his mother and, grabbing her wrists, pulled her arms down crossways to her breasts, covering them, hovering over her like an electrified storm cloud. "What are you doing here?" he said an inch from her face, red and smeared with fear. "Who are you protecting? Why are you protecting them?"

His mother was shaking her head from side to side, sucking in her lips. "Do you hate him that much?" he shouted. "Did you hate my father that much? Did you?"

"Leave me alone!" she screamed at him finally. "What are you talking . . . about? Please. You're talking crazy!" With her head back, sunk in a cushion, her tears were running down her throat, choking off her words.

Harding leaped up, pulling her arms with him, dragging her off the couch. She was sobbing, and her body, dead weight in surrender, fell to the floor. He threw her arms down like harpoons. "Get out!" he cried. "Go back to Snell. Go back to your lover!" He kicked at her empty shoe. "Go on—move!"

His mother frantically scrambled on all fours across the rug, sweeping her hand across her face to get the thick black hair away from her eyes, the lip-drawn blood out of her mouth, scooping up pieces of clothing as she scuttled along, her knees burning on the rug.

"You're crazy!" she screamed, and stood shakily.

Harding had dropped onto the couch, holding his hands out away from him as though waiting for rain from the ceiling, for something to drink from his palms. He watched her spin toward him and spit on the carpet. Harding stared into her hateful eyes a moment; he felt hollow inside, devoured from within.

"I hope," he said, and swallowed dry. "I hope whoever it is you're protecting . . . is worth your husband's life."

She started to talk over his last words in anger. "Worth more than *you'll* ever be!" she said, her voice seething. Harding didn't watch her leave; he sat and watched his hands shaking instead.

The hurried clip-clop of high heels from far away drew near, and Laura ran into the back office. "Johnny! My God, what happened?" She sat down and swung her arms around him, leaning forward, trying to look into his hidden face, which was like trying to look into an eaten-out hole in a large tree. "Was that Mrs. Harding I saw ru—"

Harding nodded.

"I don't get it. I couldn't find that store and came back to ask . . . Was she—?" Harding raised his hand. Then he looked at Laura's frightened face, felt her hands kneading his arm, his back, while still holding him. He looked back down at his hands, at nothing, while Laura dipped her head, used the flank of his arm as a cushion.

That's when the Devil walked in.

"Hey, Johnny! Whaddaya know? Nice you should come in." The Devil strutted up to Harding, rotating his black fedora in his hands. He leaned down and threw a thumb over his shoulder: "So who was the dish with the full-bloom petunias?"

Laura stuck out a chin. "Hey—shut up, Sol."

The Devil's brow furrowed into two hard humps. "Look, butter buns, don't tell the boss man what to do."

"Shut it, Sol!" Harding snapped.

The Devil put on a mock frown and nodded. "So that's how it is now. . . ." Harding watched the Devil drop into his wooden swivel chair before he turned to the girl holding him close. "How about getting me a drink?"

Laura nodded. "Scotch or something?"

Clearing his throat, Harding shook his head. "Just water. From the cooler down the hall." He really wanted enough to take a shower, or maybe drown, in.

"Sure thing." Laura looked at Sol as she rose. He was sitting beyond the splash of light from the front office, though his eyes appeared luminous and, if she thought about it, red orange. But she avoided his gaze as she passed him. Then she stopped suddenly and, stooping down, picked up a bracelet with small, blue-white gems and held it dancing in the yellow light. "This Mrs. Harding's, right?"

Standing up slowly, Harding looked at her and nodded.

"I'll put it somewhere, I guess," Laura said, and walked out of the room.

"Oh," said the Devil's voice from the dark, "it was Mommy."

Harding ignored him and gingerly tucked in part of his shirt, which had been yanked out and partially torn near his old bruises.

"This is a helluva show, Johnny," the Devil said, leaning over his desk, his hands entwined, appearing in the glow like a crystal ball. "My dance card's been filling up lately. Clients been keeping me busy. So clue me in on the details."

Harding fixed the knot in his tie, licked his lower lip and tasted blood. "Fuck you, Sol."

"Hey, buddy, I'm along for the ride, and your life's a regular loop-the-loop. That's why I gave you this setup. Now spill."

"Read your own contract. Nothing there about your good times. I don't have to tell you squat." Harding snatched his hat from the floor.

"Seems like natural curiosity to me to wanna know what you an' your mother's bazookas were doing in the same room together," the Devil said matter-of-factly. "Let alone what your old man really knows about this. Then there's the murder. I mean, who refried the beaner Romero, anyway? That's if it wasn't *you*. And what about that fire-haired sister you bumped into at the casino? What's her hand in this card deal? You see *her* bazookas yet?" The Devil's voice floated to him as if on a boiling river. Standing still and sweating, Harding didn't understand why he didn't just leave the room, why he stood there, eyes closed, clenching his fists, thinking he deserved it, wanting to hear more.

The Devil got up and moved to the immobile Harding and whispered into his ear like a lover, "I just think you should keep your partner happy . . . I can burn your ass."

Harding's muscles twitched and finally moved the rest of him toward the door.

"Johnny!" the Devil roared, Harding feeling a hot, dry wind ripple down his back, stopping him. "The ring, Johnny."

Harding nodded his head to no one, then turned to the Devil.

"Hand me the ring . . . now." His palm was open, cupped, like an empty cauldron. Harding reached into his pocket and pulled out the heavy ring. He inspected it for a second, then, glancing at the Devil, tossed it at his feet, the ring bouncing twice and landing a yard behind him.

"Bend over, Sol," Harding said. Then he marched out the door.

The Devil stood there, cut in half by the front office light, and closed his empty hand on itself, forming a fist, his thumb rubbing against his fingers like sticks of gray, hard flint.

Laura looked at the road and cars that *whoosh*ed by like blurred memories, then at Harding, who was driving. She was afraid to ask. She had handed him a mug of water when he'd rushed out of the back office and he'd gulped it down, looking at the bottom of the empty cup as if he saw his reflection or a bug. He had handed it back to her without a word and walked out and down the hall. She had shouted, "Wait!" not wanting to stay alone with Sol for some vague, fearful feeling, having glanced back in the rear office and seen only a headless fist struck by light. She had jumped into the passenger seat of the Buick without a protest from Harding, with only his eyes like misguided beacons glancing off her, then to the dashboard, to the road, to the wheel.

But in the middle of the traffic whirr, and a banking right, she asked him anyway: "Mrs. Harding . . . did you two . . . ?"

Harding didn't look at her. "No." Then he looked at her, a lingering look, one that made her uneasy if only because it felt a moment too long not to be looking at the road. "That make everything okay?" His voice cracked like the snap of a branch. She shriveled in her seat.

When they arrived at the Harding house, Laura trailed Jonathan by two steps, his gait long and fast. The maid looked perplexed at Harding when she opened the door. "Mrs. Harding isn't here at the mo—"

"I know that," Harding barked. "*Mr.* Harding I want."

"He was called to the laboratory on an emergency."

The door was closing; Harding stopped it with his body. "Where's that?"

"The factory on Millbrook Avenue." She got the door shut this time, but Harding didn't care.

The First Star Chemicals building was a massive pile of bricks, well ordered and stacked in wide stretches of windowless red until the upper floors, where multipaned windows filled with dirty, pocked glass peered out but were obviously blind. Pale green sheeting slanted off its roof, the stamp of an artless industry having listless coloring top its sturdy forms.

Harding saw but one dot of fuzzy white from a center window, a cyclopic beam. He leaped out of the car, and as Laura followed, he turned on her. "Stay put!"

"Why?"

"Do it!" he said, and spun away, moving quickly toward a corrugated metal door that cracked open like the broken jaw of a whale. Harding squeaked it open wider to fit himself inside. It was dark, and he stood listening to nothing as his eyes adjusted to the room. Nothing in particular formed into recognizable shapes, and just the slightest echo to his breathing told him it was a large, empty expanse, possibly a delivery area. He squinted and crouched, finding a doorknob with his searching hands about twenty feet away. The door led to a stairwell, which he climbed to the only other way out three flights up. The top door opened onto a hallway, dimly lit by the EXIT sign above his head and at the far end by a half-opened door that allowed a slab of pure white light to escape to the opposite wall.

As he closed in on the light's source, an acrid smell, far worse than the one at his father's home lab, struck his nose and burned tears from his eyes. Harding pulled out his handkerchief and covered his nose and mouth, commanding himself not to cough. He fought through the stench to the door and looked inside. The expansive laboratory was fully lit and completely empty of people. He grabbed a pair of goggles that sat on a workbench and held it up to his face to relieve his watery vision. This particular section of the lab had fuller vials, deeper stains, more complex-looking equipment and tubing, so that whatever activity had taken place here had been messy, intricate, and more important, interrupted.

This discovery pushed Harding back through the doorway. His rapid search up and down corridors led to locked doors and huge glass cabinets filled with canisters with unpronounceable names and unapproachable ooze.

Finally Harding hit upon an opening that almost led him into free-fall. At least it seemed so because of the sudden appearance of three stories of open air. In fact it was the companion room to the one he had first entered, only this large, cavernous expanse was filled with endless aisles of boxes down below, supplies or shipments; he couldn't tell. The only way down was from his current position—a four-foot landing atop a gray metal winding staircase that corkscrewed its way into the concrete floor far below.

From the stillness, the dim horizon of crates, Harding heard a murmur, deep, like the somber voice you hear from a distance coming from a confessional, unintelligible but full of judgment. The landing hugged the upper wall another ten feet away from the stairs, and Harding slid along the extension to possibly peer down other aisles, to locate the well-deep whisper.

Suddenly he saw a shock of white. Down the third aisle, a man stood with his hands raised talking to someone unseen, to a blackish extension that wavered near the man's face. The man was draped in white, his hands were white, as was the top of his head; from this perspective he looked as though he were a troubled ghost or a robed priest lifting his hands while preparing the sacrament. A sharper look revealed it was his father in a loose white lab smock, white lab gloves on his upright hands, a large white skullcap keeping most of his hair hidden, and a pair of goggles slung around his neck. It was *his* voice that murmured darkly, that droned within this chemical supply vault. And it was a gun-filled hand that wavered in front of his face, inches away, silent.

A different hand clutched at Harding's forearm. He ducked and swung his fist, driving off his left leg to make sure his attacker, and not he, toppled over the short railing. His muscles lurched as he adjusted his swing the second he saw it was Laura. He dipped his shoulder enough so that his fist brushed her astonished face and pounded the wall with little impact. His other hand snatched her body, which had instinctively jerked away from the blow and was about to flip over the rail. But he yanked her to him, his arm locked about her waist like a handcuff, her nose touching his.

"What are yo—?"

Harding shoved his wall-bruised hand over her mouth and shushed her. "I *told* you—" he hissed through his teeth, then stopped. Her eyes looked scared enough . . . maybe even as scared as his. "Just relax," he whispered calmly. "And keep quiet. My father is down there, and someone has a gun on him. I've got to go down and see who it is. Okay?" Laura nodded as Harding removed his hand, her lipstick having imprinted his palm like a tattooed kiss. He let go of her, but she didn't let go of him. She hugged him to her, then stepped back. Harding pulled out his gun while Laura stretched her neck to one side to catch a glimpse of what he'd told her about.

"That Mr. Harding?" she said in a hush.

"Yeah . . . so?"

"I thought you said your father?"

Harding shook his head. "Forget what I said. Stay out of sight. If they move away before I can get to them, get a good look at whoever has the gun."

"But maybe we should go get the cops, you think?" Laura held on to Harding's arm, not wanting him to go, the movie getting too big, too close, like sitting up against the screen—it made you dizzy.

"We don't need the cops."

"Why don't you keep a watch out and *I'll* get them."

"No. No cops."

"Why not?"

Harding ducked his head level to hers. "I can handle it, that's why." He almost added, "Besides, he doesn't die here. Not like this. Not with a bullet."

Harding pushed past her and began his circular descent to the storehouse floor. He glanced up once and saw this beautiful girl at the darkened railing watch him as though she were about to set out into the night on a massive ship while he whirlpooled down into the murmuring danger below.

At ground level he slipped past two quiet rows, gun drawn and upward, and poked his head around the final one. There was no way to slip behind whoever held the gun; the boxes were bunched together too tightly and randomly behind the confrontation. He would have to climb a mountain of cardboard and look as obvious as a planted flag. So, taking long, slow, graceful strides, he moved deliberately down the aisle in which his father appeared in profile, speaking to what looked like a disembodied gun barrel stuck near his mouth.

Harding smiled as he drew closer. As a cop he had noticed that when he had the drop on a perp, the farther the suspect raised his hands, the more frightened the jerk was. One fifteen-year-old tire thief had stretched his arms so high, it was as though he could grab hold of a breeze-blown, nighttime cloud and fly the bust. But his father's hands were barely at head level, his spine arched back like a rifle in a rack. His voice was clear now and defiant.

"—what the point is. So now I know. Now what? The game's over, wouldn't you say?"

Harding kept moving toward him. He hoped that he wouldn't catch his attention yet, and when he did, that his father would immediately look away, act normally, as normally as you could with a gun in your face, and would realize who Harding was and be ready for Harding's final move.

His father's gaze left the gun's barrel, dropped away and downward; his posture turned soft and sad. "I know I'm to blame for this," he said more to himself, for himself. "My damn show of standards—" Then his father saw Harding approaching, nodding.

His voice cracked. The gun hammer clicked. Harding stopped.

His father's eyes rolled up to heaven, to the black-grid warehouse ceiling, a checkerboard with only dark squares, just as the gun blasted and a bullet poured through his right ear.

Harding screamed as his father's skull blew apart, his scalp tearing off in chunks like a split coconut, his face spreading, then flying out, ripping itself away, making room for the erupting bone beneath. Harding screamed again and bolted forward. It wasn't clear if he screamed his father's name, or God's, or a loud, long, *"No!"*—but in the unsettling echo it all became a burst of vibrant white noise signifying little, changing nothing.

All that remained of the gun barrel was a wisp of trailing smoke. His father's headless torso collapsed on its legs of paper. As though in sympathy, Harding stumbled and fell to the floor midstride, cracking his chin. His hand landed on something soft, something fleshy and thick with his father's blood. He cried out, and as he shuffled to his feet, a bottle flew past him, a full bottle with a flaming tail. It exploded to his right and blew him backward, back to the floor and into a stack of boxes. Flames dove toward him as though from celestial heights, as though out of the dark ceiling, as stacks of fire-engulfed crates fell at him. The fire popped to his rear, in sequence, small, tense explosions; the smoke was suddenly dense enough to smother all the air and strong enough to burn through your eye sockets.

Harding could see nothing left of what was an aisle, could see no way to what was left of his father's body. He called out, his arm shielding his eyes as best it could, but parts of the roof were falling out of the darkness and dropping like dying stars, full of light and heat.

One such beam dropped a crooked line of flames at his feet. He jumped back, swung away to one side, and slammed into a high stack of sturdy crates yet to be ignited. Instead, as one being, they leaned forward and began to topple. Harding looked up, his eyes seared, his hot vision watching, seeing a blur of brown come at him, like the dark, oversize rock in his dream, the tree with eyes, the falling shadow. But no all-encompassing arms pulled him from its path this time, no magic lasso. One box jammed his side, another grazed his head, a third was a full body blow. Harding lay buried under the shadow-tree, a bed of fire to become his grave.

A siren floated. And skin was being stroked. Wet. He opened his eyes, and the handkerchief traversed his brow again, then down each cheek. Harding looked into Laura's tensed face. She dabbed his forehead frantically as though blotting runaway beads of ink. He jerked up from Laura's lap as more sirens whined and blasted.

"Johnny," Laura said, trying to hold him down. "I think you're hurt."

They were nearly a block away from the blaze, up a hilly street, where below stirred a billowing thicket of smoke from which another sudden blast jolted Harding, shocked him into a freeze-frame of the gunshot, the head bursting. Harding closed his eyes to escape the moment, but it only brought the sharp picture of his father's death directly on top of him.

"I got you outta there as fast as I could, Johnny. I figured from what you said before—you didn't want any part of cops and all."

Harding couldn't speak; he struggled to stand. A fire engine *whoosh*ed by, took the hilltop flying, and bounced once hard on the slope down into the fire that covered the base of the block.

"Did Mr. Harding—" Laura said, then stopped when Jonathan looked at her, tears pushing out from his eyes. It all fell in on him now. It all really happened. Shaking, he stood and watched his father's fiery grave rage on, burn his insides out.

"Makes *me* sad, too," said a voice just behind him.

Harding swiveled sharply and saw the Devil nodding, frowning at the inferno below. "Homesick, really."

Harding sobbed and looked back into the fire, trembling. He let out a loud, wretched cry, a cry of souls lost in a dance of flames, of skulls planted in dark holes. His mouth was a wide, gaping wound. Then his teeth clamped shut, and he twisted and swung at the distracted Devil, landing a hard, sharp, perfect right-hand shot to his upper jaw. The Devil flew off his feet and caromed into an adjacent stucco wall; the jagged plaster smacked the back of his head, then scraped it like so much bloody cabbage on the slide down. Laura shouted at Jonathan, but Harding—breathing heavily, looking for more—took another step toward his fallen partner. She finally pulled his arm around to face her.

"Stop it!" she shouted above the din. "We have to get the car before the cops find it sitting down there."

Harding appeared to nod as Laura led him away but was suddenly overcome with coughing from the smoke that had risen up again in his lungs. So too like smoke did the Devil rise to his feet. So quietly, in fact, Harding's heart shivered when he turned during his march down the hill and looked behind him. The Devil stood erect. His eyes glared down his nose as they would a gun sight, his face angled upward, exposing two taut veins in his neck like bars in a jail cell. The Devil raised his arm and pointed his finger at the retreating detective, Laura tugging at him, Harding stumbling forward as he gazed back. Then the Devil slowly brought his finger back until its tip touched the one vein and drew a deliberate arc to the other. Blood traced his finger's sinister path across his throat and dripped to the sidewalk, onto his black wing-tip shoes; blood spurted from each taut vein and flowed down his wide tie and sharply creased pants. When he finished, the message was delivered. The Devil wasn't smiling at Harding, but his neck was, a vile and gory grin that meant there were ways, quiet as a razor, for contracts and necks to be broken.

· nine ·

I f Laura had but grabbed Harding's tie as she led him, a distant passerby might have thought a girl was smuggling a large, upright animal, drugged and lumbering, into her apartment building for some peculiar reason. Unleashed, Harding was no more the stunned animal, but a restlessness moved his steps sideways, then forward; his hands gripping, then ungripping, his eyes dead but focused straight ahead. He had said nothing in the drive over to Ditmore Avenue; Laura was smart enough to let the silence cushion them.

"My apartment," she said, opening the door marked 5B and letting Harding enter first. His step over the landing was awkward, and his knee almost buckled. Laura wedged herself under his right arm and steadied his crossing. She sat him in a green cloth armchair with dark blue arm covers that obviously didn't belong.

She poured a glass of whiskey from a bottle she dug out from the bottom of a cluttered closet across the way. "It's cheap," she said, shrugging in apology. "I mean—hell. Think I'm talking to a Rockefeller or something." She smiled and tried to laugh for a response as she poured. Harding just took the glass and downed it, wiped his face with his other hand; his sweat felt like a coat of motor oil, though he never attempted to remove his hat.

Laura poured an inch for herself and sipped it, making a face. "I can drink. Just the real bad stuff. . . ." She squished her nose. "Funny. The good booze I like shooting down my throat. This turpentine I sip like it's brandy. Only way I can get it down."

Harding drank another glassful quickly. His memory banks were too pristine, too polished like chrome, and etched deep. He wanted to cultivate fuzz and water it with Laura's rotgut. He wanted the picture blurred, the image ghosted, the film flickering, then burned out of his skull from the middle of the jammed frame outward like an expanding circle of fire.

"I guess I lied," Laura said, then looked at Harding to see if he responded. "It's not my flat—not totally. I'm kicking in my share, or will be once I get paid. But my sister will cover it for now. That's whose flat it is, anyway. My sister, Lucy." Laura looked away and sipped her drink. No face this time, except one of reverie. Her cheeks shone. "She sings real good. She's a singer for a band. That something? Little band, but they're sharp. She's at a gig up in Frisco now. Met Gene Krupa once."

Laura, who had been sitting on the arm of Harding's chair, got up and walked to the small kitchen. She slipped the hat off of his head on the way. It was as though she'd removed the shade from a dull red bulb as the gesture revealed a face flush with anger and bad alcohol. "I got some leftover chinks from yesterday after I got home late.

Chicken chow mein or chop suey. You should eat something." The clink of bottle neck and glass was the response from the next room. She didn't know how much more of this she could take.

Harding watched Laura's hips move back toward him from the kitchen, her dress clinging to her contours with the heat. She reached behind her and pulled off one raised-up shoe by its sharp heel, then the other. There was the sucking sound tight shoes make when a woman's foot slips out, an intimate sound, a drawing in from a pulling out. She padded up in front of Harding, closer to him now if only by her drop in height, her waist at eye level.

"My sister and me, it's crazy, we're all grown up and all. But we share a room again, like it was back home, and it's like we got into some time machine gizmo and we act like kids."

Harding looked up from her waist and met her eyes, licking the taste of perspiration and whiskey from his lips. He swallowed and nodded. "I got kids," he said. And as though for the first time in years, he thought of his children, of his own failed fatherhood, thought of his children not as abstract possessions—"having kids," like having unseen money in the bank or having a job or a good time—but as real beings, real two-legged pieces of yourself. Out there. Smoky wisps of memory now formed true lines and faces. David and his mopey eyes and whippet-thin body flopping for ground balls, first left, then right. He liked eating dirt, even as an infant. Suzanne and her tousled black hair devouring her face, tickling her baby-pug nose; Suzanne grabbing Daddy's badge, "shiny Daddy," she'd say.

"Shiny Daddy," Harding said, squinting, his head thumping, swimming. Laura slipped down onto his lap and wrapped her arm about his neck. She spoke with concern. "What's going on, Johnny? You gotta tell me what this Harding business is about. You're eating yourself up. You're fading on me. I think you're going to disappear on me like some spook or something. . . . Please, Johnny. Be straight with me."

Harding's hands went under her thighs, glided over her nylons, and he pulled her to him. He made love to Laura in a tangle of clothes and with a choking of dust from her stain-mottled rug. He wasn't rough, but he was sloppy. His hands moved randomly, distracted; his mouth took in all it could. Laura tried to slow him, guide him (it was far from her first time), but the knot they formed—of legs, half-trousered, and armless dress sleeves, of panties not completely removed but hooped over a raised ankle, of scuffing, scraping shoes and ties slung over shoulders—pulled tighter, squeezed harder, until the release that unbound them laid them flat on the floor on top of one another like thrown corpses.

Laura winced in pain, trying to remove his weight from her hipbone. Maneuvering sideways on her back, she pulled free and rose up in the shadowy heat. She caught and bundled the top of her dress at her chest as she walked to the bathroom, her body feeling stiff and wrinkled. She sat behind the closed door on the closed toilet seat and dropped her head in her hands. That it was not "like in the movies" was no longer a surprise. That it was no different from in the back of Mr. Buckner's market or behind the abandoned concert shell in Hackett Park or any of the dozen places she and some boy had poked and groped their way into each other . . .

After a few minutes, she pulled the dress all the way off and dropped it on the floor. She wiped the tears from her eyes, the sweat from her upper lip. She straightened her slip. She wanted to finish her drink. She stepped outside the bathroom and was surprised to see Harding no longer prone on the rug.

"Johnny?" she said softly. She swiveled around and shivered as she realized he was gone. Her quarter-filled tumbler of whiskey sat on the rug, but the rest of the bottle was gone, too. Her jaw tightened, and she kicked the glass with a swipe of her foot. It flew up and cracked into jagged pieces two feet up the wall. Among the shards on the floor a yellowish puddle gathered like something a dog would leave behind.

Harding rode his power over Time as recklessly as he had ridden Laura's body. The liquor had risen in him, finally pouring into his brain, his loins—and now he bounced freely over years.

He remembered throwing the whiskey bottle at a statue of a naked Greek god at the entrance to Sunview Park in 1949 and scraping his cheek and nose on its base in 1986, seeing if he could smell the cheap booze in the full moonlight thirty-plus years later.

He remembered leaning against the thick glass, cupping his face to cut down on the harsh hospital glare so he could see inside. He saw his mother's face more clearly, the tubing having been removed from her mouth, the cubical demonic guards reduced by one. Her facial contours were as sunken and serene as a parched hillside. Then he let his whiskey breath fog up the glass he was almost kissing, wanting it to mist, seeing his mother, her ancient valleys, disappearing into an alcoholic fog bank, fading, fading, gone. A female voice said, "Officer?" and he ran. He ran as if he had been peeking at something dirty, forbidden. He ran so that a night duty nurse wouldn't catch a drunken policeman in uniform.

He remembered standing amid the smoldering factory, watching the acrid whispers of gas meander toward the blank-faced moon, feeling the ashes of boxes and wood inside the brick fortress, the dust of chemicals, commingling with his father's. He removed his fedora and bowed his head. And whose dented skull lay beneath the warped cellar floorboards, then?

He remembered sitting, peering over a rooftop—the station house rooftop? the rooftop of his mother's love nest?—it was a familiar perch from which he peered downward, measuring the distance to the street below, looking up to the smattering of stars, then dropping his gaze to the sidewalk, his head plunging till the snap of his neck. He remembered teetering on the roof's ledge as he sat, extending his arm and flipping back and forth in time, watching his hand that held his fedora one second that changed to a blue officer's cap the next, then back to a fedora, then to a cap, to a fedora, then cap, fedora, cap, fedora, cap—until he wondered if he could possibly cause the friction of Time to disintegrate him, to powder his soul and free him from the Devil.

He remembered the trunk. He remembered entering the dark room, removing the artifacts from his mother's shrine, and flipping the lid open, diving in with two hands, scooping out old clothes and picture books. It was as though he were shoveling a hole in the ground. He found an old World War I canteen. He found a large folder filled with canceled checks to somebody named Doris Huntsford. He found an envelope that looked as though it had documents inside. He found a gold star he'd made out of heavy paper and given to his mother from kindergarten. He found himself sadly floundering on the floor, picking up the broken wedding picture and cutting his finger on a sharp wedge of glass and dripping the blood deliberately on his father's face, blotting it out, making his head a gooey red ball atop a morning coat. He touched his own neck with his bloody hand and wondered again whose skull lay creased in the cellar if not his father's. Who had died with his father's ring on his finger? Did his father have the ring on at the factory?

He remembered all this as his head began to clear and the booze began to drain from his system, standing, weaving from fatigue in front of Laura's apartment door hours later with the dawn about to emerge at his back like a questioning onlooker.

When Laura opened the door he walked straight in, not looking at her. Then just as he turned to face her, she smacked him hard across the face. Harding took it without a word.

"You bastard! You want another shot at me or something? That what you hired me for?"

She didn't want to, but she started to cry and punched him even harder on the chest. "You liked me 'cause I don't take shit. Well, I don't take shit from *you*, either! I thought when I left home, I left the kinds of creeps who kept their shoes on just in case something better came along while they were doing it. At least I knew what the hell they were about. But you I don't figure. Except maybe you take a girl's booze and anything else she's got to give and don't say two peeps to her."

She pummeled him with wild blows, slobbering, tired. "It's not fair!" She stopped hitting him and grabbed herself with both arms as though holding herself together. "I thought you liked me," she said, weeping heavily now, her legs melting beneath her.

Harding grabbed her by her arms to keep her up, and she leaned back, pulled away with the force of her dead weight. But he lifted her to him, bowing his head to hers, holding her to his breast, feeling her tears wet his shirt, her hands grab at his back, kneading.

"I'm sorry," he said. "I'll tell you everything. I swear it."

Laura looked up at his worn, ragged face. "I swear it,"

he said again. "Let's get some sleep, okay? I gotta get some sleep."

They lay down on the large double bed, which leaned to the left, and held each other for a while. Harding dozed off with his shirt and shoes still on. Laura rose from his arms and slowly pulled off his shoes. Then she retreated back into his body, her head floating on top of his gently heaving chest.

The sun tried to sear its way into the room, but the shades, burnt orange with the midmorning heat, prevented its intrusion. Only the white-hot edges glowed through, the windows like illuminated squares squeezing light out their borders. Harding lifted his heavy eyes halfway to the sensation of a smooth leg sliding over his loins slowly and deliberately. His one popped-open eye spotted Laura beside him, her green eyes quietly caressing his face, her lips pressed together in a wry smile, spread like a conjurer's hands readying to reveal a cluster of fragrant flowers from thin air. He felt her body next to his, up against his, and realized she was entirely naked. He felt his stomach pinch as she yanked his belt end to free it from its buckle. Her leg never stopped rubbing up and down, and he gently brushed the blond web of hair that dangled sideways on her cheek, against her nose, and he dipped down and kissed her softly on the lips.

Laura smiled, then giggled once, before she pulled on his neck and head and passionately kissed him open-mouthed. Harding slid out of his pants and watched Laura lie there, angled, her hip stuck out, much the way he'd first seen her standing in the office doorway. Her toes played with his kneecap as he kneeled on the bed, removing his shirt. He leaned over and kissed her protruding thigh, his right hand following the curve of her buttocks around to the small of her back. He kissed and licked her hips to her stomach and on the way up to the eyes of her breasts, which stared tautly at him. He devoured her bosoms with desire, but without the hunger of disregard he'd showed her last night. He would caress her, feed on her, mold himself into her with tender passion, something he felt he had lost all moment for in his little cop world.

Sure Harding had picked up a woman or two since the divorce, even saw a few hookers he knew from the beat. Never on duty, but after hours; after his patrol had inspected the latest crop from the west side of town, he would return in plain clothes, uncomfortable. But the hookers he'd have picked out always thought him cute and liked his discomfort.

As he pressed himself closer to Laura, he breathed in her body; he loved the smell of her—a slight perfumed scent touched by a dewlike perspiration that grew with each movement, each passionate display. Harding loved the smell of a naked woman, how each held her own aromatic secrets. It had always disturbed him that June had no smell. She never wore perfume and never sweated during even the most heated lovemaking. He laughingly would say it added to her sainthood, until he overheard what was probably innocent, sound advice she once gave to one of her workers before a confrontational county board meeting: "Don't let them see you sweat." Afterward Harding couldn't shake that remark during their bedroom embraces (which became fewer and fewer anyway through the years), and her dryness, so to speak, her cool-skinned passion, always put him on the other side, as one of "them," as the adversary on the pillow of power.

Laura had her whimsical power over him now as she straddled him, smiling like a wicked nymph and moving with a rotational force that ground him into the dust of ecstatic extinction. He made sure her satisfaction was deep and long, and he reached for her caresses again and again, her legs and arms and tongue seeming to wrap themselves around him endlessly. Harding had finally lost himself, not in booze, or pot, or self-examination, but in this heady display of affection and need. Laura had become another pipeline across time, this time to his teens, to youth in flower, as sweet-scented as Laura's rosy lips.

Afterward they catnapped a while; then Laura got up and slipped on Harding's shirt, but it was soiled from days-old sweat and blood. She took it off and placed it in a sink full of soap powder and water. She settled for her sister's linen robe with the holes in the elbows and started cooking a few eggs.

When Harding fully awoke he propped himself up in bed, two pillows bolstering his damp torso. He swiveled his head, inspecting the bedroom and its peeling pink wallpaper. One wall had some cheaply printed posters tacked up announcing the Huey Wallace Band with singers Lucy Gabell and Irma Devore out in Hallsburg, up north. Sheet music cluttered up lots of dresser space, held down by an assortment of ladies' garments, mostly those worn to be unseen. A cot was spread out next to where he lay, taking up most of the floor between the window and the bed, which was probably where Laura slept when her sister was home from her tours.

He noticed an envelope leaning in the crease of the cot's blanket, noticed whom it was addressed to, and he bent over and snatched it from its resting place. It was already opened, so he pulled out the contents, read a few lines, then stuck the letter back into the envelope. Hearing Laura's padding feet, he calmly slid it under the sheet.

Laura entered the room smiling. Though her golden hair drooped about her forehead, it gave her eyes more allure, being half-hidden below. The top of the lime-colored robe had shifted, and her left breast had nearly escaped. "Guess what? I got a late breakfast in the works. And it's no leftover chop suey or nothing, so don't get wise on me."

"Eats, huh?" Harding nodded. "Who's Imogene?"

Laura dropped her smile as you would an unexpectedly hot pan. She brought it back up, halfway at best. "What do you mean?" Her hand unconsciously shifted her robe; her left breast fell back out of sight.

Harding shrugged. "Why the big deal? So your real name is Imogene Gab—"

"Gabell," Laura said, straight-lipped. "Imogene Gabell. So?"

"That's what *I* say."

"How'd you find out?"

Harding pulled out the envelope from under the sheet. "Your letter from home."

Laura stomped to the bedside and plucked the letter from his hand. "I think you're a swell guy, Johnny, but your manners stink." She threw the envelope back on the cot, then pulled the cloth tie with both hands, squeezing her belly with the yank. "Can't a girl change her name if she wants? Can't she change things she hates? Things gotta change, you know. And if they don't change for you the way you want, you gotta change *them*, even if it's just a stinkin' name. . . ."

Laura grew red and manic and was about to break into a fit of tears. Harding rose out of bed and kissed her, held her a minute before she spun out wildly. He sat her on the edge of the mattress and they held hands, looking at their hands squeezing each other, touching fingers, stroking palms, her fingers like pink stems delicate within his grasp; all the while she spoke about her leaving home, a town in a more rural part of the state, a town hurt by the influx of returning boys back from the war with no jobs or to depleted farmland.

Her brother, Jimmy, was one of those boys. He came home to drink his days away and let out his rage at night. Her sister, Lucy, left and came to San Marco because she was the one with talent. Her parents thought Laura smart, but that was an expendable commodity for a woman in a small town, and besides, she got too smart.

Laura told Harding about her wanting to be a quarterback, playing touchy-feely football with the high school boys at dusk. She told him about bedding down those same boys after endless nights at the movies where she'd force her date to see the feature again if he wanted what would come later.

And when she'd finally had it up to here with her life, she'd left without a suitcase since her sister was the same size and would share the world with her, left without a word to her parents who slept uneasily upstairs, left having to step over her drunken brother's tangled, inert body on the porch steps in a pose of spent anger.

She decided to leave her name behind, too; that's all. What was good for Lana Turner and Tyrone Power was good enough for her. Imogene Edith Gabell would not make it in San Marco, but Laura Gabriel might.

"But I still write home. At least, Imogene does. Laura doesn't need one." Laura rested her cool cheek on Harding's bare shoulder. "So I get letters back. My poppa sends me dough so I won't become a whore. My mother sends me dough figuring I am one already and need it to come home."

Laura raised her head and looked into Harding's face, inches away. "You'll still call me Laura, okay? Even better, I like it when you call me 'angel.'" Harding shook his head, suppressing a smile, but not well enough. "Hey!"

she said, putting her fingertip on his lips, outlining the arc. "That looks kinda swell on you. Wear it a lot more, okay?" Harding hugged her to him, kissing her neck, then her waiting mouth.

On a tray that looked as though it were stolen from a school cafeteria, Laura finally brought in the afternoon's breakfast, a spread of eggs and toast, decorously garnished with some kind of green vegetation. After she set it down between them on the bed, she grabbed a small potted flower from a dusty sill and stuck it on the tray with a laugh.

Harding nodded his head. "Looks plenty fancy."

"Not bad for a lousy cook," Laura said.

"Bet you're not a lousy cook."

"Oh, yeah?" Laura said. "Double or nothing on the two bits you owe me."

Harding poked at the garnish that sprouted near the dark brown sausage. "What's this stuff?"

"Frills." Laura took a breath and blinked her large green eyes. " 'The cheaper the cook, the gaudier the platter.' "

Harding deadpanned for a second; then they both chuckled as they dug into their respective dishes. Harding took a large bite, then looked at Laura with drooping eyes. Laura responded, worried.

Harding spoke through a mouthful of unswallowed food. "I owe you four bits."

Laura flung her napkin at him, laughing, as Harding put on a stuffed-face fool's grin.

It was late afternoon.

In the imperfect full-length mirror that leaned, unattached, against the bedroom wall, Laura was adjusting her pleated yellow skirt to the finale of a swing tune on the radio when she stopped.

Harding was sitting out on the fire escape, his pantsed legs jutting out between two bars and dangling, his chest still bare, drawing in the sun's heat, when he turned an alert ear inside.

The three o'clock news blurted its headlines on the airwaves with the name Harding drawing them both to it. ". . . when the chemicals exploded at the First Star factory, causing a fire which reportedly killed Nathaniel Harding, part own—"

Laura switched it off.

Harding's bodiless head moved into the open window. "Leave that on."

Laura stood there, her hands at her side, her lips tight.

"I said, leave it on," Harding snapped.

"No," Laura said, upset. "Only if you promise you won't go walking like you were dead or something, like before."

"Yeah, sure, now put it on."

Laura reluctantly flipped the knob. "—that it was an accident. Sources say that the company was working on a highly combustible chemical solution to be used as a lure to regain lost government contracts since our great war ended. Neither co-owner Clifford Snell nor widow Dolores Harding could be reached for comment. In other news, the mayor of—"

Laura turned the knob and watched Harding's head disappear back outside the window. She moved to the sill, saw his glistening reddened back hunched away from her, his shoulders abutting the fire escape where he sat as though in a small cage. The long, twisted black iron bars, like giant drill bits, bored holes through his fists as he ran his closed hand up and down their hard length.

"You promised," she said to the faceless back outside.

"Come out here," Harding said.

"Why?"

"Because I promised."

Laura tucked her skirt between her legs and sat beside Harding on this metal-grated overhang hovering above San Marco. He looked at her sadly, as though he were going to lose her, too.

"I said last night I'd tell you everything . . . so I will."

"You trust me," Laura said, almost as a question.

"Thing is, will you trust *me* after what I've got to say. There's a good chance I'm a fucking nut case, you know."

Laura laid her head on her hands like a bust on a pillar. "Try me. I got no corner on being crackers." She smiled but stopped when he didn't reciprocate.

Harding proceeded to tell Laura everything. From his discovery of what he thought was his father's skull, the deal with the Devil, his being hired by his father to nail his mother, the whole business, right to witnessing his father's killing seconds before the factory erupted in flames. Throughout it all—and it all took about half an hour; Harding thought it would take an eternity—Laura looked at him with awe, overwhelmed by the tale, as though reliving an amazing filmic experience. Harding saw fear in her eyes at the fearful parts, sadness at the sad parts— after a time, he wasn't sure it wasn't a myth, movie, or dime novel he was telling.

When he finished he couldn't look at her but heard her get up and go inside. Harding squinted at the wobbly sun for a minute, then moved indoors himself. He didn't see Laura right away—blue sunspots crowded his eyes—but as their dance and substance faded, he saw her standing before him, staring.

Harding picked up his shirt, avoiding her gaze as he put it on. "You haven't said."

Laura stayed quiet, bent over to scoop something off the floor.

"Do you?" Harding asked. Laura's eyebrows pushed upward.

"Do you believe me?" Harding said; he stuck out his hand as a gesture of inquiry.

Laura placed his fedora in it.

Harding looked puzzled. "You want me to go?"

"I want *us* to go," Laura said with a sly smile. "It's time we got back on this case."

"You're willing to stick with me?" Harding asked with uncertainty.

Laura sidled up to him and squeezed his chest. "Only through thick and thin. That's as far as I go, bub."

Harding laughed to himself, kissing her forehead, smelling her hair, afraid to question her further and jeopardize her faith in him. She pulled the fedora from his hand and propped it on his head, angled a bit for effect, and made an approving face. "It becomes you." She pulled away and toed a white pump.

Laura had that wrong, Harding thought. He had become *it*. He turned toward the long mirror and saw a regular, full-length private dick, except his father was murdered, his mother was no good, his partner was the Devil, and a bump in the reflection made his face wave like heat off a cement sidewalk.

"Think anybody will be working the casino now?" Laura asked.

"If not," Harding said, "that might give me a chance to poke around Harlen Gunther's office. Never made it last time. I need the link between him and my mother. Maybe it's there."

Harding stopped the car behind a low white apartment building that faced the box of bricks that housed the mob's casino. Harding and Laura approached the empty parking lot cautiously, then trotted to the doorway where the rock-jawed blond in white had put him through the frisk that rainy night. Thick flanks of wood like crossbones had been hammered across the frame, sealing the entrance either way.

"Place looks dead," Harding said.

"That's what you wanted, right?"

"Yeah, but it's been nailed up like a coffin. Business was way down. The mob might have finally shut it off."

Laura, wandering some yards away, glanced around the far corner, then upward. "Is this the right place?" she asked.

"Yeah, sure."

"I thought you said it was Rome Company."

Harding walked toward her, nodding. "That's what it said, or looked like through the rain, anyway."

At Laura's side, Harding looked up at the flat brickface two stories above them. The word ROME stood out fairly clearly in painted white letters, but only flaky patches of a beginning *D* and an ending *X* sandwiched the faint ghost of another word.

"Dromex!" Harding shouted.

"What?"

"Dromex Company. Come on!" Harding pulled Laura's hand from her hip and ran back to the car.

"What is it?" Laura asked, jumping into the passenger seat.

"Dromex Company," Harding repeated, gunning the engine on. "That's one of First Star's subsidiary companies. I saw it in Snell's office. On a plaque or something. He *owns* it, the son of a bitch. He owned it with my father, but who the hell knows if my father knew about the casino or *anything* that scum Snell did? Snell was the casino boss behind Gunther. Snell was taking the heat, which is why he looked so lost just after I left his office. This place was coming down on top of him. The mob joined in, too."

Harding screeched around the corner, bumping the curb, then pulled straight. "Where's the fire?" Laura asked, one hand clutching the dashboard.

"The mob doesn't like a casino of theirs having to shut down. We have to get to our pal Woodrow so we can ask him a few questions before he gets shut down with it."

"Know where he lives?"

"Yeah," Harding said, pushing past a red light. "Twelve twelve Canyon Hill Road. Saw it on a letter of his."

Laura shook her head and smiled at him. "There's those stinking manners again."

A black Dodge missed his back fender by three inches as Harding *whoosh*ed through the intersection, feeling the comforting heat of the wheel and road.

Canyon Hill Road was a literal "steppe" up from where Harding's father and mother had lived, at an elevation that nurtured cooler trees, greener foliage. A thick set of pines usually set the natural boundaries between houses, and sinewy roads were paved unlined, making it feel as though it were one long private driveway for the well-to-do residents on it.

Harding pushed the Buick up a sloping hill that had at its foot a mailbox right on the main road labeled 1212. He stopped just when the house nosed its way into sight.

"Stay here," Harding said to Laura. "And this time I mean it."

Snell's home was a jutting two-story structure with a weathered face made up of hundreds of large stones. Its angled roof spread out over where the hill sloped back down, so that an elevated wooden patio could stand on firm pillars and overlook the canyon's gradual decline into the wilderness.

Harding crouched on his approach, using the large, egg-shaped shrubbery as his shield, until he heard a tangle of branches being crushed underfoot from the back of the house, a thumping of ground, and snaps of twigs. He bolted up from his cover and ran forward. A dark-suited man was galloping down the slope at a ninety-degree angle to Harding, and in the distance flashed a gleam of green, not from a tree but from metal, flat metal, a car roof.

"Shit!" Harding spat under his breath, and ran back toward his own gray Buick.

"What's going on?" Laura said, watching Harding dive back behind the wheel and jerk the car into reverse so fast she nearly had her neck snapped off. Harding drove backward downhill as fast as he could without losing control of the car. He kept watching the woods alongside the road.

"What is it?" Laura shouted.

"There!" Harding shouted with a nod.

Laura looked toward where Jonathan was staring and spotted a blur of a man careening through the woods, losing him in one thicket, gaining sight of him through a hole in between tree trunks, as the Buick sped backward, nearly slipping off the road, swerving.

The man reached the green car, and instantaneously it moved. It jolted forward, bouncing through the uneven terrain, heading for a gap forty yards farther down the hill. Harding hit the pedal for an extra bit of juice, and his rear end caromed off a bordering slope; then, gaining control just in time, he kicked hard on the brake right in front of the green sedan, which had broken through to what it thought was empty road. The sedan hit the brakes as well and spun right. Harding spun in reverse, and both cars met side by side with a parallel clang of metal, facing in opposite directions.

Harding looked past a frozen Laura and into the passenger seat of the green sedan. The cigar looked somewhat familiar, but the round face looked even more so. It was Dooley Manson, the man in the casino parking lot trying to get at Carla's money. Or was it just Carla?

Manson raised a gun barrel to cigar level.

Harding screamed at Laura and pushed her and himself down in the seat. The bullet pierced the closed window on the driver's side, spewing glass. From his side below the window, Harding stepped on the clutch with his left foot and kicked the gear stem with his right knee. The car lurched forward enough so that the second shot missed the car completely. Harding bobbed up and jammed on the gas pedal, heading back up the hill. Laura peeked up from the front seat and saw the other car drive back down the hill and out of sight.

Harding drove right up to the stone house this time and leaped out of the car. He looked in a few side windows and saw no activity. An open window allowed him to slip inside a white-highlighted drawing room, but it was the open sliding door to the patio that caught his eye. The rest of the south side of the room was a line of screens that let the cool hillside air in, so there would be no reason for the door to the patio to be open unless somebody was using it. But it was also clear even before Harding stepped out onto the patio that nobody was there.

The sun loomed a descending ball over the treetops, an orange globe that centered above the one gap between the patio railing, above the tail end of a built-in wooden ladder for climbing below the house or down the gentle forest slope. Harding walked up to the sun, to the gap, looked down the ladder, and saw nothing related to gentility. He saw a man's body, facedown, at the ladder's base, his head oozing a dark substance.

Harding climbed down to it, turned the body over, and looked at Clifford Snell's dead countenance. His face looked tired, worn out more than shocked, by the loss of half its forehead. A convenient push saves on bullets, Harding thought. Then he saw Snell's red pen stuck in his chest, leaking either blood or ink—you couldn't tell. Might have fallen on it. More likely jammed home by Manson's gloved hand before the fall as a parting gesture.

When Harding walked back to the car, he heard a shout at his back. An old man in jeans and checkered shirt was looking at him, puzzled, from up the road a bit. When Harding only moved faster, the man started trotting toward the car. Probably the damn caretaker, Harding thought. He started the coupe and swiveled back down the hill as fast as he could.

Laura looked at Jonathan's beet-red face and cold sweat. "What was in there, Johnny?"

Harding shook his head. "Tomorrow's obit page."

On the drive back he told Laura about Manson, his probably being an arm of the mob, and Snell's demise. Harding speculated out loud, tested theories, getting angry at some, even angrier at others. Of one thing he thought sure: Snell was not only being squeezed from the top; he was being squeezed from the bottom as well.

Laura finally shook her head. "You're losing me."

Harding looked at her intently and placed his firm hand in hers. "I better not be." Laura gazed back at him and laid her other hand on top of her own, enfolding his.

It was dark by the time they hit downtown San Marco.

When Harding pulled the car to the curb, he leaned over to Laura and kissed her quickly, then spoke over the passing street traffic.

"Get this heap out of here and wait for me two blocks up. The alley off Kelso. I may be out with company."

Laura was about to say something when he kissed her again and hopped out of the car. He watched her pull away, then entered the adjacent apartment building.

The door he knocked on brought a few seconds of silence, then a muffled woman's voice answered.

Harding whispered back, his cheek near the door frame. "Open up, doll. It's me—Gunther. Hurry."

The door remained motionless, then cracked open three inches, a gap that widened considerably when Harding slammed himself against it. Carla backed off almost as fast, as the door banged into an end table and vibrated with the collision. Harding snatched its edge and threw it shut behind him.

"No, it's not your boyfriend."

Carla laughed through her large square teeth. She stood shaking her head in a red V-neck dress with jutting shoulders, her crimson hair piled up in parallel loops like twin Ferris wheels.

"What do *you* want?" she spat.

Harding spoke slowly, deliberately, watching Carla puff on a cigarette smeared with her lipstick. "You had some lucky night that night, didn't you, sister? At the casino, remember? You and lover-boy Romero working the final killing before the honeymoon? Only it was Romero's killing, and the honeymoon was really all set up for you and Harlen Gunther all along. You met Romero at your father's house, saw a moonstruck patsy you could manipulate, set him up as a dealer through your 'connections,' convinced him to swindle the casino nice and easy, then got him bumped off."

Carla pushed the nub of her cigarette into the ashtray as though she were sticking somebody's face into a pile of dirt. "You're nuts!"

Harding sat on the couch, watching her attitude, her looking away, her seething impatience.

"But let's back this story up a bit," he said. "Snell, the casino owner—as if you didn't know—sees the place dying. His second banana, Gunther, sees likewise. Snell's in deep. The mob kingpins hate losing money. Gunther sets this Romero scheme up with you so he can cash in on the downfall even though it makes Snell drop even faster. Gunther's real good at helping downfalls, too. He had lots of practice with Max Turley in New York City."

Harding rose from the couch, and Carla backed away toward the bedroom door.

"The mob probably wanted to see what the hell was going on at the casino, losing customers, losing money . . . They send a mug to check into things on the sly, and he sees you win real big that night I was there. Dooley Manson—remember him? Like me, he maybe nosed out a possible dealer-player setup. He grabs you in the parking lot, and who shows up in wrinkled armor?" Harding held out his arms. "Yours truly, sap number one. Romero had to go sometime soon, but with a fall guy like me handed to you . . . like I said, your lucky night. Besides, I knew too much and started being a pest. This sound good so far?"

Carla stood quiet until the bedroom door swung open and Harlen Gunther swaggered in waving a small, white-handled pistol. "Volume was low in the bedroom, but sounded okay, factwise." Gunther chuckled.

"About time," Carla groused. "What were you doing in there?"

"Listening, doll," Gunther said. "Listening to our crack-erjack shamus catch on."

Harding shook his head toward Carla but directed his anger more to himself. "I knew you let me in too easy. Too easy the last time, too."

"What's this about last time, smart guy?" Gunther asked.

"Getting to talk to Romero," Harding said. "I had threatened your sweetheart here unless she got me to see him, but she still relented pretty damn fast. When I caught her on the phone in the bedroom, I assumed she was talking to Romero. That's what she made it sound like, anyway, when I walked in. Dumb move. It was you. She was setting up the evening's entertainment—Romero taking the bullet and me taking the rap. I should have smelled something wrong at Romero's when he opened the door and acted surprised to see us. Only he wasn't acting since Carla hadn't called him in the first place." Harding let out a stale breath. "I got to get better at this private eye biz, what do you think?"

Gunther frowned, tilted his head. "I don't know. I think you're pretty good now."

"Only there's one gun showing and it's pointed at *me*."

"Yeah, not *that* good, sure," Gunther said. "Which reminds me, toss your piece to Carla like a good Joe, okay?"

Harding removed the gun from his holster delicately with two fingers as though it were a four-day-old flounder and tossed it on the couch.

Gunther smiled. "So tell me some more about my great scheme, okay?"

Carla fetched the gun. "Just plug him already," she said as she marched into the bedroom to finish packing a small valise.

"No. You get ready," Gunther said. "A little praise first. I like hearing about my success from other people. Not a lot of what I do gets appreciated."

"Gets too hot to hang around for the bows," Harding said.

"You got it."

"Did you always have your mitts in Snell's pocket?"

Gunther shook the gun along with his head as though they were attached. "No. But Snell was a jerk, and I saw that the mob boys weren't pleased with things. Snell got desperate, and desperate men got soft spots guys like me can poke at."

"And he was desperate enough to try some kind of blackmail scheme on his partner's wife," Harding said, hoping to hear the details.

Gunther nodded proudly. "I gave Snell that idea. 'Cause I knew the dope."

"And somehow you got your paws into that money bin, too. You got the jewels from Ridley the pawnbroker, and the money delivered to the casino by Mrs. Harding would get into Carla's winnings through the dupe Romero. Long way around, but a nice double dip: the jewels *and* the money."

"Easier than fooling with the books, you see?" Gunther said. "They catch on to that, those business guys, real quick."

"Lots of dough," Harding commented.

"You need it these days if you plan to go underground for a while."

"Hiding from the mob?" Harding asked.

"They'll catch on. Too late, but . . . right?" Gunther said with a grin. "We'll have new names, jobs . . . maybe faces, who knows, huh?" He chuckled and his free hand fished into his green suit pocket and pulled out a shiny gold wedding band. Harding stiffened: though no outer markings would ever tell him so, the knot in his chest told him it was his father's.

"See?" Gunther showed Harding. "We're going legit." Then Gunther, though facing forward, yelled behind him. "Right, honey?"

"What?" Carla said from the open doorway, still busy.

With his eyes boring in on the ring between Gunther's leathery fingers, Harding jerked forward, a sudden reflex of anger. But Gunther jabbed his gun toward him. "Hey! Keep still there, peeper. You'll catch a slug soon enough."

Gunther shouted behind him again. "I said, we're starting over, right, doll? Got the ring and everything." He glanced inside the band and addressed Harding. "Got initials, but what the hell, huh? N. H. and D. H." Once more over his shoulder: "How about Huntsford, Carla? Like that one?" His voice softened as he eyed Harding. "Like the rich family what lives up the coast. That them? Nick Huntsford. That's me. Distant cousin or such." His free hand straightened his silk suit and brushed across his gray mustache at the image.

Harding tightened. "Where'd you get that ring?"

"I didn't get it," Gunther said. "Dunbar got it for me. Offa the Harding stiff when he torched the factory. Thick always takes what I call 'souvenirs' off his hits, okay? Sort of his proof to me he done the deed. Nice habit. I like trinkets."

"So it was Dunbar who slugged me, plugged Romero, and took the watch the cops couldn't find . . . not you."

"Hey, I don't do such things," Gunther said, looking slightly insulted. "I'm the requester, remember?" He stuck out his free hand, allowing the sleeve to rise above his wrist, revealing a silver-plated watch, and put it to his ear. "Keeps good time, too."

Harding's voice sounded harsh. "Why did Dunbar have to kill Nathaniel Harding? Or torch the factory?"

Gunther shrugged. "Well, you know, I still worked for Snell. I had to keep it looking that way, anyway. And Snell wanted to collect some fast bucks on fire insurance, mob on his back, you know. Harding was working late, that's all. Besides he suddenly knew everything, and he's the type would probably stop his wife's little payoffs. Maybe even go to the law. Snell told me Mrs. Harding couldn't take it no more. That she had to spill everything to her husband no matter what. Snell even went to her flat the other night to strong-arm her not to tell. Didn't work. So we bumped Harding and burned the place." Gunther's face lit up in discovery. "Another 'double dip' job, right?"

"What about the blackmail?" Harding said, persisting. "What did you have on Mrs. Harding that you told Snell about?"

Carla came out of the bedroom with the lightweight valise slung over her shoulder.

"Don't matter," Gunther said. "Thick is taking care of Mrs. Harding and her secret right now. Tie up loose ends, like that."

Harding's face faded into a dense white as his stomach dropped.

"What's wrong, Hard?" Gunther said. "You look like a lost pup."

Carla set the valise at Gunther's feet. "I'm ready. Nail him and let's blow."

Harding stared at Gunther's smug features, his pressed green suit, his newly acquired ring flickering in the brutal light from the shadeless bulb of a stand-up lamp. He noticed that the light cast a thick, shadowy outline on Gunther's face, ringing his eyes in black, his cavelike nostrils rounded black, the deep valleys in his cheeks sunken black, and suddenly Harding saw fingers turn bone, face turn skull, and he knew: he had met such a face.

"Ever go to a fortune-teller, Gunther?" Harding asked.

Gunther snorted. "No. Why?"

"My crystal ball tells me you got one, maybe two years to live. Then you're going to meet a tall, dark cylinder of lead." Harding nodded toward Carla. "She'll introduce you."

"Shut him up already," Carla said.

"Yeah," Harding continued. "You both go underground all right. Only she pokes her head back up. You stay for keeps."

Carla's eyes flared at Gunther. "Shut this bum up!"

"Cool off, baby," Gunther said, smiling. "Condemned men always talk bullshit before they die. It's funny."

In disgust, Carla stepped away from the other two and happened to glance out the window below. Disgust was shoved aside by fear.

"Damn it, Gunther! The cops!"

"What's that?"

"The cops. The cops," Carla said, annoyed. She looked closer now at two cars double-parking out front, one a black-and-white with two uniformed officers spilling out, the other a brown, unmarked, humpbacked heap unloading another uniform and a plainclothesman.

The moment Gunther had turned his head toward Carla's concern at the window, Harding jumped. His fist pumped upward, knocking Gunther's pistoled arm toward the ceiling. He grabbed his wrist, and a shot exploded, its kick jerking the held, taut arm even farther back, allowing Harding even further leverage. He laid a short, quick punch with his left hand into the ribs of the arched-back Gunther and felt Gunther's forced breath on his face with the blow.

Gunther swung his weight to the left, however, and his bulk forced the grappling men against the wall, stumbling over the shadeless stemmed lamp that now was pressed to the wall with them by their wrestling arms. Another gunshot split the plasterboard two feet above Harding's head.

Carla immediately ran for her handbag, sitting on the card table. Not bothering to remove her weighty club, she swung the bag at full-arm extension toward Harding's face in a one-handed hammer throw.

Harding bobbed his head and felt the force of the impact bang across the top of his shoulder and alongside his neck. It stung him enough that he almost lost his grip on Gunther's arm, but not quite. In fact, in lowering his center of gravity, he now lunged forward and pressed Gunther's exposed wrist on the blinding bulb that was jammed against the wall between them.

Gunther screamed and dropped the gun before he could find out what his smoking flesh smelled like burning. Harding tried to bend for the pistol, but Gunther's knee came up and met his forehead at an angle, and Harding bounced back against the wall with the base of his spine.

Gunther snatched his own seared red wrist, closing his eyes quickly with pain. Carla bent to pick up the gun when Harding realized that though he couldn't beat her to it with his hand, his foot was close enough to side-kick it. His hard swipe sent the small gun spinning across the wooden floor like a fleeing whirlwind and under an upholstered armchair.

Unfortunately, the move also left Harding open to another blow from Gunther, who seething now with clenched teeth over what was done to him, drove his toe into Harding's side, forcing him to the floor.

From down the hall, a woman was heard screaming for the police as if she were the one being shot at. Carla threw her valise strap over her shoulder and pulled at Gunther.

"Come on! We gotta move."

"Where?" Gunther said, still holding his wrist.

"The roof," Carla said. "I got an out."

Both of them were through the door before Harding even rolled over. He stumbled upward and, crouched forward, moved toward the doorway. He briefly leaned up against the frame, his arm out holding the other side as a brace, catching his breath, pushing back the stab in his ribs so that he could run.

Two long strides down the hall, a voice shouted, "Hold it!"

Harding almost didn't stop but did.

"Turn around—easy!"

He followed the booming voice's command and turned around. A stout uniformed cop was holding his pistol on him, its barrel waving toward Carla's apartment.

"Inside," he said.

"The people you want ran to the roof," Harding said.

"I said, inside," the cop repeated calmly.

Harding complied, his guts churning, thinking of his mother dancing in her white dress and Thick Dunbar's gun barrel stuck in his father's ear, firing. The moment they both entered the flat, he turned toward the officer, about to plead with him, to explain his urgency, explain the murder about to happen, when footfalls rushed toward the doorway and a familiar face appeared. Then a fist, and a short, pulled-back right hand struck Harding on the chin, snapping his head back and his bottom teeth into his top in a sudden, unnaturally hard bite.

The face belonged to Lt. Butch Stone as well as to his son, Dale, a fact that had again frozen Harding before the short, swift blow. The lanky detective nodded his head at the deadbeat before him. "Don't get worked up. Everybody's got their own way of saying hello."

"You dumb jerk!" Harding said, not wanting to rub his jaw as a show of strength. "Gunther and his girl are on the roof."

Lt. Stone jerked his head toward the man in blue next to him. The cop stuck his head out the doorway, shouting something to the two other officers, who then bolted up the next flight of stairs. Meanwhile, Lt. Stone was frisking Harding down, spinning him around roughly, then pushing him away with his thick, springlike fingers.

"What happened, Hard?" Lt. Stone snickered. "Somebody snatch your heater? Officer Sujeck and me heard some rounds on the way up here. Figured you'd be wearing either the gun or the bullet. You miss him again?"

Harding's pain was less physical than it was emotional, the stress breaking him down. "Listen," he said, "one of Gunther's hoods—Thick Dunbar—you know him, I know you do!—he's on his way to kill Mrs. Harding. You've got to stop him. I don't care what you do with me. Just stop him! Or let me!"

Lt. Stone raised his eyebrows with a grin toward Sujeck. "Hey, what luck, huh? We've been trying to pin Harlen Gunther's butt to the floor for months, and now we got one of Max Turley's boys here to sing for us about it."

"What?"

"Don't play asshole with me, Hard."

"I'm not one of Turley's boys!" Harding shouted. Lt. Stone smacked him across the face with a loose fist. Officer Sujeck looked away as though he saw an unwanted fly in the room.

"Remember how I like lying? Huh?" Lt. Stone shook Harding by the shoulders and pushed him down on the couch, face first. "So how come I hear from H.Q. that a call comes in from up the canyon from an old guy who tends Clifford Snell's joint? Says he sees a gray Buick outside the house on his way back from the woods up there. Sees a big-shouldered Joe in a trench and fedora bolt outta there when he calls to him. Then he finds his boss all sorts of dead offa the patio. So that's one Snell pal gone, right?"

Harding opened his mouth to speak, but Lt. Stone pushed his face into the musty cushion, Harding feeling as though he were drowning in embedded dust, suffocating.

"Then a local prowl car perchance spots same gray sedan stopped outside this apartment building. Spots same trench and fedora being dropped off. We've been keeping a lookout on Gunther lately. I figure it's my move. So you guys have a swell reunion, or what? Maybe you tried to hit Gunther and missed. Maybe you tried to deal with him. You tell me."

Lt. Stone picked up Harding's head from the cushion, which was soiled with spittle. Harding gasped and coughed. "Look, we can run through this crap all you want later," he sputtered. "You've got to stop Dunbar, *now!*"

Lt. Stone drove an extended knuckle into Harding's side. "Don't tell me what I gotta do, slime."

A freckle-faced cop came rushing into the apartment. "Looks like we got somebody pinned on top. Can't tell."

"You and Dugan handle it," Lt. Stone said. "Call in a backup, you want. Me and Sujeck and this scumbag here are going downtown for some more tea-party talk."

With that, Lt. Stone lifted Harding by his arm and threw him toward the door. Still coughing, Harding stumbled and fell to one knee, his arm grabbing the arm of the upholstered armchair. Harding realized he wanted to go down, flat to the floor. He turned and spit at the lieutenant who was about to yank him up. The saliva caught him on his green-striped tie and part of his shirt. Officer Sujeck made a low groan in his throat and stepped just outside the hallway; he had ten years invested in this job. What he didn't see wouldn't be allowed in a courtroom.

Lt. Stone lashed his foot out at the kneeling Harding, his shoe smacking him flat on the shoulder blade, driving Harding down to the floor, just where he wanted to be, as his arm slid and disappeared under the chair in the fall. Then Lt. Stone landed, knee first, on Harding's back and pulled his head up by his chin, the neck tendons to his chest stretching out like leather barber straps waiting for the razor. Groping under the chair, Harding fingered wads of gathered dirt and torn bits of paper. He tried to edge his body forward, a rooted-out earthworm seeking his hole again, but Lt. Stone threw Harding's head back down toward the floor, mashing his nose in the boards. The taste of blood came quickly to Harding's scraping lips.

"The captain don't like when my suspects trip and fall downstairs 'cause they get clumsy, but what's a cop supposed to do when some shitface loses his balance, huh? Come on!" Lt. Stone commanded, pulling Harding by the seat of his pants, sliding him on the floor.

Harding tensed and felt his hand, empty, smeared with dust, start to slide out from under the chair. He swept his hand back along the darkened floor just before Lt. Stone's final yank, and his fingers touched something cool, something hard. The white handle appeared out from under the chair, like a found bone, firm in his grip.

Harding spun on his own axis, face up, as fast as he could, in spite of his ribs crying in pain. His left hand pulled at Lt. Stone's dangling, spit-soiled tie, bringing the surprised detective down to his knees and Harding up to his face. Harding's right hand shoved Gunther's gun against the lieutenant's cheek hard enough to hurt Stone's back molars.

"You son of a bitch," Harding snarled into Lt. Stone's face. "Get up."

Harding swung the detective away from him and had his left arm wrapped around his throat, keeping the gun barrel pushed into him as though he were trying to tunnel through his flesh with a blunt piece of metal. Lt. Stone could barely speak with his Adam's apple so squeezed. "You'd better kill me now, slick," he whispered. "You're dead meat later."

"I don't make my friends orphans," Harding said, "even if it'd be doing him a favor. Move."

Officer Sujeck appeared in the doorway with his gun drawn. "Anything wr—" He took a step back, his face sunk.

"Back off!" Harding yelled.

"Shoot him!" Lt. Stone said, straining his voice.

"Shut up!" Harding said, pulling his arm back a notch on Lt. Stone's throat.

"Shoot him," Lt. Stone still managed to get out. His face flushed red with the effort. "Shoot him, you fat tub of guts!"

Officer Sujeck, who had a beer belly but a strong upper body, watched Harding's eyes, held his gun steady, not sure of what to do.

Lt. Stone could somehow smell it from Harding's beading forehead, or hear it in his short, anxious breaths, but somehow he sensed that Harding wouldn't kill him, was afraid to for some strange reason, sensed it as one animal senses the fear in another. And Lt. Stone was right. Harding's mind was flashing all over the place. What he'd said before about orphans was true, but he also realized that Dale Stone was younger than he was, and quite possibly wasn't even born yet. Killing Stone's father meant killing Dale, didn't it? Lt. Stone had no idea of the reasoning, but he played off his sixth sense.

"Sujeck, you take fuckin' aim and shoot this bastard's head off," he said.

Harding cocked the gun hammer and watched Officer Sujeck lick his lips, take a step forward.

"Back off, I said!" Harding shouted, backing off himself.

"Shoot him!" Lt. Stone screamed, strangely feeling in command, even in such a position.

Officer Sujeck moved forward still.

Harding was delirious; Dunbar shot into his mind, his mother, his own kids again—why now? He pressed the gun into Lt. Stone's temple, hoping to indent his brain.

"You wanna die or something?" he yelled into Stone's ear. "Huh? You trying to pay back for the young cop you got killed? For your lieutenant friend's kid who was wasted 'cause of you? Is that it? That why I should plug you?"

Stone quieted, though his body remained tense, his mouth open as though stunned. Officer Sujeck still moved slowly forward, but in the brief quiet, Harding's mind cleared for an instant, like a sudden bathing of sunlight through blanketing storm clouds.

He turned his gun toward the approaching officer, who then stopped. "Deep down, this fucker may want me to blow his head off," Harding said to Officer Sujeck, "but how about you?"

The balance had shifted. Sujeck figured that at best it was a gutted belly, his girth a good target for at least two rounds of lead. At worst . . .

"Drop the gun," Harding said.

Lt. Stone started to shake his head as best he could.

"Drop it!" Harding shouted.

Officer Sujeck's head dropped, as did his gun.

"No," Lt. Stone said, "you asshole."

"Now move toward the john," Harding said. "Let's go. Move."

Officer Sujeck walked toward the bathroom and went inside when Harding nodded his head. "Close the door," Harding said. The door closed. "Now turn the key that's in the lock and slide it under the door."

Harding heard the click of the lock and saw the key peek out the crack below. He kicked it into the bedroom, heard it rattle under the bed somewhere.

Lt. Stone shouted hoarsely at the shut wooden door, "Forget it, Sujeck. Flush yourself down the toilet while you're in there, you piece of shit."

Harding grappled with the squirming homicide detective but got him away from the bathroom, out of the apartment, and at the staircase, his forearm tight on Stone's throat, not allowing him to shout out his self-destructive cries to the cops combing the upper levels.

"We head out of here quiet with you as my shield," he said into Lt. Stone's ear. "Then I let you go. Downstairs." One step down and Lt. Stone threw an elbow behind him, knowing he was lower, and just missed a direct blow into Harding's loins. The shot did, however, force Harding to bend at the waist, but in doing so, he grabbed Stone's head like a boulder and twisted it. Harding's fingers dug into and mutated Stone's facial features into a grotesque mask of effort and agony. Before Stone could swat at Harding's groin again, he rammed Stone's head into the wall above the banister. Still unsatisfied and raging, Harding then threw the homicide detective down the stairs. Stone's body struck each step awkwardly, bounding down, a tumbling sack of bones and bricks. At the bottom landing, Stone moaned, flinched, then lay still.

Harding ran down the flight and saw a discarded mannequin, Stone's mangled torso with his left arm clearly dislocated and stuck behind him at an unnatural angle. Harding thought of pulling a hank of Stone's thinning, greasy hair and sending it to the old man who sat in the basement of his retirement bungalow, sending it as an addition to his collection. Instead, he put his free hand under Stone's hidden face and lifted it by his chin to see if the homicide detective was near consciousness.

The passive, almost peaceful, face came alive, eyes popped, mouth springing open, then clamping down on Harding's hand. Harding screamed. He pulled once, then threw a knee into Stone's forehead. He pulled again, but Stone's bite wouldn't give; meanwhile Stone's untangled arm came up and grappled with Harding, yanking him down, punching, his jaws biting harder, like a snarling, bloodsucking hound, foaming with madness. Harding thought Stone's teeth would meet in another second and spit out a third of his hand, but through the pain he hammered the gun down on Lt. Stone's skull. His hand was released, and Lt. Stone flopped to the floor, the dark-suited mannequin returning to its twisted, lifeless state.

Harding, backed against the stairwell, pulled the handkerchief from his pocket and wrapped his gnawed, bleeding hand. He then heard male voices, commotion, about three flights up, his painful screams probably having carried throughout the building and maybe half the state.

He ran down the stairs as fast as he could, hearing clattering footsteps from far above. On the first level, he spotted a back door, one used to dump garbage into the back alley by the landlord, and rushed to it. The alley was deserted and narrow. He ran down its length and headed for Laura, who would be waiting off Kelso, and for his mother, who would unknowingly be waiting for Dunbar's gun. And what of his own existence?

The stale air *whoosh*ing past, his feet striding, flying, Harding sped through the brick-lined valley toward the dark opening onto Kelso Street, hoping to be born.

Thick Dunbar rubbed the barrel of his .38 with the tips of his fingers, waiting, stroking the nub of his gun sight like a hardened nipple.

He sat readied, sat in a parked black DeSoto, looking at the five-floor walk-up across Nuart Street, angled so as to see also the rusted fire escape that climbed the tan, blank wall in the adjacent alley. Dunbar liked the feel of his pistol and was patient, incredibly so for an enforcer, which is why Gunther liked him better than Frisky, besides the fact that Frisky Jeeter had no funny bone whatsoever. That didn't bother Thick any; in fact, after tonight's job, he was meeting Frisky at the back of Teddy's flophouse, and they (along with the nice cut Gunther sweetened their wallets with) were taking the train to Mexico for a few months, going to catch up on a few cons he knew on the lam there. He'd work his way back into the States eventually, once he'd had his fill of cheap booze and even cheaper señoritas.

It also didn't bother him that Dolores Harding had left the apartment ten minutes ago just when he had gotten out of his car to fulfill his obligations. He just watched her cross the intersection diagonally and enter a late night grocery, watched her pick up a can of evaporated milk and bread and whatever before he became uninterested and sat back in his car again, sunk back into his oversize brown suit jacket. He wanted her back in the apartment, wanted to do things all at once, a professional job.

Dunbar barely lifted his head when Dolores Harding reentered the building with a small, full paper bag cradled in her arm; he merely tested the weight of the gun in his large hand. The moment she disappeared from the vestibule, Dunbar pulled himself out of the car. His gun holstered up against his breast, he walked quietly into the bordering alley. At the base of the looming fire escape, he looked up at the tall, curtained window on the fourth floor that faced the alleyway, the window he knew was hers, and saw it was alight, as it had been before, only now he saw it flicker, saw a shadow pass, a body eclipse its luminance, and he smiled, hunched, muscular, like a prehistoric cave dweller acknowledging the existence of a star's burning light and wanting to attain it.

He touched his suit, pressing the gun to his chest as a reflex, then began his climb.

Harding was beyond explanations. Laura was quickly deposited at the door of the Helmsley Building and told to call the Harding house, to tell his mother—if she was there—to hide, to lay low somewhere safe, that she was in danger. Harding, meanwhile, would go to her secret apartment, where she was probably hiding in the first place, hiding from the death of her husband and the questions of reporters.

The drive was full of fears and speed. Harding's eyes watched more for police, for teeth-bearing traps laid by a vengeful Lt. Stone, than for obstacles like corner street lamps and the occasional night stroller. He flew onto Nuart and left his car almost before it came to a stop, a honking motorist behind shouting curses at him. He ran into the alleyway, then slowed, pulling out the white-handled gun, thankful he even had it.

In the alley's quiet he heard the faint echo of slowly struck metal, vibrating a sour thunking tune, fading upward. Harding looked skyward at the fire escape. It shot up like a twisted spine, and halfway up, as if on an X-ray, was a dark smudge, a shadow that grew, spread upward, a sign of impending death.

Harding immediately tried to snatch down the ladder, but Dunbar had pulled it up from ground level and put it out of reach. The mirror-twin fire escape ladder across the alley was also inaccessible.

In hurried strides, Harding circled to the front of the building, climbed the stoop, and entered the vestibule. He swung his pistol, and its handle smashed the glass over the inner door, Harding flinching away at the strike. The glass fell over him like vicious rain. He reached in and turned the inner knob, letting himself inside.

Harding ran up each flight of stairs, taking two steps at a time, each landing's quarter turn spinning him upward. He didn't bother looking down the hallway on either the first or second floor, but on the third Thick Dunbar's frame appeared at the open, far hallway window, right to left, like a dark, passing cloud.

Harding scrambled down the dim hall when suddenly Dunbar stuck his head back into the square frame, having seen a rushing figure from the corner of his eye, and raised his gun to fire.

Harding dove to the floor, his arms extended, landing uncomfortably hard on the thin pine slats; he rolled left once, then braced his elbows down and took aim. Dunbar was gone. No shot had been fired, either.

Dunbar was mad; it was going to be sloppy. He had to speed things now, and it was at high speed that jobs go wrong. He held off taking a shot at the onrushing dick because that would start the time clock as to when the coppers would show. Some neighbors would figure it to be some none-of-our-business commotion, but there was always some Joe calling the law if somebody sneezed hard outside his door, let alone cracked off a couple of slugs. Of course, Dunbar had no way of knowing that the last thing Harding wanted to see was a squadron of police.

First duty was to complete the hit; the victims get the first slugs. Then you can start counting the seconds till the coppers show; then you can litter the floor with interfering gumshoes on the way out. But for now, Dunbar scaled the next three steps up the rickety fire escape and stopped. And when Harding stuck his arm and head out the hallway window, Dunbar flew—one hand on the metal rod banister, the other vaulting (along with his two-forty-plus poundage) over the side, back toward the window.

Harding thought the top floor collapsed upon him. Fortunately, it was only Thick Dunbar's thigh, followed by a more directed elbow to the back of the head. Unfortunately Dunbar's foot caught Harding's gun, and it clattered on the metal grating and slipped down one of its openings, then clattered again a story below, this time to a halt.

Harding blindly wrapped his arms at whatever body

parts became available so as not to tumble over as he fell outside the window, and he used his momentum to twist himself and the body part with him. It was a leg, and Dunbar crashed down on the fire escape floor. Quickly, Dunbar kicked out with his shoe and tagged Harding on the shoulder. Dunbar felt the grip on his leg loosen, and he stood up with amazing speed for a man with such bulk.

From all fours Harding pushed off and drove himself into Dunbar's stomach, his right shoulder as battering ram, and pressed Dunbar to the far railing. In the first instant, it seemed Harding would be able to rise up, lift himself, and in turn Dunbar, and send the weighty thug over the side. But the balance tipped, the point of release fell short, and Dunbar's weight, as well as his blows to Harding's back and ribs from on top, weakened him. His knees suddenly wobbled, and Dunbar encircled Harding's waist with his arms and flipped him sideways. Harding fell to the fire escape floor, rolling to his side. Again, the fire escape shook and sung its metallic tune with the toss, its rusty structure reverberating in the moonlight like an orange winding strand, a genetic molecule in decay.

When Harding tried to rise, Dunbar's foot pushed him toward the landing's hole, and Harding skidded down the iron steps, trying to grip the banister or a passing stair, but the tumble only ended at the bottom of the short flight to the second landing. His head pulsing, Harding spotted the white-handled gun in the far corner.

Dunbar moved forward, his big strides jarring the thin metal steps like measured beats upward, toward the fourth and final floor. He maneuvered his body through the hallway window, marched down the hall with sure steps, gun drawn. At apartment 4D he thrust out his left leg and, snapping the lock with the force of his kick, watched the door fly open, swing away as if by explosion.

Dunbar took one step forward, just outside the door

frame, and half smiled. Everybody was there for him, all in one place, all in one fatal grouping. An old woman, a retired schoolteacher with a bad leg, stood in back and upon seeing the bulk at the door cried out feebly due to watery lungs, then cupped her mouth with her hand. In front of her stood Dolores Harding, who, after jumping back, fell to her knees as her eyes widened in recognition and terror. Before them both wavered a little boy, almost three, who looked at this man, looked with bulging, fascinated eyes, wondering.

Thick Dunbar raised his gun. Youngest first was another rule.

"Dunbar!"

The voice caromed down the hall just before the blast of bullets. Dunbar felt one slug pierce his shoulder as he turned toward the hallway window and fired at Harding, but the damaged shoulder also damaged his aim, and the shot flew into the ceiling. Harding cracked off two more shots. Both caught Dunbar in the side this time, bit into his stomach and left lung like parasites. He turned back toward the apartment doorway, feeling the job slipping away from him, unless . . .

Dunbar, raised up tall, unnaturally stiff as though being lifted by the bullets rather than felled by them, gazed down at the small boy and brought his gun up again. The boy, squinting at the noise, raised his own hand up and pointed his finger at Dunbar, poking it twice in the air.

"Pah. Pah," the boy said.

And with that Dunbar's eyes looped up into his head, his blood draining out, his gun hand unworkable; he began to fall. Harding appeared in the doorway just as the large tree of a man started his descent toward the little boy, who watched the growing shadow loom over him, darkening his vision, bringing fear, the seed of a lingering dream.

Dolores Harding shouted out: "Jonathan!"

Harding looked up at her in response but soon realized it was not for him she called as she swept the young child into her oversized green sweater just before Thick Dunbar fell at the boy's bare feet, dead.

Harding looked at his mother sobbing, rocking the little boy from her knees. The old nursemaid touched Mrs. Harding's shoulder and said something to her, but Mrs. Harding just shook her head and kept holding the boy from behind and crying. The boy, meanwhile, was facing away, staring at the man in the doorway, panting, his half-eaten hand bleeding again, his head leaning against the frame, looking down. He was looking down there at himself looking up here, looking up with heavy green arms wrapped around his neck. Harding moved his shoulders in pain as he lost himself in his own child eyes.

Mrs. Harding finally stared at Harding wilting at the doorway, still holding her secret tightly to her; it was hers to bear, her sin to hide, her burden for life. She hugged Jonathan to her as Harding slid to the floor, his back against the molding, and wiped his face with his bloody hand.

"It'll be . . . okay," he said, nodding. He put his head back on the hard wood. He could stop running after ghosts now.

· ten ·

It was just past midnight as Harding slowly entered his
mother's kitchen to prepare a cup of instant coffee.
He took off his officer's cap and sat it on the white
Formica table, sat himself down, too, waiting for the water
to boil, thinking about Laura, how she might still
be waiting for him in the office thirty-seven years away,
but there was something missing, something about
his mother. A final link. He thought he knew where it
was.

He was climbing the stairs to see if he was right when he
noticed a flashlight graze the front window to his mother's
home. Harding opened the front door, and a white beam
blinded him for an instant.

"Jonathan!"

Among the swirling blue dots stood Stone, flashlight

lowered in one hand, gun up in the other. His facial expression jumped from astonished to reprimanding. "The hell you doing here? And where have you been? Jesus Christ! I was gonna plug you, man."

Stone holstered his weapon and flash and moved inside. "I been keeping an eye out on your mom's house, and when I saw the light on I figured I was in for a fight—if the jerk was dumb enough to switch on the lights, he was dumb enough to want a shoot-out. Geez, you look like a shit hole. Man! Where *were* you? You still on sick time or what? Why you wearing your blues? What the fuck is this all about, Jonathan? You're driving me bat shit lately, you know?"

Harding started to smile and hugged his friend, his partner, the face with the right body this time, the right soul. Stone patted Harding's back in response. "Hey, you okay, man?"

Harding broke away, nodding. "Almost," he said. "Almost, man. I'm getting there."

"Where the fuck you getting? That's what I wanna know," Stone said.

Harding became somber. He still needed an out from his deal with Sol. "I can't tell you everything now. Maybe I will someday." Stone shook his head, made a face. "It's almost over, though, I swear. At least about the murder. One last step. I think I got something."

"About what?" Stone asked.

"The guy we found in the basement. The guy whose skull was hammered."

"Your father?"

"That wasn't my father." Harding would tell Stone about Harlen Gunther later, let the department research the hood's disappearance, dig deeper and maybe find some teeth, something to identify the skull further, but right now he wanted to go upstairs.

"Come on," Harding said. "Grab a cup of coffee. Help me piece something together."

Harding and Stone sat among the yellowing envelopes, pictures, and wrinkled clothing that Harding had tossed about the previous night. They brought a large table lamp into the private sanctum from the adjacent bedroom, and in the bright, full light, somehow the room became what it was all along, a storage place for mementos and junk. Propped against the trunk, Harding pulled a carbon copy from a manila folder. "My mother should have been pretty well off. Half the company fire insurance went to her from the partnership. Her being the heir to my father's half. See?" Harding passed the copy of the fire claim adjustment to Stone. "But then it all slips away in dribs and drabs."

"Your mom a spender?" Stone asked, still reading the report.

"Look around, man," Harding said. "Stuff is prehistoric. I know she bought this house with a lot of what was left of the dissolved company. Snell owed a bundle; so that cut in. But shit—where'd it all go? Why is my mother always struggling for money? Nothing put away. . . ."

Harding picked up a thick, yellow eight-by-fourteen-inch envelope and dumped its contents on the floor: stacks of canceled checks, the ones he'd found the other night, the ones with a now recognizable name.

"They are all from my mother made out to a Doris Huntsford. At least this first set are. Near a thousand a month went to this woman for a while. Insurance money gets dried up slowly but surely with this kind of payoff."

Stone was looking wide-eyed, but not by what Harding just said. "Holy shit."

"What?"

Stone fumbled into his back pocket and removed a

folded piece of paper. "I forgot. I got those names of previous owners finally, of the house where we found the skull and all. The owners before the city took over, and look. . . ."

Stone's finger pointed at a line on the sheet, third line down; Harding didn't have to look. "Doris Huntsford," he said.

Stone glanced up at him. "Yeah. How'd you—? Fuck it, you're not going to tell me anyway. Yeah, Nick and Doris Huntsford were one of the owners. No forwarding address."

"No surprise," Harding said, his mood sobering, his calmness becoming a growing rock in his chest.

"Then come the next set of checks," he said.

"What?"

"Another set. Sure." Harding tossed a few bound packs on the floor. "A few years later, a lot less money given, but—"

"Same woman?"

"Same woman," Harding said. "Different name."

"How do you know?" Stone said, quickly feeling suckered again, answered with silence again, a silence that he knew well from Jonathan, a silence that meant a building determination, a forewarning of action.

"They go up to now. Current," Stone said, surprised. "Your mother's been paying this"—he looked at a check —"Betty Carlisle–Doris Huntsford broad for almost thirty years?"

Harding nodded. And Stone knew better than to ask why. For now. For now he watched Harding pull out his police issue and check its readiness. Dolores Harding had written an address on an envelope that was never sent because of a tear, just using it now to stick some more canceled checks in. Betty Carlisle, 427 Roberts Road,

Tolina. Two towns east, but still within San Marco County jurisdiction. Forty-minute drive, tops.

Stone watched Harding rise. "You know this woman?"

"Oh, yeah," Harding said, snapping his loaded holster closed. "She's like a sister to me."

The woman lay in bed at two o'clock in the morning watching a bad old movie, half-drowsy, half-drunk, her hair spilling over her face, and thought she heard something. She dragged her hand across the clumpy wads that displayed a strange color of orange that you could associate with neither hair nor fruit. Her eyes bagged low, victims of gravity, but her teeth were strong, though some shone as yellow as corn. The noise came from the living room, she thought.

She climbed out of bed, already in her thick red cotton robe, and shut the TV on the dresser. The room grew dimmer, the woman not realizing the picture tube provided most of the room's light at the time, her night-table lamp emanating an anemic glow. Then she saw a shadow at her bedroom doorway. She stumbled backward, her head still pumping the burgundy through its channels, fogging her senses and her fear, though it was gradually crawling to the surface like a persistent spider.

"What?" she said to nothing at the moment. "Who is it?"

The shadow grew in the doorway, then an indistinguishable body filled it.

"Who's there?" the woman shouted. "Who is it?"

Harding couldn't resist. "I'm the ghost of killings past," his voice said coldly.

"What?" The woman moved near the open window, where a slight, warm breeze was pushing the yellow curtain away ever so slightly. She was ready to get the hell out of there. She always thought this a safe neighborhood, one of the best—

"Betty Carlisle?" Harding said. "Doris Huntsford? . . . Or is it Carla Harding? Depends what year we're in, doesn't it?"

Carla blinked her eyes slowly, then straightened up defiantly. *"Who are you?!"*

Harding stepped closer to where the brush of light from the night table could reach him.

"A cop!?" Carla said, then spit out a laugh. Her shoulders were as formidable as ever. Her legs seemed more spindly, worn down. Her skin was bone white against the shock of orange hair. "What kind of game is this? You got no right to enter this house like that. You got a warrant or something?"

"You had the door open," Harding said.

"Yeah, but the screen door—"

"The screen door was unlocked. I knocked a few times, but your television was loud, I guess. I came in." Harding lied easily. The white wooden door had been open, as the screen door was being used to ventilate the house, but the latter was locked just as Carla had said. He'd used a simple credit card to jimmy the screen lock open and made sure Stone didn't see the maneuver from the distant car. Harding had mimicked speaking to someone at the door just in case so that the report would state the suspect allowed him entry without a warrant.

"Figures. Told you the neighborhood was safe," Carla said. Harding didn't remember her telling him that at all. "It's so safe, only the cops break in." She let out a laugh, which looked more like one of her youthful sneers only with less sex appeal and a lot more bitterness. She coughed up a bit, then swallowed. She patted her chest twice, then said: "Okay. Get lost. It's friggin' two in the morning. I don't talk to no cops at two in the morning.

You'd be lucky to get a peep outta me at two in the afternoon, you fuck. Now scram"—she chuckled, helped by the booze—"before I call a cop." She coughed up another laugh, sat on the bed.

"Still peddling the rough stuff," Harding said. He moved a stride closer. "I'm your alleged stepbrother. Jonathan."

Carla squinted at the young officer, though she really couldn't tell his age from the light, his uniform the only thing apparent to her, nor did she care.

"Jonathan, huh? So . . . you finally know the score, I guess. Good for you. Now get the hell out of here. I hate family reunions."

"Guess the checks won't be coming anymore," Harding said.

"Checks?"

"The checks you get," he said. "The monthly payments from my mother—"

"Well," Carla said, giving her hand a queenly wave. "If she's down on her dough, she's down on her dough. She can pay up what she owes me whenever she can get th—"

Harding boomed, *"Don't* dish out lines older than your goddamn dentures, big sister. Not to *me!"* He pulled her up by a reluctant elbow. "Especially not to *me.* I don't play the sap nearly so well as Romero did."

Carla pulled away from the irate cop and nervously poured more lukewarm wine into her coffee mug. Harding quickly cased the room: old furniture, but classy old, good for a long time; a portable color TV on the oak dresser; and in the corner the jade-green elephant, all by himself on a stand, a white frill doily at its feet, its trunk forever raised.

Carla gulped down the alcohol loudly, then, putting the mug back on the nightstand, tightened her jaw.

"So what do you want from me? Money? I'm not rich, you know."

Harding had walked to the porcelain animal on display. "Just you and your lucky elephant, right?" he said, touching its smooth trunk. Then he turned toward her sharply. "I want to know what made you the way you are. Why did you want to bring my family down? Why my father murdered? My mother persecuted?"

Carla was dazed by the questions. Did he know . . . ? But she shook her head and snickered. "Some people. You asshole types. You think everything is a mystery. Sooooo complicated. All that hidden psychology bullshit." She blew out some air; her smirk disappeared. "Your mother was a slut who got rich. I was a slut who wasn't. Things needed evening out." She nodded her head in a "that's it" gesture.

"When did you first even find out about my mother's past?"

Carla sat back down on the bed, getting even more tired, tired of this dumb cop and everything. "That stuff? Yeah. My husband. Ha! Just after I met my husband—"

"Harlen Gunther," Harding said for effect.

Carla froze. The spider was starting its slow crawl up her spine again. "You knew my husband?"

"Keep talking."

"But what—"

Harding grabbed her face and pulled it toward his. "I said, keep talking!"

He let her go, and she swallowed hard. "Sure, whatever. After Gunther came from New York, I met him at a casino. We got close, and he found out he knew your mother, my stepmother. He couldn't believe his eyes, he said, when he first saw her in the papers married off to Nathaniel Harding, some big shot. I mean, who was she kidding? And no mention of a kid, either. Well, he knew he had her cold. His casino boss, Snell, was real pleased, too. Get his hands into the Harding cookie jar." Carla's speech slowed; she squinted at Harding. "I was pleased, too." Harding's face was looking familiar, a lost imprint somewhere deep in her memory.

Harding said, "So Snell and Gunther got her to steal her own jewels and fence them to pay for their silence."

"Sure," Carla said, and snorted, forgetting his face for the moment and picturing her father's. "Can you imagine what Daddy would have done finding out he married an ex-hooker with a kid?"

"She was afraid," Harding said.

"Your jerk of a mother was afraid of *everything!*" Carla said. "The cops, your daddy, God—all the same in *her* head."

Harding was almost speaking to himself, thinking about the factory, what his father had said before Dunbar . . . "Yeah, but he wouldn't have left her. He finally knew— and he wouldn't have."

During Harding's momentary reverie, Carla's eyes darted up and back, finally settling on her purse, which was on the floor beside the night table. She inched toward it but stopped at Harding's sudden gaze and strong voice: "And all the money from the jewels and the gambling scheme and whatever else Gunther had stashed away—it still wasn't enough for you."

"*Gunther* wasn't enough for me," Carla sneered. "His dough was just fine for a while. We changed names, even got a new nose." She turned toward the dresser mirror. "Pretty good bob," she mused. "We figured the mob, if they came looking for us 'cause of our scam, they wouldn't be looking real close in their own backyard."

"So you bought a house in Winston Beach," Harding said.

Carla broke into a sweat; that spider was creeping up

her neck now, pinching nerves at the base of her skull. "How—?"

Harding was fiddling with some of her dresser debris. A hair net, a phone bill—he picked up a small iron jewelry box, looking at the relief work: sweet little angels blowing long, loud horns. "I know plenty," he said, not paying attention to her rump shifting on the bed, her maneuvering toward the nightstand. "I know you probably lived pretty high, not too, because you didn't want to be noticed. After a while, the dough was gradually going, but Gunther was there to stay. So you parted his hair with your lead pipe routine and laid him out under the cellar."

Harding looked at her this time. "I shook his hand down there three days ago. He lost a *lot* of weight."

The disclosure had stopped Carla's maneuvers for a moment; fear began poisoning her brain. Then she got a better look at Harding's face in the dimness. Why'd he look so . . . young?

"So you move out," Harding said, watching Carla shift on the bed more openly now, looking at him with hatred, panic. "Supposedly with hubby. Maybe after some time you say he left you—I don't know. But you need some money . . . *and* you still hate my mother. Now you blackmail her so that *I* don't find out the truth about the past. For thirty years you make her pay constant penance for her one great sin—*me*."

Carla's shaky hand reached down, almost lunging, and grabbed her purse, opening it in the same motion.

"The pipe trick is getting old," Harding said.

Carla pulled out a small .22-caliber gun and pointed it at Harding. "There are other kinds of lead, you know. Pipes get real heavy at my age."

Carla gestured "hands up" with the pistol. Harding raised his arms, still holding the small box in his hand, but not very far up, not for this woman, not for the woman who lurked in his mother's shadow, who became her mother's shadow through time.

Carla arched her back straight; the gun gave her aging hand youthful heft; she felt weight in her legs, muscles in her shoulders. The gun killed spiders and cops and captured pieces of an aggressive past; she looked good for a woman nearing sixty.

"Drop the box," she said coldly, "and give me your gun."

Harding didn't move.

"*Now!*" she yelled, raising her hand, setting her eyes down the short sights of the .22.

"You are one—murderous—evil—bitch," Harding said.

Carla almost laughed. "See? Life's that simple sometimes."

Harding flicked his wrist at the green smudge he saw out of the corner of his eye, sending the small iron box directly into the porcelain elephant. The box struck the animal's fragile bulk, smashing it on impact. Shattered into dozens of pieces, the elephant toppled to the floor along with the narrow stand, decimated.

Carla cried out and turned for an instant, allowing Harding to dive to his left toward the end of the bed and its thick mahogany footboard for cover. Carla turned away from her fallen charm and shot at where Harding stood a second ago.

"Drop it, lady," came Stone's voice from the open bedroom window. His arms were propped on the sill, holding his gun steady.

Carla swiveled again, like an out-of-control whirligig, this time toward the cop in the window, and fired. Stone returned the shot, almost overlapping. Her bullet splintered the painted molding to Stone's right. His bullet splintered her spine as it drilled through her body and out her ribs.

Carla fell back against the nightstand, wobbled, blinked, then fell to the floor. Gun drawn, Harding crawled over to Carla, saw her breathing slightly, her eyes blinking still, erratically as though in secret code. Her fingers shook as she touched her wound and lifted her hand to her face. She stared at the red on her hand, felt the red oozing from her, the red soaking the back of her robe.

"That's it," Harding said to her with quiet contempt. "That's your luck . . . all run out."

Carla stared at her hand for another moment before it fell to her side, as lifeless as the rest of her.

Stone was standing above them both now, angry, upset that he had had to shoot an old lady, upset that she had shot at him in the first place. Harding stood and grabbed Stone by the side of his shoulder. "Thanks, man. I guess that's why you have backup, huh?"

Stone nodded. "Yeah, that's why," he muttered, sadly looking at Carla, and although her hair was unnaturally orange and her upper body was far more square and brutish, Carla made Stone feel as though he had shot his own mother.

"Bet the investigating squad will find plenty here," Harding said, referring to the house, "to link her up to Gunther. She was probably fucked enough to keep the pipe."

Stone remained silent over Carla's body. Harding noticed his partner's grief, thinking she didn't deserve it, thinking how Stone's father would be dancing around the corpse, drinking to her demise. Maybe Harding was thinking of himself in the same vein.

"I'll call it in," Harding said.

Stone nodded.

On the way out of the bedroom, Harding crunched small green pieces of porcelain underfoot and unknowingly kicked the remnants of a once defiant trunk across the floor.

The Devil's eyes were shifting and searching.

He had passed a sleeping Laura, scrunched into a fetal posture on the tiny reception room couch, and marched into the back office, the feathery rays of dawn seeping through the shades. He had had to take care of a full day's business before he could return to such "recreational" matters. At least that's how it all started out three days ago.

The back office was empty; he peeked out the shades, annoyed at the impending sun, but saw a car pull up across the street, a bulging yellow car that lay below like a fried egg. The Devil smiled as he sat at his desk and lit a cigarette. He would wait. He had an eternity of practice.

Less than an hour would pass before Harding entered the front room. His vision was weakening, his head unclear, as his need for sleep grew through the night of precinct house questioning, of paperwork (that Stone did, mainly), of strange looks from the graveyard shift. Desk Sgt. Walcott had kept shaking his head at the story of two cops (one off duty, the other off his patrol route) and the dead old lady. Walcott just made sure it was all down on paper and made sure he would be on coffee break when Captain Schulman got the report handed to him in the morning.

But even after all that, Harding had to come back, had to return for Laura. He had tried her apartment first, and now he saw her breathing softly, tucked into herself, on the grungy office sofa. He wanted to join her, position himself with her like twins; he wanted some peace.

Harding bent over her and kissed her nose. It crinkled

once, twice; then her hand went up to scratch it blindly. Harding grabbed her long fingers, and her eyes popped open fearfully at first, then softened seeing Harding inches from her, on his knees above her. She ran her arms around his neck, kissing him just below the ear, and hugged hard.

"I thought maybe you got hurt," she whispered, near tears. "I thought maybe the cops or the mob—"

Harding pulled her away from him to see her puffy but glowing, girlish face. "It's okay. I'm all right."

They kissed each other softly, tasting each other's desire and fatigue. The Devil appeared quietly from the back office and, unnoticed, leaned in the doorway, watching the openmouthed embrace as he would a brutally murdered child—with dispassion.

Breaking away, Harding pushed a blond sprig from Laura's eyes and forehead. "Tell me what happened— okay?" Laura said. "Tell me everything." She grabbed his forearms, guiding them around her. "But don't stop holding me."

Harding smiled wearily and helped her stand up. "Let's go to your place."

The couple moved toward the smoky-glassed front door and opened it when the Devil spoke. "No time for that, kiddies."

Startled, Laura jumped and Harding jerked his head behind. The Devil took two steps toward them with hands open, adjusting his cuffs.

"Sol," Harding said, feeling Laura draw nearer to him. "I thought we'd had enough of each other."

"We have, Hard-boy," the Devil replied. "That's why I've decided to collect."

"What are you talking about?"

The Devil raised an eyebrow, felt the cool silk of his tie

between his fingers. "I'm calling for payment due on the contract, lover."

"What for?"

The Devil stopped adjusting the shoulders in his suit jacket. "Let's say you've lost box office appeal for me, Johnny. You're stale. You're no fun anymore. Besides"—Harding thought he caught the red spark simmering in the Devil's eyes again—"nobody hits me, Johnny," the Devil said. "*No*body."

The Devil waved his arm in a tight arc near his chest, and the smoky-glassed door slammed shut, the back office door slammed shut, and two lamp bulbs burst in a puff of flame, which vanished just as quickly, only smoke remaining. Harding felt heat sweep his face from the Devil's wave, as did Laura, who started shaking, becoming unsure of her senses.

Harding remained unmoved. "Don't threaten me with your carnival stunts, Sol. You can't demand payment now. It's too early, and you damn well know it." He took Laura's arm and grabbed the front-door knob. "Contract says I get to keep my powers *and* my soul—"

The Devil nodded his head to Harding's words as if following a tune. "Until . . ."

"Until I die," Harding said, and opened the door to leave.

Two bullets pumped Harding in the stomach, following the hollow-sounding shots.

"You got it," the Devil said.

The sudden impact pushed Harding five feet, stumbling backward in short steps. Laura screamed as he fell onto the reception desk, then to the floor, banging his head.

Frisky Jeeter stood in the doorway with a hot pistol in his hand at waist level, stood there just long enough to have yanked on the trigger twice, then say, "That's for breezing Thick, shamus." The next moment the thin, quirky thug was gone.

Laura was picking Harding's bruised head up off the floor, crying out his name, as his eyes opened and fluttered like a trapped butterfly. Laura propped him up against the side of the desk, his bloody shirt painting her arms for her effort.

The Devil sniffed and crossed his arms. "Forgot about Frisky, didn't you?" Then he thumb-pointed to the window. "Didn't you see that big yellow beast of a car sitting out there when you came in, partner?" The Devil shook his head at Harding, who was looking back at him now, holding his stomach, trying to keep his insides from erupting.

"Always can find the fatal flaw in you tragic hero types," the Devil went on. "Yours is that you're fucking stupid."

Harding felt a little strength returning to his arms, and he pushed himself up straighter, licking his lips to speak. "You still don't have me," he said, shaking his head.

The Devil snorted. "So give it, say . . ." He made a show of checking his watch. "Ten minutes."

"Give it all eternity, you fuck," Harding tried to yell, but pulled back, the pain pulling him back. "I'm *still* not yours. Ever."

The Devil pulled out the red vinyl-bound folder from apparently nowhere. "It's in the contract, kiddo."

Harding nodded and managed a phony smile. "Damn right it is." He coughed, and Laura, dazed, helpless, held him tighter, sobbing. "'Cause there's something you didn't figure on. You see, 'kiddo,' before my mother came to San Marco and married respectable, she was a fancy-ass prostitute in New York City. Yeah. The sort of lowlife I used to throw in the can every week downtown."

The Devil looked bored and tapped his fingers on the vinyl to prove it.

"She somehow got in good with a big-city crime boss," Harding continued steadily. "A guy named Max Turley. From what I hear, a real bastard. One of *your* kind, Sol—pure shit. Still—who knows why?—he marries my mother. And they even have a kid together—named Jonathan."

A veil of darkness fell over Harding's face. "After Turley was bumped off, my mother fled here, married Nathaniel Harding, and hid me from my stepfather when I was small. When I got older, she hid me from myself and the knowledge of my *real* father. I figure part of the early blackmail bargain with Gunther must have been a doctored birth certificate, but my mother had also kept the real one."

Harding struggled but pulled a small envelope from his suit and held it out to the Devil. The Devil took it suspiciously, unfolding the document tucked inside.

"Hidden in her sacred trunk," Harding said. "Proof positive. That gangland monster Turley was my father. Which means—"

The Devil's eyes had scanned the New York City birth certificate dated 1946 in an instant, then held it out to Harding in his fist, his face turning fire red. "Wait a minute here!"

"*Which means*," Harding asserted, "my real, *legal*, binding name is Jonathan Turley. Not Harding. Check the dotted line, hot-stuff. I might as well have signed that contract Holdberg as Harding for all it's worth. . . ." Harding couldn't help but laugh, even knowing the tunneled wounds in his body would spit blood. "Legal loopholes," he said sardonically. "Ain't they a kick in the ass?"

The Devil stood motionless, enraged, his face fuller, redder, enflamed, holding the contract feverishly tight in his fists. Harding and Laura watched the flames, almost in slow motion, devour the folder in the Devil's hands from the bottom up while at the same time the Devil's eyes grew wider, redder, like dirt pits filled with sun-bursting hot rocks, and his mouth opened gradually, viciously, a scream coming out, a cry of anger and pain, getting louder, filling the room, driving Laura's hands to her ears, Harding's face to the wall of the desk. The temperature rose dramatically, and a fiery wind blasted at them, searing their vision, scorching their skin, a wind swirling from the smoky rage, bursting eyes, and crying mouth of a hell-bent twisting pyre that used to be Sol Berner and was now suddenly, ferociously, a whipping, blinding flash of light and noise and eternal agony. And gone. Instantly gone. The Devil had vanished. The Devil left no sign.

Overwhelmed by the spectacle, Laura became hysterical, crying loudly and shaking. Harding held her as tight as he could, the pressure of her body actually feeling good as though shoring up the damage, holding back the constant ebbing of his life. She shivered over what she had witnessed, the unearthly display, and wept in fear. Harding realized that that was the first time she had seen the Devil in action, had seen anything at all that proved his story to be true. When she calmed down after a minute, Harding asked her: "You didn't believe me until now, did you?"

Laura shook her head, wiping tears from her face, her cheek on his shoulder.

"I don't blame you," Harding said, "but then why—"

"I fell in love with you," Laura said, almost angry. "I didn't care that you were crazy maybe." She thought of Sol, of his death-mask expression, his power. "Now I wish to God you were."

Laura looked down at Harding, who was fading, turning pale. "I can't let you die here." She pulled at him, swung herself under him, and lifted the bulk of his body a few inches. Harding pushed off his legs and stiff-armed the floor and actually stood, leaning against Laura clumsily.

He looked at her tear-streaked face and touched it as if making sure it was real.

"I fell for you too, angel," Harding said. His head felt woozy.

"Don't make me cry again," Laura said, helping him toward the door. "I gotta get you to the hospital. I can't watch you die here."

Even to the doorway, both of them knew there was little chance they could make it down the hall, let alone down the stairs. But even as they struggled, Harding thought of something.

"I have to go back," he said.

"What?"

Harding pried himself from Laura and braced himself against the door frame. "I have to go back to 1986."

"What are you saying? Why?"

"They might be able to save me there." Harding shook his head, felt the steady morning sun as it angled in from the hallway window to heat his legs. "It's a different world, Laura."

"Better?" Laura asked.

Harding shrugged one shoulder limply. "Different," he said.

"They got medicines we don't and things?"

"Yeah, that's it," Harding said. Even if his plan didn't work, he didn't want her to see him die here, either.

"How do you know you *can* go back?"

"I don't," Harding said, "but I remember Sol saying that once he gave me the power, he couldn't take it back. I remember him saying that." He shook his head at her. "I have to give it a shot."

Laura's chin trembled; she grabbed his hand. "Will you come back, if . . . ?"

"Of course, I will," Harding said. "I'd try, anyway. I might even look you up there."

Laura half smiled. "But I'll be old. In my fifties. God." Her eyes glazed over with age, her inner vision adding years to her life.

"That's okay," Harding said. "I like older women."

Laura chuckled despite her grief; she drew up to him, held him again. "I can't leave you."

"You have to. It won't work in your presence. In anybody's. That was the deal." Those were his words, but his arms didn't want to let her go.

Laura kissed him and saw Harding's eyes dissolving, becoming watery. She wiped her face with her wrists, her hands the color of dried blood. She wobbled as she backed away from his shivering form. The pain in Harding's stomach moved into the core of his heart as he watched her turn and walk down the hall to the stairwell. Before she descended, she glanced back at Harding, his body like a leaking paper sack, but his face full of adoration. She blew a kiss with a shaky hand, and before the pain tore into her eyes again, she left.

Harding heard the clip-clop of her shoes down the steps, the echo of throaty sobs fading, the sad sound gripping his nonexistent stomach that suddenly bore no pain, just numbness, which drifted upward; only his heart thumping was felt, otherwise his arms tingled, and his back and neck fell to numbness, too, and he closed his eyes and felt himself falling to the floor through the doorway, falling what seemed farther than the few feet he was above the floor. When he finally landed, he heard his shoulder cap pop and the sound of squeaky wheels.

The two nurses getting ready to prepare Mrs. Worrell for surgery were discussing their escalating rents and cheap boyfriends. The younger nurse was holding the necessary pills needed before the bladder operation; the other, prematurely gray, pushed a gurney down the antiseptic-smelling corridor. They passed an alcove near an isolated fire exit when the right wheel of the gurney ran over a reddened hand. It was stuck out in the hallway, and it belonged to a uniformed cop who was bleeding from the abdomen, his body sprawled out across the alcove.

The younger nurse froze and let out a small scream, more from the surprise than from what she saw, while the older one was already yelling down the corridor for assistance, touching Harding's neck for a pulse, assessing his bullet wound. Obviously he had been shot, but how did he get up to the third floor in this condition? She could not assess that he had really almost fallen *down* a floor and had dislocated his shoulder as well, since the floors at San Marco County Hospital were seven feet lower than the floors in the old Helmsley Building.

Harding barely made out the nurse's heavyset face above him, barely had breath enough to fill his lungs, but he did remember that this was his hope, that his power over Time still existed; that he had remembered that San Marco County Hospital (one of his ex-wife's primary spoils in her battles with the county and cause for many of their own during their collapsing marriage) had been built on the site of his office, the Helmsley Building, torn down years before. He had almost pointed out the fact to Stone the other day.

The nurse furrowed her brow when she saw the wounded police officer smirk and mumble something to himself. Even if she had heard what he murmured, she still wouldn't have understood.

Harding had mumbled: "Bless Saint June."

It was two weeks in the morphine fog of convalescence before Harding ventured forth from his lumpen hospital bed to visit his mother. Not that the nursing staff or doctors allowed it: the wide swaths that wound about Harding's midsection were still compressing sensitive, tender tissue. Any attempt at getting out of bed risked rupture. But the wait was too long, and as the drug was eased from him, his need to see her grew; his misty consciousness cleared, and the image of his mother's bedridden body was burned in it.

Harding shuffled down the hall in a pair of corduroy slippers Stone had given him, palming the peach-colored wall for balance as he moved. The night nurse was flipping over report binders, checking off items on taped index cards inside, not noticing the man hugging the wall at the end of the corridor as he used the fire door.

Harding grimaced at each concrete step downward, the cold of his dark descent chilling him, the pulling at his stomach making him sweat.

He thought of his children, David and Suzanne, coming to warm him. They would jump on the bed, with him usually in his half-robe fresh from a shower, sitting there, then pretending to be freezing from being wet, his head shaking, spraying sharp beads of water at them, the children screaming and laughing, then jumping on him, rubbing his bathrobe on his body and a towel on his head, getting him dry.

Harding had the letter from June with him in his pajama pocket, the one he'd gotten three days ago saying she was sending them down to San Marco with his mother-in-law next week to see him. As her letter had got around to his injury, he thought there was an I-knew-this-would-happen-one-day tone behind it. But he wasn't sure. Maybe it was just his own belittling insecurity he steadfastly nurtured to this moment.

Harding made it to the floor below without his guts falling like fruit from a torn, wet shopping bag. He poked his head out of the exiting fire door, wishing he had Stone to cover for him. Stone always covered for him.

He thought of how Stone had taken the heat of Carla's shooting in the report, how Stone told him about the talk he had with Captain Schulman, how the investigation team, headed by Lt. Neery, backed up the murder story. Sure enough, they found the pipe in a box, along with secret bank books and pictures of her and Gunther, even a cheap seaside snap of Romero. All in a box in an upstairs closet. Like mother, like stepdaughter, Harding had thought.

Stone was less optimistic about Harding's career with the force. Harding had explained nothing about his own shooting besides that it was by an unknown assailant, and when asked how or why he'd climbed to the third floor of San Marco Hospital, he'd just said he didn't remember. Stone knew the shots had to be still from the "father business," as Stone put it, but he kept mum. Harding promised himself he would tell Stone everything one night back home over a few strong joints and lots of drink and see how much of the tale he bought. Harding knew one thing for sure: like Laura, no matter how much Stone thought Jonathan was losing it, he'd be there.

Harding saw no white uniforms in the corridor, so he slid not far along the wall and into Intensive Care. The private enclosure still showed his mother bedridden and attached to life support systems, the glass front now reminding him of a giant television screen. He quickly made the image real by walking into the dim room and looking intently at his mother's wan frame barely filling the center of the bed. Harding wanted to tell his mother it was over.

He thought of Stone, telling Stone the same thing. Harding had at first handed him a piece of paper with the name Laura Gabriel on it with a sparse description of what Harding thought she might look like at middle age and the few facts he knew about her. He asked Stone to look her up in the files, see if she still lived in San Marco, see if she was still alive even. Stone shook his head.

"She involved with this mess?" he asked, pointing to Harding's stomach bandage.

"Only with me," Harding said.

"That's a pretty big mess right there," Stone replied, and they laughed. Then Stone grew quiet.

Harding knew that after recuperation he would eventually venture back to see Laura again, to live out their new identities, their shared secrets, in spite of Lt. Butch Stone's dark and threatening presence. But Harding needed to be here for his mother right now, needed to reestablish his roots in her heart, needed to convalesce with his one true friend who solidified the dreamlike present.

Stone nodded. "You mean it's over, man?"

"All over," Harding said. He grabbed Stone's hand as his partner stuck Laura's name in his breast pocket and smiled.

Stone went on to tell Harding about how Sgt. Fowler had just been put back on duty after his "rest," and how the sarge said how great it was Harding wasn't around so that he could prolong the vacation, but Stone also said that Van Dam was screwing up Fowler's head by hiding his pork 'n' beans can on him from time to time with the sarge staying quiet and steaming, probably afraid to announce any more disappearances.

Harding had smiled at Stone's story as he now smiled down at his mother, whose eyes were half-open, seemingly all along. She was still paralyzed badly, and her face was like an encrusted mask from a Greek drama. Harding moved to her side and, not being able to bend at the waist, dropped to his knees slowly. He stroked her dried gray hair and felt his throat constrict. His left hand fumbled at his pajama-top pocket, but it finally produced the gold band found below the cellar boards. He picked up his mother's unresponsive hand and placed her husband's ring on her finger alongside her own.

He thought of his parents together as old people, a tableau only in his imagination, never to be. He thought of Stone's parents together in a pushed-aside bungalow, of the bizarre invitation.

"My parents want you to come to dinner with me when you get out," Stone had said just before he concluded his hospital visit.

"What?" Harding tried not to sound incredulous.

"My father liked you. He wants you for dinner when I go next time."

Harding sickened at the thought; he thought of Stone's father as a sign of death, a killer of sons; then thought of his own real father as the true godlike, prime mover of events, the spirit behind his family's whole tortured ordeal, the fire he had borne within himself that had been found and purged. Max Turley—never photographed, never bending, faceless and powerful and the scum of the earth. Harding was about to tell Stone that his father, Butch, was of the same ilk, that to dine with his father was the last thing he ever wanted to do.

Then, as Harding was about to say it all, he looked at Stone's expression; he looked at Stone's hopeful, open face, a face whose brow carried tiny, nearly unnoticeable scars barely a quarter inch long, but a face genetically innocent somehow. Harding felt his insides soften and thought about how one's own genes aren't so much inherited as grappled with, microscopic snakes you must wrestle within you, you must squeeze the poison out of. Angels begat devils begat devils begat angels . . . and vice versa and once around for good luck.

Harding told Stone it would be fine to have dinner with his folks, and Stone couldn't have been happier if you'd told him he'd made chief of police.

Harding now leaned over to his mother, hoping she could hear him, understand him just this once. Holding her hand tightly, he whispered to her.

"I'm sorry, Mom," he said. "I know everything now . . . and I love you." In the following silence, Harding thought he saw his mother's eyes well up in the shallow light, but it didn't matter. He put his head on her chest and held her as if the years of childhood and old age were one, and as he clasped her hand he saw the wedding rings touch in a golden double loop, saw them glimmer softly together in the darkness.

Harding had almost said to Stone about dinner, "Just tell your old man one of Turley's boys is coming." But he thought better of it.

Harding thought better of a lot of things.